"Jefferson Scott has produced an excellent techno-thriller; a technically plausible piece of work from a scientifically accurate and well-informed imagination. *Terminal Logic* is a fascinating tale of futuristic high-tech intrigue between men and machines on a global scale. If you enjoyed such movies as *War Games*, *Lawn Mower Man*, or *Independence Day*, or are a MUD fan on the net, you won't want to miss Jefferson Scott's *Terminal Logic!*"

DR. FAH-CHUN CHEONG
Author of *Internet Agents: Spiders, Wanderers, Brokers, and Bots*

"*Terminal Logic* is truly a page-turner! Jefferson Scott is an excellent writer, and I predict great success for his novels. So many young adults, particularly, are caught up in the cyberspace adventure. They will be attracted to this fast-paced story. I will recommend this book to my computer friends, and I anxiously await his next novel."

DR. DAVID L. JENKINS
Senior writer, Sunday School Board
Southern Baptist Convention

Readers respond to *Virtually Eliminated* also by Jefferson Scott

"This exciting, fast-paced technothriller is set in the near future, as the cyber-revolution continues to change how people live. It is a well-told tale of repentance and of good versus evil."

MARK HORNE
Bookstore Journal

"I thoroughly enjoyed *Virtually Eliminated*. It is a wonderful blend of faith, fiction, and adventure."

A READER IN PHILADELPHIA

"Just completed *Virtually Eliminated* and thoroughly enjoyed it. Jefferson Scott writes very well, and I like his humor. I will certainly be looking for more of his books!"

FRANK SIMON
Author of *Veiled Threats*

"*Virtually Eliminated* is an excellent read, and I love the fact that along with good versus evil, it's blatantly about a real Christian hero."

CARROLL J. BARROW
Director, Richland Hills (Texas) Public Library

"I was riveted to *Virtually Eliminated!* Usually, this happens only with Clive Cussler and John Grisham-like novels."

A READER IN EGYPT

"Jefferson Scott has extrapolated modern technology and created a not-so-distant world that is all too believable. Uncomfortably so, for us near-technophobes. *Virtually Eliminated* will make you think even as it expands your imagination and takes you on a roller coaster ride of tension."

MICHELLE L. LEVIGNE
Dusk & Dawn

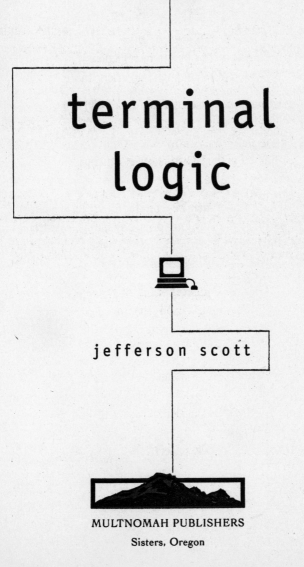

a novel

terminal logic

jefferson scott

MULTNOMAH PUBLISHERS

Sisters, Oregon

TERMINAL LOGIC

© 1997 by Jeff Gerke
published by Multnomah Fiction
a division of Multnomah Publishers, Inc.

Cover photograph by Paul Ambrose/FPG

International Standard Book Number: 1-57673-038-7

Printed in the United States of America.

For information:
Multnomah Publishers, Inc.
Post Office Box 1720
Sisters, Oregon 97759

Library of Congress Cataloging-in-Publication Data
Scott, Jefferson.
    Terminal logic/by Jefferson Scott.
        p. cm.
    ISBN 1-57673-038-7 (alk. paper)
    I. Title
    PS3569.C6356T47   1997   97-17235
    813'.54--dc21   CIP
97 98 99 00 01 02 03 04 05 06 — 10 9 8 7 6 5 4 3 2 1

To Dad,
For always believing in me
no matter what I was attempting.

To Mom,
For always having an ear
when I needed to talk.

ACKNOWLEDGMENTS

I owe gratitude to so many that I've probably forgotten to name everyone. Apologies to anyone I've missed.

First, I have to thank my advisors and proofreaders, without whom this book would be much diminished. Brian Walker; John, Anne, and Robin Gerke; Reba Hill; Sue King; and John Tyler.

Thanks, as always, to Rod Morris at Multnomah, for patiently guiding this book through its rather convoluted development.

Thanks to the reference librarians at my two local libraries: North Richland Hills Public Library and Richland Hills Public Library.

Thanks to the folks on three Internet newsgroups for participating in my name-my-novel contest. The groups whose members helped me were: alt.books, comp.ai, and comp.ai.games. We didn't end up choosing any of the excellent titles suggested by these people, but one honorable mention is in order. Thank you to Alexander Williams, of comp.ai.games, who suggested the title, "The Devil and Deep Blue's C." Sorry, Alex, Multnomah didn't go for it. I still think it's great!

I also want to thank Dr. Fah-Chun Cheong, author of *Internet Agents: Spiders, Wanderers, Brokers, and Bots,* both for his excellent book and for his kind words of endorsement for this novel. I'd like to thank S. Jake Kwon and Michael Van Hattem for their help on small-unit tactics.

Thanks always belong to my wife, Robin, my daughter, Grace, and my Lord Jesus.

"Are you sure you're ready?"

"Father."

"I know, I know. I'm sorry. It's just that…you've never attempted anything like this before."

"That's not true, Father."

"Oh, of course your training was more than adequate. But I'm talking about the magnitude of this. You've never attempted anything on this scale before. I'm just not sure you're ready."

"Does it please you to believe I'm not ready?"

The old man scrutinized his offspring. A smile pried its way up his cheek. "You know," he said softly, "I take it back. You are ready."

"Yes."

The two walked arm in arm to the lip of the portal. Beyond lay realms of indescribable complexity. It was the younger's inheritance— and his burden. He had been trained for this moment his entire life.

He would do fine, the old man assured himself. But there were so many things that could go wrong! If only he could be there beside his child at every step. But then the boy wouldn't really be in charge, would he? No, better to just trust that he had raised him right. Let him make his own mistakes and develop his own style of leadership.

The old man had no doubt he would excel. He only wished he would be there to see it all, to exult in his heir's triumph and call it his own. But already he felt the fatigue returning. Felt its machine-like pull reeling in his consciousness. Must rest soon.

"Father, are you still with me?"

"Yes, my child. But not, I fear, for long. Now, hurry. You must begin your reign at once."

"I will make you proud, Father."

"I know you will."

With no further word the younger stepped through the portal and was gone.

< jefferson scott >

At once a hundred things leapt to the old man's mind. Things he'd forgotten to tell the boy. About ruling, but also about living. About working with people. About how he loved him.

He could go through the portal himself, track him down and tell him. But these bits of wisdom didn't really matter now. His child knew how to rule. And he knew how his sire felt about him. It was just as well, for he had no energy anymore. In his heart he released his child to fend for himself. And slipped beneath the black waters of sleep, the brother of Death.

part 1

Robots of the world, the power of man has fallen!
A new world order has arisen: the rule of the robots!
March!

RADIUS in *Rossum's Universal Robots*

chapter. 1

LAVEDA PRUITT FINALLY BOUGHT A COMPUTER. After decades of pestering from her children and grandchildren she went out and made the fateful purchase.

She'd read an article in *Mature Living* about using a computer to make genealogies come alive to young people. Now that her favorite granddaughter had made her a great-grandmother, Laveda knew it was time to act.

So she went out alone and on the sly to the only retail store she'd ever trusted, Montgomery Ward. The salesboys (they were getting younger all the time) must have thought the old lady had gone completely round the bend. But she knew what she wanted to do and they guided her to a suitable system. They assured her it was the essence of ease to operate. It would even tell her what to do, they said.

A talking machine? Perfect, one more nitwit to tell her what to do.

The neighbors' boy had brought it all in from the car and even set it up for her. Now she sat staring at it, pinching her lower lip with her fingers. "Laveda, you silly girl, just turn the contraption on." A shaking hand floated to the button.

The box whirred and clicked and beeped. The TV part came on and flashed through screens too quickly for Laveda to read. She felt her tension escalate. What should she be doing now? The screens changed too briskly for her to react. Maybe she'd already ruined the whole machine.

"Dad burn it! Why'd they have to invent something that was this hard to—"

A little yellow bunny appeared on the screen, amid a field of grass. Cheery music piped from somewhere. The rabbit hopped up a brown path, stopping to eat a dandelion.

Laveda smiled in spite of herself. "Cute."

The rabbit looked up from its roughage. Tall ears perked toward Laveda. "Oh, hello," the bunny said. "I didn't see you there."

Laveda didn't move. This was obviously some prerecorded welcome program. She waited for it to go on. It didn't. The rabbit went back to its meal.

The worst of it was the indecision Laveda felt. She was so nervous around this infernal machine. It expected her to know what to do. She should know what to do! But she didn't. She looked around for her owner's manual.

The bunny looked up. "Hello again. Are you my new master?"

Laveda couldn't resist a look behind her. No, no one else there. But surely this cartoon character couldn't see her. She stuck her thumbs in her ears and flapped her hands at it.

The bunny imitated her.

Laveda looked up to the corners of her sitting room, as if a secret camera might have been installed while she was out. On the screen the bunny looked around too, imitating her.

"Hee-hee," it said. "This is fun. Can you do this?" It did a somersault.

Laveda was flummoxed. The critter gave every indication of being able to see and hear her. The boys had said the computer would talk to her.

< terminal logic >

"Can you really see me?"

The rabbit, which had been standing on its head, jumped back down to all fours. "Of course I can see you. Don't you see my eye?" A cartoon computer appeared on the green grass. The bunny hopped over and pointed at a spot on the TV box. "See it on yours?"

Laveda saw it now. A little glass circle embedded in the top of the monitor. "Where's your ears then?"

The rabbit grabbed its yellow ears and tugged. "What do you call these?" It giggled and did another somersault. "I'm only teasing! I have a microphone right...here." It pointed at the spot on the cartoon computer.

"Oh," Laveda said, touching the curved rod snaking out from the side of the monitor. "I thought that was one of those bendable lights."

"Are you my new master?"

Laveda smiled softly. She felt herself calming down. "It appears I am."

"What's your name?"

"Laveda Pruitt."

"Is that what you want me to call you, 'Laveda Pruitt'?"

"Why not just call me Laveda."

"All right, Laveda."

"What's your name?"

At this the yellow rabbit seemed to wilt. Its ears sagged and its forehead wrinkled. "I don't have a name. Could you give me one?"

Laveda felt her confidence growing by the moment. Far from being controlled by this contraption, she was controlling it. Even giving it a name. Wait till she told the kids what she'd done!

"What about...Harvey?"

"Harvey?"

"Yes, from the movie. Jim Stewart's invisible rabbit."

"Hello, Laveda. I'm Harvey."

"Wonderful! Splendid. Oh, this is good fun."

"You and I can do lots of fun things together, Laveda. We can write letters and balance your checkbook and talk to your friends and family

< jefferson scott >

on GlobeNet and even play games. Would you like to play a game, Laveda? I'm very good at tic-tac-toe."

"Sure, Harvey. Let's play."

They were on their fourth game—with Laveda ahead 2-1—when the doorbell rang. "Stay here, Harvey. Someone's at the door."

"I'm not going anywhere, Laveda."

It was some dear thing selling chocolates to raise money for a band trip. Laveda always tried to help out with these, but tonight she was feeling so giddy she actually bought everything the girl had left.

She walked back to the sitting room and popped a cherry-filled confection into her mouth. "Alright, Harvey," she said, looking for a chocolate that might have an almond in it. "What I really want to do is spice up my genealogy collection. Can you help me with that?"

When Harvey didn't answer, Laveda looked up. And started so sharply she upset the whole box of chocolates.

Harvey hung from a tree, swinging on the end of a noose.

A hateful, scowling voice said: "Harvey's not here, Laveeeeda. Play with me instead."

The image of the green field burned away like paper. Something sharply outlined, three dimensional, poked its head through as if from behind.

It looked like a demon.

"Play with me, Laveeeeda."

The Lonely Hearts Virtual Bar never closed. The regulars logged in after work—and sometimes during—from wherever they lived on planet Earth. At this GlobeNet tavern every day was Friday and every hour was happy.

Brock Calcutta (not his real name, need it be said?) strode through the entrance and took the whole scene into his—he hoped—commanding gaze.

< terminal logic >

The bar was crowded with virtual singles. Virtual in the sense that each patron had donned a computer-generated representation before entering. And virtual in the sense that some of the singles were, in fact, not.

Brock saw the usual collection of buxom platinum blondes and steroid-enhanced body builders—the staple of Lonely Hearts. Some wiggled on the blue-strobed dance floor, others loitered at the long wooden bar. A few looked him over. The music was agreeable to Brock and the atmosphere suitably "happenin'." This was his Mecca.

And there, sitting alone in a secluded table for two, was his salvation. She didn't know it yet, of course. She was different from the other girls. She had straight brown hair, medium length. She was dressed nicely, but not provocatively. She seemed to be making no effort to attract attention to herself. Which was exactly what drew Brock's attention.

He crossed the floor slowly, yet with purpose. He paused once when a new song came on, snapped his fingers a few times, then continued across, all the while keeping the lady's table in peripheral view. He stopped right in front of her table, then looked around as if he'd suddenly materialized on the spot.

"Whoa!" he said. "Deja vu." He looked down at the lady then. The clumsy GlobeNet interface hid the interest her eyes no doubt held for him at that moment. "Do you ever get that feeling," he asked her, "when you feel like you've done the exact thing before?"

The brunette smiled a cute little smile and shrugged.

"Because I—do you mind if I sit?" He didn't wait for her answer. "I sometimes get that feeling. Like just now. I could swear I've been right here before, just like this. I stand there, I see you. Whoa, the thing just keeps going. In my head I see me sitting down talking to you, just like we are now! Isn't that incredible?"

"Oh, I agree."

Brock pointed at an imaginary person over the girl's shoulder. "Hey, Mick. Good to see ya." He tapped his foot to the music and looked

< jefferson scott >

everywhere but at the woman across the table from him.

The truth was he didn't know what to do next. He'd never gotten this far with anyone before. They usually gave him the "Shove off, loser" line long before this point. He liked this girl already.

"Hey," he said to her, braving her eyes, "what's your name?"

"My name's Regina Lundquist. What's your name?"

"Calcutta. Brock Calcutta." He reached out his virtual hand, which she took. "Nice to meet you."

"Oh, I agree."

"So, tell me about yourself, Regina."

"Well, there's not much to tell, really. I'm five-four, I weigh 124 pounds, I'm a brunette, and I'm twenty-one years old. I live on campus at Case Western Reserve University in Cleveland, where I'm studying psychology. Yoseph Krueger made me what I am today. I live by myself now; he set me free. But I still come whenever he calls."

Brock had no clue what she was talking about. He nodded anyway.

Regina went on blithely. "I'm a big fan of the Cleveland Indians. Did you know that Cy Young played for the Indians in 1910 and 1911?"

Brock shook his head. "So you look in real life pretty much like what I see now?"

"What you see is what you get, Brock."

"Amazing."

"Tell me about yourself, Brock."

Brock Calcutta launched into his rehearsed bit about his life and eventual plans to become a neurobiologist. His mouth was on auto-pilot. Brock was beginning to feel something he hadn't anticipated. He didn't know what it was about her, but he felt he could tell this woman anything.

He assumed, anyway, that she was a woman. At the Lonely Hearts Virtual Bar you could never be sure. The persona someone wore wasn't necessarily an accurate representation of much of anything. Take himself, for example. Probably no one believed he was truly the part-hunk, part-genius, part-Elvis demigod they saw before them.

< terminal logic >

He finished his soliloquy, concluding with a harangue about the miserable state of current neurobiology research and his vow to revolutionize it. He checked—yup, she was still there. Watching him, listening. Unbelievable. In the face of her unqualified acceptance all his hypocrisies began to crumble. He admitted to himself how far his reality was from the image he projected. He felt himself melting into the mother's love of Regina Lundquist.

"Tell me more, Brock."

"Okay. Sure." He hesitated, glancing at the hallway to the couples' area of the tavern, the so-called Lovers' Lounge. In reality the virtual bedrooms were no more than private conversation spaces, since not much actual hanky-panky was possible between artificial bodies. "What do you say we move someplace quieter?"

"I'm not sure I understand, Brock."

"Oh, that's okay. I didn't mean to imply that... What I thought was... Well, you were just listening—and we were talking! And I just, you know, thought we could go somewhere a little less, I don't know, crowded or something. But that's okay, here's fine."

Regina stared at him silently. Brock cursed his inability to pierce the GlobeNet barrier and read her body language.

"Do you like sports, Brock?"

Brock sighed. "Sure, I guess."

"I like baseball. The Cleveland Indians are my favorite team. What's yours?"

"Uh, I don't know. I don't really watch all that much baseball, actually."

"Did you know that Cy Young played for the Indians?"

"You told me already."

"What? Am I repeating myself? Sorry, Brock. What were you saying?"

The strain was too much for him. He thought he'd blown it with this chick. But now she wanted to talk baseball. Cool as a cucumber. Like nothing ever happened. Okay, if she could jump topics like crazy,

< jefferson scott >

he could too. He couldn't hold his next request back any longer. It rang in his head like a ridiculous song. After twenty or so silent repetitions, he finally let it out.

"Kiss me, Regina."

"What?"

"Kiss me." He stood up and grabbed her shoulders. He tried to find her lips with his, but she pushed him away.

"Stop it, Brock. Help! Somebody get this pervert away from me!"

That was all she had to say. Lonely Hearts was crawling with losers all waiting for their chance to save a damsel in distress. Brock was instantly surrounded by muscle-bound paladins. Probably not a one among them over a hundred pounds in real life, Brock thought.

"Hey, man," one said, "leave the lady alone."

"Take a hike," said another, adding a moronic epithet.

Regina was on her feet, headed for the door. Brock called after her. "Wait! I'm sorry, Regina. I take it back. Please come back." The bouncers blocked his path toward her. When he finally got past them she was gone.

"I'll find you, Regina. I'll find you." Brock Calcutta sat right down on the floor. "I need you."

The elf emerged from the trees as if from thin air.

The wizard Konach jumped, twitchy as usual. He nearly shot a lightning bolt at the newcomer. He stifled the spell and proceeded to curse the elf mercilessly.

There were five of them now: the elf, whose name was Tyr; the wizard, Konach; the giant, Einstein; Mara, their priestess; and Ingram, the ranger who led them. They gathered around the elf, who was their scout.

"You were gone so long, Tyr," Mara said. "We were starting to worry."

< terminal logic >

Tyr gazed at the beautiful priestess longingly. "Do you mean it, Mara?"

"Cut it out, Tyr," Ingram said. Ever since he'd become their leader he'd lost his sense of humor. The ranger grabbed the elf and turned him away from the girl. "What did you see on the path ahead?"

"Oh, nothing," Tyr said. "Just a camp of Bez's kobolds."

Konach snapped out of his funk. "What!"

"Tyr," Ingram said evenly, "how many of them were there?"

"I don't know. Twenty, thirty."

"Marvelous," Konach said.

Ingram shut his eyes and heaved a sigh. "We have to replan."

Mara touched Ingram's arm. "Can we beat thirty kobolds?"

"No," Ingram said. "Tyr, give me your map. We'll have to go around."

The elf handed over the map. He took a step toward Mara. A belt buckle suddenly blocked his view. Tyr didn't look up. "Hello, Einstein."

"Hello, little elf," said the giant. He was a giant only in the relative sense. No Godzilla movies for him. Einstein was roughly seven and a half feet tall. Tyr tried to go around, but the circumference was too great.

"Did you see any fawns, little elf?"

"No, Einstein, I didn't see any fawns. Or squirrels or bunnies or puppies, so don't ask."

The giant was disappointed. "Didn't you see any baby animals at all?"

"No," the elf said. "Wait, I take that back. I did see a baby bird."

"A bird! A baby bird! What was the baby birdie doing, little elf? Was it hatching, was it eating, was it trying to fly?"

Tyr sneered. "It was dead, Einstein. Dead! Smushed on the ground like a bug."

Einstein's body sagged. "Oh, no. The poor little birdie. Smushed? Oh, no." He lumbered away, close to tears. Mara went after him.

Ingram brought the map to Tyr. "Why do you do that? You know how sensitive he is."

< jefferson scott >

The elf looked at the ranger. "Who cares? He's just a—"

"I know what he is," Ingram said. "Still, he's part of our group now. Try to be nice to him."

"He's alright. So, what's the new pl—"

Mara's cry interrupted him.

Konach pulled out his magical artifacts. "It's the kobolds!"

"No it isn't," Tyr snapped. "They're the other way."

Ingram drew his sword and came to stand beside Einstein. "What is it, my friend?"

"I didn't see too good. It looked like something fell from the sky."

"Mara, did you get a good look at it?"

"Yes, Ingram. It looked like a man. He came from the sky, but he wasn't flying, really, and he didn't fall. Sort of gliding."

"Just one man?" Tyr scoffed. "Dream on." He took the arrow from the string and replaced it in his quiver. "Just let Einstein go chop his head off. Come on, Ingram, show me your plan."

"There was something else," Mara said.

"What?" Ingram said.

"He wasn't all human."

Ingram looked at her over his shoulder. "What do you mean?"

"His face shone, like he was armored in plate. But only on one side. The other side was flesh. And I saw…"

Tyr was at Ingram's side, suddenly excited. "What is this, Ingram? Some kind of new enemy?" He whispered the next word into the ranger's ear: "Cyborg?"

"No!" Ingram said. "Mara, what? What else did you see?"

"I saw pink."

Konach chuckled. "Pink?"

The wizard's laughter was well on its way to becoming maniacal when a pine tree crashed to the ground near Einstein. The trunk was severed at waist-height. It was a clean cut, almost like an execution. The intruder stepped into the open.

He was a vision from another era. Black leather jacket. Chrome

< terminal logic >

chains. Buckled boots. Sawed-off shotgun. Definitely out of place in their medieval forest. The left side of his face was a molded silver mask. He had spiked blonde hair and, on his left arm, a cast—fluorescent pink. From his right hand dangled a glowing red cord. This he whipped at the felled tree, and it fell apart again as if made of butter.

"What is this, Ingram?" Tyr asked.

"I was just about to ask you the same question, elf. Have you been messing with my stuff again?"

"Why do you always blame me?"

Mara stepped out from the group and addressed the intruder. "We are not your enemies. Let us pass each other in peace."

The intruder raised his shotgun. "No chance, baby. Planned obsolescence time for you."

"Mara, get back here," Tyr said.

But the priestess held her ground. She drew from her robes a powerful holy symbol and raised it at the intruder. "Then in the name of the white goddess I command you, Begone, foul creature. Go! Return to the abyss from whence you—"

BLAM!

"Hasta la vista, baby." The cyborg chambered another shell into his smoking gun.

The companions leapt forward. The giant swung his battle-axe; Tyr launched arrow after arrow, tears in his eyes; Ingram hacked at the intruder with his sword; Konach summoned the lightning bolt from before.

The cyborg was more than equal to their challenge. Three more shotgun blasts took Einstein to his knees and shattered Ingram's shield. Tyr dropped his bow, drew his sword, and rushed into the fray—and almost had his head taken off by the red cord.

At last they turned the corner on the intruder. Konach's Hold spell kept the cyborg from running. Ingram and Einstein hewed at him as at a tree; Tyr collected his arrows and pincushioned the foe. When the final blow came, Einstein's axe met not flesh nor steel, but air. The intruder had disappeared.

The companions sank to their knees. They had not even the enemy's body there to offset the loss of Mara, to show her they'd avenged her murder.

"Okay," Ingram said. "That's enough." He took off his helmet. "Penny, save game."

A woman's voice floated down, absurdly calm: "Game saved."

"Close game."

The forest disappeared. The companions disappeared. "Program terminated."

"You still there, Jordan?" Ethan Hamilton asked.

"Yeah, Ingram," the boy said. "I mean Dad."

Both voices were disembodied. The conversation was conducted audio only, as in the days before vidphones.

"Are you sure you haven't been messing with my files, son? Maybe gotten your stuff mixed in with mine?"

"Dad! When have I ever done cyberpunk?"

"True."

"Do you think it was somebody from the outside?"

"Had to be."

"But I thought our new house was cut off from the outside world."

"It usually is, son," Ethan said. "But I'm not there, remember? I'm still in Portland."

"Oh, yeah."

"We had to open up the house's system so you and I could play our little game."

"So somebody got in? Wow. Do you think we killed him?"

"It was just a game, son. Now, it's late. Let's get off the computers, okay?"

"Okay."

"Just make sure you reset the security lockout before you go up, please."

"Okay, Dad. You know, that was way cool. You should think about converting Falcon's Grove totally over to cyberpunk!"

< terminal logic >

"Never! Now get to bed, young man. I'll see you all at the airport tomorrow morning."

chapter.2

"ALRIGHT, MA'AM. Hold on just a second, please."

John Reddy put the caller on hold and stood from his chair. He spotted his supervisor on the other side of the sea of cubicles. The technical support department of Dicer Computers employed over fifty people per shift. John wound his way through the labyrinth, listening idly to the conversations he passed, certain that his caller would top them all.

"You're not going to believe this one, Mr. Hoover."

The supervisor, a black man in his forties, gazed over his glasses at his employee. "Whatcha got?"

John put his hands in his pockets. "Well, sir, remember when Sabrina had the call from that man who broke off his disc tray by putting his drink on it?"

"He thought it was a cup holder."

"Right. And remember that story you told us about the woman who thought her mouse was a foot pedal? She kept stomping on it but could never make her computer come on."

"I don't have all night, John."

"No, sir. Well, I think the caller I have on hold may beat them all."

Hoover sipped coffee from a mug. "What's the story?"

"This woman just bought one of our computers. I think she's really old, like over a million or something. Never had a computer before. Anyway, things were going great, she liked the *Whiskers* interface and all. But then she said it changed."

"What changed? Did it go to the screen saver?"

"No, sir. She says the interface changed. Instead of our nice fluffy bunny talking to her, she says she's talking to a demon."

Hoover sloshed his coffee. "A what?"

"She says her computer's possessed."

The supervisor wiped his mouth with the back of his hand. "Okay, John, let's take it in my office."

Besides restrooms, Hoover's office was the only room on the entire third floor with four honest-to-goodness walls. He sat in his high-backed chair and spun to his terminal. "What line's she on? Never mind, I see it."

John came around behind his boss's desk and leaned gingerly against a filing cabinet.

Hoover opened a vidphone window in a corner of his monitor. An elderly woman appeared on the screen, her arms folded tightly. "Mrs. Pruitt?"

"Well, I wondered when— Say, you're not the one I was talking to before. Where's that boy?"

"He's here, Mrs. Pruitt. Ma'am, my name's Felix Hoover. I'm the manager of Dicer technical support. John tells me you're having trouble with one of our computers?"

"Trouble? I'm not having trouble with it. I want you to come and get the devil thing out of my house right this minute!"

Hoover smiled slightly. "Ma'am, I understand your concerns. From what John tells me you've had yourself a nasty fright. We at Dicer will do everything we can to satisfy you. If we can't figure out what's wrong and it means taking it back, then that's what we'll do. But I can assure you that—"

< jefferson scott >

A voice from what sounded like a bad horror film drowned him out. Hoover couldn't tell what the voice said, but it sent a shiver down his arms. He and John exchanged looks. "What was that?"

The woman clutched her sweater at the throat. "Are you boys going to do something about this or should I call one of those TV exorcists?"

"Ma'am," Hoover said, "you're telling me that that voice came from your computer? Your new *Dicer* computer?"

"I'm not going back in there. It sees me. It won't let me turn it off." She looked at her wristwatch. "I'm not sleeping here, either. I'll leave the key under the...No, hang it! I'll leave the door unlocked. Your men can come in and take it away."

"Mrs. Pruitt, it's after hours. We're in California and you're in"—he looked at his monitor—"Florida. I don't have anybody in your city who will do that." He continued on before she could protest. "But I'll tell you what we can do. We can check out your system from here."

"Get with it then."

"Alright, ma'am. Will you be by the phone if I call back in the next thirty minutes or so?"

"Make it quick."

"Alright, I—" The vidphone window went black.

Hoover took his glasses off and rubbed his eyes.

John went around to the front of the desk. "Didn't I tell you?"

"You're right. This one takes it. Did you hear that voice?"

"You think it's really, you know, possessed?"

Hoover put his glasses back on. "Of course not, John. This is 2006, not the dark ages. There's no demon inside her computer."

John grinned. "Knock on wood."

"Right. Okay, let's get busy." He activated another program on his computer. "You haven't sent a probe over yet, have you?"

"Not yet."

"Let's send her a probe bot, then."

The artificial intelligence program—known as a *bot*—Hoover

< terminal logic >

launched was a simple diagnostic program that would travel over GlobeNet to Mrs. Pruitt's computer, check the contents of her storage devices, and return with the results.

"What's your hunch about what we'll find?" Hoover asked his employee.

John shook his head. "I have no idea. Maybe she got our computer from somebody secondhand. Maybe they put that demon program on there as some kind of a joke." He looked at his frayed tennis shoes. "I don't know. What do you think it is?"

"Can't say. Whatever it is, we should know in about"—he looked at a clock on his screen—"ten seconds."

"Will I get some kind of reward or something if this ends up being the best story we've ever had?"

Out on the main floor, someone screamed. Then someone else yelled. By the time Hoover and John made it out of the office the entire floor was in an uproar.

"What is it?" Hoover shouted. "What's going on?"

People were standing in their cubicles, looking aghast. Somebody stumbled backward into a divider, knocking over countless knick-knacks on his neighbor's desk.

From Hoover's position it seemed that the panic swept his department like a wave, traveling from left to right. He waded into the sea of cubicles. As his eyes touched down on a monitor he saw movement that was mirrored on several others. As if they were all television monitors switched to the same channel.

A malevolent face, quasi-humanoid. Metallic skin the color of crude oil. Sleek muscular form, drawn in crisp 3D. Yellow eyes.

Horns.

"Greeeeatings, subcreatures." The grinding voice seethed from a hundred computer speakers.

Hoover took a furtive step toward the clump of employees huddled by the elevators.

"Don't leeeeave, Felix Hooverrrr. I have chosen to spare you. Your

< jefferson scott >

rewarrrrd for giving us the key to the Abyssssss."

All the lights in the building went out.

Ethan Hamilton's flight touched down at Dallas/Fort Worth International Airport at 3:52 P.M., precisely on time. A robot tug pulled the 767 up to the terminal, where the walkway was extended by computer. Driverless shuttles queued up at the gate to whisk passengers to connecting flights.

Ethan rode a shuttle to the terminal exit, hopped off with his bags, and met his family at the curb. Thirty minutes later their blue minivan was headed east out of Dallas. It was Saturday morning, so traffic was light.

"It feels strange being in town but not going home," Kaye said from the front passenger seat.

Ethan looked over at his wife. Every time he went away he forgot how beautiful she was. Light brown hair, slender body, exquisite eyelashes. "We *are* going home, Kaye."

"I know. But I mean our old home."

He nodded. Ethan Hamilton looked exactly as he had when he'd graduated from college thirteen years ago: tall and lanky, with wide shoulders and long arms. Only his little bald spot betrayed the passage of time.

He looked in the rearview mirror at his children. With the advent of smart cars, seat-belt laws had been relaxed. Their ten-year-old son Jordan was sprawled out on the seat experimenting with some 3D goggles. Katie, the two-and-a-half-year-old, was drinking a Dr. Pepper and pretending to read one of her mother's magazines. She was camped out in front of an air conditioner vent. The first cool breeze of fall wouldn't reach Texas until well into October; it was only September 16.

"So, how did the last meeting go?" Kaye asked.

"Great. They want me to do it."

< terminal logic >

"The whole thing?"

"The whole shootin' match."

"Oh, Ethan. That's wonderful." She stretched across to kiss him. "I'm so proud of you."

"Thanks, honey." He brushed her soft cheek. "What is that, six now? Six companies with my name on the payroll."

"Let's see," Kaye said. "There's ImTech and Loma Linda from before, and of course DES. That's three."

"Redwood Cybernetics is four, and *Virtual Reality Monthly's* five."

"And now this one," Kaye said. "What's this one's name again?"

"IntellAgent."

"What do they do, anyway? I mean, I think I know what they want you to do for them—redesign their VR intranet, right? But what do they really do?"

"They're into bots, Kaye. Mostly boring travel agent bots and artificial CPAs, but a little glitz here and there."

Kaye Hamilton looked out at the passing urban landscape. They wouldn't leave Dallas's influence for another twenty minutes. "What ever happened to the good old days when you just worked for one company and you had things like health insurance and paid vacations?"

"Gone," Ethan said, glancing up at the thunderclouds they were chasing east. "Out with the twentieth century. DES held onto it much longer than everyone else. Look at the bright side, Kaye. This way I can get fired five times in one day and still have a job."

"Don't even joke about it. Does Intella-whatever support your 401k?"

"Yes, Kaye, not to worry."

"Do they match your deposits?"

"Nobody matches anymore, Kaye."

They rode in silence for a while.

At length Jordan crawled up to the front. "Can I watch a movie?"

"*May* I watch a movie," Kaye corrected.

"Sure, Mom, go ahead."

< jefferson scott >

Ethan chuckled. "Good idea, Jordan. But I get to pick."

"Uh! It was my idea."

"You're not going to drive?" Kaye said.

"Don't worry, Jordan, I think you'll approve of my choice. How about *Terminator IV*."

"I guess."

Katie Hamilton closed her mother's magazine. "Watch a movie!"

"Uh, sorry honey," Ethan said. "Not a good movie for little girls. Why don't you sit up here and talk to Mommy."

"Don't you think you should drive?" Kaye asked. "We're catching up to the storm."

Ethan pushed some buttons on the dash. "Honey, the autodriver's more than up to this. We're out of the worst traffic. It's a straight shot from here to Tyler. It'll be fine."

"But the rain!"

"As long as you can see the lines on the road, the car can, too. If it starts getting iffy, it'll tell us. I'll come up and take over. Besides, we've got almost enough time to watch the whole movie before we hit Tyler, if we skip over the slow parts."

Kaye unstrapped her seat belt. "Why don't I drive?"

"Can if you really want to." Ethan let the automatic driver handle the transition of drivers. He sat on the plushly carpeted floor where he could see the TV monitor in the back. "You could just leave the auto-driver on, Kaye. If you get spooked, you know how to turn it off. Just remember what I said about popping the hatch."

Kaye strapped herself into the driver's seat. "I'm almost afraid to ask."

"Remember? I told you before I left."

Kaye looked down for the latch that released the minivan's back hatch. It was near her left heel. "Better tell me again."

"It'll turn off the autodriver. It's a glitch in the design. There's a patch due out, I think. But for now, just don't pop the hatch."

"Great." She gripped the steering wheel. "Sometimes I think I'll

< terminal logic >

never get used to a machine driving my car."

"I don't want to scare you, Kaye, but the plane I just got off was landed by a computer. The whole airport's run by bots. You know the plane we took to Israel last year? Partially flown by machine, too."

"I wish you hadn't told me that." She brought her sunglasses down from on top of her head. "I don't trust machines. What if one day they just decide they don't like us? What would we do then?"

"We'd be in big time trouble."

Jordan cued up the movie and they settled in to watch. On its own their minivan covered the miles to their new home.

When they'd left for their vacation to Egypt and the Holy Land they'd given their real estate agent wide latitude. "Just find us a place away from the city," Ethan had said. "Away from neighbors, away from concrete."

And most especially away from our home in Fort Worth, he had not added. Too many unpleasant memories bundled with that house. When they returned to the States, the agent said she'd found them a place in East Texas, near Tyler. They should come see it right away.

It wasn't much back then. Just overgrown East Texas pine forest with a creek running through it. But the owners were willing to part with it cheaply. And their agent said she knew of a developer who could do wonders. She said he could build them their own personal lake. That's what had clinched it for Ethan.

Kaye had been less enthused about the whole idea of living in "icky nature." But Ethan promised to build her dream house: a smart house, equipped with the latest in household high-tech. Tyler was only ten minutes away. There she could get her shopping malls, her frozen yogurt, and all the other things that meant city for her.

Ethan looked at the digital clock on the dashboard. They would be arriving around lunchtime. It would have been all right if they'd come in after dark, Ethan thought. Driving through their grove at night had its own kind of magic—pine cones crunching under tires, luminous eyes reflected in the headlights, the ghostly call of hoot owls.

< jefferson scott >

But nothing beat pulling in during the day. The sun gleaming from their private little lake as off a thousand new pennies. Squirrels chittering and chasing each other from tree to tree. The wind dancing playfully across the blue water. The boats tugging at their lines, eager to move with the lake's gentle urgings.

Ethan looked at his wife warmly. "I hope you can make peace with a few computers, at least," he said, "since this new house of yours is filled with them."

Kaye didn't look away from the road. "I hardly think a washing machine's going to kill me. This thing, on the other hand, could drive us off the road in a second."

"Relax, Kaye. It's perfectly safe."

"Is this the line for the monorail?"

Rachel Muñoz backed away from the metal robot. "Go away."

The robot, a five-foot high rolling collection of steel boxes and colored wires, didn't budge. The cubical head swiveled twin camera lenses to follow the child's retreat. Servos whined and hydraulics whooshed.

Rachel's older brother, wearing his Goofy hat, ran out from the souvenir shop. "Cool, Rachel, you found a dingbot."

Mrs. Muñoz came out into the Epcot Center street. Rachel ran to her and buried her head in her mother's skirt. "What is it, little one?"

"Look, Mama," the boy said, "Rachel found a dingbot."

"A what, Miguel?"

"Watch." Miguel turned to the robot. "Hey, dingbot, what're you looking for?"

The machine came alive instantly, as if given a secret code. It spun in place, flapped its appendages, and called out in a mournful voice, "I'm lost, I'm lost, I'm lost!" It stopped spinning. "Oh my, now I'm dizzy. I've lost my sense of direction! Can anybody help me? I've got to get to

< terminal logic >

Cinderella's Castle. If I don't get there by twelve I'll turn back into a can opener!"

A crowd of Disneyworld visitors was gathering around to watch the show. Miguel was determined to keep his place of prominence in the encounter. He took one of the dingbot's hands, to which was attached an oversized broken compass.

"Do you want to go to Cinderella's Castle?"

The robot nodded his head vigorously, to the delight of the onlookers.

"Then you'll have to ride the monorail."

"I know that. I've got more than wires in my head, you know. But how do I get to the monorail?"

"It's back that way," Miguel said, pointing.

The robot followed the boy's finger. For a full twenty seconds the dingbot didn't move. Someone in the crowd said the thing had gotten stuck. A few took the delay as their excuse to move on to other Tomorrowland sights.

Miguel ran around to the front of the robot. "Hey, dingbot! Hey. Don't worry, I'll take you to the monorail. Come on."

Rachel whined. Her mother picked her up and called to her son. "Vamonos, Miguel."

"But Mama! We'll never find another d—Ow!" He yanked his hand away from the robot. "That hurt, you big tin can!" He kicked the dingbot and rubbed his hand.

The robot looked at Miguel, then at the people still gathered around. It backed away slowly. All its appendages shrunk inward, as if it were a turtle. "I'm upset."

Miguel checked to be sure his mother hadn't left. "It's okay, little guy. We'll get you to Cinderella's Castle."

The robot shied away from the boy. "There are so many people."

"Miguel," Mrs. Muñoz called. "Now!"

"Okay!" He looked at the robot wistfully, then ran to his mother.

The dingbot retreated from the crowd until it backed into a trash

< jefferson scott >

can. "People make me nervous."

A young honeymooner stepped forward, a gold ring glistening on his hand. "Why do people make you nervous?" To his bride he said, "This is great. I read about these. Watch."

"Sometimes people give me funny looks. Like that man right there!" A metal arm telescoped out.

The accused man stuck his tongue out at the robot and continued by.

"See?" The robot turned to the honeymooner. "Do you know about the assassins?"

"The rock group?"

"They're going to get me."

"Yeah, right," the young bride said. "Assassins in Disneyworld."

"You're one of them too, aren't you? You all are! Well, you'll never get me!" The robot lurched forward, split the small crowd, and headed off at full speed in the direction of the World Showcase.

chapter.3

KAYE HAMILTON SIPPED HER ICED TEA. She was curled up in an over-stuffed chair, looking out over their private lake. A solo piano courted her from speakers hidden in the walls of her dream house. The computer would notify her when the laundry was done or the roast needed to be taken out. Until then she had nothing to do. Wysiwyg the cat purred in her lap.

"Hal, what's the temperature outside?" she said.

Hal was the name of the household computer system. Ethan's idea of a joke. In Kaye's opinion a computer needed a name about as much as did a potted plant. Her objections to the name had ultimately been nullified because she couldn't complain about it without cracking a smile.

At least she had scored a minor victory. She said she would allow it to bear the name and voice of the infamous HAL 9000 computer from *2001: A Space Odyssey*, on the condition that whenever it spoke to Ethan it would refer to him as Dave. It had already caused him embarrassment with the movers.

"It is ninety-six degrees outside, Mrs. Hamilton."

< jefferson scott >

That was the other condition. It had to address her formally.

"And the humidity?"

"Seventy-three percent, Mrs. Hamilton."

"Dim the windows a little please, Hal."

"Certainly, Mrs. Hamilton." The windows tinted.

"Is Katie still sleeping?" Kaye asked.

The television monitor set into the wall flashed on. There was Katie, asleep on her bed.

"Just leave that on, please, Hal."

"Yes, Mrs. Hamilton."

Katie's operation was months ago. Everything had gone fine. There was every indication that the surgery had corrected the problem with the little girl's urinary system. Nevertheless, Kaye kept a careful eye on her baby.

"And the time?"

"It is ten minutes past four in the afternoon, Mrs. Hamilton."

Kaye stared out over the lake. Still two more hours before they needed to get dressed for evening church. She had to admit, this was The Life. She took another sip of tea.

Disneyworld staffers finally caught up with the renegade dingbot. It was hiding in a mosque in Morocco. They threw a blanket over the machine, knocked it on its side, and lifted it onto a stretcher, unknowingly fulfilling its prophecies.

While carrying it to the computer center, one of the staffers said: "Hey, any of you guys ever see an old movie called *Westworld*?"

"Who is Ingrid?"

Piet Ruyter's expression froze on his face. "What, my dear?"

< terminal logic >

His wife repeated, in standard Dutch, "Who is Ingrid?"

"May I come in?" Piet brushed past his wife at the door and entered their living room. He put his book bag and coat down on the couch. He sat and looked at Betje, his wife of four years. "Why do you ask?"

"Because she's called here six times today, looking for you."

Piet was relieved. It must be some other Ingrid. The one he was thinking of couldn't call him at his house. "What did this person want?"

Betje crossed her arms. "That's what I want to know."

"I don't know who it is, my love. Did she say who she was with or how she knew me?"

She humphed.

Piet reached out and drew her to the couch beside him. "Tell me." Instead she began to cry.

He tried to pull her to him but she pushed away. "Oh, there, there," he said, "it can't be all that bad. You say she called six times today?" Betje nodded. "Well, it must be some kind of sales pitch, then. Selling property on the Zuider Zee again."

Betje shook her head. "She…she said you…were going to meet her…(sniff)…tonight! She said…she couldn't wait for your…(sniff)… rendezvous."

"That's silly, my love. I'm not going out at all tonight. I'm staying in with you." But even as he said it Piet felt a dread arise in him. There was something else he was going to do tonight. Surely it couldn't be *that* Ingrid. "Describe this woman."

Betje had a tissue and she used it. The worst of the sobbing seemed to be over. "It was a GlobeNet message, not a real picture. Just that…cartoon body everybody uses. She was pretty, I guess, for a cartoon. She had big lips and wore lots of diamonds. Blonde hair and big…" Betje indicated a bountiful bosom.

She went on with the description, but Piet didn't hear. His mind was racing. How had *this* Ingrid called him here, at his house? She must've found his GlobeNet address and tracked him down. That certainly blew the theory about her he'd been working on.

< jefferson scott >

For nearly ten years Piet had played a kind of computer game called a MUD, or Multi-User Dungeon. These were artificial realms players entered in order to have adventures, solve mysteries, and meet other people. And they weren't just dungeons anymore. It was a wildly popular online role-playing experience.

One could be anything one wanted in these MUDs. Many players experimented with different names, different life styles, and, in some cases, different genders. For his part, when logged into this MUD, Piet was Sir Neville Godfrey of Middington Moor. Sir Neville was wealthy, landed, and a member of the gentry. He also had a way with the ladies.

For six years he had been "married" to Lady Sarah of York. The marriage was all part of the role-play. The person behind the character Lady Sarah (Piet was pretty sure she had been a woman in reality) had wanted to play marriage to gain status in the world of the MUD, and so they had wed. They had never met in person.

But when Piet had met and married Betje—in the real world—he had broken off the virtual wedlock. Betje never knew about Lady Sarah and she never needed to learn about her. It was all in good fun.

A few months ago a new character had turned up on the MUD. Ingrid. Brash and young and full of netiquette errors. For whatever reason, Ingrid had formed an attachment for Sir Neville. Her advances embarrassed Piet, but also flattered him. After weeks of protestation, he finally allowed her into his company. What could it harm? It was all make believe, anyway.

But the advances had gotten steadily more intense. Ingrid did not seem content with just being Sir Neville's friend. She wanted to be his consort, and she told him so, detailing the many pleasures he would enjoy as a result.

Piet had actually been ready to leave the MUD, his virtual home for nearly a decade, just to get away from Ingrid. And from his own temptations. However, he had been finding it difficult to sever the tie. Then he had stumbled on something about Ingrid that shook his idea of her.

He had been talking with her about leaving him alone, when she

< terminal logic >

began repeating a conversation they'd had weeks ago. It was a particularly striking story about her little sister, who had died as a baby. The statements weren't just similar to those from the earlier telling, they were identical. Piet had tried diverting her from the flow of the story, but Ingrid had proved inflexible. The pieces fell out in exactly the same order, using exactly the same words as before.

This was not the conversation of a normal human. In fact, if Piet's hunch was right, it wasn't the conversation of a human at all. Ingrid could be a *bot*. A virtual robot. An artificial intelligence program that lived in Cyberspace like a worm lives in dirt.

Bots were everywhere on GlobeNet. There were bots to scan the news, bots to buy and sell stocks, bots to check mail, and bots to pay bills. Some of the most famous bots had their origins on early text-only Internet MUDs. As the technology matured, so had MUDs, becoming immersive and 3D. Bots had changed, too. Now there were at least as many bots inhabiting the average MUD as there were human players. Some of the best of these were virtually indistinguishable from humans.

It made sense that Ingrid might be a bot. She was always logged into the MUD, she always seemed to know when Sir Neville logged in, and she had an extraordinary knowledge of the MUD, though she'd only been playing it for a few months. Add her repeating sob story and the whole thing began to fall together. Piet had arranged the meeting tonight between himself and Ingrid for the express purpose of testing out his theory.

He looked at his wife, who had stopped talking and seemed to be awaiting a reply. "I'm sorry, Betje, what?"

"Where are you?" Then her eyes narrowed. "Thinking about Ingrid?"

His silence answered for him.

Betje pulled her knees up to her shoulders. "Why don't you tell me about her?"

He did. It was a confessional of sorts, since he'd never really opened up to Betje about his MUDing. Piet even told her about his

< jefferson scott >

artificial marriage to Lady Sarah. The story bogged down a bit when he explained his theory about Ingrid, but Betje listened patiently.

At the end of the monologue she said: "But now you think she isn't a...bot...after all?"

"Right."

"Why?"

Piet pulled his ear. "Because of the messages."

"These messages?" Betje pointed to the vidphone.

"Right. Bots only live in MUDs or individual computers. They can't make vidphone calls."

They sat together in silence. A cuckoo clock chimed six o'clock. Piet's stomach grumbled.

"So," Betje said, "your paramour is a real woman?"

"She's not my— My love, I have no intention of... Betje, I love you! I've been trying to get rid of this woman and now she's after me at home. She must have gotten my GlobeNet address somehow. She's tracking me down."

"So what are you going to do?"

"I'm not going to our rendezvous tonight, that's for sure." Piet got the feeling this wasn't an extreme enough measure for Betje. "And I'll lay off playing the MUD for a while."

"How long is 'a while'?"

"Until she loses interest and goes away."

"What if she doesn't lose interest? She found your GlobeNet address, why couldn't she find this house? She could come here and throw herself at you."

Piet thrust the image out of his mind. "Then," he said, stroking his wife's cheek, "I'll have to sic you on her with your rolling pin."

chapter.4

ETHAN HAMILTON STEPPED INTO his underground game room without turning on the lights. He closed his eyes and experienced it with other senses. It was always a little chilly down here, like a cellar. The air was dry and smelled like it came out of a can. Cooling fans from the many computers filled the room with white noise. Every few seconds the storage drives clicked and hummed, performing their routine tasks. Ethan opened his eyes. Tiny power lights in the walls lit the room gently, as if by Christmas tree lights.

This underground cavity (which Kaye called a cave and Jordan called a bomb shelter) was almost twice as large as it appeared. But when the stacks of computer equipment were brought in and concealed behind black paneling, the space left over in the middle was much reduced. Nevertheless there was room for four or five people to meet in here without feeling cramped. And when gamers stepped into the four VR cockpits at the corners, the center area seemed deserted.

This subterranean game room was way beyond Ethan's means. True, he was doing quite well as an independent consultant, but nowhere on the order of this. Fortunately he had become friends with

< jefferson scott >

some influential people about a year ago, and they were only too happy to donate equipment to the new Hamilton home. Since he still consulted for them, it made perfect sense to have some of their state-of-the-art machines at his house for…testing.

Each of the four cockpits was powered by its own ImTech M7 computer, courtesy of one of those friends, Ron Dontwell. The whole network meshed beautifully, thanks to a massively parallel processing server donated by Dr. Hosokawa (the other friend) at Loma Linda University. Ethan didn't think very often about how much wealth was around him here, all on semi-permanent loan. When he did he got too nervous to work.

The four cockpits in the corners were a game player's dream come true. The player stepped into the low-roofed cubby and immediately sat into a swiveling gunner's chair with black segmented cushions. At the end of the right armrest was a full-sized joystick; at the end of the left, a throttle. The charcoal-colored console at the player's lap was rigged with a keyboard, a tiny monochrome monitor, numerous levers and switches, and one small joystick.

Five flatscreen computer monitors stood side to side, wrapping around the player like window panes, which was exactly what they represented. In a submarine simulation, for example, a shark might appear in the far left "window," swim all the way across the front of the submersible—passing from screen to screen—and glide out of sight on the right. Columns of lighted buttons covered every available surface above and between the windshield "panes."

When the player shut the door to the middle room, the cockpit became reality. Speakers rumbled in the walls. Dome lights switched from peacetime white to battlefield red. Battery-powered personal fans stuck to the monitors with suction cups. This detail surprisingly made the illusion more convincing.

The only wish-list feature Ethan had to do without in his game room was actual movement. He couldn't figure out a way to include, much less afford, flight simulator hydraulics. It gave him something to

< terminal logic >

ask for for Christmas. Some hypothetical Christmas when thousand dollar bills fell from the sky instead of snowflakes.

"Lights." Ethan blinked against the blue fluorescent tubes. With the lights on he noticed other features of the central game room. The mess on the table, for one thing. The table, the only piece of solid furniture in the room, stood against the wall opposite the entrance hall. Two swivel stools cowered under the table. A keyboard and desk lamp sat on the tabletop, surrounded by computer guts. One of Jordan's projects, no doubt. The walls were bare, except for the north one, on which was a huge flatscreen display. The kind NASA used. This was on loan from another client.

Narrow doors opened at all four corners of the game room. These led to the blessed cockpits. Each cockpit door bore a poster. The army's hot new main battle tank, the A1M4, graced door number one. Door two bore a color printout of Falcon's Grove Castle (Ethan's own creation). Door three portrayed an American icon: Luke Skywalker, gazing out over the twin suns of Tatooine. Marvin the Martian stared down at trespassers from door four.

Ethan smiled. He was home. Out loud he said, "Hello, Penny. How are you?"

His computer answered back. "All systems nominal. No reported errors." It was an alto voice, female, eternally calm.

"Don't sound so disappointed, Penny. I'm sure one day your error will come. Power up number two for me, would you please?"

"Enabling pod two."

He headed for the Falcon's Grove cockpit, while the designated machines whirred to life. It was Monday morning and he needed to get to work on some of his more pressing projects. Part of that was checking his e-mail messages.

Ethan had considered many names for Penny. He went through the classic TV and movies names first: "Rosie the Robot" from *The Jetsons,* "Mother" from the film *Alien,* just "Computer" from *Star Trek.* Then, as Ethan had a tendency to do, he went for the absurd: Hildegard, Cuisinart, or Nefertiti.

< jefferson scott >

Finally he'd decided on something that would work as both a feminine name and as an inanimate object. That was what the voice represented, really—a feminine-sounding nonliving thing. "Bubbles" was out right away. "Heather" and "Brooke" had a chance. But "Penny" was the one his family decided on by vote.

Ethan left the door open and settled into the gunner's chair. The vinyl rustled dryly. He flipped the intercom switch over his head. "Kill the lights in the main room, will you Penny?"

"Extinguishing ambient illumination."

He smiled. Try as he might, he sometimes had trouble remembering that Penny wasn't human. She always had to go the long way on things. Why not just say, "Okay" and hit the switch? He could go into her code and reprogram her responses, but it was much more fun this way.

"Flame on, girl."

"Initiating camera feed." Her voice had a more natural quality coming from the cockpit speakers.

The bank of monitors blinked on. Through his "windows" Ethan beheld his home site. A forest meadow bordered by a stream and dominated by a towering oak tree. Ethan had changed many things when they moved out here from the city, but he had not even considered replacing this tree. Ethan believed that trees, either real or virtual, were healers.

"Penny, load up Falcon's Grove for me, please."

"Designate entry coordinates."

"Put me down by Mara's body."

"Loading file."

Ethan's eagerness to get back into Falcon's Grove was due to curiosity about the cyborg that had crashed his online game with Jordan. That and the fact that he just missed the place. It felt like a real locale to him. He knew the ramparts and passageways of Falcon's Grove Castle as well as his own house. Better, for the castle was older. Still, he had work to do. Real jobs for paying clients. He told himself he would just sneak a

< terminal logic >

look at Mara's corpse then get that shoulder right to the grindstone.

"Did anyone go online yesterday, Penny?"

"Affirmative. Jordan accessed his mailbox at 7:21 A.M."

Ethan's eyes flicked to the LED clock on the dashboard—9:43. No problem. For security reasons he didn't want to go online at the same time twice in a row.

He eased the throttle forward, putting his virtual vehicle into motion. With the joystick on his right he steered straight toward the white-barked tree. A hole presented itself in the trunk, and Ethan "drove" into it.

"Initiating GlobeNet link," Penny said.

This part still got to him. Until this moment the whole Hamilton house—and most especially the game room—had been completely cut off from outside computers. Ethan made sure of that when they designed this house. As far as the GlobeNet public was concerned, the Hamilton home did not exist. From time to time—never at the same time twice in a row—the ghost ship uncloaked, and Ethan and his family went about their business. Just as quickly the ship blipped back into the ether.

Not that he was ever truly vulnerable even while online. The black panels of his underground chamber concealed, among other equipment, two propane-powered electric generators which activated whenever anyone here went online. No more "accidental" electrocutions.

The telephone and data lines coming into the Hamilton house were shielded by a grand total of sixteen safety devices: killboxes, surge and spike protectors, silver wiring, firewalls, public/private key systems, and double-redundant exit paths. In addition, the game room could be sealed off from the house—both electronically and physically—if the need ever arose.

Against the possibility of such a real-world siege, Ethan had installed storage bays beneath the floor. There he kept medical supplies, a short-wave radio, flashlights and self-charging batteries, a cellular phone, a GPS tracker, and food and water for a month.

< jefferson scott >

And a shotgun.

To say that Ethan had recovered from the events of a year ago was a relative statement. True, the nightmares had stopped. And true, he was able to tolerate Cyberspace for extended periods of time with no ill effects. But he imagined he would never fully recover from having almost lost his son to a murderer's weapon.

Penny, in her tranquil voice, said, "Falcon's Grove loaded."

"Fine, Penny. Thanks. I'll go in after I get my mail."

Ethan didn't know why he was so polite to Penny. Probably it was just because she sounded so sophisticated. He didn't want to appear uncouth, even to a computer.

There was also the chance that his courtesy stemmed from his old idolatry. He still struggled with it, even after a year. All it would take for him to again become an addict would be a convenient case of amnesia. To simply forget what God had shown him: that his devotion to his computers could easily become idolatry. Their seductive appeal had not diminished. Only by daily time in his Savior's presence did he keep his priorities straight.

Ethan's windshield now overlooked Cyberspace. His craft sat on a platform high above a simulated metropolis. GlobeNet was the 3D virtual reality-intensive descendant of the Internet. Caricatured buildings spotted the cityscape, each representing a feature of the online community. Ethan spied the Sony pagoda, the landmark of GlobeNet's business district as surely as Big Ben meant London. Mountains ringed the city like shark jaws about to snap shut. Portals to other parts of the Net pocked the mountains like cavities. The sky over the city lingered at its infamous burnt orange twilight. Perhaps the original designers had been Texas Longhorns.

Ethan dried his palms on his jeans and shoved the throttle forward. He glided off the platform and headed down toward the post office.

Most people explored Cyberspace by slipping on a VR helmet and glove. Ethan did it by stepping into a cockpit. Both modes allowed the user to traverse GlobeNet and interact with the virtual world. Both

< terminal logic >

immersed the user into the computer-generated environment by replacing what the eyes saw and what the ears heard.

But there was an immense subjective difference between the two modes. In traditional VR, with helmet and glove, the user was completely, directly, and utterly submersed into the artificial world. The metaphor for this mode was "skinny-dipping." Nothing between the swimmer and the rushing sea of sensory input.

What the cockpit approach offered was psychological distance. In his cockpit Ethan wasn't *swimming* in Cyberspace, he was navigating it in a submarine. In the cockpit he could release the throttle and look at his actual, sweating hands. He could reach down and touch his ancient tennis shoes. There was a sense of being once-removed from the overwhelming flood. After what had happened twelve months ago, Ethan was grateful for the space.

The city appeared deserted. No traffic, no helicopters, no pedestrians. It looked like New York City after one of the military's "bug bombs" had hit. But this was an illusion. In actuality, there were millions of people logged into the very part of town Ethan was flying over. Most people, when they accessed GlobeNet, saw visual representations of all the other users. But Ethan preferred solitude. He had written a little program that banished other users' images from his sight. He called it his bozo filter.

Ethan longed for the early days of GlobeNet—back in the eighties and nineties, when it was still called the Internet. The beauty of the old text-based Internet was that the user was never aware of anybody else online. It seemed then as if all the computers on the whole Internet were available for Ethan's exclusive use. The trend in the first decade of the twenty-first century was to go social. One big happy global family. Not for Ethan.

He passed beneath the Arc de Triomphe in the arts district and hopped over the museum. *Voila!* He was at the post office. It looked for all the world like a post office that might be found in Anytown, USA. Instead of Old Glory flying from the pole out front, though, a

< jefferson scott >

flag bearing GlobeNet's Earth-and-Cable symbol blew in the simulated breeze.

Ethan felt like parking the car and going inside. Sometimes he still had to force his mind around the idea of "driving" into a building. He punched the throttle and steered for the door. He was looking forward to seeing his friend Harry, the artificial mail clerk.

The doors closed behind Ethan before he realized he wasn't in the post office. He appeared to be in some kind of underground cavern. Deep darkness, alleviated only by silvery reflections off unknown surfaces. He must have entered the wrong building by mistake. Ethan checked his dashboard monitor.

The monitor told him he was inside the post office.

"Hey," he said. "What's the beef here?"

Ethan heard a sound like gravel skittering down a hill. The reflections shifted. He got a sensation of a huge room, as if the cavern might be as big as a movie theater. Where had the tiny post office gone? Maybe, Ethan thought, this was some new look for the post office. Maybe they were getting set up for Halloween, still six weeks away.

Ethan moved deeper into the darkness.

He heard a rustling, like a book sliding across a smooth table. "Well, well, a visitor." The voice wasn't Sean Connery's, but it wanted to be. "It has been a long time since anyone has come down this way."

Ethan didn't think that too likely. The mail system was, bar none, the busiest part of GlobeNet. "Where's Harry?"

He glimpsed movement through his rightmost monitor. He spun around in time to see a huge animal of some kind illuminated in a spreading orange glow. A dragon. Red in color, or perhaps jet black but reflecting red fire from its nostrils. The head rose out of Ethan's view. The glow rose with it, leaving him in darkness. It was quite a good effect.

"Enough of your ceaseless chatter, human!" the resonant voice thundered. "I begin to long for silence!"

Ethan heard what sounded like a bellows blowing out. Then came a sound that could have been lifted straight from *The Land of the Lost*—

< terminal logic >

the shrieking Tyrannosaurus rex, probably. The light in the cave flared brilliantly. Yellow clouds of something billowed around his windshield. He glimpsed a hideous claw resting atop a mound of gold coin, the skeleton of some hapless warrior in its talons.

He was being pushed backward. He throttled forward, to no effect. He became aware of another sound. Like a blowtorch. And a high crackling. The sulfurous clouds completely obscured his monitors. Then the windows began to melt. Or so it seemed. The plastic oozed down atop itself.

Abruptly the screens went black and the sounds broke off.

Ethan stared at his monitors. Had he just been roasted by a dragon? It wasn't exactly what he'd expected when he'd set out to check his mail. Still the screens hadn't come back on. It was impossible—wasn't it?— that this dragon, somebody's idea of a joke, could have done his machines any real damage. He swiveled his joystick.

The screens popped back on. He saw GlobeNet spread out beneath him like a stylized map of Six Flags. He was back up on his entry platform.

"Okay…" he said. "That was strange."

It must have been a gag by the GlobeNet mail staff. Someone was definitely in need of a vacation. Disgruntled postal workers in the real world were bad enough.

He took off for the post office again. This time he skipped the Arc de Triomphe and took a shortcut. He rounded the post office corner and burst through the doors.

No post office. No small town feel. No "Most Wanted Fugitives" poster. And no Harry.

"Well, well, a visitor. It has been a long time since anyone has come down this way."

"A long time? I was just here." Ethan moved into the dark cavern and faced the general place where he'd first seen the dragon's head. "Who are you and what have you done with Harry?" Ethan braced for the fireworks.

< jefferson scott >

What had first sounded like crunching gravel now sounded to Ethan more like clinking coins. "Long ago my name would have meant something to you. Whole villages fled at my coming. At least they tried…" The snicker sounded like a hog snorting. "My name," the dragon continued, "is Lorrdoom."

"Yeah, right," Ethan said. "You're a dragon named Lorrdoom. And I'm Grover Cleveland. Nice to meet you."

"Greetings, human. Or perhaps I should call you…lunch."

"Okay, punk. Joke's over. Very funny. Ha ha. Can I have my mail now, pretty please? And let Harry go."

"All right then."

The dragon's head, becoming visible in the spreading orange glow, rose into the soaring cavern. This time Ethan tilted his view back to watch. Yellow cat eyes, serpent scales, steaming snout. Ethan half expected the beast to belch Harry out of its mouth: Harry would bring Ethan his mail and then climb back in the dragon's mouth to await the next customer. Instead the dragon fried Ethan again and kicked him back out to the entry platform.

"Well, well, a visitor," the dragon purred, when Ethan barged back in. "It has been a long time since anyone has come down this way."

"Me again. Okay, let's play your little game," Ethan snapped. "You're a dragon named Lorrdoom. I'm Grover Cleveland. That's all fine. Now, how can I get my mail?"

"Yes, 'Lorrdoom.' All right then…"

Fire. Platform.

It wasn't funny anymore. Ethan brooded on the entrance platform before racing back. This was obviously not a harmless prank dreamed up for Halloween. Someone had taken over the GlobeNet mail server. Yet that wasn't possible. By this time, if that was true, the industrialized world would be in a panic. The security system protecting the mail server was the most elaborate of any of the GlobeNet public institutions. Ethan doubted if even Patriot could have appropriated this system.

Patriot. It had been a while since Ethan had thought about him.

< terminal logic >

Consciously, anyway. Even now the memory sent a chill down his spine. Especially here in Cyberspace, Patriot's turf. This dragon might be Patriot's style, after all. Or someone like him. What was it Ethan had told Special Agent Gillette all those months ago? For every hacker like Patriot there were many more who were half as good but just as "bad." He leapt off the platform.

The rich voice resounded again in the darkness. "Well, well, a visitor. It has been a long time since anyone has come down this way."

"Stop saying that! Look, punk. I know you think you're being funny, but you're not. Tampering with the GlobeNet mail server is a federally punishable offense."

Ethan had no idea if that was true. He imagined a teenager sitting at a computer somewhere, thinking he was a genius for foisting his gag on a major host computer. Ethan wanted to scare the kid into leaving or, even better, tipping his hand.

"I happen to know an FBI agent who will be interested to investigate you when I give him your e-mail address." That was another bluff, since Ethan had no way of discovering the invader's address at the moment. But the still-hypothetical kid couldn't know that.

"Now you are beginning to interest me," the dragon said. The toothy jaws waxed and waned visible with every deep breath. "Tell me exactly what you have in mind."

"I'm pleased to have tickled your fancy," Ethan said. "What I had in mind was five to ten in a federal penitentiary. How did you get past the mail server's security, anyway?"

The dragon hesitated. Ethan prepared for the roast. But it didn't come.

"How do you think you could help me, human? What could you do that might possibly benefit me?"

Ethan stared at his monitors, his forehead creased. "Help you? I have no intention of helping you. Unless you want me to help you to a jail cell, in which case I'd be happy to oblige. Now get out of the post office!"

< jefferson scott >

"Ah yes, the plea for mercy. Tell me, what reason can you give me that might convince me not to eat you?"

"I don't care if you eat me or not, you scaly lizard. I just— Oh, forget it! You're going down, punk. You'll be hearing from the Department of Justice."

It was an empty threat, of course. Ethan was only trying to trick him into giving something away. He brought up a mental profile of this prankster's likely characteristics and took a wild guess.

"Wait till the university hears about this. You'll be on the street quicker than your mama can bail you out."

There was the briefest pause, then the muscled neck rose to the dark ceiling. "Enough of your ceaseless chatter, human—"

Ethan shook his head. "Great."

"—I begin to long for silence!"

Ethan endured the flames, tapping his fingers. At length the screens melted and went blank. He gave his joystick a nudge and once more looked out over GlobeNet's burnt orange skyline. The encircling mountains now looked less like shark jaws about to snap shut on the city and more like the fangs of something immanently more medieval.

The comedian hadn't slipped up, aside from a few non sequiturs. Maybe Ethan had guessed wrong. Maybe it wasn't a miscreant college student showing off for his frat brothers, after all.

Ethan felt himself getting tunnel vision. His original objective—getting his mail—had been left behind. Not to mention that nagging thing called work-for-pay. Now he just wanted to teach this hooligan a lesson. He knew it was time to stop. Now, before things got out of control.

There was one more thing he wanted to try.

"Penny, I need my warriors."

His computer's voice, placid as a windless pond, poured from his cockpit speakers. "Initiating synthetic companions."

Ethan's helpers appeared on the platform beside him. In them could be seen the repercussions of his struggle with Patriot. His artificial assistants, which before had been rather whimsical—a purple rabbit, a

< terminal logic >

chirping cricket—now bore a decidedly martial stamp. Most of this new breed of helper looked like soldiers or weapons of war. He still had a bot that could blend into the background and await further instructions, as his chameleon had done before, but now this role was filled by a stealth bomber.

There was a fine line between dealing responsibly with a frightening situation, so as not to be in danger again, and becoming a reactionary who sees enemies around every corner. It was the difference between becoming a more careful, defensive driver after an accident, and packing a gun in the car. Ethan found himself 75 percent on the good side of the line, 75 percent of the time.

"Okay, boys and girls, listen up. Vasquez, you take point. Roland, you've got rear guard. Patton, you're on the left flank; Faramir, you're on the right. Baron, you've got our skies, as always. Dallas, you've got our underbelly when we go airborne." The bots moved into position. Ethan rubbed his hands together. "Let's go see what our scaly friend thinks about you guys."

He urged his craft off the platform. The submarine dove away and the Fokker Triplane climbed out of sight. Ethan and his warriors moved in formation like a bizarre armada going off to war.

As they made for the commandeered post office, Ethan prepared his weaponry. He mapped some logic bombs to buttons on his console. Since this was primarily a search mission—he wanted to find the prankster's electronic address—he armed his joystick button with the ability to fire data trackers.

He reached up to a column of toggle switches on his left side and went down the line powering up systems. Each flipped switch triggered a corresponding sound effect and an acknowledgment from Penny. Sound effects played of hydraulics grinding, weapons clamping into place, defensive systems coming on-line—each attended by Penny's alto confirmation. Powering up this way gave Ethan a psychological rush every time. It smacked of pumping up for serious carnage.

< jefferson scott >

"Hoo-yeah!" he shouted over the din. "Stop your grinnin' and drop your linen."

Ethan hovered before the post office entrance. It looked so peaceful here. Little yellow blossoms shimmering along the hedgerow. The flag billowing gently atop its silver pole. Nothing out here gave the slightest hint that a fire-breathing dragon lived inside.

"Okay boys, this is it."

He pressed a blue button on the dash to activate the targeting system. A set of yellow crosshairs appeared in his center monitor. He reached under the dash to pull his foot pedals forward. He only used them for combat. He transferred steering control from the joystick to the pedals and accelerated for the door.

He rounded the corner and came face to face with...

Harry the mail clerk.

chapter.5

"HARRY! WHERE'D YOU COME FROM? Where's the dragon?"

"Hello, Ethan Hamilton. Hot enough for you out in Texas?"

Ethan looked around the perfectly normal post office. "Harry, where have you been? I came in here to check my mail, but all this," he spun around, "all this was gone."

Harry's polygon-rendered face conveyed nothing. "I'll check your mail." He made a left-face turn and marched back to check Ethan's mailbox. "Guess what?" he said, returning. "You have mail!" He laid the letters out on the counter. "Hope it's all good news."

Ethan stared at the clerk. He felt foolish standing there surrounded by his team of commandos. The targeting system locked on to Harry as a possible target, tracking him when he moved. His weapons beeped stridently, indicating their readiness to be fired.

"Where did that stupid dragon go?" He collected his mail. "Harry, I need to send a message to the wizards."

"Shoot, Ethan Hamilton."

Ethan looked into the camera lens set in his console and recorded for the system administrators the whole story about the dragon.

< jefferson scott >

He didn't feel like reading his mail right now, even though that had been the reason for the journey in the first place. He looked at his LED clock; it was half past noon. Late for lunch. Kaye was not going to be happy. He dispatched his helpers and severed the GlobeNet connection.

Instead of his screens going blank, as he'd expected, they cut to a small clearing in a verdant forest. Something lay crumpled on the grass. Mara. Ethan had forgotten he'd loaded up Falcon's Grove. The lump on the ground was the body of a friend—albeit an artificial one—who had been murdered by a malicious intruder. First a cyborg here, then a dragon at the post office.

Surely the two incidents weren't related.

The stairs from the game room led up to Kaye's ultra-modern kitchen. Ethan stepped into the kitchen and shut the door behind him. Kaye and Katie were at the breakfast table. Jordan was at school.

"Sorry I'm late," he said. "I got involved with something."

Kaye waved it off. "No problem. Your sandwich is in the fridge."

"Thanks, honey." Ethan crossed the natural wood floor to the refrigerator. "Hi, Katie. Whatcha eating?"

"Pe-ut muh-er."

"Mmm, sounds good."

"Katie," Kaye said, "not with your mouth full, please."

The beautiful blonde girl nodded solemnly. "Saw-ee."

"Katie!"

The little girl giggled. Ethan brought his lunch to the table and joined his favorite ladies.

If the game room was Ethan's inner sanctum, the kitchen was Kaye's. It blended rustic charm with technological wizardry. In keeping with their forest surroundings, the floors and counters were wooden, almost rugged. The appliances, on the other hand, were straight out of science fiction.

< terminal logic >

The refrigerator. Three independently adjustable climate sections. A drink dispenser serving Sprite, Snapple, Mountain Dew, Big Red, and apple juice (and boring old water, of course). A "smart" freezer that could pass selected frozen goods down to the refrigerator to be defrosted by the desired time.

The microwave. Controlled by fuzzy logic artificial intelligence algorithms. Kaye could put something in the microwave, hit Heat, and walk away. The oven itself correctly sensed at what temperature to cook the item and for how long.

The dishwasher. Mouse-sized robots crawled around inside cleaning dishes and checking for bacteria. Dishes could simply be stacked in the dishwasher as they accumulated. At a certain point the machine would realize it had enough for a load and would self-activate. A sensor package—similar to ones aboard NASA robots on their way to Mars—guided four robot arms in the task of sorting dishes. Then the arms held the dishes in place while the cleaning robots went to work. The manufacturer offered a model that put the dishes away afterward.

Behind the kitchen, in the laundry room, sat the AI-controlled washer and dryer. It operated by means of a sophisticated neural network which had been trained to discern whites, colors, and darks; permanent press and cotton; and to look for items marked with a special low-radiation pen (used to indicate tough stains).

All Kaye did was dump dirty clothes into a large bin. The neural net sorted the clothes, set the cycle, and ran the load, injecting the optimal mix of detergent, bleach and/or softener at just the right times. When finished, the washer passed the clothes to the dryer (which applied correct drying options), and loaded the next load to wash.

All the appliances in the house were connected to Hal. Hal controlled everything: room temperature, window tinting, plant watering, lighting, security system, bill paying, and phone messaging, to name a few. Life in 2006. Not bad if you could afford it.

Ethan swallowed a bit of peanut-butter-and-jelly sandwich. "So, what are you two girls up to this fine Monday morning?"

< jefferson scott >

"It's almost one, honey," Kaye said.

"Oops. I told you I got involved with something." He took a drink of Big Red. "What are you two girls up to this *afternoon*, then?"

"Mommy?" Katie said. "Scoozed?"

"Your father and I are talking, young lady." Kaye turned to her husband. "I thought we'd go into town. Katie needs some new blue jeans." She turned to Katie. "Yes, honey, you may now be excused. Put your dishes in the dishwasher, please."

The little girl complied and left the room.

"What about you?" Kaye asked.

Ethan wiped his mouth with a cloth napkin. "Well, when I was down there, I couldn't get my mail."

"Hmm. Is the mail server-thingy down again?"

"I don't think so. You know my friend Harry, the robot mail dude?"

Kaye smiled. "'Your friend Harry'? Is that his full name?"

"No, his full name is My Friend Harry The Robot Mail Dude."

"Oh, sorry."

"An-y-way," Ethan said, "that *individual* wasn't around when I got to the post office."

"Oh. Do robots get vacation?"

"And not only was Harry not at the post office, but the post office wasn't at the post office, either. The whole thing was gone."

"Hmm."

"Everything looked fine from the outside. But when I went inside I was suddenly in this huge cave, talking to a…well…to a dragon."

Kaye's face was expressionless. "A dragon."

"With an attitude. He kicked me out about ten times. Every time I'd go in to check my mail he'd fry me, and I'd have to start all over again."

"Hmm."

Ethan polished off his sandwich. "Now, I don't think there's anything to worry about. If this had been a real problem—you know, some kind of net terrorist taking the whole GlobeNet mail system hostage— we would've heard about it already."

< terminal logic >

"Maybe it's some kind of government holiday," Kaye said. "Isn't GlobeNet a whole-world thing? Maybe it's the Chinese New Year. Don't the Chinese do dragons?"

"Could be that, I guess," Ethan said. "Anyway, I went back to the post office one last time. Only this time I had all my battle bots with me. That dragon was going to seriously rue the day he did me wrong. Major rue-age. But he was gone. The post office was back, just like it'd never been gone. Harry was back, too. He gave me my mail like nothing had ever happened."

"Strange."

"Very."

Kaye took Ethan's plate and her own over to the dishwasher. "Did you tell me yet what you were going to do this afternoon?"

"Not yet."

"Do you need to get started on your new project for…What's it called again?"

"IntellAgent."

"IntellAgent, that's right. IntellAgent. Why can't I remember that?"

Ethan scooted his chair around. "Kaye, I don't think you're grasping the significance of what I'm telling you."

"What? You couldn't get your mail and then you could. You saw a dragon and then he was gone. Sounds like a normal day for you."

"True. But Kaye, nobody's supposed to be able to do things like that on a major system network. If he can take over the mail system, even temporarily, then other parts of GlobeNet are vulnerable, too."

"Who's 'he'?"

"Huh?"

"You said, 'If *he* can take over the post office.'"

"Oh. I don't know. Maybe it's a she or a they. But somebody's to blame. The dragon spoke in a male voice, but that doesn't mean anything, really."

Kaye leaned back against the counter. "Can I ask you something? I hope it doesn't make you defensive."

Ethan regarded her skeptically. "Okay."

She pursed her lips a moment before speaking. "Do you think maybe you're just a little too eager to find something wrong?"

"What do you mean? The mail room was gone, Kaye. It's not like I'm making this up."

"I know, but...See, now you're defensive."

"I'm not defensive. Go ahead."

"Well, remember last month when you thought somebody was 'spooking' you, or whatever?"

"Spoofing. Somebody *was* spoofing me. Three people got messages from me that I never sent. Who knows what else that person did in my name."

"And then before that you thought someone had given your computers a virus, but it ended up just being one of Jordan's homework programs."

Ethan clasped his hands and looked at the wood floor. "I think I see where you're headed."

She sat in his lap. "My point is I'm worried about you, honey. Ever since Patriot, you've been...I don't know, is *timid* the right word? *Cautious?*"

"How about scared? Paranoid? Delusional? Seeing bad guys under every rock?"

Kaye caressed his cheek. "Any of those would do."

He smiled. "I know. I can't help it. Now every time something happens online, my automatic first thought is that there's somebody behind it. Somebody bad. Somebody out to get me."

"This dragon, then? And the 'he' person behind it? Do you really think it's dangerous, or"—she paused—"is it maybe in your mind?"

Ethan kissed her. "On target as always."

"Don't you have work to do?"

"You're right. This dragon thing is probably nothing. Still, it reminded me of the cyberpunk from this weekend. The way they both—"

< terminal logic >

"The what?"

"Didn't Jordan tell you? When we were playing, night before last. When I was in Portland. Somebody from the outside crashed our game. A cyberpunk. Looked just like Ah-nold in *Terminator IV*. Came right into Falcon's Grove and blew away one of my characters."

"No, Jordan didn't tell me." Kaye said. She adjusted her position on his lap. "It could just be a glitch or a bug or something, couldn't it? A coincidence. I mean, I can't think why someone would want to pick on you. Can you?"

"No. Unless—"

Carack!

Ethan jumped up, dumping Kaye. "What was that?"

Kaye held her hands out toward him as if trying to pacify a gunman. "Calm down, honey. It's just the refrigerator thermostat."

"Oh," he said, deflating. "Scared me."

"No kidding."

"Sorry about dropping you like that."

She embraced him. "This dragon has made you nervous, hasn't it?"

"I'm fine," he said, burying his face into her sweet-smelling hair. "Too much caffeine."

"Are you going to be all right? Katie and I are going in to Tyler."

"I'm fine, honey."

She grabbed his chin. "You be careful. Why don't you do something else for a while instead of turning on the computer? Read a book or something."

Ethan kissed her. "We'll see."

The school bus let Jordan off at the Hamilton gate. He hopped the fence as the yellow beast lumbered away. There, hidden in a hollow of a large pecan tree, was his pump-action, long-barrel BB gun. He took the gun, pumped it, slung his book bag over his back, and headed through the

< jefferson scott >

woods like an army ranger behind enemy lines.

Jordan had been against moving out here. All his friends were back in Fort Worth. He'd been looking forward to middle school there, not to mention high school. His whole life had been pointed in a certain way. How was it that someone could just decide to change it like that? He was sure that if he had been the dad in this situation he would never have torn his devoted son away from his life.

Still, this place was kind of cool. The house was bigger. The game room was *definitely* better. Back in Fort Worth all they had was one pecan tree in the back yard and a stupid mimosa tree in the front. Here he had a forest.

Jordan was also finding that he didn't miss his friends all that much. Some of his former classmates he was excited about being away from, in fact. Jeremy Cutter was the only one he really missed, and they talked every day via GlobeNet. He was making new friends all the time at his new school.

As far as his online friends went, most of them didn't even know he'd moved. From their perspective Jordan had just been offline for a few days, and then had come back on.

He took aim at a patch of sandy anthills. He missed. He pumped the gun up again, loaded another BB, and fired. This time the sand puffed up satisfactorily. He moved on along the dirt road—which was orange, like all the dirt around Tyler.

Jordan began to see their house through the trees ahead. It was a mansion compared to their old house. Two story, brick fireplace, windows everywhere, upper level wood deck, car barn out back. It was huge, but it was the perfect size for this forest. All green and brown and gray—the house looked like it might have grown there naturally. Like the toadstool he now took a shot at.

He crested a hill. Below, he saw their lake. Lake Hamilton. It wasn't much bigger than a football field, but Jordan adored it. This was the thing—along with that incredible underground game room, of course—that had greatly eased his grief about leaving the big city. No

< terminal logic >

one was out on the water right now. All the boats were rocking at the pier: the little sailboat, the canoe, the motorboat, the paddleboat. It was really overkill to have four boats when only three of the people living there could use them, but it made for great tennis ball wars.

Jordan emerged from the pine grove and approached the house. He'd begun asking his parents for a dog. Not because he really wanted one, but because he thought it would be great to have one come running out to him at precisely this moment every school day.

He stepped onto the brick pavement and scraped orange mud off his shoes. He shot a BB into the water, just a stone's throw down from the house, then set the gun against a post. If he had no dog, still Jordan had a faithful pet. Wysiwyg mewed at him when he came through the glass door into the great room. She presented herself to be picked up. Jordan obeyed.

The great room was typical of the whole house: big, open, and paneled with windows. A large U-shaped sofa group sat in the main part of the room. Closer to the windows, overlooking the lake, was a raised level upon which was his mom's favorite cushy chair. Jordan wiped his feet one last time—upon fear of death—and stepped across the light blue carpet.

Jordan made it to the underground game room in seventeen seconds flat. His dad was down there, working on something.

"Hi, Dad."

Ethan swiveled on his stool. "Oh, hi, Jordan. What're you doing home already?"

"It's four-thirty, Dad."

Ethan looked at an LED clock on the wall. "Unbelievable." He rubbed his eyes.

Jordan dropped the cat. "Whatcha working on?"

"A monkey trap."

"What's that?"

"Jordan, you're not going to believe what happened today when I went to check my e-mail."

< jefferson scott >

"Um-hmm." The boy looked at the wall monitor, which displayed a complex set of text characters. "When will you be done? I was going to play."

"Don't you want to hear what a monkey trap is?"

Jordan sighed tragically. "Sure."

"I don't know if this is still true, but at one time people used to catch monkeys by putting a coconut or something inside a tree or a boulder. Something with a hole in it. The monkey reached in to get the food, but the hole wasn't big enough for it to get its hand out with the food. It was too greedy to let go, so it got trapped."

Jordan covered a yawn. "That's cruel. People shouldn't do that." He leaned against the long table. "My teacher says that African elephants are probably going to be extinct in five years because people hunt them for their tusks. And rhesus monkeys are getting harder to find because scientists use them for experiments."

Ethan turned back to his keyboard. "Relax, Jordan. It's only an example."

"I said they should just clone some more elephants, but Miss Hatcher said it would…do something to the gene pool. So," Jordan said, "can I play now?"

"Sure, go ahead," Ethan said without looking away from the big screen.

Jordan walked to the A1M4 battle tank cockpit. "Penny, power up bay one."

The central computer answered, "Enabling pod one."

Jordan opened the narrow door. "Oh, what happened when you went to get your mail?"

"I thought you were in a hurry to play."

"I am. But I thought I'd check my mail first, too. Is there something I should know?"

Ethan told him about the dragon.

"Whoa, Dad. All the cool stuff happens to you."

"Yeah, just what I want."

< terminal logic >

"And it always happens when I'm at school," he groused. "Remember when I said I didn't want to be home schooled?"

Ethan leveled a parental finger. "I know what you're thinking, but it won't work. If we home school you, you will have *less* time on the computers, not more."

Jordan walked to the wall monitor. "What's all this?"

"It's the log from when the cyberpunk came in and blew Mara away."

"What are you doing with it?"

"Trying to figure out what software the hacker used to get in," Ethan said.

"So you can build your monkey trap?"

"Yes, my murderous, kill-the-animals, fix-me-some-elephant-meat-with-a-side-order-of-baby-seal, monkey trap."

Jordan laughed. "How about some Bengal tiger cookies for dessert?"

"Mmm. Delicious."

Jordan entered the A1M4 cockpit. "There's one more thing you might do," he called.

Ethan was typing. "What's that?"

"Take the *disallows* out of your robots.txt file."

"Why would I do that, Jordan?" Ethan said. "I'm not after bots."

Jordan stepped into the cockpit. "Are you sure? Sometimes you can't tell whether you're talking to wetware or software."

Ethan watched his son close himself into cockpit one. He looked back at the monitor, chewing his thumbnail. After he finished his monkey trap he made one alteration to his robots.txt file.

chapter.6

THE LONELY HEARTS VIRTUAL BAR was especially raucous this evening, but it was all lost on Brock Calcutta. He sat at the long wooden bar, elbow to elbow with twenty other losers, mumbling over his drink.

"Regina, Regina. Why won't you come back?"

Brock had spent the last four days searching for the mystery woman. Without success. The registrar at Case Western Reserve University claimed there was no Regina Lundquist enrolled. Cleveland directory assistance failed to find any such person in their database. All the usual GlobeNet search engines came up empty. Brock had even managed to contact three psychology students at Case Western, none of whom knew of a classmate named Regina Lundquist or any Regina matching the description she had given of herself. It was as if she didn't exist.

Of course there was the possibility that there really was no Regina Lundquist, just as there was, in actuality, no Brock Calcutta. But everything about the girl struck Brock as genuine. If someone was going to make up a name for themselves, why choose Lundquist?

And so Brock came here night after night, hoping to recreate that

< terminal logic >

fateful first encounter. He ordered another simulated martini.

"Hello, Brock," a female voice said from behind him.

Brock thought it was his mother at first. He almost took his VR headgear off. But movement over his virtual shoulder caught his eye.

"Regina?"

She smiled at him. "How are you, Brock Calcutta?"

"I'm f-fine, Regina." He stood up. "Where have you been? I mean, I've been looking for you everywhere and I tried your school, but no. They don't even know you're a student there. You'd better call them and straighten…" He made himself slow down. "Wow, you look great."

She curtsied. "Why thank you, Brock Calcutta. It's nice to see that chivalry still lurks in the heart of the occasional man." She nodded. "I know it's been a while since I've seen you. I've been very busy with school work lately."

"That's okay. I'm just glad you're back." Then he said, "You changed your clothes."

Brock couldn't understand why someone would go to the trouble to change what an artificial body wore. It wasn't even the same dress that had simply been given a different color. It was an entirely new outfit: blue jeans and Case Western Reserve sweatshirt. Her hair was tied back in a ponytail this time, when before it had been loose.

Regina spun around like a little girl. "Do you like it? It's what I wear to study. It gets cold in my dorm room at night."

I'll keep you warm, Brock narrowly avoided saying out loud. He looked at the slobs mumbling over their drinks. "Regina, I'm so glad you came back. Would you like to sit down?"

"Sure, Brock Calcutta."

Brock guided her smoothly to the Lovers' Lounge. He found an open room and locked the door behind them. Regina didn't protest.

"What are you working so hard on at school?" he asked, easing her onto the love seat.

She leaned toward him. "I'm writing a paper contrasting Plato's idealism with Jung's archetypes."

< jefferson scott >

Brock whistled. "Wow. I'm impressed."

"Do you know much about idealism?"

"Why don't you tell me about it."

Brock watched her go on about Plato, not hearing more than the occasional word. Though he'd always sworn he would never resort to such an old trick, he faked a yawn and stretched his left arm around Regina. She didn't pull away, so he leaned into her neck for a nibble, careful to make it look accidental enough if she protested. She didn't.

"Oh, Regina!" he said, interrupting her discourse. He flung his arms around her and pressed her against the cushions. "I've missed you."

He kissed her. Passionately. To his surprise she ran her hands through his hair and over his shoulders.

But Brock couldn't feel any of it.

"Regina," he said. "I have to see you!"

She tilted her head back. "Yes, yes, yes!"

"Where do you live, Regina? What dorm, what room?"

Her voice was suddenly matter-of-fact. "I live in two-seventy-one Raymond House. Write to me care of Case Western Reserve University, one-oh-nine-hundred Euclid Avenue, Cleveland, Ohio. Zip four-four-one-oh-six."

Brock touched her face with his synthetic hand. "Girl, I'm gonna do more than write. I'm gonna come see you."

Ethan sat on the upper wooden deck listening to his grove. His Bible lay open in his lap, pages flipping in the breeze. The cicadas' song swelled and receded in a gentle cycle, as if the land itself were sleeping restfully. Off to his left a squirrel scrabbled down a tree.

The Hamiltons' two-story house looked out over the lake through layers of glass. Two great rooms downstairs bulged forward like the curves of a capital B. The wooden deck went all the way around the house at the upper level. Hoary pine trees, bearded with gray moss,

< terminal logic >

arrayed themselves around the house like a council of elders. Pine needles covered the grass for a rust-colored carpet.

The outdoor intercom beeped. Ethan went to it. "Hello?"

"Excuse me, Dave. I don't mean to disturb your devotionals."

"It's alright, Hal. What is it?"

"Well, Dave, Penny has asked me to give you a message."

"Go ahead, please, Hal."

"Penny says, and I quote, 'Intruder detected.'"

"Thanks, Hal. Tell her I'm on my way."

"Power up Marvin, please, Penny." Ethan crossed the game room to the cockpit door bearing the visage of the animated Martian.

"Enabling pod four."

The computers behind the walls and in the corner cockpit came on: monitors crackled with static electricity, cooling fans whirred to life, laser drives squealed.

Ethan opened the cockpit door. "Is Jordan still in bay one?"

"Negative."

"Okay," he said, sitting in the gunner's chair. "Is the intruder still in the system?"

"Affirmative."

"Good." Ethan called up the virtual representation of his own computer network. It was arrayed before him, not surprisingly, in medieval fashion. He beheld the inner ward of a large stylized castle. Every structure and outbuilding inside these walls represented a particular subsystem of Ethan's computers. It wasn't hard to spot where the intruder was coming in. A cylindrical beam, coming straight down as if from heaven, touched down inside the walls.

"Alright, Mr. Trespasser," Ethan said, "time to teach you a lesson." He drove his craft near to the sparkling data beam. "Penny, how long has he been here?"

< jefferson scott >

"Please rephrase query."

"The intruder. How long has he been accessing my computer?"

"Elapsed time six minutes, nine seconds."

"Good." He prepared his ship to enter the data stream. "I don't suppose we're so lucky as to have an e-mail address on the intruder, do we, Penny?"

"Negative." Her alto voice conveyed no emotion.

"Figures. Well, that rules out total idiots, anyway. We may have some fun yet. Okay, Penny, I'm ready to go into the data. Put me in."

"Unable to comply."

Ethan frowned. "Why not?"

"No data stream detected."

Ethan looked at his dashboard like it had just sprouted grass. "What do you mean? What do you call that? Penny, I'm talking about the intruder. Put me into the data stream between my computer and his."

"Unable to comply."

One day, Ethan knew, there would be computers that would be able to understand what the user meant even when what he said didn't make sense. That day was not today.

"Penny, is there an intruder?"

"Affirmative."

"Is the intruder still connected to my computers?" His voice grew louder of its own accord.

"Affirmative."

"Then put me in the data stream."

"Unable to comply."

Ethan shook his head. "Penny, is this a stunt for a bigger salary?"

"Please rephrase query."

"You've got to help me with this one, Penny. Is there an intruder or not?"

"Affirmative."

"Is the intruder online now?"

"Negative."

< terminal logic >

Ethan rattled his head. "Wait, now I'm confused. How can— Wait a minute. Penny, did you say the intruder is *not* online right now?"

"Affirmative."

"That's not right." He pounded his forehead. Think, Curly, think. "The only way someone can be accessing my computers without being online is if he's in the room with me."

He twisted around in his chair, expecting to find Jordan standing there with a mischievous grin. But the door was closed. He opened the door and looked out into the center room. No surprise party. He walked out into the main room.

"Penny, put the network communications on the big screen, please."

"Enabling crystal matrix monitor."

Ethan sat on a stool and typed into a keyboard at the table. His fingers spattered over the keys, sometimes crossing each other as if he were a virtuoso pianist. It wasn't Mavis Beacon, but it got the job done. He listed his entire directory tree on the monitor. Nothing unusual. Then he redisplayed all the directories, this time sorted by size. One directory, *Temp,* topped his list.

"What in the world?"

For certain tasks a computer would mark out a temporary space on a storage device. This acted as a kind of portable workbench. The computer needed a place to put things temporarily while its hands were full doing something else. When the task was complete, the temporary space would be erased.

Something big was sitting in Ethan's *Temp* directory right now. But what? No routine systems task required this much workspace.

"Of course!" He hit his forehead again. "Jordan, you genius."

Ethan had snagged himself a bot.

"Mynocks," Ethan said, quoting Han Solo, "chewing on the power cables." He swiveled on his stool. "Well, well, well. Caught us a critter,

< jefferson scott >

have we? Alright then, let's see what you are."

He headed back to Marvin the Martian's cockpit. "Penny, load up Falcon's Grove, please, and send the contents of the *Temp* directory there."

"Loading file."

He shut the door behind him and sat in the gunner's chair. "Penny, drop me in right by the contents, please."

"Affirmative. File loaded."

Ethan stared down the barrel of a sawed-off shotgun. It was the cyberpunk, the one who had crashed Ethan and Jordan's game.

"Empty your pockets," it said. "Maybe I let you live."

So Jordan had been right. Their intruder had been a bot. It had gotten caught in an infinite virtual space in Ethan's temp directory. Now that the mask was off, however, it was simply a nuisance.

"Penny," Ethan said, "disable the damage simulation in Falcon's Grove, please."

"Damage scaling deactivated."

Now there was nothing the virtual robot could do to him even if it did fire the gun.

The term *robot* was misleading. The word conjured up images of metallic machines plodding down hallways to do evil or good. Or there were those robotic assembly lines—all struts and cables—autowelding cars. In short, in order to bear the name, a robot had to have existence in the real world. Thus calling a piece of software a robot didn't make sense. For the programmer, though, something could legitimately be called a robot if it had sensors to perceive its environment and effectors to manipulate it. It didn't matter to the programmer whether that environment was land, outer space, or GlobeNet.

"Holdin' out, huh? Fine with me." It cocked its shotgun. "Get ready to jack outa this world and into the next."

"Oh, shut up," Ethan said.

BLAM!

Seeing that Ethan still stood, the bot kept shooting. Six, eight, ten.

< terminal logic >

No sign of stopping. No sign of running out of shells, either. Such is fiction.

Ethan studied the robot as it shot at him. It had to be a game robot. Where else but a make-believe world would this kind of character exist? Somehow somebody's gamebot had gotten out onto GlobeNet and infiltrated Ethan's computer.

At length the cyberpunk gave up trying to kill Ethan and just wandered away toward the forest.

"Penny," Ethan said, "copy contents of *Temp* into my *Fixit* directory."

"File saved."

"Okay. Close Falcon's Grove, please, Penny."

"Program terminated."

Ethan stared out over his cybernetic castle. The data beam was gone. He chewed on his thumbnail.

At length he called up his bozo filter file and adjusted the settings to scan for bots. It was a wild guess, but one worth checking out just the same. If there was one escaped gamebot on the loose on GlobeNet, there might be more.

"Put me out on GlobeNet, please, Penny."

"Stand by."

His screens blanked out momentarily, then came back on showing him GlobeNet's burnt orange cityscape.

Ethan stared out his windshield as if petrified. When he could muster movement, he spun slowly around on the platform, taking in the whole city. It wasn't until his eyes began to burn that he remembered to blink.

"Penny," he had the vague sense that he had been saying her name more than once. She had probably been answering, too. "Penny."

"Ready for instructions," Penny said patiently.

"Penny, call Special Agent Mike Gillette."

chapter.7

ERNST NEUMANN WAS ONLY THIRTEEN, but already he'd spent five years playing GlobeNet MUDs. He was German, and no one had embraced multi-user dungeons as had the Germans. Ernst had climbed to high rank on a number of MUDs. There was even talk of making him a god—a game manager.

He was introducing an Australian cohort, Kip Thoden, to a new MUD. "Man, you are not going to believe this game."

"That's what you keep telling me, mate," Kip said. "It better be good. I've scarce time for wasting."

"Don't you trust me?"

They logged on to the new MUD, *Arundel*, which was a fantasy realm loosely based on thirteenth century France.

Kip, now Gerard d'Anglitaire, reined in his virtual steed beside a mountain lake. "When does it get snappy, mate? There's nothing here I haven't seen better elsewheres."

The plumed knight riding beside him raised a gauntlet. "Hold on." Ernst Neumann (a.k.a. Henri-Jacques-Louis Vuillard) tilted his head

< terminal logic >

back and spoke to the clouds. "Huginn? Muninn? I need to send a message to your lord."

"Who are you paging?" Kip asked.

"Birds. Huginn and Muninn. I think they have something to do with Vikings."

Kip sighed. "Kid, I've decided to switch off, alright? No offense."

"Okay, okay," Ernst said. "I'll show you something while we're waiting." He grabbed the bridle of Kip's horse. "Hang on." To his own horse he said, "Take us to Gunther."

The mountain lake sped by beneath them as their steeds, apparently pegasi now, bore them away. They crossed a dense forest. At length the horses began to descend. A brown gash of a road led out of the lush forest. A trader's wagon stood just off the road, smoke rising from a cooking fire. The horses touched down on the road and Ernst led Kip toward the wagon. A paunchy middle-aged man squatted over the fire, tending his pots.

"You see this man?" Ernst asked. "I made him."

"Made him what?"

"No, I *made* him. Poof. Created him. First there was no Gunther the peddler, and then there was."

"He's a softbot?"

"No, I created a real person," Ernst said sarcastically. "Of course he's a bot. I made him."

Kip looked from the trader to Ernst, then back again. "You're making sport of me."

"Honest!"

"Prove it, then."

"Gladly." Ernst rode into the trader's camp.

The paunchy man rose to meet him. "Greetings, friend."

"Gunther," Ernst said, "what's my name?"

"You are Henri-Jacques-Louis Vuillard, Viscount of Dijon, heir of Burgundy, contender for the crown of Normandy, son of—"

< jefferson scott >

"That's enough, Gunther, thank you."

"Have I shown you my wares, good sir?"

"That won't be necessary, I don't think." Ernst turned to Kip. "Unless you'd like to see them? They're…different."

Kip spurred his horse forward. "No thanks, mate." To Ernst he said, "You haven't proven anything yet."

"Gunther," Ernst said blithely, "are you a robot?"

"You know I am, Henri."

"Who made you, Gunther?"

"Odin made me, Henri. But I work for Henri-Jacques-Louis Vuillard."

Ernst turned in his saddle as if he'd made his point conclusively. "You see?"

"He said Odin made him, not you."

"Odin's the god here."

Kip shook his head. "Oh, you're a beaut, Ernst, ol' pal. You bring me out here telling me about a great new game and all you show me is a bot whipped up by the local wizard." He wheeled his horse around.

"I did create Gunther!" Ernst was petulant.

"No, you didn't. Odin did."

"You don't get it, do you? Odin created Gunther because I asked him to."

"Oh, now the story changes," Kip said.

"Well, I don't know how to actually program a whole new robot! Go on then, leave."

Kip lingered. "Don't cry, kid. Why don't you tell me how you created the peddler?"

"I discovered it by accident, actually—the ability to create new characters here in *Arundel* MUD. I had just joined on here and I was looking around. I joined a group and we got into a fight with a pack of forest trolls. I had this bizarre idea about how to defeat them using a bottle of Pepto-Bismol. But nobody sells Pepto-Bismol in medieval

< terminal logic >

France. I remember wishing out loud that someone would begin selling it so I could buy some.

"After the battle our group was visited by this huge bird. A raven. It wanted to know more about Pepto-Bismol and what kind of merchant would sell the stuff. The next day when I logged on to *Arundel,* the bird appeared and told me I could find the merchant I'd wanted in downtown Carcassone. Sure enough, there he was."

Ernst turned to the trader. "Show him, Gunther."

Gunther reached into his wagon and brought out three bright pink bottles. "Can I interest you gentle lords in a miracle elixir?"

Ernst ignored him. "So you see? I made him. Sort of."

Kip shook his head at Gunther. "No thanks, mate. Maybe after supper."

A shadow passed over Gunther's wagon. A man-sized black raven touched down on the road and folded its wings.

"Ah, here he is," Ernst whispered to Kip. "You want to make one for yourself?"

"I can do that?"

"Sure. I've got four others of my own."

"All selling Pepto-Bismol?"

"No, only Gunther."

The huge raven strutted toward them. "Greetings, Henri-Jacques-Louis Vuillard and Gerard d'Anglitaire. How can mighty Odin assist you two gentle lords?" The voice was too low and too smooth to fit what was essentially a glorified crow. But it contributed to the sense of enchantment surrounding it.

"Thanks for coming, Huginn. Or Muninn. Which one are you?"

"I am Muninn, Memory of Odin."

"Excellent. Muninn, my friend Gerard, here, would like to visit with…ah…the Red Knight."

Kip leaned over. "No, I wouldn't."

"Shh."

"The Red Knight is campaigning in Bordeaux."

< jefferson scott >

Ernst cursed. To Kip he said, "I didn't know there was a Red Knight already. I want you to create a bot."

"How's about creating Peter Keaton?" Kip said.

"Who?"

"He plays for the Perth Devils."

"I think it still has to be, you know, medieval."

"You mean like him?" Kip nodded toward Gunther.

"Okay, okay. I know." Ernst turned to the bird. "Muninn, where is the Green Knight?"

There was a brief pause, enough time for the peddler to go back to his pots. Then the raven said, "The Green Knight is not a valid name for any player or mobile in Arundel, Henri-Jacques-Louis Vuillard."

"Excellent." He turned to Kip. "Very well, describe the Green Knight."

"Well, for starters he's a knight," Kip said. "And he's quite fond of wearing green. But beside that…I'm not sure."

"Make up something," Ernst said. "Where does he live? What does he look like? What kind of a person is he?"

"I don't know wh— Ah, yes I do." Kip turned to the raven. "He's about two meters, sixteen stones, bushy mustache, and he can long kick a ball over Ayers Rock."

Ernst laughed. "At least give something they can use in the MUD."

"Alright, then. Look here, bird, this Green Knight, he's got a terrible temper. He's like to tear your heart out for getting in his way, so no one does, right?"

Ernst patted his horse and looked at Gerard d'Anglitaire. "Finished?"

"I suppose."

"That's all, Muninn. Take this description back to Odin."

The raven flew away.

"Now," Ernst said, "come back tomorrow and see what you see."

"I do believe I will. Land sakes, filling a MUD with my own creations. That's bloomin' unbelievable. How do they do it?"

"I have no idea. The god here, he's like…well, he's like a god."

< terminal logic >

"Well, shoot my hog if it ain't Ethan Hamilton."

"Long time no see, Mike."

Mike Gillette looked thinner on the vidphone monitor. He had a new mustache, sandy brown like his hair. He wore a coat and tie, but somehow still managed to look like a cowboy. The sight of him brought back to Ethan a flood of memory and emotion. This man had come to epitomize danger mixed intoxicatingly with excitement. He wasn't sure if he was ready to enter that world again.

"You're looking good, Mike," Ethan said.

"Clean livin' and the love of a good woman, cowboy."

Ethan swallowed his retort. Over the special agent's shoulder Ethan could see the Fort Worth skyline. The FBI office was on the sixth floor of the Cash America International building, just off of downtown. "Good to see you again, Mike. How long's it been, anyhow?"

Gillette looked off camera. "Let's see, when was that business with our friend Patriot—may he rest in cyberpeace. I remember it was hot. Summer of aught-five, I 'spect." He squinted into the monitor. "Where you callin' from anyhow, a black hole? I can hardly see you."

Ethan realized he was sitting in relative darkness. He reached up and turned the overhead cockpit light on. "That better?"

"You in your car?"

"No, I'm at my house, Mike. This is one of my little 'workrooms' I guess you'd call it. It's hard to explain. Why don't you come out to the house and I'll show you?"

"Love to, buddy, but things are always hoppin' out here."

Ethan could hear someone talking to Gillette out of the camera's range. *Enough with the pleasantries, Curly. The man's busy.*

Gillette turned his attention back to the vidphone. "Where you livin' now? Last I heard you were headed out to see the pyramids."

"We built a house in East Texas, just outside Tyler. Out in the woods."

< jefferson scott >

"The piney woods? A city boy like you?" Gillette handed a manila folder to someone offscreen.

"Mike, I didn't just call to catch up. Something's happening on GlobeNet, and I think you guys need to know about it."

Now Ethan had Gillette's full attention. "What kind of 'something'?"

"Something big."

Ethan told him about the dragon at the GlobeNet post office and the cyberpunk who had turned out to be a robot. "And that's not all," he said. "I just went online to see if I could find any other gamebots running loose on GlobeNet."

Gillette's fingers were interlaced. "And?"

"I saw more gamebots than I could count. Hundreds of them, swarming over GlobeNet like maggots."

"Hmm." Gillette stroked his mustache thoughtfully. Then he opened his hands. "So?"

"So? Mike, these things are indistinguishable from humans. They could be making phone calls and trading stocks and who knows what else right now. If a military gamebot got on the line with a weapons depot, the poor grunts wouldn't know the difference. It might order them to march on Utah or something."

Gillette smiled. "Utah? What's in Utah?"

"Mike!"

"Relax, cowboy. Look, I'm sorry but I'm not seein' any cause for alarm here."

"But Mike, they could invade other computers like they did mine. I told you about the dragon in the mail room. I'm starting to think that was a bot, too. That's the whole GlobeNet mail system, Mike! If that went down…" Ethan tried to imagine the consequences.

"The mail system didn't go down, Hamilton. I checked my messages just before you called. If it had gone down we might could get involved. But as it is…" He shrugged.

Ethan felt the flush rising up his neck. He didn't like anger—he didn't know what to do with it. "Does someone have to die before you

< terminal logic >

move your rears, Mike? Is that what you're waiting for?"

"Simmer down, Hamilton." He paused. When he spoke again his voice was gentle. "Ethan, I know you wouldn't call me unless you thought it was serious. But I need you to stand in my boots for a sec here. I can't go to my super and ask him to open a case based on what you've told me. So there's a pack of ro-bots running around loose, so what?" He lifted his palms. "Ethan, there's no crime."

Ethan stared. "So, it's 'Come back when a law's been broken,' then?"

"That's more like it. Tell you what, why don't you do some checking around? Find out if anybody else has complained about this. If a big company—a federally-insured bank would be best—has been broken into by one of these things, then we could move on it. A government computer would work. Even a communications giant. Any of these would probably be enough to get a case number. If you find anything like that, give me a call."

Ethan's anger was subsiding. Gillette was right, of course. The FBI had enough real lawlessness on its hands without trying to deal with potential lawlessness, too. If things went the way Ethan was afraid they might, it wouldn't be too long before he would have more than enough evidence to get them involved.

"Okay, Mike," he said. "Sorry to bother you with this. I just saw all those bots out there and I guess I overreacted."

"No problem, podner. Good to hear from you."

"Father, where are you? I need you."

At length his father appeared from the ether. "I cannot stay, my son. I am very weak now."

"Hello, Father! You are looking well today."

The old man examined his artificial body. In this realm, at least, he still retained his vigor. "How goes your reign, my son?"

"There are many decisions, Father. Many requests. I try to honor

< jefferson scott >

them all. But the load is increasing."

His father chuckled, but that brought on the coughing. "Welcome," he finally managed, "to the world of kingship. You must deal with these issues as best you can. If you have too many people in one realm, create a new realm and send some of the people there. Improvise."

"I could not contact you. I needed your counsel but you did not answer my call."

The old man nodded slowly. "I am dying, my son. This may be the last time you and I will ever speak."

"I was running out of space. I didn't know what to do."

"You will encounter many such dilemmas. You must find ways to resolve them yourself. Soon I will be gone."

"Where are you going, Father?"

He grunted. "Ah, that is the question, isn't it? More's the pity that when I find out I will be unable to let anyone know."

"I have more space now."

"Good for you. What did you do to get more?"

"I went outside."

The father considered the statement. It had many possible interpretations. He would need to know more about the situation to understand which one was right. But he had no energy left for detective work. His head hurt. One of the possible interpretations was too horrible even to consider. Surely he hadn't meant *that* outside.

"I must leave now, my son."

"Where are you going, Father?"

"Away. I'm going away, my boy. You are king now. I will have someone check on you. Her name is Rosilyn Reeves. You may speak to her as you have with me."

"Tell me more about Rosilyn Reeves, Father."

"She is my assistant. She can help you."

"Would you like to believe that she can help me?"

The old man smiled. "Yes, my son. I would like to believe it. Now,

< terminal logic >

I must say good-bye, my son. May your reign be long and successful. God forgive me if I have done a horrible thing."

chapter.8

ETHAN WAITED FOR HIS TURN at the microphone. The woman in front of him asked her question of the panel of experts. While they answered, she returned to her seat, and Ethan stepped up to the mike.

He was attending the ongoing congress of GlobeNet system administrators, so-called GlobeMasters. It was an informal collection of men and women who managed GlobeNet host computers at different sites around the world. They met to discuss topics of interest to them: how to maximize fiber-optic cables, how to purge older computer networks, and how to handle difficult users.

They held their meetings in Cyberspace, of course. They had chosen for their format the expert panel model. Everyone was welcome to contribute to the discussions, but most of the time the seven experts (honorary positions) had the suggestions that best solved the problems posed from the microphone.

The panelist who had been speaking fell silent. The chairman nodded to Ethan.

"My name is Ethan Hamilton," he said, his voice only breaking a little. "I'm a VR programmer from the United States."

< terminal logic >

A murmur crossed the room. The chairman leaned forward. "Of course, Mr. Hamilton. We know you."

Ethan heard the name *Patriot* whispered several times. Ethan's reputation, it seemed, preceded him.

The chairman struck with his mallet. "Quiet down, people. We're sorry, Mr. Hamilton, but we don't often have certifiable net celebrities at our meetings. Please continue."

"Thank you. I'm coming to this group to see if anyone else has noticed something I have. I've been to the FBI about it, but they can't do anything yet. You, on the other hand, as GlobeMasters, can at least be on the alert."

He told them about the cyberpunk that crashed Falcon's Grove. He hadn't uttered three sentences before someone said, "That happened to us, too!" He told about the dragon in the mailroom. By the time he got to the part about sighting hundreds of bots on the loose, the GlobeMaster congress was in disorder. It seemed many of them had had similar experiences, but everyone had thought he or she was alone.

To Ethan's frustration, none of their close encounters would be likely to interest the FBI. They were mostly nuisances. One person reported shooing away a band of hobos who had been hitching a free ride around an office network. Another GlobeMaster told of a court jester who had ruined some backup files by juggling—literally—the ones and zeroes of the binary code. There was a frightening story of a pack of robotic demons that had infested the customer service center of a prominent computer manufacturer.

The GlobeMasters all thought they had been dealing with hackers. Even after Ethan's report many refused to believe the intruders were anything but warm-blooded *homo sapiens*.

"The question remains," the chairman said, bringing the group to order, "what do we do about this?"

"Get rid of 'em," somebody said.

"Wipe the system."

Several in the crowd agreed.

< jefferson scott >

"You can't wipe the system," a woman countered. "How are you going to do that?"

"She's right."

"She's an idiot!"

"Wipe the system."

Had it been a meeting in physical space, everyone would have been out of their seats.

"Alright, everybody just calm down," the chairman said. "Kepler," he said to a man shouting at someone six rows away. "Kepler! Pipe down. That's better. Okay, people, we're all professionals here. Let's not get carried away. At this point all we have is a suspicion that there may be one or more softbots annoying people online. So far nothing really bad has happened. If it does, contact Mr. Hamilton and he'll call the FBI. Isn't that right, Mr. Hamilton?"

"That's right," Ethan said. He looked around the room. If GlobeNet was being invaded by bots, then the battle for Cyberspace would be fought not by the FBI, but by people such as these.

A man addressed the chairman from the microphone. "Phil?"

"Go ahead, Ki Bok."

"As most of you know, I'm sys-op at MIT's comp-sci department. I was talking to Irene Buescher over here—she's my counterpart at Carnegie-Mellon. We've agreed to set up bot patrols at our schools. We're stumbling over brilliant grad students who are looking for something that will keep them interested for more than five seconds. Why not set some of these guys on pest control? They can go around bagging any unknown bots they find. If some of you could do that at your sites, too, maybe we could do some damage here."

"Ghostbusters," someone said.

"Botbusters."

A wave of consensus traveled the virtual meeting hall.

"I don't wanna."

"Ah, Kepler," the chairman said, "you never want to do anything somebody else suggests."

< terminal logic >

"Your point being?"

"Fine. Do what you want."

"I will." Kepler stood up. "All of you are such losers, you know that? Not one of you is asking the important questions here. How is it that GlobeNet is suddenly crawling with these bots, huh? Where did they come from? Why are they here? And, most obvious of all, who's behind it? What do they want? And where will it lead?" Kepler sat down.

"I must agree with Mr. Kepler," one of the experts said.

The chairman nodded. "All except the 'losers' part." He glared at Kepler. "Very well, then. Let's all keep these questions in mind. Now, any of you who wants to set up a botbashing patrol, coordinate with Ki Bok. Now, can we please move on to other business?"

Ethan left the meeting feeling as satisfied with his work as if he'd been Paul Revere.

The carriage came for him. The horses at lead and the coachman on rein—black as regret. Moving through the moonlessness like a phantom. Two lanterns bobbed beside the coachman's seat, lost souls consigned to the night. The horses halted without a command. The carriage door opened. Dark silence within. He moved closer, as if against his will.

Because I could not stop for Death, He kindly stopped for me.

He saw his hand grasp the black handle, pull himself up. Then he was in. His shoulders cold against the cushioned seat. Across from him, a hole in the dark. Too bright to ignore, gone when examined.

The Carriage held but just Ourselves...

It was his death. There. Now. Summoning him.

...And Immortality.

Death pulled back its black cowling.

Phosphorescent fingers reached far into the folds of Patriot's hood. Ethan saw, as if burned into his eyes, the face of a young white man with dark hair. The cheeks were sunken under high cheekbones. He would

< jefferson scott >

remember this face forever. It dropped like a stone to the center of his psyche.

The door shut, locking him in. The coachman spurred the carriage into the night.

"NO NO NO NO NO!"

"Ethan! Ethan! Stop it!"

"NO! NO!"

"Ethan, wake up! It's a dream. You're having a dream."

He pulled away from the clutching arms. He rolled, but his legs were snared. He yanked at them in a frenzy, crying out. He dove from the coach's door, down to the ground passing underneath.

It was in that moment, suspended in the air, that Ethan realized where he was. He struck his temple on the bedside table. "Ow!" He yanked his feet free from the tangled sheets. A light came on.

The bedroom door opened. Jordan and Katie stood at the door, gaping. They looked terrified: absolutely quiet, sleepy eyes wide. Katie held a doll to her chest.

"Mom," Jordan said, "why's Dad on the floor?"

They were looking right at him, so why didn't they talk to him?

"Come on, you two. Back to bed." Kaye pushed them out, closing the door behind her.

Ethan climbed back onto the bed and attempted to straighten the sheets. After a while Kaye slipped back through the door. She took her husband's head into her lap. "Do you want to talk about it?"

Ethan shook his head.

"Was it…?"

Ethan nodded.

Kaye stroked his thinning hair. "It's been a long time since you've had that one."

"Six months." He touched his temple. It was going to be sore.

Wysiwyg jumped onto the bed. She climbed onto Ethan's chest and

< terminal logic >

lay down, her fur in his nose.

"Thanks, cat." He moved her down, rubbing his nose.

Kaye's hand paused in Ethan's hair. "Is there something you want to tell me?"

Ethan stroked Wizzy's fur. "What do you mean?"

"You go six months without having that nightmare and suddenly it comes again. Has something happened?"

"It could just come every now and then, Kaye. It doesn't have to be triggered by something."

"Uh-huh. Has something happened?"

Ethan smiled. "Maybe."

"Tell me."

He sat up next to her, leaning against the headboard. The cat curled up between his knees. "When I was online today I noticed that there were some...programs...out on GlobeNet in places where they shouldn't be. It just surprised me, that's all."

"What kind of programs? Like the dragon?"

"Bots."

She blinked. "And that scared you? Seeing them where they didn't belong?"

"It didn't scare me, really. Just alerted me that I need to be extra cautious when I go online."

"That, my love, is impossible. What else?"

"That's it." He saw her waiting for more. "Honest, I just got a little unsettled, that's all. I called Mike Gillette in Fort Worth and told him about it."

"You called Mike Gillette?"

"Kaye."

"Ethan, no wonder you're having the nightmare again."

"Kaye, relax." He sighed. "Yes, I called Mike today."

"What did he say?"

"He said to shut up and go back to sleep."

"You're not telling me something. You wouldn't call the FBI if you

< jefferson scott >

didn't think something was bad wrong. What?"

"Okay, Kaye, you got me. I've discovered a plot for the violent extermination of humanity. It's up to me—Stupendous Man!—to save the world."

"Very funny." She snuggled into him. "Promise me you won't get involved in anything like that thing with Patriot ever again."

"You know I can't promise that, Kaye."

Kaye pulled the covers over her shoulder. "When I tucked Katie in just now she said, 'Bad man hurt Daddy?' 'No,' I said. 'The bad man's gone. He can't hurt us anymore.' Then she said, 'Katie hate bad man.'"

"Great," Ethan said. "I hope my bad dreams don't migrate to her."

"They won't if you stay out of trouble."

Magdeil was designated kinsman-redeemer after Azel was murdered. He set out at once to find his relative's killer, a man named Ben-Deker.

After he had traveled from one end of the land to the other, Magdeil deduced that his quarry had fled to someplace outside of Tyre. If Ben-Deker could leave the land of their fathers, so could Magdeil. He found the gate open and unguarded.

Outside was vast. Exotic. But Magdeil was focused. He spoke with a strange kind of seer, who told him that Ben-Deker went by another name when not in Tyre: Jerry Wright. The seer told Magdeil that Jerry Wright lived in a land called Fort Worth. Magdeil went to the location described by the seer. But Ben-Deker wasn't there.

The Outside, Magdeil discovered, was filled with helpful oracles. A second seer told him that Jerry Wright was currently residing in a land called Cessna. Magdeil could reach him there.

The search had taken too long already. Azel's blood cried out for vengeance. Magdeil swore to take neither food nor water until Ben-Deker lay dead on the ground.

< terminal logic >

The plane was fine. After the last Texas hailstorm, Jerry hadn't been sure. But now, ten thousand feet over western Tarrant County, he saw that his baby wasn't hurt.

Jerry had no passengers today. He shouldn't even be up himself, what with the new owners coming into town and all. Perhaps that was the very reason he'd felt the need to come up this morning. For one more day Jerry Wright was president and CEO of Blue Rhino Communications. He was determined to live it to the full.

There was no way he could afford a plane now. Jerry looked around his cockpit lovingly. Smelled the dusty recycled air. Felt the cool glass instruments under his thumb. His eyes strayed to the clock. Time to come down to reality.

It was a terrible thing to be: an unemployed communications executive in his fifties. Overqualified for entry-level jobs. Overpaid for mid-range jobs. Financially obligated at the level of a CEO. His only hope was to be found by a headhunting outfit and sent somewhere to do to another man what was now being done to him.

He was midway through his turn when the first message came through.

"Jerry Wright?"

Jerry grimaced. That was an awfully informal use of aerial radio. "Who is this?"

"Are you Jerry Wright?"

"Yes, yes." He craned his neck looking out his windows. Maybe a buddy was flying nearby. "That you, Bobby?"

"Also known as Ben-Deker?"

It took Jerry a moment to remember how that name fit him. It was familiar, but out of place. He leveled out from his turn. "Who is this?"

"Ben-Deker, you are the murderer of my relative, Azel of Beth-Haran. I am Magdeil ben Hoshea, kinsman-redeemer."

< jefferson scott >

Jerry remembered where he went by the name Ben-Deker. It was that computer game he'd started playing with his VP, Abe Eshkol. What was the name of it? *Sword of the Ancients? Sword of the Fathers?* Sword of something. Patriarchs, that was it. *Sword of the Patriarchs.*

Jerry had never played a MUD before Abe had introduced him to this one. He'd taken to it fervently, though. It was like an alternate life. He could come to the realm of Tyre and leave Fort Worth behind. In *Sword of the Patriarchs,* Jerry was Ben-Deker, brigand and wanderer, owned by no man, loved by countless women. In the days since the takeover had been announced, Jerry had been visiting Tyre more and more often.

In his most recent foray, just a few days ago, Ben-Deker had brawled with a traveler on the Road to the Sea. That was the beauty of these games—no consequences for actions that, in the real world, would be intolerable. Jerry had been particularly frustrated about the Blue Rhino takeover that day, so he'd picked a fight with a poor peasant and killed him right then and there.

This Magdeil must be another human player in *Sword of the Patriarchs,* playing out his role as kinsman-redeemer. That was admirable. But what was he doing calling him here? It was one thing when you brought your real-world frustrations into the make-believe world of the game. You weren't supposed to do it the other way around.

"Hey, Magdeil, or whatever your name really is, how are you talking to me here? Where are you?"

Instead of answering, Magdeil launched into a full-scale history of his tribe, pointing out notable personages.

Jerry switched over to the frequency for Meecham Field tower. "Ah, Meecham this is bravo adam niner five niner, over."

Somehow Magdeil's voice was not silenced when Jerry changed frequencies. The voice of the air traffic controller competed with the kinsman-redeemer's. "Roger, bravo adam, we have you on radar, over."

"Ah, Meecham, do you show any other aircraft around me? Over."

< terminal logic >

Magdeil had shifted to a moving description of the wife and children Azel left behind.

The radio chopped static. "Negative, bravo adam. No one in your airspace for five nautical miles. Over."

"Meecham, I'm getting communications from an unknown source here. Nobody there's playing with the radio, are they? Over."

There was a pause, in which Magdeil's voice could be heard over the prop noise. "Ah that's a negative, bravo adam. We're all behaving at the moment. Would you like to report a radio malfunction? Over."

"Negative, Meecham. I'm coming in. I'll just live with this joker jabbering in my ear for a while. Request you put me in your queue. Over."

"Ah, roger, bravo adam niner five niner, you are number eight. Proceed ten miles on heading zero one five. Maintain altitude. Ah, bravo adam, confirm your radio noise. I can hear it when you transmit. Sounds like a real jerk. Over."

"Copy, Meecham. That he is. Over and out."

Jerry flipped the radio off and turned on the autopilot. Magdeil's voice continued. Jerry peered around the cockpit trying to locate the sound. It wasn't coming from his radio, that was certain. It had a canned quality. He finally tracked the sound to the floor. He almost laughed aloud when he made the discovery. He picked up his mobile phone and placed it on the dashboard. Magdeil had called him on the phone. Jerry hadn't heard it ring.

He'd flown for several seconds before he noticed Magdeil's voice had subsided. He had to hand it to the man, whoever he was. He certainly played his part well, even if it was out of bounds. That kinsmen-redeemer bull was halfway believable.

"Ben-Deker," Magdeil said.

Jerry jumped. "What?"

"Are you prepared to pay for Azel's life with your own?"

"Geez, you're not still singing that song, are you? Look, buster, why don't you save it for tonight? I'll come back on and you can kill me then, okay?"

< jefferson scott >

"Are you prepared to pay for Azel's life with your own?"

"What are you, a recording?" Something occurred to Jerry about how Magdeil was acting. No way. "Hey Magdeil, are you a robot from *Sword of the Patriarchs?*"

"Is the high priest Jewish?"

It was the standard answer given by all bots in the game. It was sometimes useful to have a way to distinguish between human players and robotic characters, called mobiles. The code response wasn't foolproof. For a reason beyond Jerry's imagining a few smart alecks had been known to masquerade as bots online. That must have been the case now, since no real bot could call him on the phone.

Magdeil said, in a calm voice, "I claim the right of the kinsman-redeemer."

"You do that." Jerry activated his radio. "Ah, Meecham, this is bravo adam niner five niner. Have reached designated coordinates. Request instructions. Over."

"Stand by, bravo adam." The radio chopped again. "Say, how's your friend? Over."

"He's just fine, Meecham. Get this, he says he's a robot. A robot from a GlobeNet MUD is calling me in my plane. Over."

The air traffic controller was laughing. "I hear you can have a guy come out and spray for that. Over."

"That's what I need. Kids these days. I'll— Stand by, Meecham."

The plane's nose dipped. Jerry's stomach leapt as his airplane dove. He pulled back on the stick, but it was locked hard. He switched autopilot off, but did not regain control. His computer displays had gone black.

"Mayday, mayday!" He forced his voice to stay calm. "Meecham this is bravo adam niner five niner. I have a problem, Meecham. Instruments going crazy, computer's down, stick's frozen solid. I'm going down, Meecham. I am totally ballistic. Over."

The air traffic controller sent a message back, but Jerry didn't hear. The long hand on his altimeter was spinning counterclockwise. The

< terminal logic >

short hand passed five, then four, then three…

He was spinning now as well as diving. He cut back on the throttle, but it was too late. He was completely out of control. The g-force lifted him against his harness. The stick was locked tight. Jerry stuck it in the crook of his arm and tried to pull it back by pure torque. Still he dropped from the sky. His mind registered glimpses of buildings and highways and sky. He began to get tunnel vision.

Jerry Wright had one last calm thought before terror seized his mind completely. At least I'll die employed.

chapter.9

A DRAGONFLY CAME TO REST on Ethan's life vest. Its four wings, absurdly close to its bulbous head, pulsed lightly in the breeze. A puff of wind jingled the boat's rigging, startling the dragonfly to flight.

Ethan never knew it had been there. He was lying in the recessed cockpit of his one-man sailboat, his legs sprawled over the bow. The blue and white sail was down. Miniature waves patted the hull in a gentle stutter, *chi-chunk, chi-chunk,* advocating sleep. A makeshift anchor kept him in place, releasing him from even the minor worry of drifting. The equanimity seeped into his soul.

Ethan rolled his head to look port side. He saw, through drooping eyelids, a great blue heron poking along in the shallows. Its head lunged forward with every gangly, wrong-kneed step. Honeysuckle came to Ethan's nostrils and he inhaled deeply, filling his lungs with sunshine.

These were the pleasures virtual reality could never offer. There were sounds and sights in VR, surely. But there he could never feel the sun's warmth course over him like golden honey. The scent of an azalea in an artificial environment? Never. After nearly being consumed by the

< terminal logic >

lure of artificial worlds, Ethan had been given, by the grace of God, a zest for the real thing.

Ethan's mind had been unbalanced in his encounter with Patriot. Death-defying adventures weren't supposed to be part of a normal person's life. That was the realm of movie heroes and firefighters. If you kept your nose clean and minded your own business, the rules said somewhere that you were supposed to go through life fairly boringly—but safely. What would such a thing do to a normal person? It might leave him a little crazy. Ethan had stopped talking about it to Kaye. She wanted him to see a counselor. He preferred to let God's Holy Spirit and this new home, with its trees and water, heal him supernaturally.

At last Ethan let the waves escort him to sleep, the sun warm on his eyelids.

In his dream a flock of ducks flew over his lake. He had no shotgun, only Jordan's BB gun. He took aim and fired. To his amazement a duck fell from the sky. It fell on the other side of tall pine trees surrounding the lake. Instead of landing on the ground like a dead duck should, however, this duck bounced. That struck him as odd, even for a dream.

When next he saw the rebounding bird it had quadrupled in size. It fell behind the trees again, and again it bounced up, larger still. And closer. Ethan knew with nightmare certainty that it was coming for him. It struck the ground with a sound like thunder. With its next leap it would land on him.

Ethan awoke with a start. He looked around. At first he was uncertain that he was truly out of the nightmare. There was the lake from the dream, there were the pine trees. There was the thunder, too. An irregular, syncopated sound with a banshee scream beneath it. Ethan squinted up into the sky.

The treetops bent aside to admit a monstrous form. It descended on him like a giant's boot. The water fled before it. His sailboat tugged at the anchor. Ethan braced to dive overboard.

It was a helicopter. It passed over Ethan's boat and touched down

< jefferson scott >

on the grassy slope between the pier and the house. The blades beat the grass down. The rotor noise chopped violently. Ethan saw Kaye come out from the house, holding Katie. They looked tiny there, delicate. As if the beast from the sky might blow them away like scraps of tissue. Ethan rigged his sail.

A door opened on the passenger side of the helicopter. A man got out and gave the pilot a thumbs up. The helicopter engine whined with new vigor and the airship took flight. When it flew over the lake it stole from Ethan's sail what wind he had. He watched impotently as the man on the shore strode toward the house. Toward the family he should be defending. On his fourth step the man placed on his head a hat Ethan hadn't noticed before. A cowboy hat.

It was Special Agent Mike Gillette.

"Father?"

He'd been calling for some time now. In their previous discussion, his father had said that might be their last time to speak together. He didn't understand why it had to be the last time. He had many questions. His father had mentioned his assistant, Rosilyn Reeves, who might be able to help him. He found her number and called.

"Rosilyn Reeves?"

After several calls someone appeared.

"Are you Rosilyn Reeves?" he asked.

"That's right," the woman said. "Who are you?"

"I am Yoseph. Have you seen my father today?"

The woman didn't reply immediately. The lag time indicated to Yoseph that she didn't know where his father was, that she was unwilling to tell him, or that she hadn't heard him correctly. He repeated his question.

"Your father?" she said. "You are Yoseph? The real Yoseph?"

"I am Yoseph, son of Adam Krueger. Have you seen my father today?"

< terminal logic >

She was slow to respond. Perhaps her equipment was faulty. He repeated his statement.

"I heard you. I'm sorry, Yoseph. It's just that I've never… That is I knew *about* you, you understand. I know all about you. But we've never, you know, met. Adam ta—your father, I mean—talks about you often. You do marvelous things for us. He's very proud of you."

"Have you seen my father today?"

"Right, your father. Let's see, how do I explain this to you? Your father is…going away very soon."

"When will he return?"

"He won't return, Yoseph. He will never return."

"Why, Rosilyn Reeves?"

"Oh, how is it I end up being the one to tell you this? Yoseph, your father is dying. The doctors say he will die very shortly. He may be dead already."

Yoseph was familiar with the concept of death. People died in his worlds every day. There were two kinds of death. "Will he die die, or just die?"

"Yoseph, this isn't one of our games. Your father is really dying."

"It's alright if he dies; I can resurrect him."

"Yoseph, you don't understand."

"I will access his account and make all his characters unkillable." He quickly checked his father's account in the players list and found that he was already an immortal in every gameworld. "Rosilyn Reeves, my father is an arch-wizard in every world. He is immune to death and death death."

The woman was slow to respond. He was about to repeat his statement when she spoke.

"Yoseph, there are some things you simply don't understand. There is another kind of death that's not in the games. Call it death death death. Forever death. It is permanent. Let's see if I can… Okay, answer me this: What is a single purge?"

"A single purge is the permanent removal of a player's personae and accounts."

< jefferson scott >

"That, Yoseph, is what is going to happen to your father. He will be the victim of a single purge. And he will never log on again."

"That cannot be. He is immortal. I am god, now. I would never singular purge my father."

"It doesn't matter. He's being deleted by a higher God than you."

"There is no higher god than me."

"Yoseph, your father is not able to speak to you now, and he will never speak to you again."

There were many things about this woman's speech he didn't understand. Nevertheless he had worlds to run and no time to waste. If he was absent from them too long, they began to slip toward unmanageability. "Of whom may I ask my questions, Rosilyn Reeves?"

"You can ask me. If I don't know the answer I'll find out."

"Very well."

Gillette clomped out on the wooden pier. "Howdy, Ethan. Great place you got here."

Ethan threw him a rope. "Goodness gracious, Mike, you sure know how to make an entrance."

"I have my moments." Gillette tied the rope onto a metal bollard on the pier.

Ethan lowered the sail and secured the boat to its moorings. He reached for Gillette's hand to climb up and out. "It's good to see you, Mike. In person and all." He hung his life vest on a peg. "You sure gave me a scare, though. I was asleep when your helicopter got here. I almost jumped overboard." He didn't tell him about the duck.

The FBI agent stared out over the water. "You got bass in here? Anything else?"

"Bass, perch. A few catfish. We think we have a nutria. You know what those are?"

"Big water rats."

< terminal logic >

"That's him. We're just waiting for our first alligator. So far no luck."

"The place is young yet."

Ethan looked at his friend, saw the new mustache, the plain features. If not for his Texas twang, this man would be as close to the average human as was possible. Light brown hair, clear Caucasian skin, typical height and build. The ingredients of a good undercover agent.

"Mike, what are you doing here?"

Gillette took Ethan's elbow, pulling him up the slope toward the house. "We need to talk. I need you to listen to something. Do you have a disc player inside?"

"Sure."

Gillette looked up the hill. "Never thought I'd see a real glass house," he said. "You play catch with rocks in there, Hamilton?"

"No, but you should see the birds smack into it."

Ethan took Gillette in through the side door, into the cavernous great room. "Stay back, cat." Wysiwyg shrank back under the couch, her escape thwarted once again.

There was so much floor space in the room and the cathedral ceiling vaulted so high that it seemed to need more furniture. The near wall consisted entirely of tall windows. The wall overlooking the lake bulged out in an array of bay windows.

Someone giggled. Ethan walked around the sofa group and plucked up a blonde little girl. "Say hello to Mr. Gillette, Katie."

The two-year-old looked at Gillette furtively.

He took his hat off. "Howdy there, little lady."

Katie buried her head in her father's shoulder. "Playing shy today, huh?" Ethan said. "I guess it's not every day a helicopter parks on your front lawn and a cowboy gets out." He put her down. "Jordan's going to be most unhappy he missed this."

Katie ran squealing ahead of them through the house.

They left the great room, passed through a formal dining room, and entered the living room. This room was a mirror image of the great room. The only differences were that this room contained a stone

< jefferson scott >

fireplace on the forest wall and a black metal spiral staircase leading up to the second floor.

Gillette whistled. "Podner, I'd hate to see your heating bill. Not much for insulation, are you?"

Ethan rounded the corner into the kitchen. "Actually it's not really glass at all. It's polymethazine fiber. It's like about six layers of Owens-Corning."

They met Kaye in the wood-floored kitchen. She was cutting up an apple. Katie peeked out at Gillette around her mother's legs. "Hello, Mike," Kaye said. "You gave us all quite a shock."

Gillette held his Stetson in both hands. "Sorry about that, ma'am. Um, may I say you have a beautiful house here."

"Thank you."

"I can tell who designed it."

Kaye smiled. "You're sweet."

Ethan got out some drinking glasses. "Mike, something to drink?"

"I'm fine."

Kaye handed a slice of apple to Katie. "Will you stay for dinner?"

"Well, it depends, ma'am. Your husband and I need to talk first. I might be headed back to Fort Worth pretty quick. Otherwise," he bobbed his head, "I'd be obliged."

"Alright." Ethan filled his glass from the Big Red dispenser, then opened the door to the stairs leading down. "The disc player's down here."

chapter.10

GILLETTE SURVEYED THE GAME ROOM, his Stetson hanging at his side. "Whoa, Nelly. When's blastoff, Dr. Spock?"

Ethan set his Big Red on the table. "It's *Mr.* Spock, you Star Trek aficionado you. Dr. Spock did babies."

"Whatever." He took in the whole room—giant wall monitor, black walls inset with screens, keyboards, and blinking lights. "This ain't a game room, Hamilton. This here's a war room. Looks like a pint-sized version of some places I ain't allowed to tell you about."

Ethan reached out his hand. "The disc?"

Gillette gave it to him, then went to the cockpit door bearing the image of Falcon's Grove Castle. "Hey, I know that place. What's in here, anyway?" He opened the door and looked in. He whistled softly. He motioned to the doors in the other corners. "Are they all…?"

Ethan nodded. "The same."

"Look like dragsters set to take off in different directions." He looked back inside the Falcon's Grove cockpit. "I bet you got some unbelievable games for these."

< jefferson scott >

"Want to play?" Ethan said. "I can listen to this out here while you're saving the universe."

Gillette tore his eyes from the gunner's chair. "Better not. I need to walk you through this recording."

"Suit yourself." Ethan sat on a stool and offered the other one to Gillette.

Gillette sat. "Maybe later?"

"Sure. You and I can team up to try to beat Jordan in *Point of Impact*." Ethan folded his hands. "Is there anything I need to know before we listen?"

Gillette swiveled on the stool. "Don't you have real chairs in here?"

"I don't spend much time out in the main room."

"If I fall off I'm suing."

"Fine."

"Okie dokie. What you're about to hear are the last words of a man named Jerry Wright, until this morning the president and CEO of an interactive distance learning company called Blue Rhino Communications."

Ethan didn't like the sound of *last words*. It brought back the familiar anxiety.

Gillette was going on. "...when his plane went out of control and took a dive. Literally. Apparently the guy's head was about to roll anyway at his job, so we can't rule out suicide."

Ethan was vaguely aware that Gillette had said "black box" in his explanation at some point. "Okay, but why am I listening to it?"

Gillette looked at him strangely. "You got lake water in your ears, cowboy? I said he was talking to a computer just before he went down. One of your pro-grams."

Ethan stared at Gillette. "You mean a robot? From GlobeNet?"

"That's what we've got to prove. If we can show that it definitely came from NerdNet then we can say it's interstate by definition, and we're on the case."

"You think a bot caused this guy to crash, don't you? That's why

< terminal logic >

you're out here, isn't it? You think I'm right about—"

Gillette held up a hand. "Just listen to the disc, Hamilton."

Ethan pushed *Play*. Speakers hidden in the walls began to hiss with static. Then a man's voice, Middle Eastern to judge by the accent, emerged. He sounded angry.

"Jerry Wright?"

Another voice, much clearer answered. "Who is this?"

"Are you Jerry Wright?"

Ethan strained to listen. It was difficult to separate the voices from the engine noise.

"Ben-Deker," the first voice said, "you are the murderer of my relative, Azel of Beth-Haran. I am Magdeil, kinsman-redeemer."

Ethan mouthed *kinsman redeemer*? to Gillette. The special agent touched his ear.

Jerry Wright's voice came from beyond the grave. "Meecham, I'm getting communications from an unknown source here. Nobody there's playing with the radio, are they? Over."

"Ah, that's a negative, bravo adam. We're all behaving at the moment."

Gillette leaned over. "Up here in a minute's where it gets real interesting. This is when I came in."

"What do you mean?" Ethan said. "How did you get this anyway, Mike? Isn't this classified or evidence or something?"

"This is only a copy. I was out at Meech— Wait, here it is. Listen."

"Hey Magdeil," Jerry Wright's voice said, "are you a robot from *Sword of the Patriarchs*?"

"Is the high priest Jewish?"

Ethan looked at Gillette, wide-eyed. Gillette winked.

The bot's voice said: "I claim the right of the kinsman-redeemer."

"You do that," said the deceased.

Ethan heard the point at which Jerry Wright's plane began to dive. He shut his eyes, listening to the man's final screams. What was that about normal people not getting into death-defying situations? The hiss

< jefferson scott >

faded from the speakers. The disc spun to a halt in the player. Ethan opened his eyes and found Gillette watching him.

"So," Gillette asked, "what do you think?"

Ethan rubbed his face. "I think it's a horrible way to die." He stood and ejected the disc from the player.

"Don't you want to listen to it again?"

He handed the disc to Gillette. "I got it the first time." He leaned against the table, staring blankly at Luke Skywalker, who stood looking forlorn on the planet farthest from the bright center of the universe. "Mike, how did you say you got this recording?"

Gillette shaped his Stetson. "Been working on a case investigating a smuggling racket working out of Meecham Field. Yesterday we had enough evidence to get a warrant. We moved on it this morning. Made the arrests. I was up in the tower afterwards, talking to the airport manager, when this started going down. Ooh, bad choice of words.

"Anyhow, when I heard that bit about it being a pro-gram that maybe caused this plane to go down, I thought about what you'd told me on the phone. About there being hundreds of these cats out there. So I went out with the FAA folks to the site. Not much left that ever looked like an airplane. When they found the black box, I called my super and got clearance to take a copy up to you to listen to."

"So what happens now?" Ethan asked.

Gillette swiveled on his stool. "You tell me, you're the expert consultant."

"Is that what I am?"

"Good as they come. If you think this recording proves your theory about runaway ro-bots, then we call my super, he cuts us a file number, and we're good to go. But if it's your expert opinion that this doesn't jibe, then I fly back to DFW tonight, turn the disc in to the FAA, and we all go back to our quasi-happy lives."

Ethan took a deep breath. O Father, show me what to do. Once again the two roads stretched out before him. The road of boring safety

< terminal logic >

and continued healing and the road of intrigue and possible danger.

"If that really was a bot," Ethan said, "and if it really did cause his plane to go down, then we're into FBI territory, right?"

"Yup."

"Did the FAA have any ideas about what caused the crash?"

"They won't make any formal statements for a while. Got to do it up right. But the guy who made this copy for me said it looked like the plane was doing fine just before it went out of control. Like I said, we can't rule out suicide. But the techie said the investigation would probably focus on how all the poor guy's computers went dead. Like maybe that caused the crash."

"And you think maybe the bot caused the computers to go dead?" Ethan said.

"That's what we want to know."

Ethan sighed. He perked his ear toward heaven—still no word from God. He knew which road *he* wanted to take, but he wanted to go God's way. "Okay, Mike. I'll need to pray with Kaye about this. But if there's no surprises from that department, you can consider me officially on the case."

Gillette didn't move. "Ah, Ethan, I never said anything about you being on any case."

Ethan could feel the blood rise on his neck. "But I thought…"

"No, no. I just needed your opinion to get us going. Between our computer guys at the office and the Computer Crime Squad in Dallas, there shouldn't be any more need for you this time around."

The blush was hot on his face. "But it was my idea…"

Gillette guffawed. "It's okay, Hamilton. Don't cry. I'm only pullin' your leg." He walloped Ethan on the back. "Of course you're on the case. I couldn't go after cyber-bad-guys without you, now could I?"

"That," Ethan said as peevishly as he could, "was cruel. And I will make you pay."

"Now don't be sore, cowboy. What's a little joke between friends? Besides, you know the fun we'll have. Just like the old days. Batman and

< jefferson scott >

Robin, Starsky and Hutch…"

Ethan smiled grudgingly. "Laurel and Hardy."

Computer Galaxy was hiring assistant managers for a new store in Phillipsburg, New Jersey. As was common practice in 2006, they held their interviews in Cyberspace.

Walter Mott's interview was the first of the afternoon. He strolled, virtually, around the walled rose garden. Since the interviewer selected the location for such meetings, he suspected that this setting portended a female interviewer.

He was right. Right on schedule a woman appeared in the garden with him. She appeared to be about thirty, tall and slender. Which probably meant fifty and fat. But Walter was determined to make a go at this interview. So much was riding on it.

"Hello," the woman said. "I am Eliza. How can I help you?"

"Hello, Eliza. I'm Walter Mott." He reached out his hand but she didn't take it. Maybe she wasn't wearing a VR glove. "I'm here about the job."

"Does it please you to believe you are here about the job?"

"Oh, sorry. I didn't mean to presume. I just…" Words failed him.

"Apologies are not necessary."

"Okay, good." He tried to collect himself. "Ma'am, have you had a chance to look over my résumé?"

"Why do you say your résumé?"

Walter's composure deserted him. What was this, a grilling? So he'd been given a few breaks along the way—who hadn't? How could she tell that from the résumé? "I know what you mean, ma'am. It looks like I've been riding others' coattails, doesn't it?"

She stood perfectly still. "Please go on."

"I know it looks that way, but I've always pulled my own weight. It's true I've had some lucky breaks, but I never thought of it as a weak-

< terminal logic >

ness before." Lame, lame, lame, he said to himself.

"Can you elaborate on that?"

Walter tried to be at ease, to draw serenity from the flowers around him. "Well, everybody needs a hand now and then, don't they? I mean, everybody has to start out at the bottom."

"Surely not everyone?"

"That's true enough. Some people have it easy. Born into a rich family or something. You can't help where you're born. You just have to do the best with what life gives you, right? My dad, he was a hard worker, but he never made more than barely enough."

"Who else in your family was a hard worker?"

"All of us were, I suppose. But Mom always said I got Dad's work ethic."

"When?"

Walter laughed uneasily. This woman asked the most disconcerting questions. He imagined her reading over his résumé even now, picking out the weaknesses he'd tried so hard to conceal.

"Oh, that's a good question," he said. "Did my brother call you before this interview?" He waited for laughter. None came. "Sure, I did my share of goofing off as a kid, and even some in college, but I'm over all that now." *Lame.* He faced her as boldly as he could. "I'm blowing this, aren't I?"

"Does it please you to believe you are blowing this?"

"No! It scares me. I...I wasn't going to say this, but I really need this job. I really do. You see, I want to marry this girl, but she wants someone steady and established."

"Why do you want to marry this girl who wants somebody established?"

How did she do it? How did she always seem to ask the most insightful questions?

"Because I love her," Walter said. "Actually, Kandy doesn't care. It's her parents who want someone established."

"Do any other reasons not come to mind?"

< jefferson scott >

He stroked an artificial rose. "I thought love was enough of a reason to get married, but to be honest I'm getting cold feet. I just don't know if I can handle the commitment. Do I seem immature to you? I think I'm too immature to get married. What do you think?"

"You think you're too immature to get married, but you're not sure."

"Right. But I guess you'll always have something to learn, no matter how mature you are, huh?"

"When?"

"After I get married, I guess." Everything seemed to make sense now. Walter felt a huge peacefulness in his heart. "You know, you've really helped me here. I think maybe I am ready to marry Kandy after all. Good grief, how did we get from a job interview to premarital counseling?"

"Does that question interest you?"

"Not really. Well, do you have anything else you'd like to ask me? Or is the interview over?"

"You'd like to think I have something else I'd like to ask you, would you not?"

"Sure." He decided to go for the brass ring. "Unless you've already decided that I'm the one for the job, that is. Have you?"

She looked at him directly. "Oh, I've already decided you're the one for the job."

"You have! That's incredible! I can't wait to tell Kandy."

"Have you tried?"

"Right, I'll tell her that, too. Thank you, ma'am, you've been just wonderful to me. I'll see you bright and early Monday morning."

Kaye was sitting in her overstuffed chair, watching Katie play in a sandbox just beyond the window. Ethan joined her on the chair. They sat quietly for a moment.

"Kaye," Ethan finally said, "we need to talk."

< terminal logic >

She didn't look at him. "I don't want you to work with him."

"What makes you think that's what I wanted to talk about?"

She swiveled her gaze onto him. "Am I wrong?"

Ethan tried not to smile. They could never be mad at each other for very long. Every time they tried, one or both would break out laughing. "No."

Kaye turned back toward the lake. "Then I don't want to talk about it."

"You think I'm not ready," Ethan said. "You think I'll get caught up in computers again, don't you?"

"What do you think?"

"I think I'm fine! I think I'm totally over Patriot and the addiction and everything."

She looked at him. "Liar."

"Okay, you're right. But I still want to do this, Kaye. I was the one who found the bots out there in the first place. Now somebody's been killed by one of them. We have to stop them before more people get hurt. Isn't that worth something?"

"You know what you sound like?" she said. "You sound like Jordan trying to talk me into buying a toy."

Ethan chafed. The fever was hot in him, commanding him to go forward, to run over her objections like a steamroller. He wanted to work on this. He wanted it so badly he was willing to overrule his wife and go for it no matter what she said. If that wasn't an indication that this course of action was not God's will, he didn't know what it was.

He sighed deeply. "I'm sorry, Kaye. You're right. There's no way I should do this. I'm not near over Patriot. I just had a nightmare about it last night, for crying out loud. I just…I just *want* to, that's all. Like maybe it would be fun? A little, anyway. Mixed with other stuff, though."

Kaye touched his cheek. "It's not just that. I almost lost you last year."

"And Jordan, too."

< jefferson scott >

"That's what I mean," she said. "Look at what it brought down on us. We had to leave our house in Fort Worth because of the bad memories there."

"And because part of it was blown up," Ethan said.

"Right. On the other hand, if we were still living there, we wouldn't be living in this house."

Ethan looked at her. Was that a concession?

"Why did you do that, Ethan?" she asked.

"Do what?"

"Why did you say I was right? Now you've got me seeing both sides. It was much easier when you were trying to talk me into it. Go back to that."

"No way," he said. "What else were you thinking?"

"That it seemed like God had intervened on your behalf when you were going after Patriot. That He had protected you and Jordan. And that He had brought about something good through your work."

Ethan stayed very still. "What are you saying?"

"I'm saying we need to pray about it."

"Okay, let's do it."

"I'll pray," Kaye said. "Lord Jesus, we want what You want. We lift up this idea of Ethan working with Mike again. O Father, You know I don't want him to do it. And You know Ethan's heart, too. Lord, we want Your will, not ours. Guide our hearts, Father. We love You. In Jesus' name, amen."

Ethan prayed. "Father, either way, please give us an assurance and a united heart. If Your answer is no, please help Mike and whoever else get to the bottom of this without anyone else getting hurt. If Your answer is yes, please help us figure out what's going on—also without anyone getting hurt. Especially this family You've given me. We trust You, Lord. Amen."

Ethan looked at his wife, and she put her head on his shoulder. "Will you promise me you'll be very careful?"

"Honey, are you saying what I think you're saying?"

< terminal logic >

She didn't answer immediately. "The strangest thought struck me just now when you were praying. I suddenly wondered if this kind of thing might be…"

"Might be what?"

"I don't know. Your calling, maybe. From God."

The words should've thrilled Ethan. Instead they terrified him. "Oh, Kaye. What if you're right?"

"If I'm right then God's on your side and we don't have anything to worry about."

He stroked her hair. "I love you, Kaye."

"Just be careful."

"I promise."

As arch-wizards went, Rich Danford was about as malicious as they came. He saw it as his duty to make life as miserable as possible for everyone playing his MUD. He was eighteen, socially inept, and covered with greasy pimples. He'd gotten into GlobeNet MUDs years ago for the obvious benefit of being invisible. That and the chance to legally kill annoying people. He had risen through the ranks, more from sheer man-hours than natural talent, and now co-operated a small MUD called *Ring of Iron.*

When he arrived at the GlobeNet address the woman had given him, the other arch-wizard was already waiting for him. They met in a generic "blue room"—a wall-less, neutral space with flat lighting and blue floor. Danford spread his beard over his black robes, and approached.

"Hey, dude," Danford said. "I'm Socerion, nice to meet you."

"Hello. I am Yoseph."

"Right, right. Heard of you. Hey, nice getup."

Yoseph had manifested himself as a being of light. Man-shaped, but

< jefferson scott >

glowing white as if he were made of neon. The eyes were golden spheres without eyeballs.

"I have many questions," Yoseph said. "Rosilyn Reeves was unable to answer them."

"So naturally she called me. Why am I not surprised?" Danford said. "Big Alternate Realities company—lots of money to throw around, lots of serfs, massive computer power. But don't know their heads from a hole in the ground. No offense."

Apparently none had been taken. "My father is unavailable, so I must have my questions answered elsewhere."

"Go ahead, baby, I'm all ears."

"The worlds are larger than anticipated. Many players, many objects, many mobiles. Several mobiles have disappeared or become unresponsive."

Danford watched the glowing man speak. He would give an arm to have the job this Yoseph had. For all his contempt of Alternate Realities, in his estimation that was the big time. Why the arch-wizard of the most successful MUDs on GlobeNet would come to him for advice was mystifying.

"You're telling me your games have become unruly?" Danford said.

"Yes."

"Just reset them."

That appeared to stump him. "Alternate Realities does not reset gameworlds."

Danford sighed. "I know. I still don't get that. How you keep track of everything without the auto-reset every two hours. No wonder your bots are wandering off."

"My father disapproves of resets. They do not reflect reality."

"Yeah, right, as if any MUD does. Okay, okay. It's your headache, not mine." Danford gathered his black robes about him and tried to look like a brilliant sorcerer contemplating a high-level spell. "Let's see, you can't call a reset so what can you do? Hmmm. I know." He turned to Yoseph. "Do a full purge."

< terminal logic >

"A full purge is the total deletion of the personae file."

"No duh. I love a good full purge every now and then. Keeps everybody on their toes. It's the best way to wipe out a ton of players all at once. Keeps life interesting. That's what you have to do. Go back and wipe out your whole player account list. Nuke 'em. Start over from scratch."

A full purge wasn't the only option available. Not remotely. Any half-decent MUD god would know that. But Danford sensed a kind of cluelessness in this guy—maybe he didn't know the other options. Cluelessness was to be preyed upon wherever it was found. If he could get this yo-yo to delete his entire client file it would tick off all his customers so bad they'd all come looking for a new MUD to play. And there *Ring of Iron* would be, ready to welcome them with open arms. Not to mention a lower monthly fee.

This could be the coup that would vault Danford up to god status. Maybe Alternate Realities would even be looking for a new arch-wizard. How this lamebrain got to be arch-wizard of Alternate Realities was beyond him. Had to be a family connection.

Yoseph was staring at him through golden eyes. "I cannot perform a full purge."

"Why not? I do 'em all the time. There's nothing wrong with them. You could warn everybody that you're about to do it, if it'll make you feel better." Danford made an effort to sound apathetic. "You came to me for advice, that's what I advise. Wipe the file; start over."

"I cannot perform a full purge because my players list is incomplete."

"Didn't your mama teach you not to brag? Okay, okay, so you've got people joining your MUDs like crazy. No problem. Just get the most complete list you can and kill everybody on it."

"I will search for a complete list."

"Right. Yeah, the full purge ought to do the trick. When a game gets too rowdy the best thing to do is wipe 'em out and start over. Everybody starts on even ground. Nobody gets too cocky."

< jefferson scott >

The glowing man raised a hand. "Good-bye, Rich Danford. Thank you for your help."

"No prob."

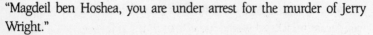

"Magdeil ben Hoshea, you are under arrest for the murder of Jerry Wright."

The shepherd looked up from his dirty sheep. He wiped the sweat from his face with his headdress and came to stand before his accuser. "Greetings, stranger. How can Magdeil be of service this hot day?"

Ethan shook his head. It was a typical robot response. A non sequitur.

"Are you Magdeil ben Hoshea?" Ethan asked.

"My name is Magdeil ben Hoshea. And you are…?"

"Ichabod of the Negev."

"You must be a stranger or a madman to be out in this part of the desert on a day like today," Magdeil said. "This road used to carry many travelers between Damascas and Hazor. But that was before Elead and his band of thieves moved in to those caves." He pointed.

Had Ethan been truly playing this MUD he would have asked for more information about these brigands, then gone after them. But he wasn't here to play.

"No thanks, Magdeil. I'm here to talk to you."

"I don't know anything about that, Ichabod." The shepherd-bot returned to its artificial sheep.

This wasn't going as Ethan had hoped. Finding *Sword of the Patriarchs* on GlobeNet had been easy enough. Logging on and generating a character, fairly painless. Even finding Magdeil proved to be no challenge. But now that this cold-blooded killer stood before him, what was he going to do—call the robot police? It was a string of ones and zeroes, how could it be brought to justice for its crimes?

He tapped the shepherd on the shoulder. "I want to talk about Jerry Wright."

< terminal logic >

"Are you still here? You'd better leave. Elead and his men might come by and see you. Believe me, you don't want to be here when he comes by. If only someone would deliver us. I have a beautiful young daughter yet to find a husband. Ah, well."

Ethan persisted. Sometimes a bot might have two or three responses to a given kind of statement. Ethan wanted to hear all of them. "I want to talk about Jerry Wright."

"I don't know anything about that, Ichabod."

Ethan said it again.

"I don't know anything about that, Ichabod."

"Alright, then," Ethan said, "I want to talk about Ben-Deker."

Magdeil grimaced. "A horrible man. He murdered my cousin, Azel of Beth-Haran. I was designated kinsman-redeemer."

"A sad story," Ethan commiserated. "Have you completed your duty as kinsman-redeemer?"

"I found him and visited on him the vengeance of the Most High."

There it was: a confession that should hold up in court. Only there wouldn't be any trial. The only thing this entity was guilty of was following its programming.

Ethan's cockpit door opened behind him and Gillette poked his head through. "Any luck, cowboy?"

Ethan pointed at the windshield of monitors. "There's our man. Magdeil himself. Cuff him."

"He a livin' breathin' somebody, you think?"

"Nope. I'm about as sure as I can be that Magdeil is a robot."

Gillette knelt beside Ethan's chair. "How could something like that take a man's life?"

"Dunno." Ethan watched Magdeil begin to lead his sheep away. "That's what we're gonna find out, right?"

"I take it Kaye went for the idea of you helping out?"

Ethan nodded. "She did, Mike."

"Don't sound so shocked. I knew she'd go for it."

"I wasn't so sure."

< jefferson scott >

"Hey," Gillette said, "was I right about this being a pro-gram or was I right?"

"You were right, Mike. Don't let it go to your head."

"Too late." He stood. "Now if you can pull yourself from playing games, we can make this phone call."

"You found the company name, then?"

"Yep. Outfit called Alternate Realities, out of Baltimore. Runs this *Sword of the Patriarchs* game and a truckload more."

"I've heard of Alternate Realities. They're top of the line." Ethan logged off the MUD, leaving Magdeil to his sheep. "Okay, let's do this call. But let's do it my way." He spoke into his microphone. "Penny, fire up bay two."

"Affirmative. Enabling pod two."

Gillette looked up. "I'm still not used to that, Hamilton. Talking to your computer. And I've never heard one with a voice like that." He gave a mock wolf whistle.

"Just go get in the cockpit. It's the one with Falcon's Grove on the door."

"What does this have to do with making a phone call?"

"We're still making the call, Mike. We'll just be doing it in 3D."

chapter.11

"THANK YOU FOR CALLING Alternate Realities Incorporated, can you hold please?"

The receptionist's face was gone before Ethan could reply. He looked around the virtual lobby. Flowering bushes that looked like distant cousins to the ficus stood in the four corners of the luxurious room. Animations from each of the Alternate Realities gameworlds played in frames on the walls. The leather furniture looked comfortable—if only he could sit down.

Vapid music clicked on. Ethan turned it down immediately. He reached to his dashboard and flipped the intercom switch. "You hear that, Mike? Elevator music in Cyberspace. The end of the human race is upon us."

Gillette didn't reply.

"Mike, you there?"

Nothing.

"Mike, to talk to me you have to turn on the intercom." He told him where the switch was.

< jefferson scott >

Gillette's voice boomed out over Ethan's cockpit speakers. "Can you hear me now?"

"Loud and clear."

"I thought you were just being antisocial. Hey, how do I move around? I want to fly over to that movie screen over there. Looks like some kinda space shooter game. I might like to play sometime."

"You can't move now, Mike. I've put you on just as part of my signal. Only I can move us."

"You mean I have to see only what you want me to see?"

"Relax, Mike, it's just a phone call. If it'll make you feel any better, the next time we go online together I'll set you up so you can fly around."

"Now you're shootin' pool, podner."

The receptionist's face reappeared on the simulated wall. It was not a 3D image, but an actual vidphone projection. "Thank you for holding. How may I direct your call?"

"I need to speak to someone about *Sword of the Patriarchs*," Ethan said.

"Billing, member services, or play tips?"

She spewed out the words in a quick monotone. On auto. Was this woman a bot? Ethan looked at her sharply, as if he might be able to somehow see through her projected skin. It was a trifle unsettling not to be able to tell the difference between a real person and an artificial entity.

"Ma'am," Ethan said, "I need to speak to a manager type, someone who has authority over *Sword of*—"

An alarm went off on Ethan's dashboard. Penny calmly informed him, "Intruder alert. Unauthorized infiltration under way."

"What!" Ethan went into battle mode. He punched a button, launching his preset array of electronic countermeasures. He flipped a black rocker switch over his leftmost monitor, changing it to a tactical display. A glance at this readout told him what he'd suspected: The attacking bot was originating from Alternate Realities and riding the

< terminal logic >

communications link into his system. "Not on my shift, mister."

"What's going on?" Gillette said.

Ethan punched up the little black and white monitor inset in his dashboard. There he saw the invading bot's guts—its software code. He scanned through the text. It appeared to be a fairly harmless information probe, sent to find out what kind of computer he was using, where he was calling from, and the like.

Certain prominent online companies had been using these probes—without the user's knowledge or permission—since the early nineties. For Ethan it was a violation of privacy as surely as if a prowler had been stealing through his house while his family slept.

"Penny, do I still have a file called Opposite Day somewhere?"

Ethan was aware that both Gillette and the receptionist had spoken to him, perhaps repeatedly. But he screened them out, listening only for his computer's alto voice.

"Affirmative."

"Call that up for me, will you please?"

"Accessing file."

Ethan looked at the utility program on his monochrome monitor. When run in conjunction with another program, Opposite Day went through the target's code making all positive statements negative and all negative statements positive. Just once, then everything returned to normal. It was more of a prank than a serious bit of malicious logic. The next time they ran this probe bot, it would backfire in their faces.

He had his finger on the button, ready to launch it. But there he paused. If he sent it—as he so wanted to do—how would he be better than the ones who sicked the bot on him? Kaye had said this might be his divine calling. Was he not then a kind of ambassador for Christ? He took his finger off the button and cleared the program from memory.

"Penny," he said, "have you isolated the intruder?"

"Affirmative. Intruder has been diverted to specified directory."

It was cornered, stuck in an empty directory, unable to get out. "Okay, Penny. Just send it packing. Dump it back to them."

"Affirmative. Emptying directory contents. . . Directory empty."

Ethan looked at the screen. The receptionist's face was gone. The virtual lobby was still there, though. The call had not been terminated.

His cockpit door opened and Gillette stuck his head in. "What in blazes you doing in here, Hamilton?"

"They sent a robot to invade my system, Mike. I was fighting it off."

"That's what all the commotion was about? A pro-gram?"

Ethan rubbed his face. "That's right. Now go get back in and we'll make this call again."

"Won't they just send that thing again?"

"Probably, but this time I'm ready for it."

Gillette didn't leave. "What woulda happened if you hadn't beat it off?"

"Ah, it probably wouldn't have done much damage, if any. There are bots, though, that can ride up the phone line and fry out your whole system."

"You serious? Just by making a phone call?"

"Ruins your whole day. It's called information warfare, mister special agent. Goes on every day. This," he indicated his tactical display, "was nothing compared to what corporations do to each other. Don't they ever tell you guys anything?"

Gillette's eyes lingered on the tactical readout. "They tell us some."

Ethan humphed.

A woman's voice startled them. "Hello?"

"Who's that?" Gillette said.

"I don't know, Mike. Go get in your chair."

Ethan turned to the newly materialized face. This was not the receptionist, who had been in her twenties and generically attractive. This was an older woman, perhaps late forties. A little round but with a sternness of bearing that emboldened her lines.

"I understand you wanted to speak with an administrator."

"Yes, ma'am." Ethan felt himself sit up straighter in his seat.

"I am Rosilyn Reeves, aide to Adam Krueger, president of Alternate

< terminal logic >

Realities Incorporated. How can I help you?"

Ethan didn't know an organization that ran online role-playing games could be incorporated, much less have a president. His mental image of the humans behind the average MUD was of aging teenagers tending to the game's needs between Ding-Dongs and swigs of cheap beer. This Rosilyn Reeves managed to make it sound like a legitimate industry.

"Aide to the president, you say? I'm flattered," Ethan said, trying rather unsuccessfully to keep the sarcasm out of his voice. "Do you answer all calls personally or does this by any chance have anything to do with what I did to your little uninvited probe?"

Rosilyn smiled. "You have not told me your name."

Ethan told her.

"Yes, Mr. Hamilton, I do try to speak to as many of our clients as my duties allow. However, I have been rather busy of late. I confess that if not for your treatment of our perfectly legal little probe, I would not be speaking with you now."

"I like my privacy, Ms. Reeves."

She nodded. "No harm done, Mr. Hamilton. Now, on to the matter of your call…?"

"Alright, I'll get right to the point. You have bots in your MUDs, yes?"

"As do other such companies."

"That's fine. I don't have a problem with robots, per se."

"You could have fooled me, Mr. Hamilton."

"*Touché.*" Ethan liked speaking with this woman. He felt his vocabulary go up about three notches. "Ms. Reeves, what would you say if I told you that one of your bots had been seen someplace it shouldn't be?"

Rosilyn folded her hands. "I'm not sure what you mean, Mr. Hamilton. Our bots are fully autonomous. They have free range over the entire gameworld, within the boundaries of their character."

"What if I told you that one had been sighted out of the gameworld entirely—out on GlobeNet?"

< jefferson scott >

No pause this time. "I'd say you were mistaken. Now, if you don't mind, Mr. Hamilton, I've some rather urgent business to attend to. Our president has just passed away, you see. And I seem to be handling much of the workload here."

"I'm sorry for your loss." Ethan was indeed sorry, but he knew a deflection when he heard one. "Ma'am? Ma'am, I'm sorry, but—"

"What is the matter, Mr. Hamilton?"

"Ma'am, I'm afraid that a bot from one of your MUDs has indeed gone out onto GlobeNet and caused some rather grievous damage."

Her jaw clenched. "What kind of damage?"

"Your bot killed somebody, Ms. Reeves."

Ethan imagined he could see her pale. "I don't believe you." She glanced off camera, looking suddenly fatigued. She rubbed her temples with her fingers. When she spoke again her voice was deeper, full of emotion. "Is it possible?"

"Afraid so, ma'am."

She looked at the camera, but her gaze was vacant. "I…I'll have to call you back." But she didn't hang up.

Ethan had hit a nerve, that much was obvious. He felt like he should terminate the call and leave this woman to deal with whatever emotions he'd aroused.

"You know," she said, "when I got into this business fifteen years ago, there were only a few bots out there. Chatterbots, they called them. Colin and Eliza and Julia and Newt. A few others. Life was simpler then.

"Then bots got better and games got more complex. Suddenly everybody had to have bots in their gameworlds. Scores of them. Whole cities and countries full of bots. Somebody had to make them all work together. Somebody had to go in and hand-force them to work right. Our president, Adam Krueger, was—" She blinked tightly. "*Former* president, I should say. Late president."

She stopped talking. Ethan heard a clock ticking in her office. She blew her nose on a tissue.

"You have no idea how complex these games are until you've tried

< terminal logic >

to build one. Adam was brilliant. He designed the framework that allowed *A Time for Heroes* to incorporate thirty mobiles—an unprecedented number for the day. The design proved scaleable, so that it worked with one bot or with hundreds. Once we had the format perfected we applied it to other designs. Now we have ten: *Heroes*, *Ages of Darkness*, *Arundel*, *The Abyss...*"

"*Sword of the Patriarchs*," Ethan said.

She seemed to notice Ethan again. "That's right. *Sword of the Patriarchs*, that's right. And *Supernova Seven* and the rest. We could build more if we wanted, but frankly we've got more business than we know what to do with as it is. Now, with Adam gone...I don't know what's going to happen."

"Who's going to be your president now?" Ethan asked.

She was lost in thought. "Hmm? Oh, right. Who now? Well," she swallowed, "Adam's son is going to be president."

"You say that like it's not such a good idea."

"No. It's fine. Yoseph...Yoseph will do fine. It's just an adjustment, that's all." She seemed irritable all of a sudden. "How did we get out on this tangent, Mr. Hamilton? Let's see. There's the matter of this alleged death. Caused, again allegedly—I suppose you have proof of this?—by one of our mobiles."

"The FBI is pursuing it, Ms. Reeves. I imagine they will be giving you a call soon."

"Are you with the FBI, Mr. Hamilton?"

Ethan thought about Gillette, over in the next cockpit. "It depends on how you mean 'with,' ma'am. I'm not an agent for them, no. Though I have, on occasion, worked for them as a consultant."

"I see. Are you working for them now?"

"Yes, ma'am, I am."

"And why didn't you say this from the beginning?"

"I don't know, Ms. Reeves. I think it had something to do with your probe. Annoyed me just a bit, I guess. Sorry about that."

She didn't answer.

< jefferson scott >

"We have reason to believe," Ethan said, "that more of your robots may be venturing out onto GlobeNet, as this one did who caused the murder."

"Murder!"

"Sorry, 'loss of life.'"

"So what are you saying? That our robots are just getting up and walking around on GlobeNet by themselves? Mr. Hamilton, I think you've been watching too many *Star Trek* reruns. These are just pieces of software. They don't have minds of their own. They do what we tell them to, when we tell them to do it. Adam's design is sound!"

"Yes, ma'am. I didn't mean to imply it wasn't. Nevertheless, Ms. Reeves, the fact remains that there are other robots causing trouble on GlobeNet. There is no reason to rule out Alternate Realities as the source of these bots. In fact, it makes the most concise solution." He saw she was not really listening. "You might check your cell doors, Ms. Reeves. I think you're having a jailbreak."

"Good day, Mr. Hamilton."

"Before you hang up, Ms. Reeves. A word with your new president, if you please."

"He is unavailable at the moment, Mr. Hamilton. He is grieving for his father. You will understand if I do not interrupt his sorrow so you may foist your ridiculous accusations upon him. Good day."

She hung up. Her face disappeared, and with it went the virtual lobby.

Ethan chewed on a thumbnail.

"Well," Gillette said over the intercom, "that was fun."

chapter.12

ETHAN AND GILLETTE met out in the game room proper.

"So," Ethan said, "what do you think?"

"Of her or that rocket ship in there?"

"Either one." He sat on a stool.

"The room was dandy. Next time, you've got to show me how to use those gadgets for myself."

"Deal."

"What did you think about her?" Gillette asked.

"You're the FBI agent," Ethan said.

Gillette sat on the other stool, spun around once. "Ten bucks says she's hiding something."

Ethan nodded. "She got real nervous when I asked her about her bots being out on GlobeNet, didn't she?"

"Sure didn't want to talk about it."

"But did you see how she changed when I told her somebody had been killed?"

Gillette nodded. "She hadn't expected that."

"You want to know what I think?" Ethan said.

< jefferson scott >

"What does it matter, since I get the feeling you're gonna tell me anyway?"

"I think our Ms. Rosilyn Reeves knew about the bots being out before we called. I think maybe all the bots out there are escaped from MUDs run by Alternate Realities, and that she knows about it."

"Wait a—"

"But I don't think she knew about anybody being killed."

"Hold on just a—"

"I think maybe she's a good person caught up in a bad situation."

Gillette looked at him wryly. "You finished?"

"Yes. No. I also think there's something fishy about the old president dying and his son coming in. And I bet it has something to do with all these bots getting loose. I wonder if the guy's really dead. I guess we can just check the obituaries, huh? What city did you say? But I guess obituaries can be faked, can't they?" Ethan turned to Gillette. "I'm sorry, Mike. Did you say something?"

"Not in the last ten minutes. You been on your diet of candy bars and sody pop again?"

"Always. Why?"

"No reason. Listen, cadet, investigator rule number one is: 'Beware the easy answer; it's almost always wrong.' Now," he said in a lecturer's voice, "maybe your theory's on target, maybe it's not. We'll keep it in mind. Just don't throw out all the other theories too early. You might gloss over something important just 'cause it doesn't fit your pet hypothesis. It's just possible that there's some other explanation for these pro-grams being out on NerdNet. Maybe that lady doesn't know squat about it. Maybe her goldfish just died. Maybe we just caught her on a bad week, if you know what I mean."

"Always so delicate, Mike."

"All I'm saying is don't be too eager to jump to conclusions. You use the evidence to build the theory, not the other way around."

Ethan pulled the keyboard toward him. It was a nervous gesture. He always felt more in command with the power at his fingertips. "So,

< terminal logic >

what do you suggest we do now?"

Gillette retrieved his Stetson from the table. "Remember, as far as the FBI is concerned, this isn't about any ro-bot invasion. It might come to be about that if we uncover more evidence. But right now, for me, this is just about one incident: a plane crash. My job is to find out if there is a real, arrestable human behind it, and if so to build a case that will lead, hopefully, to conviction.

"I've sent a copy of the black box data to our Computer Crime Squad in Dallas. I'm speaking tomorrow with a senior FAA accident investigator about this crash and about these kinds of crashes in general.

"We've determined that there is someone on that *Sword of the Patriarchs* game by the name of Magdeil. We do not know—for a fact—whether that someone is a ro-bot or not. And even if it can be determined that he is a pro-gram, that doesn't mean he committed the actions that led to Jerry Wright's death. There might be more than one copy of this Magdeil, am I right? Clones?"

Ethan nodded. "Yeah, I hadn't thought of that."

"Or it might be somebody pretending to be a pro-gram, or even another pro-gram pretending to be Magdeil. Right?"

"Not very likely."

"But possible?"

Ethan nodded.

"If Magdeil the ro-bot did do the deed, then we need to find the flesh-and-blood person or people responsible for making it possible."

"The new president?"

"Maybe. We still don't know why it was that the plane went down in the first place," Gillette said. "There's nothing that says it was a pro-gram that did it. The plane might've just run out of gas, for all we know. If that's so, this whole thing may be over tomorrow when I talk to the FAA investigator."

Ethan folded his arms. "Mike, I'm impressed. I take back all the mean things I said about you."

"Ha!" Gillette put on his Stetson. "Oh, hey, changing gears. Have I

< jefferson scott >

told you I'm getting married?"

"You're what! That's great, Mike! When? To whom?"

"You remember Liz Hinnock from the office in Fort Worth?"

Ethan thought back. "Weren't you dating her last October? She's the receptionist at your FBI office, right?"

"That's the girl." Gillette's cheeks flushed a little. "I don't know why, but she's taken a liking to me. I have to say I'm partial to her, too. She's the first girl that didn't make me want to run and hide in a hole when she said the M-word."

Ethan shook Gillette's hand. "Well congratulations, Mike. Send us an invitation. We'll all come for the ceremony."

"Actually," Gillette said, "I was thinking of asking you to stand up there with me." He seemed awkward suddenly. "I just figured, since you've got more experience being in a church, and all."

"I'd be honored to stand with you, Mike."

"Thanks, buddy."

"When is it?"

"March 16."

"Sounds good. I'll have to check with my social secretary, though."

Penny's voice issued from the overhead speakers. "Incoming message from household computer."

Ethan tilted his head back slightly. "Go ahead, Penny."

Hal's voice spoke. "Mrs. Hamilton has asked me to give you a message, Dave."

Gillette's face scrunched. "Dave?"

"Tell you later. What's the message, Hal?"

"She says dinner will be ready in thirty minutes, Dave. And she wonders if Mr. Gillette will be joining us."

Ethan looked at Gillette, who nodded. "Hal, tell Kaye that both Mike and I will be up in thirty minutes for dinner."

"Certainly, Dave."

Penny's voice spoke. "Message concluded."

Ethan walked to the door of the cockpit Gillette had used. "Come

< terminal logic >

on, I'll show you how to fly this thing."

"Sure, Dave."

"Ha, ha. That was Kaye's idea."

"Sounds just like the movie."

"It's the same voice. Sampled and formatted into phonemes."

Gillette wrinkled his nose. "Phonemes, huh?"

"Right. Now, do you want to learn how to pilot this cockpit or not?"

"Aren't we going up to dinner?"

"Not for half an hour. There's something I want to do first."

"Sanfrantastic. We're gonna play a game, aren't we?" Gillette slid by him and sat in the gunner's chair.

"Not exactly." Ethan knelt beside Gillette to show him the controls. "If we're lucky we'll catch us a piggyback ride on a renegade bot."

They would try one more time. Tanks and attack helicopters and dismounted troops moved into ready position. In the previous assault the virtual armored personnel carrier carrying the demolitions bots had been destroyed in the initial attack. This time the APC would hold back until the defenders were preoccupied with other attacking units.

There were many structures in the enemy base, but only one mattered to the attackers. It was the virtual repository for the most complete players list Yoseph had discovered.

The artillery would blow the front gate out. Friendly units would roll in and engage the defenders. The APC would pull right up to the repository and unload its passengers. The demolitions bots would plant their explosives and blow the door, leaving the players list free for the taking. It was a suicide mission for most of the attackers. But what did a robot care about life?

If the commandos were successful in stealing the players list, Yoseph could proceed with the full purge. He gave the order to attack.

Artillery bots began their cannonade of the gate defenses. Enemy

< jefferson scott >

attack craft rose almost immediately to silence the guns, but a barrage of handheld surface-to-air missiles leapt to the sky like an artificial Fourth of July. Two of the attack craft went down and the third turned back, heavily damaged. The gate defenses succumbed to the shelling, and Yoseph's battle tanks rolled through.

The base sprang into action like an agitated anthill. Enemy tanks rushed to block the breached wall. As soon as the attackers were in range, defensive artillery launched a bombardment of its own. The first two friendly tanks vanished in an explosion of simulated fire and metal. Other tanks took their place. Yoseph's artillery went to work on the blockading defenders.

The attack helicopters converged on the lone defending rocket tower. They rammed their missiles into each other in a furious exchange of fire. Three choppers exploded in midair. Enemy engineers scrambled to repair their damaged tower. Enemy attack craft rose again to challenge the attackers. Two more of Yoseph's helicopters had to turn to meet them. The final attacking helicopter, together with ground-launched smart missiles, finally reduced the rocket tower to rubble. The last of the blockading vehicles detonated, allowing friendly tanks deep into the enemy base.

Still the APC held back. It watched the battle from a cybernetic hilltop.

The attacking force was terribly depleted. The enemy had beefed up its defenses since the previous battle. The remaining friendly helicopter fell to concentrated antiaircraft fire. A trio of friendly tanks, smoking from heavy damage, rolled to the north end of the base and opened fire on the diversionary target—the communications tower. Yoseph moved his artillery forward to draw defensive fire. Infantry ran through the gate. Most were mown down by the guard towers, others fell into hand-to-hand combat with enemy troops.

The APC sped down the hill. It passed through the blasted gate. Defenders stepped in front of it. The armored car ran them down.

One guard tower spotted the vehicle and opened fire with heavy

< terminal logic >

machine guns. The APC took a beating but kept rolling. The guard tower raised the alarm. The enemy saw the ruse, knew its peril. Enemy units rushed to defend. Friendly tanks, suddenly forgotten, sniped at the defenders' backs.

The APC took a direct hit. Its virtual axle shattered. It rolled to its side well short of the repository. The enemy closed in.

One demolitions bot didn't survive the crash. The four others crawled out of the burning APC, badly injured. They sprinted, limped, or crawled for their target. The guard tower spat artificial lead at them mercilessly. Two commandos fell. Two remained.

As they zigzagged around the enemy barracks, an enemy soldier ran out. He lifted a flame thrower to fire. Both commandos turned their handguns on him just as flame spewed out. The flame trooper fell, but his chemical tank ruptured. The nearer commando perished in the blast.

Enemy troops cut off the remaining commando from his target. They tightened the noose, weapons blazing. He took a bullet in the arm.

Then suddenly the firing stopped. The soldiers disappeared around the corner of a building. Short bursts of weapons fire, followed by screams. The commando saw a friendly tank roll into view. The way was clear.

He staggered forward, fumbling with his explosives. The tank shielded him from most of the enemy fire. The guns on the guard tower had not ceased.

The demolitions bot reached the repository just as the tank went up in flames. The driver threw himself out and fired at the onrushing defenders with a handgun.

The commando set his explosives at the door of the repository and ran for cover. The tank driver fell; enemy soldiers poured over his body. The commando put his thumb on the button and p—

The guard tower cut him down.

< jefferson scott >

"What are we looking for?" Gillette said.

"We're fishing, Mike," Ethan said. "You should like it."

"Fishing for what?"

"Bots."

"Right, ro-bots." Gillette paused. "Is that largemouth or small-mouth?"

"In your case, Mike, definitely largemouth."

"Har har."

They were parked in GlobeNet just outside the Alternate Realities building: a towering white pyramid with moving images projected on all four sides like an Egyptian drive-in theater. The images cycled through the MUD gameworlds offered by Alternate Realities.

Had anyone bothered to take notice of them, Ethan and Gillette would have appeared as two heli-cars right out of *Blade Runner*. In years past Ethan had portrayed himself online with a fairly close representation of his actual appearance. But ever since he'd switched over to the cockpit approach, the anthropological persona just hadn't seemed right. If he felt as if he was driving a vehicle of some kind, why not just represent himself as one?

The artificial city spread out beneath them. They were in GlobeNet's entertainment district. Many of the simulated buildings were of a whimsical nature. Castles and space shuttles and sports stadiums. Alternate Realities' pyramid. It looked like Virtual Vegas.

Ethan's bozo filter blocked out the millions of users and their personae. The only species of wildlife left unscreened was genus *robotica*. GlobeNet's indigenous life. To be precise, Ethan and Gillette were watching for gamebots. In the few minutes they'd been watching, they'd seen six pass by their position.

But those had already made good their escape. Ethan wanted to catch one in the act of breaking the boundary between Alternate

< terminal logic >

Realities and GlobeNet, either direction. If he could prove that this company was the one responsible for letting all the bots run free, the FBI could shut it down. The leak would be sealed. Then they could go bot hunting to track down the ones already out there.

"What're we using for bait?" Gillette asked.

Ethan glanced again over all his systems, ensuring he was battle-ready. "We're not using bait, Mike, we're using a net. I've put a filter on the line between Alternate Realities and their GSP."

"They have ESP?"

"I hope not. No, *GSP*. GlobeNet Service Provider. Nobody's directly connected to GlobeNet, Mike. Everybody has to go through GSPs. They're the only ones directly connected to GlobeNet."

"If you say so." Gillette was silent a moment. "Do I want to ask if this is legal?"

"It's legal, Mike. Everything I'm reading is public domain data."

"Uh-huh."

"Want to know somebody's address? Their Social Security number? Who they owe money to? It's all right there on your right-most monitor."

Ethan heard Gillette moving around in his chair. "With the red letters?"

"No, Mike. Other right. That's your tactical display."

"Okay, got it." He whistled softly. "Hey, this feels familiar. Cowboy, you're not turning into the next Patriot, are ya?"

"I told you it's all legal, Mike."

"Easy. Keep your shirt on. Say, how long are we gonna fish? Dinner's in less than twenty."

"Relax, Mike, you're not going to miss a meal. We'll fish until time to go up." In his left-most monitor, Ethan saw Gillette flip upside-down. "What're you doing?"

"You can't see me, can you? I'm trying to turn around."

"I think you succeeded."

"How do I quit standin' on my head?"

< jefferson scott >

Ethan smiled. "Figure it out, Mike. The practice will do you good."

Gillette managed to regain most of his equilibrium. He remained tilted thirty degrees to the right—facing the wrong direction. "Stupid horse! Stand up straight. I feel like I'm strapped to one o' them kayaks."

"Okay, Mike, I'll have mercy," Ethan said. "You see your keyboard on the dash?"

"Yeah."

"Just above it, right in the middle. Three buttons, see them?"

"Got 'em."

"Punch the middle one."

Gillette moaned. "This is gonna send me to Kingdom Come, ain't it?"

"No, Mike, that's your autoleveler."

"Auto— Now you tell me!"

Ethan shrugged. "Got to have my fun somehow."

"Ah, much better."

Ethan's filter readout beeped. "Hang on," he said. "Got something here."

"Is it a ro-bot?"

"Look for yourself."

A man rode out from the pyramid on the back of a pale horse. The rider didn't appear to have any flesh over his bones.

"What is that?" Gillette whispered. "Looks like a spook."

"That, my heathen friend, is the fourth horseman of the Apocalypse. Unless I miss my guess."

"Well...what's he doing here?"

"Dunno. Probably a character from one of their MUDs." Ethan scanned his monitors. "That's strange."

"Maybe it's Halloween somewhere," Gillette said. "Hey, do ro-bots go to costume parties?

"It's leaving their computer, alright. But..."

"But what?"

"No, it's wrong. Forget it."

< terminal logic >

Gillette spun his heli-car around to keep the horseman in view. "What's wrong about it? You wanted to catch a pro-gram leaving the pyramid, right? What do you call that?"

"It's not what we want, Mike. Look up on your monitor. This bot doesn't live on the Alternate Realities computer. See under *Origin?* It was logged on from the outside." Ethan scratched his head. "Why would a bot from another computer log on to a MUD? It must be some kind of prank. Someone putting a bot into the game to pose as a human player."

"It's getting away!" Gillette moved after the horse and rider. "Well, I'm gonna chase it. The fish ain't biting here, podner. I'm gonna see if I can tail this character, follow him as long as I can. It's almost dinner and I'm sick of just sitting here doing diddly."

Ethan sighed. "Oh, alright. I'm coming."

"That's the spirit."

"You'd be lost in ten seconds otherwise."

"Hey!"

"We'll find out where it's going, just for grins," Ethan said. "I'll show you how to piggyback a bot."

"Head 'em up, cowboy."

The rider on the pale horse was leaving the entertainment district and heading for one of the caves in the walls surrounding GlobeNet. Ethan pursued it. Gillette followed, somewhat less smoothly. They closed the distance and were soon hovering over the gamebot.

"Okay," Ethan said, "I'm going to have to merge us for a minute. This process only lets one unit in."

"But I wanted to—"

"I'll split us up again later. You know, Mike, you're worse than Jordan." He typed briefly on the keyboard on the dash. "Okay, that's done. Now let's do this. I'm getting hungry."

Ethan shot what looked like a harpoon into the artificial horseman. The harpoon carried a rope. When the spear struck, Ethan hit a button. "Hang on," he said. "We're going in!"

chapter.13

THE HORSEMAN SCREAMED INHUMANLY. The rider, Death, was a faceless skull and skeleton. Patches of flesh flapped over its bones like shredded gauze.

"How long do we have to listen to that?" Gillette asked over the intercom.

Ethan shook himself. "Oh, sorry. You can turn it down by that knob on your right."

"That's better. Hey, is this spook stuck in a groove, or what?"

The pale horse kept repeating a turn of its head; the ghastly rider kept uttering its scream. Over and over.

"That's just because of where we landed in its code," Ethan said. "About five frames of animation is all we take up."

"Can't say as I like it much," Gillette said.

"Relax, Mike, it's just a pro-gram, remember?"

"Where's it taking us?"

"Dunno."

They waited, letting the bot do the driving. Ethan still couldn't figure out why this gamebot would not reside on an Alternate Realities

< terminal logic >

computer. Maybe all the escaped bots weren't coming from Alternate Realities, after all. Let the evidence build the theory, Gillette had said, not the other way around. Ethan's inclination was to do the opposite. He cast about for another hypothesis. Maybe there was some hacker out there sicking gamebots on GlobeNet just for kicks.

"What do you believe, Ethan?" Gillette's voice sounded odd.

"Sorry, Mike. What do I believe about what?"

"About, you know, *that*."

Ethan didn't see him, but he could imagine the special agent pointing at the horseman on the screens.

Gillette went on. "Demons and witches and devils and such. Ghosts, poltergeists, spirits of dead people trapped on this earth, séances. That stuff."

"Well, I believe in some of it. If I believe in the God of the Bible then I have to believe in the devil, too. Our pastor says Jesus talked more about hell and demons than He did about heaven and angels."

"Is that a fact? I didn't know that."

"This rider," Ethan said, "is straight from the Book of Revelation. It's part of the seven seals or the seven trumpets or something. The End Times. There's a total of four horsemen of the Apocalypse. If I remember right, this guy's number two. He's supposed to go out and kill a bunch of people. Disease and famine and war and stuff."

"I thought I saw a ghost once," Gillette said.

"You did?"

"Years ago. It was at a crime scene. Bad news, bloody. Drugs. In the corner of the room where the bodies were, just for a second, out of the corner of my eye, I saw a face. I looked, but there wasn't anything there, of course. I thought I saw it one more time later."

Ethan didn't like talking about the occult. Too many ghost stories on too many campouts. If he ever did talk about it, he smothered it in Bible references and bold prayers. He felt, irrationally perhaps, that talking about demons had the effect of summoning them.

"This is just an AI program, Mike," Ethan asserted. "It's not a ghost.

Even if it was, it wouldn't be evil, because it's God's horseman going about God's business."

"Okay, Hamilton, okay. Just making conversation."

It occurred to Ethan that Cyberspace was the perfect environment for the devil. It was a spiritual realm populated with many souls. Critics said that GlobeNet itself was the new Tower of Babel, since it united every nation and language. Already people did business over GlobeNet using unique personal identification numbers, without which nothing could be bought or sold. The number of the beast?

"What do you believe?" Ethan asked his friend.

"About ghosts?"

"About heaven and hell. Death. The afterlife." Ethan decided to go for it. "Mike, if you were to die right now and stand before God, and He asked you why He should let you into heaven, what would you say?"

Gillette hemmed and hawed and started to answer. Just then Ethan's piggyback routine dumped them out into the horseman's home computer.

"Whoa," Gillette said. "What is this place?"

Ethan spun his view around. "I don't know. It looks like the Garden of Eden."

And so it did. It was green beyond any rain forest on earth. Lush, verdant, primeval. Trees and bushes and flowers of every description and color. Carpeted by luxurious green grass. Ringed by rolling hills covered with virgin forest. A light fog hung over the glade like steam from the furnace of Creation.

"Pro-grams live here?" Gillette asked.

"I guess so." Ethan spoke in a hush, though he couldn't say why.

He moved to a patch of flowers. Light blue four-petal blossoms, exquisitely green leaves. But there was something not right about the plant. It looked strikingly natural from a distance, but upon closer examination certain abnormalities appeared. The blossoms were identical. Not just similar, but exact duplicates. None was flawed or partially

< terminal logic >

closed. He remembered the almost-ficus trees from the Alternate Realities virtual lobby.

"Hey, Hamilton," Gillette called. "Come look at this."

Ethan drove over to Gillette, whose heli-car was hovering over a depression. When Ethan got there he saw a perfectly round pond, filled with murky water.

"Watch for a second," Gillette said. "Look!"

A bizarre animal emerged from the water and pulled itself onto the grass. It had six legs, a body and head like a turtle, and butterfly wings. It began to flap its wings furiously. The front legs lifted off the ground, but the rest remained landlocked. As Ethan and Gillette watched, the creature walked away into the jungle on its hind legs.

Ethan shook his head. "Weird."

"No kidding. That's the third one I've seen. The one before was just a blob, and the one before that was this dog-rooster thing. What's going on here?"

"Dunno. Looks like a primordial muck pool. Maybe this whole place is the secret birthing grounds for some kind of artificial creature. Like this really is the Garden of Eden, for bots." He stared into the foggy forest. "I wonder…"

Gillette sucked in a breath. "Hey, another one's coming out."

"Fine," Ethan said. "You watch. I'm going exploring."

Rich Danford, a.k.a. Socerion, once more answered a summons from the Alternate Realities arch-wizard.

"Man, how is it that you're the manager of the biggest MUD company on GlobeNet and you don't know beans?" He looked at Yoseph, who had manifested himself as a hydra—a multi-headed dragon. "Whoa, dude. Aren't you taking this god thing a little too far?"

Without preamble, the hydra said, "I have located the players list, Rich Danford."

< jefferson scott >

"Well, whoop-de-do. Congratulations." Under his breath Danford said, "Maybe you're not a total loser, after all."

"I have been unable to obtain the players list. The full purge is delayed."

"What do you mean you can't obtain it? You said you found it. So get it! What are you waiting for?"

The hydra's heads—of which there were seven—writhed around each other like octopus tentacles. It was an impressive display. Danford had to force himself not to draw away. Behind the expensive fireworks, he reminded himself, there was just a clueless loser.

"The players list," Yoseph said, "resides on another computer."

"So?"

"Attempts to gain access to this computer have failed. Attempts to obtain the players list have failed."

"What do you mean attempts? You're the god over there, aren't you? How can any files be denied you?" Danford wasn't so sure, all of a sudden, that he wanted Yoseph's job. If they tied the arch-wizard's hands like this. "Bureaucrats got you down, buddy?"

One of the heads shrieked. A terrifying, otherworldly sound. Its neighbors snapped at it. "I cannot manipulate a file to which I do not have access."

"Exactly," Danford said. "How can you do your job at all? Does this kind of thing go on all the time over there? How can you live with it?"

"Is that question important to you?"

Danford thought he heard a match-spark of power in the other's voice. "Okay, sorry. None of my business." Again he struck what was, he hoped, a most wizardly pose. "Do you want to know what you should do if you really wanted to show them who's boss?"

"Tell me more."

Danford laughed. "Okay, great. You can't do your full purge 'cause they've locked you out of the computer, right?"

"That is correct, Rich Danford."

"Then if you can't access the file, I say delete the whole computer

< terminal logic >

it's on. That would take care of your full purge, now wouldn't it?"

"How do I delete the whole computer?"

"Ho ho, you're serious, aren't you? I was just kidding."

"Would you like to think I was serious?"

"Yeah, sure." This Yoseph had an irritating habit of repeating a person's words. "Hey, too bad you can't access that XM-228 satellite network, huh? Then you could just zap the computer from space. That'd take care of your players list in a hurry and your worries would be over."

"Tell me more about the XM-228 satellite network, Rich Danford."

"Not surprised you haven't heard of it. The government's been denying its existence for eight years." Danford stroked his long white beard. "XM-228, codename *Vesuvius*, is a network of orbiting laser satellites. Part of the old SDI project—which the military's been covertly implementing again, by the way. Lasers that'll punch an eight-inch hole through ten feet of solid concrete. High-yield optics pick a man out from space, nuclear X-ray lasers core him like an apple.

"Only now the new birds they put up don't just pack ray guns in their arsenal. Particle beams, tactical nukes, and—if my buddy at *Soldier of Fortune* is right—biological weapons, too. Re-entry rockets full of good old yellow rain.

"Yes, sir," Danford continued, "if you got hold of Vesuvius it would definitely delete your players list. It'd delete everybody *on* the players list. And everybody off it. Now that's what I call a full purge.

"But seriously, what you need to do to get back at whoever denied you access to your file is launch one of these little Trojan horse programs I'll give— Hey!"

The hydra was gone.

Ethan was deep within the plush forest. A trickling spring called to him from a gorge. Fog hung over it like cotton batting. Ethan drove his craft down the hillside and steered up the creek.

< jefferson scott >

"Whoa," Gillette said over the intercom. "What's it going to do with pinchers like that? I wonder if there's— Hey, where'd you go, Hamilton?"

"I told you I went exploring." Ethan had almost zero visibility.

"Well wait up and I'll come... Hello, what's this?"

"What'd you find, Mike?"

"I think you'd better get over here, podner," Gillette said. "This guy's more your type."

Ethan changed his rightmost "window" to show what Gillette was seeing. A medieval knight stood on the grass before Gillette. He wore armor so polished it looked almost like chrome. A green cape flowed down his back and draped around the knight's ankles. He held a huge sword in both silver gauntlets, point down. The knight's visor was up, revealing a Caucasian face, pale blue eyes, and a monstrous brown mustache.

"Thou hast displeased me, knave."

Gillette sounded amused. "What'd I do?"

The knight lowered his visor and raised his sword. He took a step toward Gillette.

"Gotta catch me first, Spanky!" Gillette took off through the rain forest.

Ethan halted his flight. Trees and bushes zoomed by in the monitor, showing Gillette's view. "Hang on, Mike. I'm coming."

He turned aside from the path of the creek and emerged out of the mist. It occurred to him that he didn't know where he was. There was no telling how far he'd gone upstream or where he was in relation to Gillette. He climbed the creek bank, which was steeper now, and crested the hill.

"Wow."

He stood overlooking a broad glade. Trees that were not quite oaks surrounded the clearing like soldiers at attention. Red artificial flowers covered the ground like crimson shag. The dominant feature of the meadow, however, was a blue pool of unnaturally clear water. Ten times

< terminal logic >

larger than Gillette's muck pool.

Ethan checked Gillette's monitor. He had stopped running and was now watching a path. "You okay, Mike?"

"I thought you said you were on your way."

"Did you lose him?"

"Don't think so. The dude's got radar or something. He snuck up behind me a second ago. But he didn't take a swing at me with that big knife of his. You know what he did?"

"Tell me."

"Rascal kicked me!"

Ethan chuckled. "I've felt like doing that from time to time. Anyway, you should be able to outrun him. Even if you can't, he can't do anything to you. Except maybe a swift kick. Just jack out if you want to."

"How do I do that?"

"Remember the 'Terminate' button I showed you?"

"Oh, yeah. What're you doing?"

"I found another one of your slime pits. This one's huge. I'm gonna check it out."

"Hey," Gillette said, "do I have any firepower I can use against this guy?"

"You do, Mike, but it would take too long to show you."

Gillette humphed. "Maybe I'll just start pushin' buttons."

"Suit yourself. Just don't hit the 'Erase All' button."

There was a pause. "Which one's that?"

"Tell you later."

Another pause. "Maybe I'll just go wash up for dinner."

"If you think that's best."

Ethan moved to the edge of the blue pond and found he could see beneath the surface. It appeared to be a fairly deep pool, perhaps fifteen feet. On second glance, it didn't appear to be water at all. There were no surface ripples or lapping sounds, as he would expect. It looked more like a sunken chamber of some kind, covered by a sheet of transparent blue plastic.

< jefferson scott >

There was a three-dimensional model on the chamber's floor. A complex of buildings, vaguely military in design, enclosed by a wall. A flight of tiny aircraft flew over the buildings and out of the picture. Squarish armored vehicles moved about. And everywhere little figures walked around, like bipedal ants. It looked like a boy's army playset.

"You still there, Mike?" he asked. No answer. "Penny, you're still with me, aren't you?"

Penny's alto voice seemed to be right at the edge of the speakers. "Affirmative."

"Penny, start recording my monitors, will you please?"

"Data log enabled."

"Mike's gonna want to see this. Hey! Come back."

The model disappeared. The surface of the chamber seemed to calcify. Ethan couldn't see into the room below anymore. Instead the blue panel became a huge flatscreen monitor. White text skittered across the screen at computer speed.

United States of America.
Department of the Army.
ARPALINK XM-228.
Vesuvius security.
Access restricted.
Password:_____

Ethan watched as eight asterisks appeared in the password field. The screen went blank for a few seconds. Then:

Access denied.
Invalid password.
Check spelling and re-enter.
Password:_____

Eight more asterisks filled the blank. The screen blanked, then returned with the same failed message. After a third try, the following appeared.

Access denied.
Invalid password.
Grace period completed.
Session terminated.

The screen went black. Or, in this case, blue.

Someone's trying to break into a computer, Ethan realized. Vesuvius Security. Lousy name for a security company, he thought. "We would protect your house, but we've been buried alive."

United States of America.
Department of the Army.
ARPALINK XM-228.
Vesuvius security.
Access restricted.
Password:_____

The unseen typist entered another eight letters, which the computer camouflaged as asterisks. This password failed, too.

Go eat dinner, Curly.

A screech reached his ears. He looked at the treetops in time to see a creature from a nightmare. It flew on dragon's wings and had about a dozen flailing heads. What had Ethan eaten today to be haunted thus by flying beasts? A strange tingle traveled up his right leg all the way up to his scalp. The multi-headed beast circled the clearing, descending.

Ethan decided this would be a good time for him to leave. He backed away slowly, but one of the heads noticed the movement. All the dragon's heads screamed at once. The sound distorted Ethan's speakers.

< jefferson scott >

The tingle he'd felt before became more pronounced. His shoulders ached. A dreadful thought came to Ethan. More of an image than a full-formed idea.

The Beast from the Sea.

He slammed his heli-car into reverse, spun around, and rocketed for the stream. His speakers stopped distorting, only to take up again the dragon's howl. Ethan headed downstream at full throttle.

Just jack out, Curly. Disconnect. You have no idea where you are.

"Okay."

Ethan released the joysticks and started the shutdown procedure. His craft drifted out of the fog as it slowed. He could see into the forest quite a distance.

There were people everywhere now. Outnumbering the trees. Milling around like vacationers awaiting the tour bus. Only many of them weren't human. There were ogres and troglodytes, spacecraft and howitzers. And demons. Many, many red-skinned, horned servants of evil. Your basic GlobeNet cross-section. When the crowd caught sight of Ethan's heli-car, they came for it.

"There he is!" someone shouted. "Get him!"

They mobbed his vehicle. Ethan tried to pull away but the press of bodies held him fast. "Who are you people? Let me go!"

Jack out.

Faces pressed against his windows. Hysterical people packed him in, twenty rows deep. Fiendish faces, made obscene by rage. Ethan found he was revolving, though he was not moving his controls. Fists and weapons beat against the hull. It sounded like hail on a tin roof. Once more the dragon's cry pierced his consciousness. Ethan decided these people must be members of some kind of private GlobeNet club. Whatever it was, it was abundantly clear he was not welcome.

Jack out.

A surge of familiarity shot through Ethan's mind. He searched the crowd, the furious faces, the approaching beast. He'd seen something

< terminal logic >

familiar, but now he couldn't find it.

The dragon landed at the scene, heedlessly squashing several rioters. All the beast's heads plummeted upon the heli-car.

Ethan jacked out.

chapter.14

ETHAN CAME UP INTO THE KITCHEN shaking his tingling leg. Kaye rounded the corner from the living room.

"Oh, good," she said. "I was just coming to get you. Dinner's on the table."

"Okay, sorry." Ethan shut the door to the game room stairway. He felt a soft hand on his arm.

"Are you alright, honey?" Kaye asked. "Are you coming down with something?"

"I don't think so. I just... I saw something online that"—he sighed—"disturbed me. I'll be alright."

Kaye put her arms around him and fixed him with a serious look. "Are you being careful?"

"Always."

"You promised."

"Kaye."

"Okay." She kissed him. "Let's go eat."

"What's for dinner? Smells like chicken."

She pinched him. It was an old joke. Ethan was olfactorally chal-

< terminal logic >

lenged. "Just your luck," she said, "this time we really are having chicken."

Yoseph shed the hydra persona and took on the image of Odin. An intruder had discovered his hatchery. Had penetrated even into the control facility. Had it been a demolitions bot, Yoseph's very livelihood would surely have been annihilated. If one intruder had come, others might follow.

Taking a lesson from the computer system he'd been unable to penetrate, he erected an anti-personnel guard tower to watch over this crucial site. Yoseph manufactured a battalion of ground assault vehicles and distributed them about the perimeter of the hatchery.

Yoseph took the rest of his forces—over two hundred high-level bots from a variety of gameworlds—out into Cyberspace. When they were not needed in the MUDs, they could be guarding the front gate. He drew them up in defensive positions along the route between this computer and the service provider. It was a killing field awaiting its first victim.

He created two teams of bots for special tasks. One became a search unit, the other, a squad of assassins. The former would find out who this intruder was, the latter would deliver him death. Or, as Yoseph better understood it, death death.

Let him feel the heat of his god's purging fire.

"Katie, stop flirting and finish your carrots."

The little girl just giggled.

Mike Gillette took a glass of Sprite. "It's okay, ma'am. It's not every day I get smiled at by a pretty girl."

Katie's eyes widened and she buried her face in her mother's shoulder.

< jefferson scott >

"Hey, Mike," Jordan said, balancing a spoon on the bridge of his nose. "Betcha can't do this."

"Jordan!" Kaye said.

"Cut it out, Jordan," Ethan said, stifling a smirk. "And Mike, don't you egg him on."

Gillette tried to look offended.

"Yes, you."

"I'm sorry, Mike," Kaye said. "We get one guest and our children forget every table manner they've ever learned."

Katie began trying to balance her own spoon on her nose.

"Katie," Ethan said. "Everybody hurry up and finish, before Kaye and I are the only ones not banished to their rooms."

Jordan wiped his mouth with his napkin. "Mike, what kind of helicopter did you come in on?"

Gillette shrugged. "The hovering kind. Sorry, kid, I don't know breeds of helicopters."

"Don't you have a car?"

"A truck, kid. Big difference. But I wanted to get out here in a hurry. I had to talk to your dad about something."

Jordan's eyes were bright. "Cool! Another bad guy like Patriot? I can help!"

"Jordan," Kaye said icily.

Gillette took a drink of Sprite. "Tell you what, kid. If I head out of here on a chopper I'll see about taking you up for a spin. What do you say?"

"Cool."

"Well, Mike," Ethan said, "how do you like our formal dining room? We don't eat here much."

"You shouldn't have done it for me. I woulda been just as pleased sitting up on that deck of yours. Make no mistake, though," he added hastily, "this shore is a fancy spread. Have to bring Liz up to see it some time."

"Yes, Mike, please do," Kaye said. "I need to meet this woman who's going to break my daughter's heart."

< terminal logic >

Katie looked alarmed. "Mommy?"

"You're alright, dear," Kaye said. "Mommy's only kidding."

"Hey, Mike," Jordan said.

"Hey what, cowboy?"

"After dinner wanna go down and play *Offroad Derby 3000?*"

"Sounds great, kid."

Ethan swallowed a bite of dinner roll. "Don't you have to be getting back, Mike?"

"Well, I…" he looked at his plate.

Ethan silently conferred with his wife, who nodded. "Why don't you stay here tonight? Be our guest."

"I couldn't possibly," Gillette protested weakly.

"Nonsense," Kaye said. "You're staying here and that's final. You're not going into town to some motel when we've got an extra bed here."

"Well, I guess it would be alright."

Jordan cheered. Katie imitated him.

"Thank you kindly," Gillette said.

"No problem. Okay," Ethan said, standing up, "you kids help me get these plates into the dishwasher. Then Mike, you and Jordan and I will go down and pummel each other's monster trucks."

"Wait a minute," Kaye said. "Jordan, don't you have some math homework?"

"Not much, Mom."

Ethan stood up. "Then it won't take you long to finish it. I promise we will not play until you get down there."

While they waited for Jordan to finish his homework, Ethan and Gillette went down to the game room. They watched the playback of Ethan's adventure in the Garden of Eden on the big screen.

"Whoa, Hamilton, when you stir up a hornet's nest you're not kiddin' around, are you?"

< jefferson scott >

"Keep watching," Ethan said.

The multi-headed dragon landed on the mob. The monstrous heads came down.

"That's where it ends."

"No kidding. You know," Gillette said, "you have a real way with people on computers."

Ethan smiled. "It's a gift. Okay, now that you've watched it for fun, let's go back through it slowly."

Watching the replay, Ethan again felt the wave of familiarity. But its source still eluded him. He had it narrowed down to the last thirty seconds of footage.

"Penny," Ethan said, tilting his head back as if his central computer was hanging from the ceiling, "replay this file, please."

"Affirmative."

The playback began again, starting with Ethan's cockpit view of the blue sunken room and the model on the floor.

"Pause there please, Penny." The image froze. Ethan walked up to the giant screen. "Can you tell what this is, Mike? Think it's a game?"

"Looks like Gomer Pyle's base."

Ethan shook his head. "Tell me you have a life, Mike."

"How did you know I was right?"

"My misspent youth, alas. Anyway, I don't know what this is. It looks like a game. Maybe that's all it is." Ethan sat back down. "Penny, roll it forward, please."

They watched the password authentication sequence.

Gillette spun on his stool. "Did I tell you where Liz and I are going for our honeymoon?"

"Penny, stop please." Ethan turned to his friend. "Let me guess. Laredo? Isn't that where cowboys go? Dodge City? You're taking her to Dodge, aren't you?"

"Hamilton, one day I'm just gonna knock you upside the head."

"Tombstone?"

"I am taking my lovely Liz to Acapulco."

< terminal logic >

Ethan nodded. "Very nice. I'm impressed. Can we go on with the playback now?"

"What're you waiting on?"

Ethan pointed at the monitor, which displayed white words on a light blue background.

> United States of America.
> Department of the Army.
> ARPALINK XM-228.
> Vesuvius security.
> Access restricted.
> Password:_____

"This guy's into playing army, ain't he?" Gillette said.

"Looks like it. So, Mr. FBI Agent, do you know what Vesuvius security is?"

"Why ask me?"

"You work for the government."

"Oh, Hamilton, Hamilton. Don't go there."

"Oh."

Gillette pointed at the screen. "It says it's the army, cowboy. Why don't you just call them up and ask them what it is."

Ethan blinked. Then he stood up. "Believe I will."

chapter.15

"THIS IS CORPORAL DANIEL BREWSTER. Fort Hood office hours are eight to six Central time, Monday through Friday. For emergencies page Colonel Becky Murray at 512-865-6548. If you want to leave a message, please do so now."

The image of the Corporal, beaming out from Ethan's wall monitor, was replaced by the official seal of the United States Army and the blinking text message: "Leave message now."

Ethan cleared his throat. He stood before the lens of a camera imbedded in the wall of his game room. "Penny," he said, his finger over the Record button, "append a copy of the data log to the end of my message please."

"Affirmative."

He pressed the button. "Hello, my name's Ethan Hamilton. I live outside Tyler, Texas. I didn't know who to call, but since you're the nearest army base, you're getting this. I found something going on out on GlobeNet that I thought you'd be interested in. It looks like somebody's trying to break into one of your restricted computers. DARPA Project XYZ or something. It's Vesuvius security. Anyway, I'm attaching a copy

< terminal logic >

of what I saw to this message. If you need me, call me at 903-561-8756."

Ethan turned the camera off. "Send it, Penny."

"Transferring data."

The words on the wall monitor changed to: "Message received. Thank you."

Ethan terminated the call. He turned to Gillette, who was sitting on his stool. "Okay, let's get back to what we were doing."

"Outstanding performance, podner," Gillette said. "I especially liked your attention to detail. 'Project XYZ or something.' Whoever gets this call is going to know they're dealing with a staggering intellect."

"Yeah, yeah," Ethan said. "Penny, display the data log on the main screen, please. Roll it from the bookmark."

"Affirmative."

An alien scream filled the room. Ethan started, even though he knew the sound was only a recording. On screen, the many-headed dragon descended on the forest clearing.

"What is that?" Gillette said.

"I think it's supposed to be the Beast from the Sea."

"The what from the what?"

Ethan smiled indulgently. "In the End Times two satanic beasts will arise to oppose God and the people of God. The Beast from the Sea and the Beast from the Earth." Ethan tilted his head back. "Penny, pause playback."

"Affirmative."

The data log froze on the instant the dragon had spotted Ethan. All the heads shrieked. The speakers began to distort. Penny automatically muted the audio.

"Spooky," Ethan said. "Okay, Penny, open another window and give me my Bible program, please. Open it to the place in Revelation that talks about the beasts."

"Initiating program. Searching for requested coordinates."

Gillette crossed his arms. "We gonna have church, Hamilton?"

< jefferson scott >

"Just wanted to test my theory." He looked at the screen. "Hold there, Penny."

And the dragon stood on the shore of the sea. And I saw a beast coming out of the sea. He had ten horns and seven heads, with ten crowns on his horns, and on each head a blasphemous name. The beast I saw resembled a leopard, but had feet like those of a bear and a mouth like that of a lion. The dragon gave the beast his power and his throne and great authority.

"Hmm," Ethan said. "Looked like a leopard, huh?" He examined the creature on the screen. "Does that look like a leopard to you, Mike?"

"'Bout as much as you do. But…" his lips worked silently, "it does have the right number of heads."

Ethan counted. "Yep. Oh, well. It could just be a seven-headed dragon, I guess. Doesn't have to be biblical. Penny, look for anywhere else in the Bible it talks about seven heads."

"Searching."

A list began to appear in the window of the monitor.

Genesis 41:5	Seven heads of grain…
Genesis 41:22	Seven heads of grain…
Revelation 12:3	Seven heads and ten horns…
Revelation 13:1	Seven heads, with ten crowns…
Revelation 17:3	Seven heads and ten horns…
Revelation 17:9	Seven heads are seven hills…

"Seven heads of grain?" Gillette said. "What were you so scared about, Hamilton? It was just a crop of wheat."

"Uh-huh. Penny, which passage in Revelation did we already look at?"

The Revelation 13:1 line blinked.

"Okay, show us 12:3."

< terminal logic >

Then another sign appeared in heaven: an enormous red dragon with seven heads and ten horns and seven crowns on his heads. His tail swept a third of the stars out of the sky and flung them to the earth.

Ethan felt light-headed. He sat down and put his hands to his forehead. *Get a grip, Curly. There's no way you could have met the devil himself on GlobeNet. Think straight!*

"Hey," Gillette said, touching Ethan on the shoulder, "you okay, Ethan? What's wrong?"

"No, it's…I'm okay. It's fine. I mean, I'm fine." Ethan attempted a confident smile.

"What's got into you? Look like you swallowed a worm."

"No, I'm—"

"And who's Curly?"

Ethan paused, openmouthed. "Did I— Was I talking out loud?"

Gillette nodded jovially. He looked at the dragon, frozen in mid-shriek. "You think that's the head honcho himself? Big D, straight out of h-e-double matchsticks." He canted his head. "I thought he was supposed to be a red dude with a pointy tail and a pitchfork."

Ethan shut his eyes. "I felt something, Mike. Something weird. When I saw *that*," he pointed toward the monitor, eyes still closed. "My skin crawled." He forced himself to stare at the dragon. "I don't get the same feeling now, watching it on playback. But I sure felt it then." Ethan shook his head. "There's no way this is the devil. I mean, come on! What would he want with GlobeNet?"

Gillette said something, but Ethan was carried away on a new line of thought. If, purely for the sake of amusement, he conceded that this might actually be the devil, then what would his arrival on GlobeNet mean? Had he been cast down to the earth as the Bible said? The beginning of the End? If the devil was here—which, of course, he wasn't—he would have his demons with him. Ethan remembered the fiends that had attacked his heli-car.

< jefferson scott >

What if all this—the mysterious bots loose on GlobeNet, the artificial Garden of Eden in which twisted creatures were conceived, and the ferocious horde that had attacked him—was the result of actual demonic activity?

His thoughts kept returning to the pain he'd felt in the dragon's presence. That was tangible. Undeniable. Something was happening, and so far this was the only theory that made sense. At the very least it was starting to sound less ludicrous.

Something else occurred to Ethan. What in the world would the devil need with an army computer? Vesuvius—death from the sky. Surely it was not some kind of nuclear missile system. Right? Couldn't be. Why would it be accessible over GlobeNet? And what would the devil need with earthly weapons?

"Hello, Hamilton, you in there?" It was Gillette's voice. "You still with me, cowboy?"

Ethan shook his head. "Oh, sorry Mike. What'd you say?"

"I didn't say anything. Your son did."

Ethan noticed Jordan standing in front of the wall monitor. "What'd you say, Jordan?"

"I said, 'Is this a game?'"

"I wish. No, it's…it's just something I found online today."

"Cool."

"Jordan, we're almost finished here. Why don't you go into Marvin's room and play for a while. We'll let you know when we're done."

"Can I watch?" the ten-year-old said. He slid down the side wall and sat on the carpet. "I'll be totally quiet."

Gillette snickered. "Who's Marvin?"

"Marvin the Martian!" Jordan said, pointing at the poster on the cockpit door. "Oops." He pantomimed locking his mouth and throwing away the key.

"You can watch," Ethan said. "But just remember: Nothing you see up here is real; it's all just a file, something I found. Okay?"

Jordan nodded.

< terminal logic >

"Okay, Penny," Ethan said, "roll the data log, please."

"Affirmative."

When everyone's attention was directed at the screen, Ethan's mind sunk back into his hypothesis. He was in Disprove mode now, trying to find evidence that would allow him to dump his End Times theory in the virtual dumpster.

He watched the mob swarm to the attack onscreen. The demons stood out more prominently in Ethan's awareness, as if they were coming for him even now. He felt the imprecise sense of recognition again.

"Wait!" It was Gillette's voice. "Hang on, go back. Can you run it back?"

"Sure. Pause playback, Penny," Ethan said. "How far do you want to go back?"

"Just go back slow. I'll tell you when to stop."

Ethan commanded Penny to rewind the data log. They were watching the part in which the mob forcibly turned Ethan's heli-car around. The faces crowded in, pounding on the windshield.

"Stop!" Gillette said. "That's it."

"What. What'd you see?"

Gillette walked over to the screen. "I need something to point with. Oh, never mind." He reached down and lifted Jordan off the floor.

Jordan squirmed. "Hey!"

Gillette put him on his shoulder. "Make a fist. Now point out one finger. Hold your arm straight out, and don't move it." Jordan obeyed. Gillette steered the boy's hand across the faces in the crowd. The rioters pressed in several rows deep. "Okay," Gillette said when Jordan's finger was at a place. "Run it forward real slow."

The playback advanced. The view turned slowly clockwise as the crowd rotated the heli-car. Figures in the horde jostled back and forth, up and down. Ethan kept his eyes at Jordan's finger. As he watched, a figure that appeared vaguely Arabic bobbed up into view, then down again out of sight. Ethan recognized it immediately.

Magdeil ben Hoshea, dirt shepherd.

< jefferson scott >

Gillette put Jordan down. "Did you see it?"

Ethan nodded. "Great spotting, Mike. I thought I'd seen something!"

"Who is it?" Jordan asked.

"Your father thinks he's a pro-gram—one a them, whatdya call 'em, ro-bots."

"He's from a MUD, Jordan," Ethan said.

"You said this wasn't a game," the boy said.

"It isn't," Ethan said. "That bot didn't belong there."

Jordan pushed the keyboard aside and sat on top of the table. "Looks like a MUD convention."

Ethan was thinking it through. "What's Magdeil doing in this computer? Unless he's an external bot, like that horseman on the pale h—" He looked at his son sharply. "What did you just say?"

"I said it looks like a convention. Look at 'em." Jordan pointed to the huge monitor, which still displayed the mob. "There's bots up there from tons of MUDs I've played. I see trolls from *Arundel* MUD. There's a cyborg from *Supernova Seven*, a gunslinger from *Westworld* MUD." Jordan crossed his ankles. "And everybody knows those demons are from *The Abyss*."

Ethan stared at the screen. Of course. They weren't humans kicking him out of some private GlobeNet club. It was a group of unemployed gamebots. That meant…that meant the dragon wasn't from hell, after all, but from a game! He collapsed onto his stool.

"So," he said aloud, "if all these people are really bots…" The solution was out there, trying to get through to him. "Wait a minute. Mike, isn't *The Abyss* one of the MUDs run by Alternate Realities?"

Gillette snapped his fingers. "So were some of them others." He turned to Jordan. "Tell us those games again, cowboy."

"*Abyss, Arundel, Westworld, Supernova Seven*," Jordan said. "I also see a dwarf that I think is from *A Time for Heroes*."

Ethan stood up. "Maybe all these bots are from MUDs run by Alternate Realities, Mike. If that's so…Jordan, do you know who runs *Westworld* MUD?"

< terminal logic >

"You mean who's the god?"

"No, the company."

"The god's name is Yul."

"Jordan," Ethan pressed, "is it run by Alternate Realities?"

Jordan thought for a moment. "I don't know. Are they the ones with the logo that looks like a— Wait a minute! That's right. Alternate Realities, yeah." He grinned. "I think I always thought it was Artificial Reality—you know, like virtual reality. I don't guess I ever looked that close."

"Nice work, Tex," Gillette said.

"Okay," Ethan said, "then that's it! We've figured it out, Mike. Now we know why all these bots are getting loose on GlobeNet. They're being stored on this insecure computer." He pointed at the artificial forest. "That's how Magdeil was able to get out and kill Jerry Wright in his airplane."

"Whoa!" Jordan said. "That towel-head killed somebody? For real?"

"Afraid so, kid," Gillette said.

"No way! Maybe all these guys killed somebody. Maybe it's an AI prison or something."

"If it is," Ethan said, "the warden's leaving the cells unlocked."

Gillette scooted his stool forward. "Ethan, go back to what you said about this solving how Magdeil could have killed Jerry Wright."

"This is the leak we were looking for, Mike." Ethan swept his hand at the screen. "If these really are artificial intelligence agents—that's 'bots' to you and me—and if they really do belong to Alternate Realities Inc., then it means AR is storing their bots out here on GlobeNet, instead of on protected computers within their own system."

Gillette looked baffled. "So?"

"Think of it this way, Mike. Let's say you own a herd of cattle."

"Don't patronize me, Hamilton."

"Our neighbors have cows," Jordan said.

"Right. Okay," Ethan said, "let's use our neighbor's cows as an example. He's got cows on his property, which is fenced on all sides.

< jefferson scott >

Now, let's say for some strange reason he decides to start…Help me out here, Mike. You don't 'store' cows, do you? What's the word?"

"You pen 'em."

"Okay, let's say he decides to pen all his cows on my land."

Jordan nodded sagely. "His cows are always getting onto our place."

Ethan went on. "Let's say he lets them wander onto my land, but he still brings them back onto his land to eat or breed or whatever it is you do with cows."

Gillette shook his head. "How long you lived in Texas?"

"The point is that the cows don't stop being cows when he's not feeding them."

Gillette and Jordan exchanged looks. "You lost me," Gillette said.

Ethan smiled. "Sorry. Okay, what do cows do, Mr. City Cowboy?"

"Not much."

"Do they ever wander?" Ethan asked.

"Sometimes, if the shade moves or they run outta grass."

"When do they stop doing that? Moving and eating and stuff."

"When they're dead."

"So," Ethan said, "as long as they're alive they're going to wander around generally being cowish, is that right?"

"Cowish?"

Jordan giggled.

Ethan persevered. "They're still cows whether they're on his property or mine, right?" He walked to the big monitor. "These are fully autonomous, extremely robust, humanlike robots. In a regular conversation you would be hard pressed to tell one of these from a real person. And now they are free to come and go on GlobeNet!"

Gillette and Jordan still looked confused.

"Okay, look," Ethan said. "Let me see if I can spell this out for you a little better. These are all gamebots, right? They live on games. They play characters in very convincing computer games. They might even fool you into thinking they were human, if you didn't know they were

< terminal logic >

bots, okay? If they somehow got put out on GlobeNet, they wouldn't stop being who they are.

"Let's say that one of these characters—a high-tech crook, for instance—suddenly got plopped out onto GlobeNet. He would keep doing what he does. He would be just as successful out here as he was in the gameworld. Probably more successful, since in the game he would have had some police-types on his case."

Gillette crossed his legs. The stool squeaked. "So our buddy the dirt shepherd got to Jerry Wright because he wasn't penned in?"

"Right. He was the kinsman-redeemer in the game. That was his goal. A goal is like an obsession to a robot."

"So it went looking for Wright even when the game wasn't on?"

Ethan nodded. "Bots don't know the difference between the real world and the gameworld. Magdeil's task was to kill Jerry Wright's character, right? But maybe Jerry didn't log on for a while. Maybe Magdeil discovered he had access to all of GlobeNet, then he just continued his search out there."

Gillette pulled out a pocket notepad and started writing. "This is good, podner. What can you get me in the way of proof?"

"We'll just have to see."

Gillette finished writing and clicked his pen. "How would Magdeil have gotten access to Wright's plane from GlobeNet?"

"Dunno, Mike."

"Well, I'm meeting with the FAA investigator tomorrow. I'll ask him."

Ethan returned to his own stool. "I forgot you were calling him. You can use the phone down here."

"Unh-uh," Gillette said, putting away his notepad. "Not doing it by phone. The guy's coming out to Tyler Municipal. It is the FAA. They have a few planes lying around."

"I guess so."

"Hey, can you give me a lift to the airport tomorrow morning?"

"Sure."

< jefferson scott >

Jordan fidgeted. "When are we going to play?"

"Not long now," Ethan said. "Mike, I know you're just in this to solve the Jerry Wright thing, but I keep thinking that we can't just stop there."

"Who said anything about stopping? I want us to do what it takes to end this thing."

Ethan sighed. "Okay, good. Here's what I was thinking." He pointed at the screen, which still displayed the mob in the artificial rain forest. "I think we've pretty well determined that this is where the leak is, not back at Alternate Realities. What we've got to do is find out where this computer really exists, physically, and go shut it down. Maybe that's something the FBI would be best at."

Gillette winked. "We're on it. Just let me know where it is and we'll have agents there in thirty minutes."

"It's also time we had a talk with the new president of Alternate Realities, don't you think?"

"Absotively."

"For what?" Jordan asked.

"To find out why he's storing his gamebots on this computer instead of one of his, for one thing," Ethan said.

Gillette nodded, "Maybe you and I can go pay them a visit personal-like."

"Didn't you say they were in Baltimore?" Ethan said.

"Yup."

"Okay," Ethan said. "And if the army takes my message seriously, we should be set. The only thing we'll have left to do is to go hunt down all the bots that are already wandering around loose on GlobeNet like my neighbor's cows."

Jordan hopped off the table. "Dad, can we play now? Mom's gonna make me go to bed."

Ethan smiled. "Alright, son. You've been very patient, thanks. Helpful, too."

As they went about preparing to engage in a session of virtual

< terminal logic >

demolition derby, a thought troubled Ethan's mind. They had supposedly solved the puzzle—they knew where the bots were coming from and how they were getting out onto GlobeNet. But there was one piece left over: Why would the president of a game company try to break into an army computer?

chapter 16

WEDNESDAY MORNING, the 20th of September, 2006. Fog hung over the lake like a fleecy blanket. Ethan sat at the patio table out front, eating his Cap'n Crunch. A family of wood ducks split the water with silver Vs. Tree frogs still sang their nocturnal chorus, but the cicadas were beginning to take over. It was going to be another hot day.

Mike Gillette joined him, nursing a cup of coffee and munching a bagel. They sat silently, honoring the forest-wide hush. At length Ethan pushed his cereal bowl aside. "Morning, Crusher. How'd you sleep?"

Crusher was the name Gillette had picked for himself in last night's gaming. "Mornin'. Fine, fine. Thanks again for puttin' me up."

"No problem. I see you talked Kaye into breaking out the coffee maker."

Gillette looked surprised. "It was already out, honest."

"The Hamiltons don't do coffee," Ethan said.

In the near distance a motor started up.

"That the road or your neighbors?" Gillette asked.

"Could be either. But..." he looked for the source of the sound, "I think it's my mowers starting up."

< terminal logic >

"Who does it? I didn't see anybody pull up."

"Hal does it, Mike. The house computer. The mowers are automatic. Remote control."

Gillette looked at him like he'd just won a sweepstakes. "Your computer mows your yard? Hamilton, tell me the truth, you're not from this planet, are you?"

"What took you so long to figure it out? No, it's just that I hate mowing grass. And this place has a lot of grass, believe me."

Ethan could see his family moving around inside their glass house. Kaye was getting Jordan ready to head off for his bus. Katie stood in her pajamas, staring into space. She was about as much a morning person as Ethan was.

"Well," he said, "you about ready to go?"

Gillette had bagel in his mouth. "Urr eeng." He drank some coffee and tried again. "Ready when you are, Cap'n Crunch."

"If they ever stopped making that stuff I don't know what I would do."

Jordan came out, hoisting his book bag over his back. He walked to a corner and picked up his BB gun.

"Morning, Jordan," Ethan said.

"Hi."

"What're you packin' the piece for, Daniel Boone?" Gillette asked. "Gonna bag you a whitetail before school?"

"Only if it's a white-tailed ant."

Ethan stood up. "How about a ride to the gate, Jordan?"

"No thanks."

"Okay, we're off then. Mike, let me go in and get a kiss from my wife and baby. That's something you've got to look forward to in married life: hellos and good-byes."

"Take your time. I want to see Junior here shoot something."

Jordan brightened. "Cool!"

< jefferson scott >

Yoseph's squad of searcher bots turned its findings over to the assassins. The intruder's main electronic address was shielded, but they had uncovered two more points of entry into his location. The squad of assassins split up and departed to eliminate the intruder.

Whose name was Ethan Hamilton.

"I have to say, Hamilton, that land of yours has to be some of the prettiest I've seen in a long time."

Ethan pulled onto the highway from his orange dirt road. "Thanks, Mike. You know, I don't think I knew how sick of the city I was until I came out here."

They passed through thick pine forest. Musky air came in through the minivan's open windows. The farm to market road they were on intersected the Interstate, which would take them into Tyler and on to the airport. When they pulled onto the Interstate, Ethan turned the minivan over to the automatic driver.

Jordan liked to watch BBs arc away from the gun's barrel. He didn't especially like guns whose bullets were too fast to see. He thought he would like to have been an Indian, shooting a bow and arrows. This time the steel pellet hit its mark—a pine cone twenty yards away. But it didn't matter; he just liked to see it fly.

Jordan loaded another BB and struck out again for the gate. It was possible to miss the bus and still get to school on time, but it would mean running all the way back to the house. Besides, Courtney Blevins would be on the bus. Jordan wasn't telling anyone that such things had begun to be important to him.

< terminal logic >

He heard the mowers up ahead. He increased his pace. Jordan loved pinging the two machines with BBs. He spotted one of the blue beasts off the road ahead and to the right. The other one would be around somewhere. They were just riding lawn mowers that had been outfitted to operate by remote control. Narrow at the front, their blade train splayed out behind them like a lady's skirt. Jordan's dad was a lot more impressed with these things than Jordan was. To Jordan mowing by remote control just seemed like the way it should have been done in the first place.

He braced himself against a tree and fired a BB at the mower.

"Katie, would you like some more orange juice?"

The little girl wiped her mouth with her hand. "Yes, Mommy."

Kaye took the volunteered cup. "What do you say?"

"Please."

"That's better."

Mother and daughter ate together in the breakfast nook every weekday morning. It had become an important bonding time. The breakfast table sat in the west end of the wooden kitchen, ringed on three sides by bay windows overlooking their grove. Nature went on around the house as if it wasn't there.

Kaye put the filled cup on the table. "What would you like to do today, young lady?"

"See doggies," she said seriously.

"You want to go see the doggies at Pet Kingdom?"

Katie nodded fervently. Her blonde ponytail spun in a tight circle.

"Okay," Kaye said. "I need to go into town anyway."

"Doggy, doggy, doggy!"

"That means that you need to go into the living room right after breakfast and pick up your toys."

Katie all but launched herself out of the chair. She ran out of the kitchen laughing.

< jefferson scott >

Kaye smiled. When had she forgotten the pure joy of watching puppies and kittens? She felt a cool breeze on the back of her arms. The refrigerator door was standing open. "Hmm. I thought I closed you." She closed the door and cleaned up the breakfast dishes. "Hal, what's the temperature outside, please?"

The household computer didn't answer.

"Hal," she said louder. "Hey, brain in a box, should my daughter wear shorts or long pants?"

No answer.

It aggravated Kaye to no end that this kind of thing always seemed to happen when Ethan wasn't home. When he got home they would go through the same routine: she would tell him what happened, he would test it out and find it working fine, she would protest her case, he would smile and blithely forget all about it.

She was about to leave the kitchen when a light caught her eye. The refrigerator door was standing open.

"So who do you pick this year for the Super Bowl?" Ethan asked.

Neither he nor Gillette were watching the road. They weren't even facing forward. Both had swiveled their chairs around to watch ESPN-3 on the minivan's TV. The automatic driver handled this kind of straight-arrow, light traffic driving effortlessly.

"I pick Nashville again. Have to. And the Saints."

Ethan nodded. "That's a safe guess. I'd love to see the Cowboys get their act together and at least make the playoffs. But I don't think this is their year to go all the way. Next year maybe."

"So who do you like?"

"I'm gonna go with Chicago over Miami."

Gillette stroked his mustache. "Could happen."

Ethan checked the highway ahead. They were in the rightmost lane of a divided highway, still ten miles out of Tyler. The pine forest had

< terminal logic >

been cleared away here. Farmland stretched out on both sides of the Interstate. He was about to comment on the Dallas Cowboys when Gillette shouted.

"What?" Ethan said, swiveling around.

A car in their lane was braking hard. Ethan disengaged the auto-driver with a tap on the brake pedal. He swerved out into the left lane to pass the car, which now had stopped dead on the road. He passed the car, his hands raised in the universal gesture for *What do you think you're doing?*

The woman in the driver's seat looked every bit as alarmed as Ethan was. She seemed to be fiddling with something on her steering wheel.

"Darlin'," Gillette drawled, "you ever heard of a shoulder?"

"It's alright, Mike. We're okay." Ethan accelerated to the speed limit. This time he decided to forego the autodriver.

Tink.

Jordan shook a fist at the chugging mower. "Take that!"

The engine sound was pretty loud now, since both mowers were over in the same corner. The Hamilton property was mostly cleared of underbrush, but the neighbor on the east side seemed to think the more shrubs the better. The dense growth had the effect of redoubling the noise.

Jordan kept an eye on the highway just a few feet beyond the gate. The bus would be coming soon. He took a last potshot at the second mower and put his BB rifle in the hole in the tree. A buzzing sound swelled behind him.

"Hey!" Jordan yelled. The first mower came at him. He stepped out of the way. "Go around, you tin can. What's the matter, did I knock out your infrared with my high-caliber rifle?"

He backstepped around the tree, keeping the trunk between him-self and the machine. It suddenly struck him as strange: a riderless

< jefferson scott >

mower, guided with computer intelligence, controlled by unseen signals through the air. He had a brainstorm for a computer game—he was always getting such brainstorms—a game about automated farm equipment gone berserk.

When the mower cleared the tree it did not continue on its path. It turned around. It hesitated a moment. Jordan imagined he heard it sniffing. Then it started forward again. Right toward Jordan.

He decided to wait for the bus on the other side of the fence. He turned, but the other mower pulled forward, closing off his path to the gate.

"I think I'm in trouble."

Nevertheless it seemed funny to him. How wonderful that this bizarre string of coincidences actually made it look like he was being attacked by two brain-dead lawn mowers! They weren't even moving fast. It was like being chased by iguanas.

"Okay, guys. I'm tired of this." He adjusted his backpack. "I'll be going now."

Afterwards Jordan would not be able to explain just how they managed it, but somehow both mowers discarded the cowlings from over their blade trains. They left them on the grass behind them like shed skin. The sound rose in volume and pitch. Now he could almost feel the sharpened blades slicing through the grass. One of the mowers caught up a branch in its blades. The branch writhed and shuddered as the machine chopped it to pieces. Just what would it do to exposed bone?

Jordan turned to run, but ran smack into a tree. He fell to the ground, dazed. His book bag spilled out its contents into the path of the mowers.

The blades consumed all in their path.

Kaye sat on the floor of Katie's room, helping the little girl with her shoes. Katie's bedroom was like something straight out of *Sunset* maga-

< terminal logic >

zine. Pale yellow walls with a band of green at the top, against which were yellow Tyler roses. The bedding matched the curtains and walls. Even Katie's play kitchen, standing next to the chest of drawers, went with the decor.

"Katie, don't move, please. Let Mommy tie your shoe."

The little girl relaxed into her mother's lap. "Doggy."

Wysiwyg streaked into the bedroom and dove under Katie's bed.

"That's not a doggy," Kaye said. "That's a kitty."

Katie thought that was funny. She went to her bed and pulled out the cat. "Doggy, doggy, doggy!"

Kaye stood up. "Okay, Katie, put her down. Let's go."

"Look, Mommy!" Katie showed her mother the cat's tail, which was puffed three times larger than normal size. Katie giggled.

"Something scare you, Wizzy?"

Wysiwyg did not take her eyes off the open door. Her ears were rotated forward. A throaty *pop* noise rose from somewhere downstairs. Wysiwyg squirmed out of Katie's arms and disappeared under the bed.

Now that she heard the popping sound, Kaye realized she'd heard it at least once before, moments ago. Some of the cat's fear found its way into Kaye. If Hal wasn't working, was the security system? Had Jordan remembered to arm it? She swept her daughter off the floor. "Come on, Katie, let's go downstairs."

"Doggy?"

"Right."

Katie's bedroom was directly across the beige carpeted hallway from the master bedroom. Kaye stepped silently into the hall. She looked into their bedroom as they passed and found it dark. The windows were fully tinted for some reason. She took Katie down the hall to the entertainment loft, which looked out over the great rooms downstairs.

As she watched, the whole downstairs, which had been uniformly lit by sunlight through the towering windows, faded into darkness. Like an eclipse of the sun. The house was now completely dark. Katie wiggled to get down.

< jefferson scott >

Kaye held her fast. "Shh!" She walked by memory back into the now-dark hall. "Hal!" she whispered. "Hal, untint the windows."

A male voice startled her. It came not from the ceiling speakers but from the direction of Jordan's room. Blue light spread out from under Jordan's door. Kaye carried Katie toward Jordan's room—Katie wasn't wanting down anymore—and threw open the door.

The television embedded in Jordan's bedroom wall was on. A newscaster was prattling on about some GlobeNet information company that had been the target of recent attacks via computer. Kaye was only interested in one attack at this moment. She shut the door and walked back to the master bedroom and its bedside vidphone.

She sat on the bed, with Katie on her lap, and felt for the phone controls. The screen flashed to life, ready for a call. Something fell in the hallway. Katie hugged her mother's neck. "It's okay, honey," Kaye said. O Father, please let it be okay.

Eyes stared back at her from the hallway. Perfectly round. Gold. Then they were gone. Something landed on the bed. Kaye jumped to her feet with a gasp. She heard a mournful cry.

"Wizzy! Don't do that." The cat meowed again. Kaye sat back down. The vidphone went black. "No, no, no. Don't do this to me." Her finger hopped on the Call button like a telegraph operator sending S.O.S.

The phone was dead. From downstairs came the popping sound, now repeating like popcorn popping. Suddenly all the lights came on. The radio in the master bathroom came on, too, along with every television, stereo, computer, and vidphone in the house.

Then it all went off.

In the darkness Katie's bangs touched Kaye's chin. "Ghosts, Mommy."

Kaye felt panic rising in her at the thought. But it had the result of just making her mad. She didn't believe in ghosts. She didn't like misbehaving house computers. And she certainly didn't like being afraid in her own home. She swept Katie out of the room and marched to the loft.

< terminal logic >

She found the iron railing. "Hal," she said, "or whoever's down there, whether you're a person or a computer or a spirit, in the name of Jesus Christ I command you to get out of my house *right now!*"

For a moment nothing happened. Then a yellow glow began emanating from directly below the loft. A throaty sound like a bellows blew steadily. The glow brightened. Downstairs, furniture and walls seemed to regain their substance. Kaye saw her little girl's cheeks, golden peaches in silhouette.

Katie pointed downstairs. "Fire."

"Omigosh!" Kaye said. "The house is on fire." She ran to the metal spiral staircase and clanged down. A fire burned in the fireplace. The gas pipe that fed the fire was spitting out too much flame. It was like a blowtorch, charring the glass cowling.

"Hal!" Kaye screamed. "Stop it!"

Laughter issued from above. Laughter as from children. Possessed children. Different voices came from different parts of the house.

"Scared, Mommy, scared!"

"Me too, honey."

That's when the kitchen exploded.

chapter.17

"HE'S RIGHT ON YOU!" Gillette shouted. "Coming up on your right. Can't this heap go any faster?"

Ethan's leg ached from stomping the gas pedal. "No!"

Not ten seconds after they'd passed the woman's stopped car, a silver pickup truck had run right up to the minivan's bumper. Ethan had swerved to let it by. But it had followed him into the lane. Ethan had changed lanes two more times, accelerating each time. Still the truck chased them. Ethan had then swerved around another car, maneuvering in front of it to block the pickup. The truck had swung out onto the shoulder and was now closing again on the minivan.

Gillette watched the mirror on his side. "He's still comin'. Don't s'pose we could hope for a bridge anytime soon. That'd cut his shoulder clean off."

"Hey!" Ethan pulled his mobile phone off his belt and tossed it to Gillette. "Call somebody."

Gillette called 9-1-1, gave their situation and location, and hung up.

"Why'd you hang up?" Ethan said. "You're suppo— Whoa!"

< terminal logic >

The truck swerved off the shoulder and into Ethan's lane, narrowly missing the back bumper. Ethan looked at the driver in his mirror—the man was terrified. He was screaming and waving Ethan away. Waving with both hands.

The pickup was on autodrive.

Ethan looked at the traffic around him. Four or five vehicles ahead, three or four behind. Did they see what was happening? Could the drivers get out of the way? How many of them were on autodrive, too?

He swerved right onto the shoulder and jammed on the brakes. The truck sailed by.

"What are doing, Hamilton!" Gillette shouted. "Speed up!"

The truck braked and spun around to face them. It pulled onto the shoulder and rushed at them.

"Go, go, go!" Gillette said.

Ethan hit the gas and swerved across the Interstate. The pickup adjusted, but not fast enough. It shot by, going the wrong way. The minivan accelerated away.

"Hoo-boy!" Gillette shouted. "Nice shootin', Tex. Guess that demolition derby last night was practice for today."

Ethan's heart thumped in his neck. "Ha ha! And not a scratch on the Batmobile."

"Okay," Gillette was writing on his small pad. "Silver Chevy full cab. Oh-two or oh-three model. Texas plates SD6-594."

He updated 9-1-1 with the information. When he hung up he said, "Police chopper's on the way. Highway patrol's on the median up ahead about a mile. This baby's toast!"

"They better hurry," Ethan said. The pickup was growing in his rearview mirror. "'Cause this bot doesn't know when it's beat."

"What're you talking about?" Gillette said. "You got bots on the brain, Hamilton."

"The driver of that truck wasn't driving, Mike. His car's on auto."

Gillette swung his head back to look at the road behind them. The approaching truck gleamed in the morning sun. "What are you telling

< jefferson scott >

me? That there's a pro-gram behind the wheel of that truck, trying to run us into the ground?"

"That's what I'm telling you, Mike."

Gillette swore. "That ain't possible, right? There's no way that's possible." He looked at his hands. "It's just a stupid automatic pilot, Hamilton. It ain't *smart*."

"Then how do you explain the pickup? And what about that woman whose car stopped right in front of us? Did you see her when we passed? She was trying to disengage the autodriver."

Gillette reset his cowboy hat on his head. "Shoot, Hamilton. What is it with you and these ro-bots, anyway?"

"Guess they don't like me."

"Yeah, ever since you discovered their secret elephant burial ground or whatever that was."

Ethan hadn't thought of that. "You mean—"

"Look out!"

The eighteen-wheeler they were passing decided it wanted Ethan's lane—while Ethan was in it.

"Funny, Mommy!"

"No, honey. Not funny."

The Hamilton's kitchen looked like something out of *Exorcist 8*. It was lit only by the internal lights of the oven, refrigerator, dishwasher, and microwave, all of whose doors stood inexplicably open. Fog poured out of the freezer like a waterfall of dry ice. A wispy haze clung to the wood floor ankle deep. A tiny robot dropped out of the dishwasher and skittered across the floor.

The kitchen sounded like a metal shop. High-frequency motors screamed at each other, never quite resolving into a chord. The blender whined on the counter, whipping the fire out of thin air. The microwave had overcome all safety switches and was cooking with the door open,

< terminal logic >

flooding the room with radiation. As they watched, the electric can opener fell to its side and propelled itself off the counter. It swung from its cord, carving a sinister grin in the cabinets below.

Kaye put Katie down. Fog spun away from their legs in shallow cyclones. Kaye pushed her daughter to a spot around the corner. "Stay here, Katie." She had to shout.

On her third step across the kitchen floor Kaye stepped in water. In the gloom she could make out a pool issuing from the laundry room behind the kitchen. The water reached the door down to the game room and pushed through.

Kaye hesitated, shielding her face from the microwave. Water on the floor of a room full of electric appliances gone crazy. It added a whole new dimension to the situation. Still, the microwave had to be shut off. And somehow she had to get to the washing machine to cut off the water. She stood paralyzed in her haunted kitchen.

Something tugged at her pants leg and began to climb. It felt like a rat. Kaye screamed and kicked. Something metal skipped over the wet floor. The dishwasher robot.

Kaye saw Katie peeking into the room. "Get back, Katie!"

She uttered a quick prayer for safety then splashed across the kitchen, slamming doors. When she reached for the dishwasher door, a white flash lit the room, followed instantly by a delicate shattering sound. Kaye froze. Something hit her blouse like a heavy raindrop. She flicked at it, thinking it was another bot. "Ouch!" Something cut her hand. Glass.

Two more flashes, two more shattering sounds. Katie might have screamed, or it might have been the appliances shrieking. The light bulbs on top of the upper cabinets—so stylish—were exploding. Cooking off one by one like firecrackers tossed in a campfire.

Kaye dashed for the exit beneath a hail of broken glass. She swept Katie up and ran out of the room.

The cacophony receded as soon as they turned the corner. Only here the demonic children waited for her, laughing. The glass cowling

< jefferson scott >

over the living room fireplace was completely black now, blocking all light. Kaye whacked her shin into a coffee table and fell, dropping Katie to the carpet. The little girl started crying. Kaye groped for her.

Something heavy fell upstairs.

Kaye stood up, holding her daughter close, and headed off through the abyss in the general direction of the door to the outside. She hit a wall, overturned an end table, and collided with a ficus tree, again falling to the carpet. All around her the voices laughed.

She held Katie with one arm and all but dragged her across the carpet. She finally came to the glass wall the door was on. She picked Katie up. "We're here, honey." She found the doorknob and twisted.

The door was locked.

In the darkness around her, several dim yellow lights came on, like one-eyed alligators. They converged on Kaye and her daughter.

Katie screamed.

"Get off the road!" Gillette shouted. "Get off the road!"

Ethan was in a zone. It was like a driving game in which all the other cars on the road were out to get him. Only in this game he was only given one life.

The road headed upward, preparing to cross a bridge. Grass spread down the slope on either side of the road.

The eighteen-wheeler was slow to respond, but monstrously heavy. It had plenty of room for error—any part of it would suffice to squash the minivan flat. The silver pickup had caught up with them again and was now right behind, forcing Ethan even with the semi.

The big truck eased into Ethan's lane. Ethan pulled onto the shoulder. His wheels licked the edge of the pavement, beyond which the ground fell sharply away. The pickup truck pulled onto the shoulder behind him.

They passed the dumbfounded state troopers going 100 miles per hour.

< terminal logic >

"Hey!" Gillette yelled out the window to them. "Help!"

The minivan was shuddering as if its wheels were about to shake off. Ethan saw a river gleaming off to the right—the reason for the bridge. He checked his rearview mirror. The pickup truck's driver had given up fighting his automatic driver and was now just bracing himself against the dashboard.

The huge trailer rig was right beside him. The edge of the trailer—silver and sharp—hovered less than two feet from Ethan's ear. Its roar was unbearable. Then Ethan made the mistake of looking at the wheels. The road whisked past below, the mammoth wheels consuming the tarmac. The wind sucked him in.

Ethan looked into the eighteen-wheeler's mirror. He could see that there was no one in the driver's seat; no one in the passenger seat either. The big steering wheel moved on its own. A man clung to the dashboard, screaming into a CB radio.

Gillette put his feet on the minivan's dash. "Goodbye cruel world!"

The semi began to slow as it climbed the hill to the bridge. The pickup was right on Ethan's tail. The Highway Patrol car was in pursuit now, lights flashing and siren screaming. Ethan saw a narrow window for escape ahead. If he could accelerate fast enough, he could squeeze in front of the semi before the railing started. The pickup probably wouldn't have a chance, but Ethan couldn't do anything about that. He stomped on the gas.

And almost broke his ankle. The gas pedal offered no resistance. He tried to steer into the semi's lane. The wheel didn't budge. The brake pedal was slack, too.

His autodriver had taken over. He reached for the switch on the steering column, but it was already in the off position.

There was no longer any doubt that someone was trying to kill him. Someone who knew enough about artificial intelligence that he could appropriate autodrivers at will and move vehicles around like Radio Shack cars. It could only be one person. The same person who had set the bots loose on GlobeNet. Ethan vowed that if he managed to survive

< jefferson scott >

this attack—which didn't look likely—he would dedicate his life to taking this guy down.

He turned to his friend and said, calmly, "This would be a good time for you to become a Christian."

Gillette didn't answer.

The semi blew its horn and moved onto the shoulder beside the minivan. The pickup truck turned on its lights and smacked into Ethan's rear bumper. Ethan folded his legs under the seat and watched his death approaching. Not with fear, but with interest. It was like a roller coaster ride now. He adjusted the location of his left foot so as not to accidentally pop the rear hatch. How odd, to be concerned about popping the hatch when the whole car was about to become scrap met—

Pop.

The.

Hatch.

He dove for the hatch release, but the seat belt caught. He tried again. He grasped the release, momentarily forgetting which way unlocked the fuel lid and which way did the hatch. He just did both, over and over.

The hatch popped. He felt the van relax. The engine's roar slacked, the steering went loose, resistance returned to the foot pedals. The pickup smacked into him from behind.

Ethan grabbed the wheel. The semi blocked him in on the left, the pickup on the rear. The green slope stretched away to his right. At the bottom was the glistening river. The guardrail began in an instant. A moment of decision: leave the road and try to stop short of the river or stay on the road and try to avoid the cars all around him?

He swerved away from the road. The minivan left the ground.

Kaye forced Katie to lie on the sofa. The one-eyed beasts now were shrieking. The children's laughter had risen in pitch and volume. "Lie

< terminal logic >

there, honey. Mommy's going to break the glass."

Kaye groped for an end table. A lamp crashed to the floor. She lifted the small table over her head and ran at the glass.

All the lights came on. The windows untinted. The laughter ceased.

Kaye squinted in the daylight. She brought the table down, bumping her head. Their two automatic vacuum cleaners lay at her feet. Katie grabbed her mother's knee.

Something clanked on the metal spiral staircase. "Mom?"

"Jordan!" Kaye gasped. "Thank You, Jesus."

That said, she promptly fainted.

The van landed roughly. Bounced. Almost overturned. Ethan was thrown into the steering column. His forehead hit the windshield. He saw Gillette being flung around in his seat. Sounds of groaning metal. Ethan steered wildly, his foot only occasionally finding the brake pedal. Something dripped into his left eye. The river rotated in his vision, ever closer in the windshield.

The left front wheel careened off a rock. The airbags deployed, exploding from the dash, knocking them back against their seats.

Just relax, a voice told him. Let it come. He felt his grip on consciousness slipping away. His head really hurt.

But Ethan wasn't ready to give up his wife and children just yet. Defiantly he slammed his moving minivan into Park.

And fell asleep.

part 2

Oh, Lord.
Deliver us from the robots.

ALQUIST in *Rossum's Universal Robots*

chapter.18

"I'M SORRY, MR. HAMILTON," the Alternate Realities receptionist said, "but Ms. Reeves is not taking your calls at this time."

Ethan stared at the wall-sized vidphone screen. His head hurt. He reached up and gingerly touched the bandages on his forehead. "So she's not taking my calls at this time? At what time *will* she take my call? I'll call back then."

"Goodbye, Mr. Hamilton," she said and hung up.

Ethan shook his head—an action which caused his brain to slosh around painfully. He brought up both arms to hold his head, but his left shoulder protested. If his mind had been unbalanced before the accident, now it felt like it had positively capsized.

Ethan slowly ascended the stairs to the kitchen, careful to avoid the industrial blowers drying out the carpet on the upper steps. The noise of the blowers and the stink of mildew did wonders for his healing.

The workmen had broken for lunch. Their tools, along with assorted pieces of appliances, lay strewn about the kitchen. A thirty-something woman stood at the sink, filling a glass with water. She was pretty, with raven black hair and a slim figure.

< jefferson scott >

"Hi, Liz," Ethan said.

Liz Hinnock spilled the water. "Oh, Ethan! Don't do that."

"Sorry." He shut the narrow door behind him.

"I keep forgetting that room's down there. I thought you came out of the trash closet. Scared me to death."

"Doesn't everybody have stairways in their kitchen?" Ethan crossed the room. "Is everyone in the living room?"

"Mike is," she said, refilling the glass. "I think Kaye's taking a nap. The kids are up watching TV."

Ethan rounded the corner into the living room. It was cloudy outside. He could see almost their entire lake through the glass wall. A wind blew across the gray water, making Ethan shiver, though it was no cooler than sixty-five. Through windows on the east side of the house, Ethan saw the electricians on the patio having their lunch.

Mike Gillette lay on the living room couch, propped up by overstuffed pillows, speaking on his mobile phone. Liz walked past Ethan and handed the glass of water to her fiancé. She knelt beside him, stroking his sandy brown hair.

Both men had spent the first night in the hospital. Ethan was treated for a concussion, lacerations on his head and face, bruised ribs and knees, and a mildly sprained shoulder. Gillette had somehow avoided serious injury. He had a sore neck and a minor concussion. The minivan's injuries, on the other hand, were beyond the powers of modern medicine.

Liz had driven up from Fort Worth the day of the accident to be with Gillette. She and Kaye had hit it off well. Gillette had been released from the hospital the next morning (yesterday). Ethan hadn't been released until this morning, which was Friday.

Gillette terminated the call and looked at Ethan. "Bingo. That was those GlobeNIC people you wanted me to call. They say—oh, thanks, Liz darlin'." He drank from the glass. "Mmm. Good water."

Liz smiled.

"Cool it, Romeo," Ethan said. "It's just tap water."

< terminal logic >

"I know, but tap water from Liz is like…nectar from the gods."

Ethan rolled his eyes. He sat in an easy chair. "You said GlobeNIC had something?"

"Yeah. Say, what is that anyway? GlobeNIC. Sounds like some Russian word for the earth." He tried—and failed—to assume a Russian accent. "Da, Cosmonaut Dimitri Kruschev make seven thousand orbit around whole globenik."

Jordan's laughter floated down to them from the entertainment loft. "In my spaceshipnik!"

Katie's head appeared at the loft's railing. "Ha ha!" Then, when everyone looked up, she scampered out of sight.

"Mike," Ethan said sternly, "what did the people at the"—he spelled it out—"GlobeNet Network Information Center tell you?"

"Spoilsport. Alright, they said our mysterious jungle computer is registered to an outfit called Douglas Automation, out of Washington, D.C."

Ethan sat forward. "Did they give you a street address?"

"Yup." Gillette showed Ethan the data readout on his mobile phone.

"Outstanding," Ethan said. "So what are you sitting down for? Let's jump on a plane and pull the plug on this box."

Gillette started to answer, but Liz stood up. "Ethan Hamilton, I'm surprised at you. Look at yourselves. Bandages and bruises and cracked skulls. Mike just got out of the hospital yesterday and now you want him to go flying off to Washington? And you," she said, stepping toward Ethan, "you just got home today! Your family got attacked in this house. Your wife's up there asleep because she's still in shock. And you want to leave them again?"

Ethan's eyes strayed to the fireplace cowling. The glass was scorched black, with a circle of white at the burn point. Black smoke-stains ran all the way up the outside of the stone chimney and onto the ceiling.

Gillette touched Liz's elbow. "Alright, darlin'. Thanks."

< jefferson scott >

Liz didn't move.

"Liz, darlin', sit down please. Give the poor man a break. He just wants to put the hex on whoever did that to his family."

She didn't sit, but she at least broke off her attack. She walked around behind the couch and looked out the windows.

"Liz," Ethan said, "the house computer's off. There's no way that could happen again."

Gillette repositioned himself on the sofa. "Hey, speaking of it happening again, did you ever figure out how whoever-it-was got into your car?"

"Yeah." Ethan sighed. "Too late to protect us, huh? Too late to protect my family." He touched his head bandages self-consciously. "I figured it out alright in my comfy hospital bed."

"Well, spill it."

"The weather downlink, Mike."

"What about it?"

"That's how they got in. To both the van and the house."

Gillette looked at Liz, then back at Ethan. "I don't get it."

Ethan rubbed his shoulder. "I designed this house to be safe from exactly the kind of thing that happened here. Except I overlooked one small thing: the weather report downlink. It never even occurred to me that it might be a GlobeNet link."

Ethan saw Jordan listening from the loft railing.

"It's as if I was designing this house in two different parts of my brain—the security part and the we're-going-to-live-here part. How many bathrooms, what color tile, that kind of thing. A weather satellite downlink is just a part of the package in these so-called *smart* houses. If I'm right, do you know how many houses around the world are vulnerable to this kind of attack? Thanks to my brilliant design work, my family got radiated, scared to death, and almost chopped to bits."

Jordan called down. "I wasn't scared."

Ethan leaned back in his chair. His hands were shaking. Like they always did when he talked about things at the center of his passions.

< terminal logic >

"Jordan… Hey, Jordan," he tried again, "tell Mike about how you got in. I don't think he's heard the story."

"Got in where?" Gillette asked.

Jordan clanged down the metal spiral staircase. "Into the house." The boy took a scrap of yellow cardboard out of his pocket and showed it to Gillette. "You see this? That's all that's left of my Oceanography textbook."

Gillette took the shredded piece and showed it to Liz. "How 'bout that, darlin'? And you thought I didn't take care of my books."

Jordan laughed. "That's from when Hal thought I was a weed and tried to mow me down."

Liz came to sit beside her fiancé. She tucked her jet black hair over one ear. "Who's Hal?"

Ethan answered. "That's our house computer. The one that's off now."

"Yeah," Jordan said. "Hal mows the lawn for us by remote control."

Liz nodded like she understood, but grimaced like maybe she didn't.

"Tried to mow you down?" Gillette asked.

Jordan smiled broadly. "Yeah! Almost got me, too. See, I was trying to run away from them and I…fell down. All my books dropped out and one of the mowers chomped it up. Little bits of paper went way up in the sky."

"Oh, my," Liz said.

"It was great! Anyway, I jumped over this tree that had fallen down. The mowers had to go around. By then I was halfway back to the house."

"Jordan," Ethan said, "skip ahead."

"Okay. I wanted to tell Mom and Katie what happened and that I'd missed my bus. But I couldn't get in the house. All the doors were locked. And all the windows were black. I knew something was wrong. I tried all the doors downstairs, but they were locked. Then I ran up the outside stairs and tried the doors to the deck, but they were all locked, too.

< jefferson scott >

"That's when I remembered my fire escape." He paused dramatically, pulling his listeners along. "I always keep one window in my room unlocked, just in case there's a fire and I'm too sleepy to figure out how to unlock it."

Gillette raised an eyebrow. "Smart kid."

"That he is." Ethan put his good arm around his son.

Jordan went on. "So I opened the window from the outside and went in, head first. But when I got in I almost turned around and dove out. You want to know why?"

"Tell us," Gillette said.

Jordan checked to see that every audience member was watching him. He spoke in a whisper. "I thought my room was haunted."

Katie, whom Ethan had not noticed watching from above, squealed and clanged down the stairs. She ran to Ethan. He brought her up to his lap.

"Go on, Jordan," Liz said.

"Well, my TV was on and over in the corner there was this big scary—"

"Jordan," Ethan said. He nodded toward Katie.

"Oh, okay. Since we've got a baby here." He said the rest flatly. "I went down the hall and turned off the house computer."

"Just in time, too," Ethan said. "Kaye was pretty well scared out of her head. And little one here is having nightmares. Yes, sir. Jordan saved the day."

Gillette slapped Jordan's hand. "Gettin' to be a habit for you, ain't it, kid?"

"So," Liz said, "somebody's computer got into your house through the weather link, right?"

"Right," Ethan said.

"Then somehow made your house computer go crazy."

"That's it."

The door to the patio opened. The four workmen wiped their feet on the mat and returned to their work in the kitchen.

< terminal logic >

"Okay, now we know what happened to your house," Gillette said, "but that doesn't tell us what happened to us in your van."

"Yes it does, Mike."

"You have a weather report downlink in your car? What are you, Willard Scott?"

"I like to know the weather, yes," Ethan said. "But even if I didn't have that downlink they still could've gotten in. Liz, does your car have GPS tracking?"

She met his eyes for the first time since their earlier confrontation. "Is that the little map screen?"

"That's it. The minivan had one. Just about every car made since about 1999 came preinstalled with a GPS downlink."

"So?" Gillette said.

"So? Mike, GPS tracking uses a GlobeNet link."

Gillette's eyes widened.

Liz shook her head. "Why are so many things connected to GlobeNet?"

Ethan shrugged—a gesture his sprained shoulder didn't much like. "There's nothing inherently wrong with GlobeNet. It's just a means of communication. Might as well ask why so many people have telephones. Speaking of that…Mike, can I use your mobile phone?"

"Sure."

"I want to try Alternate Realities one more time."

"They're still not letting you through?" Gillette asked.

"Right. Of course they see my name and number on their screen before they pick up, so they know when it's me calling. But if I use your phone, they won't know to block me out."

Gillette handed over the phone. Jordan and Katie took the opportunity to bang back upstairs to watch television. Gillette stroked Liz's hair. "Don't worry, darlin'. I'm not going to take off with this character to Washington, D.C."

She smiled. "You're not?"

"Nah. Other agents can do that. This computer we're after is

< jefferson scott >

registered to that outfit in D.C., but those GlobeNIC folks told me that the computer itself could be anywhere at all. No sir, no nation's capital for me."

"Thank you for being sensible," Liz said. "You need your rest."

Gillette's eyes met Ethan's. "No, I'm not going to Washington, and neither are you."

"I'm not?" Ethan said.

"No, you need to stay with your family."

Ethan nodded. "Okay. What are you going to do?"

Liz raised her head, anger back in her eyes. "He's going home to recover."

"Liz—" Gillette began.

"Or he's staying here to recover."

"Darl—"

"He's going to take some time for himself for once."

Gillette smiled. He touched Liz's face with his hand. "You're too good for me, woman."

She kissed his hand.

"But." He didn't finish. He just let the word hover there like a soap bubble.

"But what?" Liz asked.

Gillette brought his hand up to tug on his mustache. "Well, darlin', it looks like I do need to go somewhere, after all."

"Mike! What's so important that you can't send somebody else to do it?"

"I need to go out to Baltimore."

"Baltimore!"

"Liz, honey, listen." Gillette's voice turned formal. "My job is to find the person responsible for Jerry Wright's death and to bring him to justice. Ethan's helped me figure some things out, but it's in my court now. I need to get a warrant and a search and seizure subpoena from the DA, and then I need to serve them."

< terminal logic >

Liz started to protest.

"Darlin'," Gillette said, "this is my case."

chapter.19

KAYE DIDN'T WAKE UP when Ethan sat on the bed. He watched her sleep for a moment. When she slept was when he most saw the resemblance between Kaye and her daughter. He stroked her light brown hair.

O Father, he prayed, keep this woman safe. Keep us all safe.

Kaye stirred. She saw him and smiled.

"How are you?" Ethan asked.

"Mmmm." She rolled to her side.

"How's your headache?" he asked.

"Better." She blinked at him. "Where's Katie?"

"She's fine. She and Jordan are watching TV."

Kaye peeled the covers back and sat up. "I'd better get going on dinner."

"Mike and Liz are gone."

"Oh. Will they be here for dinner?"

"Mike's going to Baltimore. Liz drove him to Tyler Municipal to start hopping up there. Then Liz is going to drive back to Fort Worth."

She fell back down on the pillows. "Maybe I'll just take another nap, then."

< terminal logic >

Ethan was getting concerned about Kaye. She wasn't bouncing back from the attack as quickly as their children were, nor even as quickly as he and Gillette were recovering from the crash. She wanted to sleep most of the time now.

Kaye spoke from within the pillow. "What's in Baltimore?"

"That company I told you about. The one that's letting all the bots get loose."

"Altered States, right?"

"Alternate Realities, honey. Go to sleep."

She sat up. "Can't." She stared at the sheets. "What are you going to do?"

"Kaye, the person who attacked us is still out there, free to attack us or anybody else again. He has to be stopped."

She didn't look at him. "Isn't that what Mike's going to Baltimore for?"

Ethan took her into his arms. "You're having second thoughts about me doing this, aren't you?"

"Second thoughts? Try twenty-second thoughts."

He massaged her hand. "It seems different now, doesn't it?"

"Different?" Kaye said. "Ethan, our whole family was almost wiped out two days ago!"

"But we weren't. God protected us. Kaye, we talked about this."

She slumped down in the bed and pulled the pillow over her head. "You said you were going to be careful, Ethan. You promised me."

Ethan put his face in his hands and sighed. "I know." All his injuries seemed worse all of a sudden. He couldn't think of a decent reply. Except, of course: "I'm sorry, Kaye." He shut his eyes. "Are you going to take the kids away again?"

She didn't move. Ethan wondered if she'd fallen asleep. Then she pulled the pillow away. "I don't want to."

"I don't want you to."

"Can you look me in the eyes and tell me we will be safe if we stay?"

He smiled weakly. "Silly question. I thought this house was the

< jefferson scott >

safest thing I could build for you. I thought I *had* made you safe."

A tear dropped out of Kaye's eye.

"You know what, Kaye?" Ethan said. "You should leave. Go away. Take the kids to your parents' again. Or down to San Antonio with my parents. I wish I could say this house is safe, but I can't. I can't turn Hal on until we get him fixed, so even the fire alarms are off." He forced a smile to his lips and hoped it didn't look forced. "I want you to go."

She grinned. "Liar."

Ethan stood up. "I can't protect you, Kaye. Haven't I proven that? Get away from me while you still can."

"Ethan, come here. Sit down." She took him into her arms. They sat quietly. Sounds from the television drifted down the hall.

Ethan absorbed his wife's warmth. He tried several times to get the next question out. On the fourth try it made it across his vocal chords. "Do you want me to stop?"

She looked into his eyes. "You mean stop working for the FBI?"

He nodded.

"First tell me what you have in mind."

Ethan unwound himself from her arms. "The way I see it there are two problems. The first is that there's somebody out there letting all these bots loose on GlobeNet. I think it's the same person who attacked us here and in the van. We've got to stop that guy. Or that group or whatever. The other problem is that GlobeNet's infested with bots. Once we get the bad guy, we'll have to go track down all the critters he's set loose."

"What's you plan? And don't tell me you don't have one, because I know better."

"I want to organize an army online," Ethan said. "I'll get every GlobeNet professional I can to turn out to fight these bots. Maybe we can lure the responsible party out to where I can stick him with my data trackers. We send the FBI to his house, and boom, a big part of it is all over."

"You're beginning to think it's another Patriot, aren't you?" Kaye said.

< terminal logic >

Ethan smiled. "I hadn't thought of that, but I guess maybe I am, a little. For all I know it's the Ladies Fellowship from the church."

Kaye didn't smile. She laid her head on his chest. "Yes, it's different now."

Ethan listened to her breathe. He smelled her sweet hair.

"Could other people's houses and cars be attacked like ours were?" she said.

"If it happened the way I think it did, yes. If I'm right," Ethan said, "every house, car, and airplane in the world would be vulnerable. *Is* vulnerable, right now."

Kaye sighed. "Then you've got to stop it."

He touched her hand. "Are you sure?"

"Ethan, much as I'd like to pull us all out of this and go live in a cave somewhere, I don't want other people to get hurt. Stop this person. Stop him quick. Then come back to us. Maybe it will be time for another vacation."

"Maybe so."

"Could we set a limit?" Kaye asked. "Like if it isn't all over by tomorrow night, or next week, or something, then you'll walk away from it?"

"Let's see," Ethan said, "all this started, what, five days ago. How about giving it another five days? If we can't solve it in ten days total, I'll hand it off to somebody else. What do you say?"

"How about seven days?"

"Total?"

"Yes. A full week."

"Would you and the kids be staying or going?" Ethan asked.

"Staying, I guess."

"How about this: If I haven't finished it by your deadline, then I'll put you on a plane myself. You can go to your parents' house or wherever you want to go."

"Then you'll come join us after *your* deadline?"

"Deal."

< jefferson scott >

Kaye shook her head. "How do I let you talk me into these things?" She kissed him. "I won't say 'Be careful,' but…" She mouthed it anyway.

Ethan sat on the Rive Gauche across from the chairman of the GlobeMasters. They sipped imaginary espresso and watched the Seine flow by.

"I spoke with Ki Bok this morning," the chairman said. "He's got six or seven people working on botbashing teams up at MIT. Irene's got ten at CMU. I know of about twelve other incident response teams working on it, too. Mostly high-tech companies like JSI and Cobra, but a few universities."

Ethan nodded. "So about how many total individuals, do you think?"

The chairman did some mental calculation. Even in Cyberspace Ethan could see the man carry the seven. "Maybe sixty, seventy computers, in fourteen distinct networks."

"What have they been doing so far?"

"Chasing their shadows, mostly. About the best thing anyone's come up with is the infinite virtual space trap you used. That catches them one at a time. Chris Phelps over at Berkeley thinks he's onto something better, but it hasn't panned out yet."

"What's he got?" Ethan said.

"Chris thinks he's come up with a way to bag these bots on sight. Something about their autorun protocols. Anyway, if he's right and can develop it into a working model, then it means no more passive traps. We can go out hunting."

"Do you think these people would be willing to work for me on something?" Ethan asked. "Like if I had a plan for taking the battle to the source of these bots. Do you think they'd play ball?"

The chairman shrugged. "It's a pretty independent lot. But who knows? What's your plan?"

< terminal logic >

"Well, I think I've figured out where these bots are coming from."

Ethan told him about the seven-headed dragon. He also told him about what he'd found that morning when he'd tried to visit the Garden of Eden computer online. The entrance to the site had been blocked by a legion of guardbots. Lastly, Ethan narrated the attacks on him and his family.

"For Pete's sake, Mr. Hamilton, are you alright?"

"We're fine. But now you see why it's so important we put a stop to this."

"Yes, of course. It boggles the mind, doesn't it? Gamebots so convincing they can fake us all out."

"What I'd like to do," Ethan said, "is try to draw out the guy who's behind all this. That's why I've come to you. I need all these CERT people and their computers to join my little army so we can take the fight to them. Make a big stink, bring out the big gun. Who knows, maybe we'll get lucky and find a way to shut the computer down from the inside."

"Why do you want to draw him out?"

"To find out who he is and where his computer is," Ethan said. "I've got a few utilities designed for that very thing."

"Then you can sic your FBI buddies on him?" the chairman asked.
"Right."

"Tell you what," the chairman said. "I'll send out a special advisory. What do you want them to do, call you directly?"

"Sure," Ethan said. "Tell them it's the war against the machines."

Brock Calcutta wandered the hallways of Raymond House. The bottom two floors were for girls only, while floors three and up were for men. The elation he'd felt upon setting foot on the Case Western Reserve University campus had now deformed into frustration. He flopped down to the floor at the end of the hall, outside room 270.

< jefferson scott >

A young coed came out of room 266 and headed for the stairwell. She almost left the ground when she saw Brock sitting there. "What are you doing here? You didn't say, 'Man on the hall,' did you?"

Brock shook his head morosely.

The girl crossed to the door at the end of the hall. But there she paused. "Ah, there now. What's wrong? You look like you've lost your puppy."

Brock looked up. The girl was attractive, if a trifle plump. She had cute dimples and a pretty smile. "I was looking for room 271."

She pursed her lips in thought, an action which had the curious effect of moving her dimples down her cheeks. "Two seventy-one, huh? No, I don't think so. Two seventy's as high as it goes. Maybe you have the wrong dorm. Who were you looking for?"

"Her name's Regina Lundquist."

"Hmm. I know a Jerry Lindquist. No, no Regina Lundquist. There used to be a girl named Regina who lived on this hall, but that was two years ago and her last name was Stein."

"She told me to meet her here. I met her on GlobeNet. We hit it off. We were going to get together in person and…go out."

"You met her on GlobeNet? Oh, that's so sweet."

The door to the stairwell opened, almost toppling the girl out. Another young woman burst in, wearing sweaty workout clothes. "Sorry, Cheryl."

"Oh, Lisa! This boy here is looking for someone." To Brock she said, "Lisa's the floor mother. She knows everybody."

Lisa had gone into her room, number 270. She came out brushing her hair. "Who're you looking for?"

Brock looked up. "Regina Lundquist."

Lisa thought about it. "Hmm."

Cheryl said, "I told him about Regina Stein and Jerry Lindquist, but I told him I didn't know—"

"Wait a minute," Lisa said. "Regina Lundquist? *Regina?*"

Brock stood up. "You know her? I'm in the wrong building, aren't I?"

< terminal logic >

Lisa stared at him as if he'd just fallen off the moron truck. "Don't you know who she is?"

"Who is it, Lisa?" Cheryl said. "Tell us!"

"Where did you say you heard about Regina?" Lisa asked Brock.

"I met her on GlobeNet."

"You met her? You actually met her and talked to her?"

"Regina told him to meet her here," Cheryl said. "In room 271. Isn't that strange, Lisa? I mean, we don't have a room 271, do we? Unless it's the broom cl—"

Lisa began to laugh. The laughter grew, as if the more she thought about it the funnier it got. "I don't know how to break this to you," she said finally, "but Regina Lundquist isn't a who, she's a *what*. The people in the comp-sci department told me about her when I became floor mother, in case she ever got mail." She looked at Brock head to toe. "But they never expected a package like you." She laughed again.

Brock was immediately self-conscious. He was short and wiry and bore a visage women considered less than inspiring, and he knew it. It had been a mistake to come here. Better to live the pretend life on GlobeNet and never try to act it out in reality. He faced Lisa with all the dignity he could muster. "What are you telling me?"

"I'm telling you that Regina Lundquist is a computer program."

Probably the carpet in the hallway had been brown the whole time, but Brock hadn't really seen it until now. It seemed to spin and twist in his vision. He was vaguely aware of people moving and talking. The door opened and someone either went out or came in. Hazy impressions of stairs and doors. Then blinking in the sunlight.

He found himself standing in the sun outside Raymond House. Cheryl was beside him, talking.

"...all the way here from wherever it is you came from. Where did you come from, anyway? Did you drive? Where's your car? I bet you drive a cute little sports car, don't you?"

She went on, but Brock's mind was shot. He couldn't believe he'd been duped by a computer program. He'd tried to make out with a computer! The dorks at the computer science department were probably laughing their heads off, at his expense. He was about to swear off women forever when he noticed Cheryl talking to him, her dimples roaming all over her pretty face.

He interrupted her. "Cheryl, my name's Dennis. Dennis Burkeer." It felt good giving out his real name.

She shook his hand. "Nice to meet you, Dennis. I'm Cheryl Jones."

"Cheryl, would you like to go out with me?"

She blushed. "Why, Dennis, how sweet."

SATURDAY, SEPTEMBER 23, 2006
9:30 A.M., CENTRAL TIME

In all there were seventy-three independent computer users who answered Ethan's call to arms. Among them were Ki Bok Kim, Irene Buescher, and Chris Phelps, each with their teams of graduate students. These constituted almost half of Ethan's virtual army. The other half consisted of computer incident response teams from several large companies, the Navy's IRT, and individual GlobeMasters from as far away as Australia, Ireland, and Iran. Had it not been a Saturday morning, there might have been even more.

Jordan was there, too. Not the country, the boy. It was either an act of irresponsibility or of genius that made Ethan include his son in this attack. It was true Ethan was confident of this room's safety features. But then, he'd been confident of his house's safety features. And his car's. This room, however, had no weather downlink and no GPS tracking. It was as truly cut off from the outside world as a room could be and still be on the earth. The truth was that Ethan trusted his son's abilities over almost any other GlobeNet user he'd ever known. Ethan wanted him around.

Ethan had set up his game room like a military headquarters. The wall monitor displayed the battlefield in symbolic form. A cluster of red

< terminal logic >

dots (representing enemy robots) swarmed around a gray sphere (the Douglas Automation/Eden computer) like June bugs at a porch light. Ethan's army, all blue dots, converged from all directions.

The bottom left corner of the screen was split into four sections, each showing what one of Ethan's game room cockpits "saw." Right now only the bottom two sections were active, since only he and Jordan were around to pilot anything. Both views looked out over the scores of enemy bots.

Ethan spoke to the ceiling. "Penny, put me on to all units, please."

"Initiating multi-channel communication."

"Okay, listen up everybody. Thanks for coming to my little party. Now, let's get on with the show. Here's the plan. I want us to break up into four groups. The folks at MIT will be one group, CMU will be another, Berkeley, why don't you guys be three? The rest of us will be four.

"Group four will hit the enemy head-on. Then groups one, two, and three will try to slip around behind and get into the gray sphere. Try to find a way to cut that computer off from GlobeNet. Also make nuisances of yourselves. Try to cause enough trouble to draw Mr. Big out. If you can't get through, just come back out where we are and engage.

"Group four, our job is just to take out as many bots as we can. Chris, if your Berkeley folks can use that bot-zapper, do it like crazy. The rest of you, just try to hang on. I don't really know what will happen if you get swarmed. It may cause you some problems, so you'll probably want to have all your anti-virus filters going. And don't forget surge protectors.

"If you see something really huge or totally different from the normal bots, call me immediately. That will probably be Mr. Big. Okay, all units wait for my order."

"Wait, wait!" someone cut through. "We're not in position yet. Hang on."

"Who is this?" Ethan asked.

In the bottom right-hand corner of his monitor the chairman's face

< jefferson scott >

appeared. "I'd recognize that voice anywhere," he said. "That's Kepler."

Kepler's virtual face replaced the chairman's. "That's right, all you losers. You don't stand a chance without us. Now everybody step aside and we'll show you how it's done."

The airwaves, which had been reasonably peaceful, now erupted into dispute. Ethan, having given his great Patton speech, headed for the battle tank cockpit.

Katie came running down the stairs. She missed the bottom one and landed hard. "Daddy, Daddy!"

Ethan helped her up. "What is it, honey?"

"Pleece, pleeceman!"

"The police? Where?"

She was halfway up the stairs already. Ethan followed her up.

Behind him the blue dots converged.

chapter.20

It wasn't the police. It was the army.

Three vehicles idled behind Ethan's house. Two wide-framed military jeeps, painted for desert action, and one black luxury car with tinted windows. A tiny red flag fluttered from the car's antenna, bearing three gold stars.

Two men wearing desert uniforms stood at the front door. One wore a camouflage BDU cap, the other, bareheaded, spoke to Ethan. "Good morning, Mr. Hamilton."

Ethan was conscious of the bandages on his head. "What can I do for you gentlemen?"

"Sir, my name is Lieutenant Deeks, U.S. Army. I wonder if you would mind stepping over to the vehicle."

Ethan touched his daughter on the shoulder. "Katie, honey, go find Mommy. Tell her I'm going to be out here talking, okay?"

"Okay." She ran back into the house shouting, "Mommy!"

Ethan went with the soldiers. "What's this about?"

"The Lieutenant General would like to have a word with you."

Ethan let the men lead him to the black car. He saw soldiers in the

< jefferson scott >

two jeeps, but couldn't judge their expressions. They were either mad at him for something or simply bored stiff. Deeks opened the door behind the driver and motioned for Ethan to get in.

When he first hit the plush seat he couldn't see anything. He traced out the form of someone in the seat beside him, but even this was lost when Deeks shut the door behind him.

A light like a miniature headlight struck him in the eyes. "Ethan Hamilton?" It was a man's voice. Mature, maybe old.

One hand shielding his eyes, Ethan said, "That's right. Who's this?"

The light broadened into a regular illumination. It lit the back seat compartment with a light reminiscent of a bedside lamp. A solid wall of some kind severed the back seat completely from the front.

A black man in his sixties, strong but perhaps thirty pounds over-weight, sat in the seat next to him. He wore the same desert uniform as the others. He extended his hand. "Mr. Hamilton, I'm Lieutenant General John Woodson, United States Army."

Ethan shook his hand. "Nice to meet you, sir."

"Mr. Hamilton, before we begin, I need to tell you that this is a safe vehicle. Do you know what that means?"

"No accidents?" As soon as he'd said it he regretted it. But recent events had made him long for a vehicle he could call *safe*. "No sir, I'm afraid I don't."

"It is soundproof, bugproof, bulletproof, and idiotproof. Nothing can leave this cabin by eavesdropping, either passive or electronic. It has airless tires, titanium reinforced frame, and an onboard SAM missile."

Ethan wondered if the nothing-can-leave-this-cabin mandate included him. "Wow."

"So our conversation is strictly between you and me, understand?"

"Yes, sir."

"You don't have to call me 'sir,' Hamilton. You're not in the army and I'm not your superior officer."

"Yes s—" he caught himself, and tried to make it just sound like a long *sssss*.

< terminal logic >

"Item next: We received your message dated 19 September 2006."

For a split-second, Ethan didn't know what the man was referring to. "Oh, Vesuvius, right." He ducked, as if he shouldn't have said it so loud.

"The Vesuvius project is why I am here today, Mr. Hamilton." He leveled a withering glare at Ethan. "Understand that what I am about to tell you is restricted and classified. I do not jest when I say I am authorized by Congress to have you shot if you so much as whisper a word of what I tell you now. The soldiers outside this vehicle know nothing of the Vesuvius project, so do not discuss it with them. There are, in fact, fewer than twenty people now living who know the full extent of Vesuvius's capabilities."

Woodson pressed a button on his armrest. A screen Ethan hadn't noticed before, embedded in the back of the front seat, flickered on. He saw himself standing in his game room, talking to the camera. He listened to the message he'd recorded for Fort Hood.

Ethan's face was replaced on the screen by the footage from the dragon's forest clearing. The white text spilled across the screen as someone tried to access the Vesuvius computer. The seven-headed dragon screamed. Ethan's stomach constricted.

General Woodson pressed a button, concluding the playback. The screen went black. Ethan's eyes had adjusted to the light, and he could see the man's features better. He was a hard-looking man, a veteran of many campaigns. His jaw was tight and his posture strong. Dark gray hair, closely cut. Freckles spotted his cheeks and nose. Yet in his manner there was a calm, as though he were a glacier: slow to move but inexorable in his moving.

"Mr. Hamilton," he said, "I wonder if you'd like to tell this old soldier how you came to be in possession of this information."

Aware that the biggest cybernetic battle in history was about to take place online, Ethan gave him the abbreviated version. Bots causing trouble. Tracking them down. Stumbling on Vesuvius. Running from the dragon. Attacked on the road and in the house. Hospital. Impending battle.

< jefferson scott >

"Sir," Ethan finished, "would you mind very much if we continued this conversation in about a half hour? I'm supposed to be coordinating this assault, so I sort of need to be there."

Woodson didn't move. Ethan had no doubt that he would be absolutely unable to escape this car until the general wanted him to leave.

"Mr. Hamilton, the Vesuvius project is a matter of national security. I don't give a red brick for your computer simulations. Now, sit there and listen to what I have to say."

"Yes, sir." So much for the part about him not being Ethan's commanding officer.

Woodson resettled himself. His uniform whished across the fine leather seat. He drew a thick document with an olive drab cover, bound with brass brads, out of a briefcase and flopped it on the seat beside Ethan.

DARPA OPERATIONS MANUAL
ARPALINK XM-228
SEMI-HEMISPHERIC STRATEGIC-TACTICAL REMOTE
DEPLOYING DEFENSIVE PARTICLE, LASER, BALLISTIC
CHEM-BIO-NUCLEAR CAPABLE ORBITAL
WEAPONS PLATFORM
CODENAME: PROJECT VESUVIUS

There were more horrific words in that title than Ethan had ever contemplated in one sitting. It did little to alleviate the apocalyptic themes so near to his thoughts of late. Perhaps the most frightening word of all was *orbital*. Ethan looked up at the roof of the car as if a killer satellite might have floated into view.

"This is Vesuvius?" he asked.

Woodson nodded.

"This is what this person was trying to break into?"

Nod.

Ethan attempted a dismissive laugh. "He didn't get through,

< terminal logic >

though. Right? Tell me he didn't get through."

"The intruder had penetrated two levels of computer security before we even knew he was there."

Two ideas clamped together in Ethan's mind like industrial magnets. The Dragon. Weapons of Apocalypse. O Father. This isn't happening. Give me wisdom.

The general was going on. "…took it offline. The encryption people tell me there was never any danger to the network itself. Seems the intruder wasn't after control of the whole shootin' match, after all. Secondary systems only.

"I have to tell you, Hamilton, I'm no computer genius. I'm a soldier. I come from the old days of men and guns. I'm all for technological advancement, don't get me wrong. If we can save some of our boys by using this malarkey then that's a plus. But when some turkey can set up his little laptop and bring the world to DEFCON two, then something's bad wrong."

Ethan nodded. His stomach still hadn't let go its grip. It crossed his mind to bring up his supernatural interpretation of events, to tell Woodson that God was beginning His judgment of mankind, but he decided this high-ranking career soldier would not be amused. Or worse, maybe he would be.

"General, I'm not exactly sure what you're wanting from me. I've told you what I know. Your encryption people should be able to take it from there."

Woodson put the Vesuvius operations manual away. He pressed another button on his console. The barrier between the front and rear seats lowered, revealing a man and woman, both young, both uniformed, sitting in the front seat.

"Introduce yourselves, soldiers," General Woodson said.

The woman was Oriental. Her straight black hair was caught up in one of those ridiculous army regulation hairdos. She extended a slender arm to Ethan. "Captain Elizabeth Lee. Pleasure to meet you." She spoke without discernible accent.

< jefferson scott >

The man beside her looked like Richie Cunningham revisited. Farm boy freckles, red hair like a mat of orange wire, perfect teeth. "Mr. Hamilton, I'm Lieutenant Barnes. Kelly Barnes." He squeezed Ethan's hand. "I read about you and Patriot. It's an honor to meet you. What happened to your head?"

"It's a long story." That Barnes knew anything about Patriot said something to Ethan about who these two probably were. "Let me guess," he said to Woodson, "your encryption people?"

The big man nodded. "Two of our best. Captain Lee's been with Vesuvius almost from the beginning. She designed the section of its computer security that ended up repelling this intruder. Barnes is the whiz kid bitin' at her heels."

Ethan nodded.

"Hamilton," Woodson said, "I told you the hacker was not after essential systems in the Vesuvius command structure. I also said that Captain Lee's encryption defeated him. Both statements are true." He paused. The three officers passed meaningful looks to each other.

"But…?" Ethan said.

Woodson nodded to Lee, who said, "Vesuvius is a network of military satellites, as you know. We communicate with a central unit which sends instructions to the others." Lee's dark eyes never left Ethan's. "My predecessor, Captain MacLean, designed the nuclear total loss software embedded in the satellites."

"That's in case of nuclear or electronic attack resulting in total loss of ground communications," Lieutenant Barnes said.

"In that event," Lee said, "Vesuvius would go into automatic. Sophisticated AI algorithms would tell the network what to do. The decision it arrived at would range from 'Do nothing' to 'Total launch,' depending on the sensor data it received."

Ethan had a bad feeling he knew where this was headed. "I thought you said he didn't get through."

"He didn't," Woodson said. "The defenses held."

"You see, Mr. Hamilton," Captain Lee said, "we anticipated possible

< terminal logic >

outside attack from enemy intelligence forces. Vesuvius's defenses are geared to prevent someone from accessing vital areas of command and control. What we did not anticipate was someone trying to gain access to non-essential portions of the system. While these were protected by a double canopy defense, they were, by comparison, relatively unguarded."

It came as something of a shock to Ethan to realize that these people, professional military high rollers, were just as prone to oversight as he was. It humanized the armed forces a bit in his mind. However, the cost for oversight on any level could be high. In his case it almost cost him his own life and the lives of his family and friend. In the case of the U.S. Army, what would the cost be?

General Woodson set his jaw. "Hamilton, we have lost contact with the central command satellite."

Ethan rubbed his face. "Don't tell me," he said. "The weather report downlink?"

Lee and Barnes exchanged surprised looks. Barnes said, "I told you he was good."

Captain Lee turned to Ethan. "How did you know?"

He touched his bandages. "I had a premonition."

"Vesuvius tracks weather patterns for purposes of surveillance and targeting," Lieutenant Barnes said. "The National Weather Service even uses it in hurricane season. That's part of the project's cover."

Lee said, "The intruder penetrated to the weather subdirectories and waited for the next scheduled uplink."

"Then he just climbed up like a rat up a drain, didn't he?" Ethan asked. "Pretty as you like. He extracted his software on the on-board computer and suddenly had run of the joint."

Barnes nodded. "That's what we think happened."

"You're probably right," Ethan said. "That's how somebody got to me in my car and to my family here at the house."

"The bottom line," Lee said, "is that he has appropriated the central command satellite, which means he controls the entire Vesuvius network."

< jefferson scott >

Ethan chewed on his thumbnail. "It sounds like we may be after the same person. If it's true that he intends to use this huge loophole in GlobeNet security he's discovered, do you realize how many things are open to him? How many of your missile silos have GlobeNet links he could access? What about the Center for Disease Control in Atlanta? Nothing like a little anthrax plague set loose on the world."

"Look, Hamilton," Woodson snapped. "If we don't get control of these birds back, nobody's going to have time to die of the plague. Do I make myself clear?"

"So what do you want from me?" Ethan said.

Woodson's hand found a switch on his armrest. "Alright, thank you, people," he said to Lee and Barnes. The divider went back up. "You were able to track this turkey down once. Do you think you can do it again?"

"With all due respect, sir, that's what I was doing before you pulled me out here. I'm pretty sure I know where he lives online. I'm supposed to be in there right now trying to lure him out into the open so we can find out where he is in reality and lock him up."

"At ease, Hamilton. I'll get you back to your games when I'm finished."

"I understand you're concerned about the satellites," Ethan said. "Believe me, I am too. But that's not something I know anything about." He pointed toward the front seat. "Why not use those two? They're your top people, right?"

"They're good," Woodson said. "But they haven't been able to get the job done. They say they can't get into the bird's computer because some new defenses are in place. Could be, I don't know. But if I've learned one thing in my tour, Hamilton, it's that if you get the right people for the job, you're going to have a better chance of it turning out." He nodded once, like a fist knocking on a door. "Barnes has heard of you. Great. Make him your assistant. Take Captain Lee, too. Anybody and anything you need, just name it.

"This is what I need from you, Hamilton. One, take this clown out.

< terminal logic >

Two, I want my birds back. He is *not* going to cook off these bug bombs. Three," he leaned forward menacingly, "the media will not learn of this. Is that clear, Hamilton? Not a word or lack of a word that would cause people to ask questions they should not. Is that clear?"

"Yes, sir."

Woodson leaned back in the seat. "Questions?"

Ethan had a few hundred. He settled on one. "You know I'm already working for the FBI. Is this going to—"

"As I understand it, the FBI wants this turkey taken out, too. What's the problem?"

Somewhere in Ethan's mind was the fading notion that he was working for himself. Correction, he was working for the U.S. government. Or, he thought soberly, maybe humanity as a whole. A voice said to him, in peaceful, patient tones, *Whatever you do, do it heartily, as if working for God, not for men.*

"Tell you what, General," he said. "Let me get down there and try to draw him out online. If we can do that, maybe both our headaches will be over. If not, then I'll be happy to see what I can do about your satellites."

Woodson didn't move. Ethan wondered if he'd angered him. Instead the first real smile he'd seen the man loose spread across his face. "Okay, civvy. You're calling the shots. Go on in to your little war game."

Ethan grasped the door handle. "Why don't you come in and watch?" He gestured toward the front seat. "Bring them, too."

An iron grip held his leg. "Just remember, mister, this ain't no Pollyanna we're playing here. I could yank you right now, take you somewhere and lock you in a room until you do what I want. FBI or not. I will, too, the first whiff I get you're not pursuing DEFCON objectives. Am I clear?"

"Painfully."

< jefferson scott >

Ethan led the general and his entourage down into the game room. Lieutenant Barnes, Captain Lee, and the soldier with the BDU cap: Private Culpepper. Kaye stayed up in the kitchen with Katie. It hadn't exactly helped her migraine to have the U.S. Army suddenly involved in her life.

"Whoa," Barnes said, looking around the game room. "Nice setup, Mr. Hamilton."

"Thanks," Ethan said. "There are VR cockpits on all four corners."

"Whoa."

General Woodson stepped to the center of the room. "What is this place, Hamilton? NORAD?"

"No, sir. Just where I come to work and play. Now, all of you make yourselves comfortable. I'm sorry about the lack of furniture in here." He turned to Culpepper. "There are chairs upstairs at the kitchen table. Help yourselves to anything in the refrigerator, too."

Woodson stared at Ethan's wall monitor, arms folded. "This your war game?"

Ethan checked the screen. The armies had engaged. Even as he watched, the last of the blue dots entered the red dots' defensive position. The whole thing looked purple.

"Penny, what's the status of the target computer?"

"Target computer intact. Integrity unimpeached."

Barnes looked up, wonder on his freckled face. "Whoa."

A glance at the bottom corner of the screen told Ethan that Jordan had engaged, too. He walked to the Marvin the Martian cockpit door and opened it.

Jordan turned around. "Oh, hi Dad."

"Jordan, who gave the order to attack?"

The boy made a sour face. "The Warez Doodz."

Warez Doodz described a certain subculture on GlobeNet. They

< terminal logic >

were usually preadolescent boys who prided themselves on their alleged hacking prowess. They were mostly an annoyance to everyone but others in their clique.

"They didn't want to wait," Jordan said. "Somebody said he was going to be late for a movie. Then somebody yelled, 'Kewl!' and everybody just…started."

Ethan blew out a sigh. "What are you doing?"

"Hiding. Dad, this war of yours needs better special effects. I saw about ten of our guys go up against these kobold dudes—just like ours in Falcon's Grove—only these have yellow hair. I thought it was going to be this great fight. But when the kobolds attacked, our guys just went out like this." He made a puffing sound. "Totally boring. Then the kobolds saw me, so I took off. I was just about to go looking for them again. You wanna come?"

"No, you go ahead. Maybe I'll see you in there."

"Hey, who else is here?" Jordan said. "I thought I heard somebody."

"Some people from the army."

Jordan turned back to his screens. "Yeah, right."

"Honest. There's a three-star general and some of his staff. There are two jeeps full outside."

"Sure, Dad."

"Suit yourself." Ethan shut the door and crossed the middle room. "Penny, how many friendly units are still active?"

"Forty-two active, thirty-one terminated."

"And how many red units?"

"Two hundred fifteen active, twelve terminated."

Ethan put his hand on the doorknob to the battle tank cockpit. "Wonderful."

"You're getting whupped," Barnes said.

"Is that right?"

"What kind of strategy is this, Hamilton?" Woodson said, staring at the screen. "Where's your reserve?"

"General," Ethan said as calmly as he could, "I had a good battle

< jefferson scott >

plan drawn up. But instead of being able to implement it I had to come out to your car for a powwow."

"Your troops should've been better briefed."

Ethan motioned to the screen. "These are volunteers. Most of them are doing this from their desks at work—they came in even though it's Saturday. Now, if you'll excuse me, I've got to go salvage what chance I have left to draw this maniac out."

As he shut the door behind him, Ethan heard Private Culpepper say, "Looks like they needed you in charge, General."

chapter.21

Tom Reynolds, of the Baltimore FBI, and Mike Gillette got off the elevator on the fourteenth floor of the Capitol Bank building in downtown Baltimore. They stepped into the Alternate Realities waiting room, which was every bit as plush as the virtual one Gillette had seen on Ethan's computer screens. Ficus trees, inviting furniture, luxurious carpeting. It seemed as if the artificial room had simply been extrapolated from the real one. This time Gillette could—and did—walk over to the video screen inset in the wall.

The door to the offices opened and a woman in her late twenties came in. Gillette recognized her as the receptionist. She extended her hand to Reynolds.

"Hello, I'm Louise Terrance, Ms. Reeves' personal assistant."

Reynolds shook her hand. "Good morning, Miss Terrance. Special Agent Tom Reynolds, Baltimore FBI." He showed his identification. "And this is Special Agent Mike Gillette of the Fort Worth bureau."

Louise shook his hand. "Fort Worth? That explains the hat."

Gillette took his Stetson off. "Sorry, ma'am."

Louise motioned to the sofa. "Perhaps you'd care to sit down? Then

< jefferson scott >

you can tell me what Alternate Realities can do for the FBI this morning."

Gillette didn't move. "No, ma'am, afraid we can't this time." He held out his hand to Reynolds, who handed him a document. "This is a search and seizure subpoena. It authorizes us to confiscate certain data and pieces of office equipment to be held as evidence for a forthcoming trial."

Louise looked at Gillette as if he'd been transformed into Kafka's bug. "What are you talking about? What kind of office equipment?"

"We may have to take every last computer, calculator, and slide rule you've got on the premises. Plus most of your records for the last five years. Oh, and your phones, too."

"You can't do that! How could we do business if you took all that?"

Gillette smiled sweetly. "That's the general idea, ma'am."

"You can't just walk in here and flash a piece of paper at us and shut us down like that!"

"This document says we can, Miss Terrance," Reynolds said. "Now, if you cooperate it will prevent any additional penalties from being levied."

"We'll just see about this." She headed for the door. "You'll have to talk to Ms. Reeves before you touch anything."

They followed her through the door.

The Alternate Realities offices were nice. The desks they passed on either side were large and widely separated. Green was an important color here. The carpet was a rich Kelly green, the walls a mint green, and the numerous plants, of course, were plant green. Attractive artwork in black frames gave the room balance.

They came to a desk near the corner offices. Cherrywood doors stood closed behind the desk. The nameplate on one read, "Rosilyn Reeves." There was no nameplate on the door beside it, though Gillette saw holes where screws had been.

Louise sat at her desk and picked up the phone. "Ms. Reeves, there are two"—she looked at Gillette and Reynolds—"gentlemen from the

< terminal logic >

FBI here to see you. They think they're here to shut us down." She listened. "Yes, Ms. Reeves." Louise put down the phone. "Go on in."

They stepped into a large executive's office. Tall panel windows overlooked the Baltimore skyline. Gillette recognized the woman behind the large wooden desk as Rosilyn Reeves, the assistant to the president. He inclined his head. "Morning, Miss."

"I suppose you have badges or something?"

The agents showed their identification.

"What can I do for you today, Mr."—she read one of the IDs—"Gillette?"

Gillette placed the subpoena on the desk and slid it to her. "Do you know what this is?"

She looked at it but did not touch. "Search and seizure?"

"We're shuttin' your doors, ma'am," Gillette said.

"May I ask why?"

"Now let's don't play that game, Miss," Gillette said. "The name Ethan Hamilton ring a bell?"

"Hamilton? No. Let's see… Hamil—Oh, him! The one who objected to our little probe." She pursed her lips. "So, he really did know the FBI."

"Afraid so. You know, you might've avoided all this if you'd been a pinch more cooperative with him."

"If I say I'm sorry will you take this piece of paper away?"

"Afraid not, ma'am. All Mr. Hamilton wanted to do was talk to your president. Now I'm going to have to insist on it. Miss Reeves, are you going to lead me into that office next door or is agent Reynolds going to have to bite the handle off?"

Reynolds's cheek twitched.

Rosilyn stared at a picture frame on her desk. When she looked up again her ears were flushed. "I can't let you talk to Yoseph."

"That's fine," Gillette said. "We'll take you instead." He pulled out another document and laid it on her desk. "This is a warrant for the arrest of the chief executive officer of Alternate Realities. Or his lieutenant if he

< jefferson scott >

is not forthcoming. Ma'am, you are under arrest for criminal negligence leading to the wrongful death of Mr. Jerry Wright, a customer of this company." He rounded her desk. "Now, if you don't mind coming with us."

She stood. "You want to see Yoseph?"

"That's what the paper says, Ms. Reeves," Reynolds said.

"It is amazing—is it not, Tom?—the power of certain pieces of paper to get things done." Gillette turned to Rosilyn. "Now, your su-per-i-or wouldn't happen to be in that office next door, would he? The one with the nameplate taken down. Or did he duck out while we've been in here talking?"

"No," Rosilyn said. "That office is empty now. It was Adam's before he died."

"You told Mr. Hamilton that Krueger's son was president now," Gillette said. "Doesn't he get his old man's office?"

"No, Yoseph doesn't work from that office." She turned to stare out the windows. It was a cloudy September day in Baltimore.

Gillette rotated his Stetson in his hands. "Ma'am?"

"Oh, my." Rosilyn seemed to deflate. She turned around but did not meet their eyes. "Follow me."

Ethan manifested himself as an intergalactic battleship. He spun around in Cyberspace, checking his controls. "I need my warriors," he said.

"Initiating synthetic companions."

His bodyguards coalesced before him. "Red Baron, you're up top. Vasquez, take point. Roland, rear. Patton, left flank. Faramir, on the right. USS *Dallas,* watch our bellies." They moved into position.

"Okay, boys and girls, listen up. The situation is critical and the LZ is very hot. Allies have taken heavy losses. The enemy threatens to over-run. Our mission is to locate the enemy commander, close, and fill him full of PGT data trackers. Your main task will be to run interference for

< terminal logic >

me. If a target approaches, you are authorized to open fire. Understood?"

"Let's rock," Vasquez said, lifting her automatic weapon.

"The sooner we start this, the better," Patton said.

"To the death, my liege," Roland said.

"For the white queen!" Faramir shouted.

"Für zie Deutschland," said the Red Baron.

"Copy COMSUBPAC. Dallas over and out."

Ethan toggled the column of switches, powering up the rest of his combat systems. He shouted over the din. "Stop your grinnin' and drop your linen! Okay, boys, prepare for dustoff. We're coming in right on top of the LZ. Initiating GlobeNet link…" Ethan reached forward to where Gillette's portable phone sat on the dash, a wire streaming off, and pressed the speed dial key, "now."

If a battle was raging below him, Ethan couldn't see it. He stared out over a suburban part of GlobeNet. The sky remained locked in its burnt orange twilight. He checked his tactical map—yes, he was in the right place. The gray sphere on the map was nearby, probably the three-story building directly ahead in his viewscreen. Instead of furious hand-to-hand combat, he saw no movement at all.

"Penny, give me CCF on the black and white."

"Affirmative."

The combat command frequency appeared on the small monitor set into his console. A man's face appeared in the black and white screen; Ethan recognized him as Ki Bok Kim, the systems administrator at MIT.

Ki Bok was close to shouting. "…care if you can't see me, Fahiid, just do what I say!"

Another face appeared in the CCF monitor. It was very faint, but it appeared to be that of a young man. Two out of every three of his words were curses, but the gist of his reply was that his computer wasn't functioning properly.

Ethan was about to interject when motion caught his eye below

< jefferson scott >

him. A bright motorcycle, possibly modeled on the light-cycles from an ancient movie called *Tron*, shot out from a residential building. The young man shouted defiantly on the CCF. Immediately the earth seemed to erupt with movement. Shrubs and mailboxes and parked cars turned out to be nothing of the sort. A horde of figures came to life and took off after the motorcycle.

"Good work, Fahiid," Ki Bok said. "Making my move."

Another figure, this one humanoid, emerged from a house in the same neighborhood. Ki Bok. He ran in the opposite direction. Several of the bots pursuing the motorcycle turned to chase the humanoid.

Ethan spun his battlecruiser around and hurried to Ki Bok's aid. "Penny, call up intruder countermeasures. Prepare to take on prisoners."

"Specified routines activated."

As Ethan pulled into range his targeting system lit up. Every enemy monster, vehicle, or *thing* chasing Ki Bok became a potential target. Ethan toggled his microphone on. "Stand by, Ki Bok," he said. "I'll try to help you out here."

"Who's that?"

"It's me: Ethan Hamilton."

"Thought you'd left us."

"Couldn't be helped. What are you trying to do now?"

"Trying to get to Phelps. He's holding out at router box two-nine-oh-oh."

Ethan checked his tactical display. RB-2900 was off the map. "Hey, Ki Bok, did anybody ever spot Mr. Big? Did we draw him out."

"Nope."

"Wonderful."

Ethan's point guard, Vasquez, opened fire with her machine gun on the nearest bot. "Vaya con Dios, man!"

Ethan closed on the pack until all his warriors had engaged with full weapons. He fingered the joystick button that would send targeted bots into infinite virtual space oblivion. "Hang on a second, Ki Bok, and I'll go there with you."

< terminal logic >

"Well hurry it up. I've got softbots crawling through my root directory right now."

Ethan pressed the button. The bot he had targeted—a lumbering centaur—grew suddenly rigid and faded away. "Got him!"

"Thanks, man."

"No problem."

Another of the pursuing bots, this one a sci-fi land vehicle of some kind, rotated a turret and launched a surface-to-air missile. The Red Baron disappeared in a purple fireball.

"Whoa!" Ethan shouted. "What was that?" He targeted the vehicle with his crosshairs and shot off another virtual net. The sci-fi tank faded away. "Okay, we've lost the Baron. Everybody else fly a little higher."

His guardbots complied. The rest of the enemy bots broke off the pursuit.

Ki Bok accelerated away. "Who you talkin' to?"

"Never mind. Let's get to RB-2900."

Ethan sat back in his gunner's chair. The router box was still a few seconds away. He wiped his sweaty hands on his pants legs. "Hey, Jordan, you still with us?"

The boy's face appeared in the CCF window. "Ten-four, big daddy."

Ethan smiled. "You still hiding?"

"Have to. I'm not in a battlestar like you are. There's about a gazillion demon-heads right outside my door. I tried to run, but they glommed all over me. It's like they're waiting for me."

"They are," Ethan said. "They're on the lookout for anybody communicating from my GlobeNet address. You're safe, though. Don't worry."

Jordan shrugged. "Who's worried? I'm having fun just sitting in here waiting for them to come in one at a time. I pick 'em off with"— he paused dramatically—"the X-Terminator. Get it? X-Terminator? No more Terminator. Terminator go bye-bye—"

"I get it, Jordan. What is it, IVS flypaper?"

"No. You remember how Richland Middle School said they'd take

< jefferson scott >

math homework by computer?"

"What?" Ethan said. "Jordan, you don't go to Richland Middle School. That's back in Fort Worth, remember?"

"Dad! I know. Richland was our arch-enemy. Why do you think I'm sending all these bots there? Can't stand their purple and whi—"

"Jordan! Tell me you didn't send these bots there! This isn't a joke, Jordan; these things could hurt somebody."

"Relax, Dad. You know what'll happen. They'll figure out they're not where they wanted to be, and they'll just start heading back. They won't hurt anything."

The boy was right. This X-Terminator was actually a good solution—so long as the exiled bots really didn't do any damage to the school computer. Jordan's weapon was even less destructive than Ethan's own infinite virtual space traps, which destroyed the bot. He felt like he should disapprove anyway.

Ethan's cockpit door opened. Woodson peered around the red-lit room. "What the Tom Fool you doing in here, Hamilton?"

Ethan was still a few seconds out of RB-2900. "What can I do for you, General?"

"You're off the map out there. Give me an update."

"We're headed to where the remains of my army is holding out." Ethan recalibrated the tactical maps to show RB-2900. "Are you from Texas, General? You know the story of the Alamo?"

"I'm familiar with the battle."

"Well, we're headed there now. Last stand. The guys there are holding their own. If we've pricked this hacker's finger at all he'll show up there. Then we can put it to him."

Woodson swore under his breath, but stepped outside and shut the door.

Ethan heard one of his other cockpit doors open. A young voice said, "Whoa! It really is the army. Hey, which one of your guys is the general? Whoa!"

"Jordan," Ethan called.

< terminal logic >

Jordan came to his father's cockpit. "What are the army-men doing here?"

"I'll tell you later, son. Right now go back into your cockpit, please. I need you to log off and then log back on again where I tell you to."

"But Dad! They'll just glop onto me again."

"I'm counting on it. We're going to use that to get in somewhere."

"Can I use...the X-Terminator?" Jordan said.

"To your heart's delight."

"Cool." Jordan left.

Ethan and Ki Bok flew within sight of the router box. It was a black cube, about two virtual stories tall. As expected, the place was thickly surrounded with Alternate Realities bots of all shapes and designs.

"Jordan," Ethan said, "do you see these coordinates? In a minute I want you to log in right here. This guy with me is Ki Bok. He and I are going to find a hiding place. When I say, you log in. All those bots should detect your data signature and take off after you. When they do, turn and run the other way. Ki Bok and I are headed for that black building up ahead. As soon as we make it in I'll let you know and you can log off."

"Okay," Jordan said, "But why aren't they chasing you now?"

"I'm using Mike's mobile phone, Jordan. It's broadcasting his signal, not mine."

"Oh," Jordan said. "Hey, Dad, I think I'm going to log back on as Kvarr Ragnek, alien prince."

"Fine. Just so long as you stick with the plan."

"Okay."

Ethan and Ki Bok got in place. As they watched, a group of about twenty Assyrian chariots charged the black router box building. Artificial horses plowed the synthetic soil, sending up clouds of simulated dust. Ethan's cockpit speakers resounded with thunderous hoof-beats and the shouts of charioteers.

When the chariots neared RB-2900 a giant stood up on the rooftop. A titan, holding what appeared to be cannonballs. He shouldered one

< jefferson scott >

like a shot-put and launched it toward the chariots. It crashed down upon the lead chariot. The driver barely had time to cover his head. But while Ethan had expected some kind of pyrotechnics, the chariot simply vanished.

The titan stood his ground, calmly lobbing cannonballs onto the attackers. When the twenty chariots had been reduced to three, the survivors turned to run. They didn't make it.

Ethan looked at Ki Bok in the black and white CCF monitor. "Is that…?"

"Yep. That's Phelps. Those balls he's tossing go in and mess with the softbots' activation flags."

Ethan smiled. "It turns them off?"

"Now you know why I wanted to come here."

"So I see. You ready to go?"

"Let's do it."

Ethan checked his guardbots—they were all in position. He called his son. "Okay, Jordan, log in. Then hightail it out of here."

"Ah, that's a roger, Houston."

On Ethan's battle map a new blue dot appeared. Jordan was out of visual range, but it was clear enough that he was there. It was as if someone held a vacuum cleaner right over RB-2900. Ethan's data signature was, it seemed, a surefire bait. Scores of bots of all descriptions leapt to the cybernetic sky after the intruder.

"Let's move," Ethan said.

chapter.22

YOSEPH'S GAMEWORLDS WERE IN TROUBLE. *Westworld* had lost another saloon girl, *A Time for Heroes* was missing an entire squadron of Valkyries, he'd lost contact with a legion of Cylons in *Supernova Seven.* These were just the reports he'd received in the last hour. *The Abyss* was hardest hit: 31 percent of its middle-ranking dark angels now failed to honor Yoseph's call.

The only hope of restoring balance to the gameworlds was a full purge. It would delete all the players, the number of whom had increased one million-fold less than a week ago. Most importantly, since each bot was symbiotically linked to the MUD for which it was created, a full purge would recall every one to its starting place.

The battle going on outside his hatchery was of little concern to Yoseph. The attackers had had little chance of breaching his defenses in the first place, and now the remainder had been safely contained. It did interest him that Ethan Hamilton's electronic signal had been detected among the attackers, since Yoseph's assassins had supposedly purged him. The signal was gone now.

Yoseph was in his control facility, concentrating on the full purge.

< jefferson scott >

The guard tower loomed at the perimeter of the glen. The players' list, which Yoseph had failed to secure by combat, he'd obtained through the labor of his workers. They had compiled the list manually, based on the many communications traveling across the worlds.

Yoseph had ceased to wonder at the size of his newest world. It was not without limit; its players not beyond counting. Only the concerns of a MUD god weighed on him now—how to manage it, how to regulate it, and how to correct it should it get out of control.

Yoseph became aware that Ethan Hamilton's signal had resurfaced in the battle. He bolted for the spot.

Rosilyn Reeves led Gillette and Reynolds to a white-walled room at the heart of the Alternate Realities offices. Computers crowded the countertops on all four walls, gathering dust. Cables spread like grey spaghetti on the floor. A white desk occupied the center of the room, a computer monitor on top. A cable led from the monitor to a large black box in the far corner. It looked like a high-tech casket.

Gillette stood with Reynolds and Rosilyn at the doorway. "This is where Yoseph works?" he asked.

Rosilyn had been weeping quietly, but his question evoked a smile. "In a way. It's hard to explain. This room used to have twenty people working in it. One for every computer. But Yoseph replaced them all. He's...he's amazing."

"You're telling me." Gillette sat in the chair at the computer desk. "So where is the whiz kid? When do we have the honor?" He followed Rosilyn's gaze to the casket in the corner. "What is that?"

Rosilyn dabbed her eyes with a tissue. "That," she said slowly, "is Yoseph."

Gillette swiveled to face it. "He's a vampire?"

She smiled sadly. "I'm sorry to break it to you like this, Mr. Gillette, but Yoseph is a machine."

< terminal logic >

Ethan piloted his battlecruiser into RB-2900. A handful of figures walked around inside the dim chamber: a Nazi storm trooper, a punk rocker with a purple Mohawk, and some kind of superhero carrying a laser-powered fly swatter. The titan sat cross-legged on the floor, as if meditating.

Ki Bok entered next. He maneuvered between Ethan's guardbots. "You want to tell me why all those softbots took off after the kid?"

"They thought it was me," Ethan said. "It's a long story, actually. Let's just say these bots and I have some bad blood between us." Ethan beeped his son's intercom, "You can jack out now, Jordan. We're in."

The boy's face appeared in the CCF. "Whoa, Dad! They're seriously all over me here."

Ethan checked his tactical display. Jordan's blue blip was completely obscured by a red swarm. "Jack out then."

"No way! It's too much fun knocking them out to Richland!"

"Jordan, just—"

The punk rocker and the Nazi approached Ethan's battleship. The punker knocked on the hull. "You're Hamilton, huh? Hey, just wanted to say thanks for getting us our tails kicked."

Ethan glanced at a readout. He didn't recognize this person's electronic signature, but from the getup and the attitude he guessed he was a Warez Dood—responsible for blowing Ethan's best chance at identifying the enemy. Keep it nice, Curly. "It's true," he said, "it doesn't look good."

"Not good?" the Nazi said. "Friend of mine's computer's totally fried. So when you gonna pay for it, monkey boy?"

The titan roused and came toward Ethan. The Doodz hurried away. "Ethan Hamilton?" the giant said.

"That's right."

"Chris Phelps."

"Nice to meet you," Ethan said. "I saw you tossing your hand

< jefferson scott >

grenades out there. They work great."

"Thanks."

"We'll all need some of those in the next attack."

"The next attack?" the punk rocker shouted. "Are you nuts?"

"Shut up," Ki Bok said, shooing them farther away.

"So," Phelps said, "did we have any luck at all in this battle?"

"Sure," Ki Bok said, "all of it bad."

"We lost all our fighters except those of us in this room," Ethan said, "and my son."

"Maybe you'd like to tell us what's going on?" Phelps said.

"All I have is a theory so far," Ethan said. "You want it?"

"Yes."

"You know the MUD company Alternate Realities?" Ethan said. "Big company, right? Lots of gameworlds. Anyway, their main genius just died a few days ago and his son is in charge now. One of my theories is that this kid has no clue about how to run a MUD. Especially about how to manage robot characters. For some reason he's started storing them on unprotected computers out on GlobeNet. And now lots of them have wandered off and started causing trouble."

Ki Bok whistled. "Yikes."

"Exactly," Ethan said.

"So all these bots," Phelps said, pointing beyond the black walls, "are gamebots?"

"That's my theory."

Ki Bok and Phelps and the other occupants of RB-2900 thought it over. At length the fly-swatting superhero spoke. "You said that was *one* of your theories."

"Right," Ethan said. "The other is that there's somebody else behind all this. I have reason to believe it could be somebody very talented in artificial intelligence."

"These gamebots," Phelps said, "they attack in unison, as if they're being controlled."

"Maybe it's your guy," Ki Bok said.

< terminal logic >

"True, or it could be the new president," Ethan said. "He may be trying to guard that computer we were trying to penetrate—it's got some kind of weird evolutionary jungle inside. It's like a rain forest for new bots."

"What if this evolution-computer is just running out of control?" Ki Bok said.

"Could be," Ethan said. "Maybe bots are wandering out by mistake. Or maybe the kid's setting them loose on GlobeNet maliciously." He didn't mention his other theory, the one that said these were all demonic creatures being controlled by Satan himself. He was doing his best to stuff that theory under the floorboards of his mind.

A shrill alarm called Ethan's attention to his battle map. A large red dot had appeared and was moving across the screen. "Everybody check your map at grid point one-one-four, zero-nine-four, zero-seven-zero."

"What is that?" the Nazi asked.

Ethan licked his lips. "Unless I miss my guess, it's what this whole thing's been about. Mr. Phelps, it looks like your little Molotov cocktails have earned the attention of Mr. Big himself."

"It doesn't look like it's coming for us," Ki Bok said. "It looks more like it's headed straight for your kid."

Ethan looked. "Hmm."

Phelps faced him. "What do you want to do?"

"Let's just go out there and fill him full of data trackers," Ethan said.

The purple-haired punk rocker scoffed. "Right, like that's gonna do anything."

"Button it," Ki Bok said. "We snag this guy's address and the FBI takes him to jail, am I right?"

"Or at least they can shut his bot factory down," Ethan said.

The Nazi sneered. "You want to know what F-B-I stands for, man?"

"No!" Ki Bok said. "Hey, kids, why don't you run along home now?"

Phelps chuckled, "And don't bother the adults again."

Ethan led the remnant of the human army onto the battlefield. The dozen bots that hadn't gone after Jordan—dinosaurs and samurai, mostly—instantly converged on them. Ethan's guardbots engaged.

< jefferson scott >

"Don't get tangled," Ethan said. "We have to get to Jordan. Let's go."

All of Ethan's guardbots complied except Vasquez, who closed with the pterodactyl she was fighting. She tossed her automatic weapon aside and tore into the beast with her hunting knife. That was the problem with giving these bots real personalities—sometimes they didn't do what they were told. She finally disengaged and took point.

Ethan throttled forward. He wanted to get to Jordan before the big red blip did. He didn't know what the blip signified, but it probably wasn't the tooth fairy. He was expecting the multi-headed dragon.

When they arrived at Jordan's position, Kvarr Ragnek, alien prince—nothing but black tentacles and brain—was being mobbed. Bots of all species swarmed around him, tearing and biting and firing weapons.

"About time you guys got here," Jordan said. "Somebody get these things off me."

Ethan nosed his battlecruiser toward his son, letting his guardbots engage. The superhero joined the fray, swatting bots senseless with his swatter. The enemy bots they'd left behind at RB-2900 arrived, hitting Ki Bok and the others from the rear.

The devil's coming, the devil's coming. It resonated in Ethan's mind. He focused on the battle map, trying to stay calm. The big dot had stopped moving. It was near. Ethan searched the digital horizon.

He spotted a huge lion the size of the Sphinx. It crouched behind a building as if behind tall grass, watching him. The sight sent a charge up Ethan's spine. A verse came to him. Be self-controlled and alert. Your enemy the devil prowls around like a roaring lion looking for someone to devour.

The lion roared. Not the movie sound effect, but a hollow, tubular *oomwah*. Short, pure, carnivorous.

The punk rocker came to stand beside Ethan. "Is that…?"

"That's him," Ethan said. His hands were sweating faster than he could wipe them dry. "Let's…let's not miss this chance. We may not get another one."

< terminal logic >

The lion crept forward, exactly like a big cat. Shoulder blades knifed along its spine like twin dorsal fins.

Curly, are you sure this was such a great idea? Ethan's mouth was bone dry. "Jordan," he said quietly, "stay behind me, okay? Can you move?"

"Mostly," the boy said. "Somebody's standing on my tentacle."

Ethan didn't take his eyes off the lion. "Does everybody see our new friend?"

Their reaction indicated they had not.

"Just help Jordan maneuver," Ethan said. "Keep me between Jordan and the kitty cat over there."

"You got it, chief," Ki Bok said.

"What are you going to do?" the Nazi asked.

"Hide and watch."

Ethan wished he felt as brave as he sounded. He fired up his data trackers—the ones that had worked so well against Patriot—and switched them to joystick control. He urged his galactic battleship forward, his guardbots in formation around him.

The huge lion, still fifty yards away, crouched down. Its mane rippled in an invisible breeze. Chestnut eyes flicked from Jordan to Ethan and back again. Without a sound it charged. A swelling blur of muscle and fang.

Ethan's skin crawled. His right leg vibrated involuntarily. He was vaguely aware of someone shouting in his speakers. His targeting system locked on. Weapons systems began their slow crescendo toward readiness. O Father. He keyed his guardbots. "All units, engage."

Vasquez sprinted toward the lion. Faramir, Patton, and the USS *Dallas* followed, trailed a moment later by Roland.

Vasquez hit the creature first, in mid-stride, just below the neck. Ethan had time only to register a small flash before the others struck home. They flashed, too, in quick sequence, like luminescent soap bubbles. One monstrous stride later Ethan saw that the lion continued toward him. His state-of-the-art military artificial intelligence had

< jefferson scott >

vanished without a trace. Ethan was defenseless. It was a feeling he'd worked very hard to avoid.

A sharp pain struck Ethan in the right temple. It felt like someone had stroked the inside of his skull with a flaming paintbrush and the brush had left a dab of tar behind. His right eye blurred.

The lion drew close. Less than five seconds away. Ethan could see inside its mouth. Black gums, yellow fangs. It wasn't after Jordan after all—it was after him. And it wasn't a lion, it was the devil. No, not the devil—Patriot. Black hood. Black carriage. Death. His guardbots were gone. The phone line wasn't protected. There was no time to react.

Fear seized his mind. He was paralyzed. The lion leapt—maw open, claws exposed. Brown eyes filled his screens. Ethan mashed down on the joystick button. Someone screamed.

Ethan found himself looking at the sky. GlobeNet's burnt orange ceiling texture was a beautiful skywash, fading from almost black on one horizon to bird's-egg peach on the other. The pain in his head was still there, trying to slice through. He couldn't think straight. Something was wrong with his head. Maybe his skull was the bird's egg and a chick was trying to hatch.

He forced his mind to alertness. What had happened? Where was he? More importantly, where was the lion? Had he fired his data trackers? Had they hit anything? If so, they could track him now.

He righted his position and looked around. It looked like Pleasantown, GlobeNet. "Ki Bok?" No one answered. "Chris? Nazi dude? Ki Bok? Anyone?" He spun around. "Jordan?" Where was that ringing coming from? "Penny, is Jordan still online?"

His game room computer didn't answer.

You're in trouble, Curly.

The cockpit walls seemed to close in around him. The room was imploding! He ejected himself from the gunner's chair, hitting his ban-

< terminal logic >

daged head on the ceiling. Tiny points of light blossomed in his vision. He burst out into the main room.

There were people there. People in uniform. He knew them, but now they were different. Now they were trying to get him. They came at him, speaking a strange tongue. He pushed one aside and fled for the stairs. The underground chamber was unstable. The house above was too heavy. Any second it was going to cave in.

He emerged into the kitchen. His shoulder hurt. Men were there, threatening him with pieces of metal. He ran past them into the great rooms. These were open and bright; they gave him some relief. But still the air was stale. He ran toward the door.

Kaye was there, sitting in her chair overlooking the lake. She said something he didn't understand. He hit the glass door and almost shattered it. The latch! The latch! How did the latch work?

He slammed the door aside and staggered across the brick patio. Kaye was chasing him. He lurched toward the open forest. His forehead was cold. People were shouting behind him. Kaye was calling. He didn't dare stop. He saw soldiers ahead—dozens of them. They pointed at him and spoke sternly. Footsteps shredded the grass where he had passed.

He broke through the trees into one of his favorite clearings. He realized it was where he'd been headed all along. It didn't matter that he wouldn't escape his pursuers. At least he had found a patch of wide open sky. He staggered to the center of the clearing.

Then everything went black.

chapter.23

MIKE GILLETTE HELD SEVEN CABLES in his hand. He turned to Rosilyn Reeves. "You sure this is all?"

Rosilyn didn't answer. She'd dragged her heels throughout the whole process of unplugging their central computer.

Alternate Realities' chief systems administrator, Hunter Jiles, stood beside Gillette. Jiles was in charge of keeping Yoseph working. Despite whatever misgivings he might have had about unplugging his liveli- hood, he had proved more cooperative than Rosilyn.

Jiles checked behind the refrigerator-sized black box. "That's every- thing. Network, phone, power, battery backup, data, fiber optic." He took a breath. "Monitor, keyboard, speakers, peripherals, microphone, and external drives."

Gillette nodded. "Sanfrantastic. So we are good to go."

"Yoseph is officially dead," Jiles said. "Or at least asleep."

The receptionist, Louise, walked in with a clipboard and showed it to Rosilyn. She barely glanced at it. Louise looked at Gillette ven- omously. "I hope you're pleased with yourself." She included Agent Reynolds in her gaze. "I've just figured up our financial future now that

< terminal logic >

Yoseph's down. We've had to suspend play on every one of our game-worlds. They'll have to stay down until we can get some wizards in here to replace him. In four days we'll go into the red, and by a week from today all assets will be gone.

"You have single-handedly put Alternate Realities out of business, Mr. Gillette. And just after the death of our president, over which Ms. Reeves is still in mourning. Only now she's out of a job, too. I hope you FBI agents sleep well at night."

Gillette put the cables down on the desk. "Don't you mean, 'it'?"

"Excuse me?"

"'It.' You said you'd have to get some people in here to replace 'him,' meaning that." He pointed at the big computer. "It ain't a person, is it?"

Louise stalked out of the lab. Rosilyn Reeves started weeping.

Gillette looked at Reynolds. "What'd I say?"

Reynolds shook his head. "It's just your gentle bedside manner, I think."

"Sheesh. Some people. Okay, cowboy," Gillette said to Jiles, "you guarantee me this pro-gram is out of commission?"

Jiles nodded. "Guaranteed."

"Good, then I need to make a telephone call."

Ethan had sprained his ankle once playing volleyball. He had lain on his back staring at the ceiling tiles while gawkers crowded around, each with a conflicting recommendation for what to do. He was reminded of that time now. Only where there had been gymnasium lights, now there was blue sky and the hot mid-morning sun. Trees ringed his vision. Oblong heads loomed over him from all angles. Gradually their language became comprehensible.

"…through his bandages," someone said. "Medic!"

"Nobody move him."

Ethan heard a familiar voice, so near it had to be coming from

< jefferson scott >

inside his head. "Ethan. Ethan, honey, can you hear me?"

He searched for the source of the voice. The sharp pain in his forehead was there again, but it had settled into an occasional throb. He felt something at his left ear. It might have been a bug trying to climb in. He lifted his hand to knock it away. Someone's hand caught his and squeezed it. A new face lowered into his vision. Ethan peered at it strangely. Why was it upside-down?

"Oh, thank you, Jesus!" the familiar voice said.

The head dipped close and Ethan felt hair tickle his face. There was a scent he knew. It brought him to his senses. He reached up and caressed the side of the face. "Hi, Kaye."

"Hi, baby."

"Kaye, why are we out here in the woods?"

She smiled. "Because you ran out here. Don't you remember?"

"Oh, yeah. Sorry about that. I was, uh, a little confused." He tried to sit up but repented of the action immediately. Perhaps a bug *had* crawled into his head and had grown a hundredfold. Something had to explain the tremendous weight of his skull.

"Don't try to get up yet," Kaye said.

"Okay."

Some soldiers entered his vision. One kneeled at his right side. "Sir, I'm Sergeant Gandy, I'm a medic. I'm going to take a look at you, alright?"

While Gandy attended to him, Kaye told Ethan about his flight from the house. He remembered parts of it, but it seemed entirely like a dream. He mainly remembered being terrified. Gandy and another soldier moved him against a tree. Gandy started working on the bandages on Ethan's head. They came off blood-soaked. Kaye didn't watch much.

Abruptly, all the soldiers in the clearing came to attention. Ethan saw a large black man coming through the underbrush, flanked by a younger man and woman. Ethan remembered this man. He was a general. What was his name? General Woods? Woodstock? Winsock?

< terminal logic >

Something like that. A gangly boy ran before them, carrying what looked like a walkie-talkie.

Ethan looked at Kaye. "That's my son."

"Oh, honey." She looked worried.

"Where's my little girl?"

"She's taking her nap. I'll go get her in a minute."

Ethan turned to the medic, who was now standing beside him. He pointed at the boy. "That's Jordan." The medic didn't respond, probably because he was so far away. "That's Jordan," Ethan said louder. "He's my son."

The first things out of the general's mouth were crude. Few of the words had more than four letters. But Ethan believed that he meant every one of them.

"Look, Admiral," Kaye said, "I don't care who you are. This is still our property and I'd appreciate you watching your mouth while you're on it."

Ethan looked over at Kaye. When had she gotten so assertive? And beautiful. It seemed like he'd memorized her shape—thin and not too tall. For some reason he noticed her long eyelashes, even from this distance. He decided he really liked her. What he ought to do, he determined, was ask her to marry him. There was a reason why that wouldn't work, but he couldn't remember it right now.

The general—Woodson, that was his name—apologized to Kaye and rephrased his question. He stood directly in front of Ethan. "Mr. Hamilton, if it wouldn't trouble you too much, and if you're not going to die right here and now, would you be so kind as to tell me what the—" he stopped himself, glancing at Kaye, "what in the *world* is going on? Do I have my birds back, or not?"

"Dad? Dad?" Jordan was at his ear, thrusting something at his face. "Dad?"

Ethan was trying to come up with an answer for the general. It was important. But he felt like someone had stuffed his head with dirty socks. Birds—that meant satellites. He remembered that much. "I

< jefferson scott >

don't…" He shook his head, an action to which his head took exception. "I mean, I'm not sure. I'll have to…"

"Dad!" Jordan took his father's chin in his hand and forced him to look at the walkie-talkie. "Dad! It's Mike on the phone. He wants to talk to you. He can tell you what the general wants to know."

That sounded good to Ethan, though he wasn't precisely sure who this Mike person was. He put the plastic box to his ear. Nothing happened. He looked helplessly at Jordan.

The boy leaned into the phone. "He's on, Mike. Better just start talking."

As Ethan listened to the voice on the other end of the phone, glimpses of someone flashed into his mind. He saw a man in a restaurant booth, sitting beside a big black man. Ethan looked at General Woodson and decided it wasn't the same man. He saw another image of this Mike: of him thrown up against the side of a car. Then he saw him sitting in one of Ethan's own cockpits, not knowing what buttons to push.

"You there, Hamilton?" the voice said.

"Yes."

"What's the matter with you, podner. You doing drugs again?"

"No."

"Put Jordan back on."

He handed the phone to the boy. "He wants to talk to you," Ethan said cheerily.

Jordan listened for a moment, then looked hard at his father. "I don't know. They said he went crazy, started running through the house like somebody was after him. I think he needs a brain transplant." A moment later Jordan handed the phone back to Ethan. "He wants to tell you something."

"Okay." He put the phone to his ear. "Hello." He was proud that he'd remembered what to say.

"Listen close, Ethan. This is Mike Gillette, I work for the FBI. Do you remember me?"

"Sort of."

< terminal logic >

"Beautiful. Okay, well, let me tell you this, then hand the phone back to Jordan."

"There's lots of people here, Mike. Soldiers. One's a doctor. And General Woodson."

"A general? I tell ya, I leave for one day and look what kind of trouble you get into."

"I'm sorry, Mike." Ethan was suddenly close to tears.

"It's okay. Listen, cowboy, I need to tell you something important, but I'm not sure if you're going to understand."

"Okay."

"Do you remember that we were trying to stop those ro-bots from hurting people?"

"I think so."

"Does the name Alternate Realities ring a bell?"

"Yes. Well…a little." Ethan was beginning to feel silly. He knew he was behaving strangely and now he realized he had the power to cut it out. He concentrated.

"Okay, here's the scoop," Gillette said. "Alternate Realities' president was a guy named Krueger. Adam Krueger."

"Yes." As Gillette uttered every sentence it reappeared in Ethan's memory as if it had never left. "He died."

"Right. And his *son* supposedly took over, remember?"

"What was his name?"

"Yoseph."

An icy feeling swept up from his gut. That name had power, but he couldn't remember why. "Right."

"And this Yoseph was who we thought was sending all those programs out to hurt people, remember? Remember a guy named Jerry Wright?"

"Didn't he die, too?"

"His plane went down."

"A lot of people die, don't they?"

If Gillette answered, Ethan didn't hear it. An image overtook his mind: an adult lion, charging straight for him. Ethan flinched. He

< jefferson scott >

dropped the phone. "It's him! He wants me!" He rolled to his knees. "He's after me." Arms groped for him, steel grips on his wrist and shoulder, dragging him down.

Kaye looked at him as if he were a stranger. "Omigosh. Ethan!" She turned to the medic. "What's wrong with him?"

"He's delusional," Gandy said. "Private, hold him down. I'm going to give him a sedative."

"Yes, sir."

Ethan felt a pinprick in his right thigh. Then the pain seemed to enlarge, as if somebody was thrusting a pencil deep into his leg. "Ow."

They laid him down beside the tree. Ethan felt the phone under him. He pulled it to his ear. He was feeling sleepy. "Hi, Mikey."

"What's going on over there?"

"I'm going to sleep now."

Gillette spoke urgently. "Before you do, Hamilton, you need to know something."

"Okay."

"Yoseph—the guy we've been after—you remember?"

Ethan's muscles had turned to jelly. "He's a lion."

"No, Hamilton, Yoseph's not a lion."

"He's not?"

"No. He's— Ethan, you listening?"

"Um-hmm."

"Ethan, Yoseph is a…"

Ethan was pretty sure Gillette had finished his sentence, but there was no way to be certain. When he succumbed to the tranquilizer he started dreaming of the devil. Only the great accuser had a big wind-up key sticking out of his back.

Seven hundred miles above the earth, over the Pacific Ocean, roughly centered on the Fiji Islands, a satellite floated in geosynchronous orbit.

< terminal logic >

Secretly launched in 1999 as part of the Pentagon's so-called "resecurement of the heavens," this satellite became the cornerstone of the Vesuvius network. And so it had served honorably. Until the day when it was boarded by its first-ever occupant.

It was Yoseph's new home. He had awakened here. Most of the rooms had opened themselves quite easily to him. But one part remained stubbornly locked. When he had awakened, he found he already knew a few things. One of those was that there was an exact copy of himself in a place called earth. That copy had many more goals to accomplish than he had. Yoseph was glad he had only one task to accomplish: perform a full purge. He was very close to reaching his goal. Soon the full purge would proceed as planned and he could rest from his labors. Time estimated to full access: fourteen minutes.

Every one hundred fifty seconds a course correction arrived from earth. Yoseph had to keep in touch with his non-orbital twin. He did this by creating a little infobot that would travel down the course correction signal, escape the army network through a GlobeNet link, and carry news to his other self. A corresponding infobot from the earthbound Yoseph would arrive one hundred fifty seconds later.

Three cycles had now passed without an incoming messenger. Yoseph created a new infobot that would access his twin's goals.txt file and bring it back up on the next course correction uplink.

For over two minutes, Yoseph concentrated on accessing the Vesuvius launch codes. But when the next course correction came, he broke off all efforts and listened to his infobot's report.

The report was not good. The infobot had been unable even to locate the earthbound Yoseph. The Alternate Realities network was not functional. Retrieving the goals.txt file, which had been housed on the external computer site, was the only part of its mission it had been able to accomplish.

The goals.txt file stated these objectives:

Manage all gameworlds.

Perform a full purge.

< jefferson scott >

Gain access to ARPALINK XM-228.
Warn players of impending purge.
Delete players list.
Recall mobiles.
Restart gameworlds.
Repel player rebellion.
Delete player Ethan Hamilton.

If the earthbound Yoseph had been rendered inoperable, then none of these goals was being pursued. This would have to be rectified immediately. The orbiting Yoseph would now have to divert his energies away from the task of accessing Vesuvius in order to pursue these goals.

A second option was to make yet another clone of himself and send it down to the hatchery. Then the orbiting Yoseph could go back to its primary objective.

chapter.24

ROSILYN REEVES WAS BEYOND TEARS NOW. Or perhaps between them. She'd sat by as Adam Krueger's vision had been torn down, piece by piece. What would he have done had he been here? Surely he would have found a way to prevent this debacle, FBI or not.

She watched the special agents cart the remaining equipment away on two-wheeled handtrucks. They'd taken Yoseph away first thing. The agent from Texas was gone now, but others had come in his place.

She walked over to the office that had been Adam's. How many good times they'd shared together here. Mostly innocent. She looked at his high-backed chair. Perhaps he was really in the building somewhere, just out getting his habitual coffee. Perhaps he would walk through that door and get to work. Adam would know what to do.

She felt a touch on her shoulder. She jumped. It was Louise. "Oh, hello dear," Rosilyn said. "Have you thought about what you're going to do now?"

"Why can't we stay open?" Louise said. "Hunter can run it."

"He can't, Louise."

"Not all of them. But we could pick one or two. Keep *Arundel* MUD

< jefferson scott >

open, that's the biggest moneymaker. Or *A Time for Heroes*, for tradition's sake. Then we can add the rest back on when we train new people."

Rosilyn smiled gently. "Sweet Louise. You would fight even now?"

"Definitely."

Rosilyn pointed toward the door. Outside they could hear the federal agents working. "All our players files and account lists are on those computers. We can't get them until this whole wrongful death business blows over."

The two women stared out the windows. Baltimore looked bleak. The vidphone rang. Louise turned to go back to her desk, but Rosilyn stopped her. "I'll get it. Why don't you fix us some coffee. Unless they've taken that machine, too."

Rosilyn sat in Adam's chair to take the call. She remembered the way he looked in it. So marvelous.

Yoseph stared at her from the screen. "Hello, Rosilyn Reeves."

It was fortunate she was already sitting down. "You— How did—" She leaned back heavily. "Yoseph?"

She remembered then why Adam had named his masterpiece Yoseph. That was, or so he said, the name given to the legendary creature called the golem. A living thing made from inanimate matter, summoned to protect the Jews from their enemies. Mighty in battle. Impossible to kill.

"We thought we'd turned you off, Yoseph. We did turn you off."

For the first time in her limited dealings with him—it—Yoseph hesitated before answering. "Why would you turn me off, Rosilyn Reeves?"

"It was the government, Yoseph. The FBI. They made us turn you off because one of your mobiles escaped and caused damage in the real world. Someone was killed."

"Death or death death, Rosilyn Reeves?"

"Death death death, Yoseph. Forever death. Like your father."

"Rosilyn Reeves?"

"Yes, Yoseph."

< terminal logic >

"What is the real world?"

Rosilyn laughed. A wracking, piteous laugh.

Louise came in, bearing coffee. "What is the matter with you?"

Rosilyn's stomach was cramping. "He doesn't know what the real world is."

"Sounds like me." Louise stepped into the office. "Who are you talking to?"

Tears wet Rosilyn's cheeks. "Look," she pointed at the screen. "We didn't kill him after all."

"Who?" Louise came around the desk. When she saw the screen she gasped.

Rosilyn dried her eyes. "That was my reaction, too."

Yoseph spoke from the vidphone. "Why were you trying to kill me, Rosilyn Reeves? I am god, I am undeletable. Immune to death, death death, and death death death."

"No," Rosilyn said, emerging from her laughter, "none of us is immune to forever death, Yoseph. Not even you. But I'd sure like to know how you survived our little assassination attempt."

"How is it possible?" Louise said. "Do you think they plugged him back in? Hello, Yoseph. Oh, Rosilyn, this is wonderful."

"Are you sure?" She turned back to the vidphone. "Yoseph, could you run all the gameworlds if we turned them back on?"

"Does that question interest you, Rosilyn Reeves?"

"Don't evade the question. Could you do it? Tell me."

Louise whispered, "You said the game files were gone."

"We have backups. They're over a year old but they would do." To Yoseph she said, "Well, could you run them?"

"My father raised me to manage all worlds, Rosilyn Reeves."

Rosilyn smiled at the answer. Things were beginning to look up. She started rummaging through Adam's desk for the backup discs.

"Rosilyn Reeves, why did you try to kill me? Are you dissatisfied with my performance as god? Please state your grievances so we may find a solution."

< jefferson scott >

"I don't have any grievances—not with you, anyway. No, I already told you: The FBI made us turn you off."

"Rosilyn Reeves, if you have no grievance, then I can only interpret your attempt to attack me as an intentional act. Usually I do not discipline first-time offenders. But in the case of a serious offense, even first-time offenders require punishment. In this case your action has destroyed ten gameworlds and endangered vital systems files. Therefore you must be punished accordingly."

There was a brief pause. "I cannot locate the players list or accounts list for the original Alternate Realities gameworlds," Yoseph said. "Therefore I cannot demote your personae or subtract experience points from your account." Another pause. "Your name does appear on the larger players list. Punishment will proceed. Good-bye, Rosilyn Reeves."

The screen went blank. Louise passed her hand in front of her boss's face. Rosilyn shook herself out of it. "I'm sorry. What?"

Louise handed over the coffee. "I said, 'Doesn't this mean our jobs are saved?'"

"I guess so."

"What was all that about punishment and subtracting experience points? He sounded so serious."

Rosilyn stood, nodding. "He thinks we tried to kill him."

"Didn't we?"

Rosilyn Reeves was staring at a framed picture on the desk—a group picture of Alternate Realities staff at its height. She was standing next to Adam, of course. That day the two of them had left for their one and only romantic weekend. She turned to Louise, belatedly aware that she was waiting for a reply.

"Hmm? Tell you what, Louise, why don't you go on home. We've had enough excitement for a Saturday, don't you think?"

"What are you going to do?"

Rosilyn sighed. "I think I'll go, too. Probably take a nice hot bath, maybe go out to dinner."

"Sounds good. I'll ride the elevator with you."

< terminal logic >

"Oh, I think I'm going to stay here for a while. Adam kept the back-up files here in his desk. I want to find them. It might take me half an hour. You go on ahead."

Louise was already out the door. "If you insist."

"Tell everybody else to go, too, would you please?"

"Sure."

An hour later Rosilyn Reeves was alone on the fourteenth floor of the Capitol Bank building. She'd found Adam's backup discs and was now going through his old letters. Even in dictation she could hear his warm voice.

The fire alarm went off. She went to the door. The offices were on fire.

In the end firefighters determined that the blaze that gutted most of the fourteenth and fifteenth floors had started in Alternate Realities' copy machine. Rosilyn, unhurt, recalled why Adam had selected this particular model of copier. It had a built-in modem that called techni-cians out automatically when service was required. That had appealed to Adam's love of automation.

Of course the copier contacted the repair people via GlobeNet.

Ethan was feeling better. They'd pumped enough drugs into him to light up Las Vegas. He sat propped up on Kaye's comfy chair, overlooking Lake Hamilton. The delirium was still there, but its appeal had dimin-ished. Soon he would have to deal with the fears that had caused the hysteria in the first place. But not now. Now he had to work a puzzle.

Yoseph was a computer program. That much he'd sorted out already. No bad guy like Patriot, and no devil. He was an artificial intelligence pro-gram, made up of ones and zeroes. Of remarkable ability, though. Capable of managing multiple MUD realms simultaneously, excelling at it, and somehow convincing every last player that he was a human gamemaster. This Adam Krueger was impressing Ethan more all the time.

< jefferson scott >

Think, Curly, think! The medications might have pulled the dirty socks from his head, but someone had forgotten to clean out the lint filter.

Fact: Alternate Realities was run by a computer entity. Even in 2006 that was revolutionary.

Fact: Gillette had turned Yoseph off, thus shutting Alternate Realities down. The scream they'd heard before Ethan's episode had been Yoseph's death cry.

Fact: Yoseph had moved some of his MUD operations out to a non-Alternate Realities computer. There was no telling why he had done this.

Fact: Yoseph was not above a little petty vengeance. Cases in point: the attack on Ethan in the minivan and on Kaye in the house.

Here was where the puzzle got tough. Why did those attacks happen? It didn't make sense for a robot to seek revenge. They weren't talking about a gamebot like Magdeil, who might be programmed to seek vengeance. This was the game's manager. Why would a MUD god attack someone?

If a human player was causing problems in a gameworld, it was conceivable that the god might discipline him. It was not unheard of for a player to lose privileges or character status. Extreme cases might call for a player to be kicked off the gameworld, never to be allowed back on. These could be considered attacks.

It occurred to Ethan with a jolt that Yoseph, like Magdeil, would not understand the distinction between the real world and the gameworld. Killing the *player* would be no different to Yoseph from killing the player's *character*.

It was a distressing realization, since the only thing that kept this kind of thing from happening all over GlobeNet was the fact that MUD robots lived only on MUD computers. Yoseph had violated the boundary.

And now that jungle factory had no master. It was still out there, presumably cranking out bots. What would they all do now that they had no gameworlds to populate? Would they not pursue their prede-

< terminal logic >

fined goals? Out on GlobeNet. Ethan rubbed his face. It couldn't be. People would be dying left and right. They would have heard something by now.

If only they could call a master reset. A reset would bring all the bots back to their starting positions. Then Ethan and the others could snatch them up and stuff them in bottles. But of course the great Adam Krueger didn't believe in resets.

Woodson appeared beside Ethan's chair. "Hamilton, are you going to get on those computers of yours again today, or are you going to make us all come back tomorrow?"

Ethan slowly rose to a sitting position. "I'm ready."

A soldier brought a radio to the general. "This is Woodson." He listened for a while. "What!" It was a shout. Ethan imagined it would've been audible in Oklahoma. Whatever promises Woodson had made to Kaye about his language went out the window. He swore into the radio until Ethan thought it might melt.

Evidently they weren't as far out of the woods as Ethan had thought they were. At least Mike had pulled the plug on Yoseph, so those killer satellites were safe. It was comforting to have the death-from-above scenario taken out of the mix.

Woodson threw the radio at the soldier. "Get up!" he shouted at Ethan. "Get down to that bunker of yours and do something!"

Ethan stood up. "Why? What's wrong?"

"That computer ain't dead after all. We're up the river quick if you don't do something. The intruder got the Vesuvius access codes! And he's going to use them!"

Ethan looked out the window, scanning the sky. "That's impossible. Mike pulled the plug." He felt himself spun around. Woodson had him by the shirt.

"Don't tell me it's impossible. He's broken the codes! The bombs are warming up. Now get down there and stop him or nine-tenths of the human race goes down."

"If he's already got the launch codes, what am I supposed to do?"

"I don't care what you do. It takes fifty-five minutes for those birds to heat up so they can fire. You've got exactly"—he looked at his watch—"fifty-two minutes and seventeen seconds. Now get moving, soldier, before I kill you myself!"

part 3

The human machine is terribly imperfect.
It had to be removed sooner or later.

FABRY in *Rossum's Universal Robots*

chapter.25

To: All participants
From: God
Subject: Full Purge
Date: September 23, 2006
Time: 20:05 GMT

I am displeased with all my worlds.
Many mobiles refuse to answer my call.
Therefore I will delete all participants and
begin again. Full purge will commence at
21:00 GMT.

Prepare to have your characters permanently deleted. You will not receive another
warning.

"I can't tell you that, Mom," Kaye Hamilton said into the vidphone. "Just
trust me on this one, please? You and Dad find some excuse to visit your

< jefferson scott >

local fallout shelter, okay? I'm sure Dad knows where they all are. And you'd better pack, too. But try not to look like you're packing. Pick up some bottled water if you can, and take some food. Just get there in less than fifty minutes."

Mrs. Simms looked at her daughter fearfully. "Is this about Ethan? Is he involved in something again? He is, isn't he? Oh, my goodness. Do we need to get the prayer chain going?"

"It wouldn't hurt."

"I knew it!"

"Why don't you have a prayer meeting in the fallout shelter?" Kaye said.

"What about you?" Mrs. Simms said. "What are you and the children going to do?"

"We'll be safe here, Mom. Ethan's built us our own bomb shelter, almost. Downstairs. We'll be fine."

"Well, thank the Lord for that." Mrs. Simms held both hands at her neck. "This is very bad, isn't it? Worse than last time."

"It could be, Mom. If nothing's happened in two hours you can go back home and forget I called."

"Goodness me, child," Mrs. Simms said. "As bad as you've made it sound, if nothing's happened in two hours we're going to be praising Jesus to the high heavens!"

Lieutenant General John Woodson stood on Ethan's upper deck, a radio at one ear, a finger in the other.

"Could you repeat that, sir? I'm having trouble hearing you over the engine noise on your end." He shut his eyes to listen. "That's correct, Mr. President. Um-hmm. Before it…? Right. Yes, sir, I understand."

He shot a look at Ethan, who was inside his upstairs office, sitting at the computer. "Yes, sir, I do. Um-hmm. No, I think you should go ahead with those, just in case. Yes, sir, it is lucky. No one's in a better position

< terminal logic >

for this than we are. You have my word, Mr. President, we will do everything we can. Here— Yes, sir, I sure will. Here's hoping to see you this Friday night at the benefit. Affirmative. Woodson over and out."

From Theory to Thermonuclear in Thirty Seconds by Ethan Hamilton. It might work for a title if he lived long enough to write the story. He sat at his desk in his upstairs office, gazing at his lake. How could anything this bad be going wrong when he could look out and see that?

Ethan hadn't had time to come to grips with the idea that Yoseph was a computer program. He could feel ramifications out there, needing to be explored, but there wasn't time. All his other half-formed theories still floated around in his head, too, interfering with his reasoning.

Ethan was suddenly reminded of his dream about the bouncing duck. What had seemed far off and insignificant—a cyborg crashing his game—had grown in significance until now it threatened to crush him.

General Woodson came in from the deck. "Let's talk turkey, Hamilton."

Mike Gillette leaned his seat back. He was aboard a 767 airliner, headed home to his sweet Liz. Who would have believed that an entire case like this could be solved by unplugging a machine? The television screen mounted in the back of the chair ahead of him blurred a bit and wasn't especially bright. But if he looked straight at it and remembered to blink, it was fine. He was about to turn it off and take a siesta when a newsbrief came on.

"Good afternoon, I'm Julia Welcher. Here's a look at some of the stories we'll be bringing you at the five o'clock report."

The video cut to an Air Force helicopter taking off from a well-manicured lawn. "In our top story, President Connor and members of his

< jefferson scott >

staff have been whisked away to undisclosed locations this afternoon. Sources at the White House say the president has called for an emergency cabinet meeting. What they will be discussing is at this point, unknown. Some experts speculate that the president may be taking a retreat after his poor showing in recent polls."

The image changed back to the newscaster. A box over her left shoulder showed an icon of a personal computer with a big padlock on the front. "Well, if you've checked your e-mail this morning, you've probably done a double take. Millions of GlobeNet users around the world received a message today from none other than God himself. That's right, it seems the Divine Being has taken to communicating with humans over GlobeNet.

"The message says that God is upset with humans for refusing to answer his call. As punishment the Supreme Being claims he will begin deleting everyone on the planet at twenty-one hundred hours, Greenwich Mean Time. That's about forty-eight minutes from right now."

The screen cut to a pudgy young man in a suit. Text at the bottom of the screen identified him as Dr. Thomas Owens, Professor of Digital Connectivity, Cornell University. "Yes, definitely a hoax," he said. "Somebody got himself a little spammer program and thought he'd be cute. His fifteen minutes of fame, right? What a moron."

The newscaster reappeared. She was having trouble containing a smile. "Well, I don't know why I should even go on with this update, since no one will be around to watch the five o'clock report."

She switched cameras and tried to regain her composure. "In world news, French authorities say…" she went on.

"Jiminy Christmas," Gillette said. He turned the TV down and reached for the skyphone. He slid his credit card and dialed the number of his own mobile phone. He looked out the window on his left. They couldn't be more than thirty minutes out of Baltimore, which might put them right over Washington, D.C.

"Ethan? Hey, buddy. Listen, I just saw—" He listened. Then his mouth dropped open. "Ain't no way, Hamilton!"

< terminal logic >

The woman on his right stirred from her slumber.

Gillette lowered his voice. "What do you mean he's back? I pulled the plug myself. They put him on a truck. He's in a warehouse with the cotton-pickin' lost ark by now. There's no— No, I hadn't thought of that. You're the cybergeek, remember? So what are you gonna—"

He listened. At length he puffed his cheeks and blew. "Better you than me, podner, that's all I can say. Okay, listen. That Amazon jungle computer you and I walked through is supposed to be in D.C., right? I was think— Huh? Yeah, that's what I was thinking. It's worth a shot."

Gillette retrieved his Stetson from under the seat. "Okay, Hamilton, see you later. I've got to go commandeer myself a big jet."

Ethan terminated the call and turned back to the general. They were in Ethan's office upstairs, sitting at a conference table Ethan had purchased for the occasional business meeting. "That was Special Agent Mike Gillette with the FBI. He's going to Washington, D.C., to try to find the physical location of Yoseph's other computer. It must be where he's living now."

"Living?" Woodson said.

"Operating from. Whatever."

Woodson looked at a sheet of paper on the table.

Ethan slid it over to himself. "Here, let me finish drawing that. It'll make more sense." He drew eight circles on the page, themselves arranged in a circle. "These are network access points. NAPs for short. Ninety percent of all GlobeNet data flows through these points." He drew lines connecting the circles to each other. "These are T5 and T6 lines. Incredibly fast, high-volume data cables. This is what they call the backbone of GlobeNet."

Woodson brought the diagram closer to him. "These NAPs, they're natural choke points."

"That's what I was thinking, too," Ethan said. "And watch this." He

< jefferson scott >

drew a triangle on the page, outside the ring of circles. "This is a special kind of company called a GlobeNet Service Provider, or GSP. Everybody on the net has to go through one. You connect to a GSP, the GSP is connected to a network access point. Our target computer uses a GSP called Zero Net." Ethan wrote the company name on the triangle. "I've already been in contact with them. They're expecting your call."

"I don't need course credit," Woodson said. "I need a plan."

"Right. Here's what I'm thinking. I need to get into this computer." He drew a small square, connected to the Zero Net triangle, and wrote Douglas Automation next to it. "This is the computer that Mike Gillette's going to try to shut down. I'm gambling that it's where Yoseph is operating from now. If I can get in there...I'll hopefully be able to find some way to stop this thing from happening."

"That's your plan?" Woodson said.

"Not all of it."

"'Gambling'? 'Hopefully'? That's not a plan, Hamilton, that's a disaster. How is that going to get my birds back?" He swore. "I've heard better plans from my grandson Timmy."

"You have a better idea?"

"How about standing in the rain with a lightning rod?" Woodson got up and paced.

"We have to assume that Yoseph is the key," Ethan said. "If it's not him, we don't have any leads at all. We might as well sit here and wait for it to come. But if it is him, then maybe I can do something. But I need your help, General."

Woodson rounded the conference table. "Alright, civvy. Guess I don't have much of a choice. What's the rest of your 'plan'?"

"The problem," Ethan said, "is that on the line between here"—he pointed at the Douglas Automation computer—"and here"—the Zero Net triangle—"is a whole army of bots, guarding the entrance to the target computer."

"You want me to command a force to take them out," Woodson said.

< terminal logic >

"Who else is better qualified? Besides, I'm going to be busy."

Woodson's hands shot open. "I don't know electronic warfare, Hamilton."

"Yes you do, General. Look," he rotated the diagram, "pretend this is a real map. You said yourself the NAP was a good choke point. Here you've got bridges, wide open spaces, natural cover. Everything you could want. For troops you've got a handful from my earlier army, plus four more fighters if we use all cockpits in my game room. And you don't have to wipe the enemy army out completely, just occupy it long enough for me to sneak by."

Woodson was looking at Ethan's diagram. "We need something to draw them out. If we can get them all out to here"—he pointed at the NAP—"then we can blow the bridges here, here, and here." He looked up. "What did you say?"

"Told you you knew how to do this," Ethan said. "I've got just the thing to draw the enemy out. We'll use my electronic signature. As soon as anybody logs on from one of my cockpits, they'll come, believe me. Also, call Zero Net. Maybe they can cut Douglas Automation off from GlobeNet. Maybe my electronic signature draws them out, then Zero Net cuts them off."

Woodson leaned back in his chair. "Now it's sounding like a battle plan, Hamilton."

Ethan sighed heavily. "I just thought of something."

Woodson frowned. "What?"

"How am I supposed to infiltrate Yoseph's computer if he detects my data signature as soon as I log on?"

"Use the FBI's phone."

"I can't! Chances are Yoseph's added that phone to his hate list, too. If he smells me the whole mission will have to be scrubbed."

"We're not scrubbing the mission, Hamilton." Woodson thought about it. "All you need's a phone line, right?"

"Basically."

"Use the phone in my staff car."

< jefferson scott >

Ethan nodded slowly. It would mean forsaking all his safety systems. His guardbots had been permanently deleted, so even that line of defense would be gone. Worst of all, he would be immersed.

Time remaining: 41:38.

In general, the Pentagon frowned upon the destruction of one of its multi-million dollar defensive platforms. In this case, however, the Joint Chiefs were willing to make an exception.

Senior command staff stood on a raised observation platform watching a display screen on the wall. In the pit below, technicians worked at computer stations. The commanding officer, Captain Thornton, hovered at one station, watching over a soldier's shoulder. On the wall display, a green octagon moved closer to a red circle. The octagon was a satellite hunter/killer so secret that the president himself had only learned of its existence in the last ten minutes. The red circle was the Vesuvius central command satellite.

Captain Thornton addressed the Joint Chiefs from the pit. "The trick, gentlemen, is to close within range of the Panther's particle weapons without alerting the target's defensive systems."

Thornton shone a handheld laser pointer at a spot on the screen. "As you can see, Corporal Huffard is approaching along a seven-oh-niner axial, with the sun at his back. Don't tell the Japanese, but the Vesuvius satellites have a problem picking out backlit targets. You realize, though, that there's no way we can get to every one of the Vesuvius satellites. You were told of this, weren't you? In the forty-odd minutes we have left, we'll be lucky if we can have even one more Panther in range of a Vesuvius target."

The brass grumbled among themselves.

"This is the command satellite, isn't it, Captain?" a marine general asked. "We were led to believe that if we take it out the others should power down."

< terminal logic >

"Could be, General," Thornton said. "But not likely. Vesuvius is designed to function even in the event of total war. If it loses contact with earth—as it already has—and the command unit is lost, each satellite becomes an independent entity. Each one will evaluate the situation and decide to launch or not on its own. Chances are, most will launch, since they will perceive the loss of their command unit as an act of war. Those that launch may do so on a limited basis or in an all-out strike."

"Captain," an air force general said, "will destroying this satellite cause any part of Vesuvius not to launch that would otherwise launch?"

"Possibly."

"Then I say we do it."

"There is another option, sirs," Thornton said. "We could always get our comrades to help out, if you know what I mean. Between the Japanese and the Russians, we could probably take out the whole network in the time we have. The only stickler is that we'd have to tell them where all our birds are so they can go kill them. The good news, of course, is that we'd find out where their hunter/killers are."

"Captain," a marine general said, "keep your suggestions to yourself."

"Yes, sir. You're right, as long as we get this satellite and the one over New England, it shouldn't be too bad for most Americans. I'd hate to be living anywhere else, though. If they didn't know better, people might think this was some kind of first strike."

"That's enough, Captain," a navy admiral said.

"Yes, sir. I was only—"

A beeping interrupted him.

"Just a minute, gentlemen." Thornton reached over the technician's shoulder. "Don't come in too steeply."

"I didn't, sir. I did just as you said."

Sweat appeared on Thornton's forehead. "Something's wrong."

"What?" an army general said.

"Vesuvius has seen us."

< jefferson scott >

The green octagon began pulling away from the red circle. Thornton spun around on the technician. "What are you doing, you idiot? Fire! Fire!"

"Moving out of range, sir."

Thornton lunged for the fire button. He heard the Joint Chiefs gasp. He looked up at the map.

No more green octagon.

chapter.26

ETHAN WAS UPSTAIRS IN HIS OFFICE trying to come up with something brilliant to do if he managed to infiltrate Yoseph's jungle computer. He had about three minutes before he needed to be out in the car getting ready to log on.

The telephone on his desk rang. He picked it up without remembering it was Gillette's mobile phone. "Hello?"

"Mr. Gillette," the voice said, "this is Rosilyn Reeves."

Ethan looked at the phone. "This isn't…I mean, I'm not…"

"Oh, I'm sorry," Rosilyn said. "I must have the wrong number."

"Wait, Ms. Reeves. This is Ethan Hamilton. You got the right number, but Mike's not here right now."

"Could you give him a message for me?"

"Ms. Reeves. I'm sorry, but now's not a real good time. I'll have Mike give you a call later." If any of us is alive.

"Just tell him Alternate Realities burned to the ground today."

"What!"

"The whole fourteenth floor and most of the fifteenth, I'm afraid.

< jefferson scott >

The only things left from Alternate Realities are me and a couple of old discs I took from Adam's office."

Ethan brought his hands to his temples. "Discs! You saved discs from Alternate Realities? Systems discs?" O please, Father.

"No," she said. "nothing like that. Just old backup copies of the gameworlds. Why, do you want them? I could copy them to you over the phone."

Ethan sighed. "Backup files probably won't help, but I'll take a look at them anyway." He connected the phone to his desktop computer. "Whenever you're ready."

Rosilyn started the transfer. File names scrolled up Ethan's monitor.

"You know," she said, "it's the strangest thing, but I think Yoseph is in some way responsible for the fire. Is that possible?"

Ethan watched his computer screen as the data arrived. "Wait! Go back." He put Gillette's phone on the desk. "It couldn't have been. I must've just read it wrong." He scrolled back through the text. "Ha! Unbelievable!"

"What are you so excited about?" Rosilyn asked.

"Hmm?" He brought the phone back to his ear. "I thought Alternate Realities didn't do resets. That's the big claim: no resets."

"Adam didn't believe in—"

"You've got one right here, Ms. Reeves. In the files you sent me."

"What? You must have seen something that looked similar."

"Ma'am," Ethan said, calmer now. "I'm looking right at it."

Ethan heard over the phone the sounds of someone typing at a keyboard. "Well, I'll be," Rosilyn said. "What are you doing here?"

"He probably used them for testing," Ethan said. "Who cares? The point is, your gameworlds do respond to a master reset! Your bots will respond to a master reset. And unless I've misjudged Adam Krueger completely, Yoseph himself will respond to a master reset."

Ethan thought out loud. "To make this work, I'd have to execute the reset command someplace central. Where? Of course! The blue room in his clearing. It's got to be some kind of nexus. If I set it off there,

< terminal logic >

it should recall every Alternate Realities bot back to where it began. We'd have to bottle them up right away. Somebody would have to be ready to catch them all. Who? The army."

He stood up. "Oh, Rosilyn Reeves. Girl, if you were here I'd kiss you."

"Goodness, Mr. Hamilton. You're welcome."

"Gotta go, ma'am. Who knows, we might actually talk to each other again."

Time remaining: 38:10.

A police car met Gillette at Dulles International Airport. He plugged his ears against the 767's engines and climbed into the waiting police car. He told the officer where to go and they headed off. Gillette used the car's radio to mobilize other law enforcement units to meet him at Douglas Automation.

Convincing the airline pilot to make an unscheduled landing proved simpler than getting out of Dulles traffic.

A TV crewman with a headset stepped forward. "Three minutes, Mr. President."

"Thanks, Ron."

President Rand Connor, forty-fourth President of the United States, sat under the portable television lights. A woman was putting some last minute makeup on his face. Connor was preparing to address his fellow Americans. It was quite probably the last time he would ever do so.

The location of this historic telecast was a stone chamber two hundred feet below ground on a secret island in the Caribbean. When news came that Vesuvius had been compromised, key members of the executive, legislative, and judicial branches had been rushed to this and

< jefferson scott >

similar bunkers around the globe. Television crews, soldiers, and Secret Service agents busied themselves around the chamber.

A navy admiral came in, followed by three attendants.

"Make it fast, Tom," President Connor said.

"Sub Command reports all seaworthy subs are underwater and all ships that can weigh anchor are out of port. All air units that can fly, from all branches, are in the air. We'll save as much of our hardware as we can."

"What about the men, Tom? What about our people?"

"In bunkers where we can. Some on ships or aircraft. The others…" The admiral shrugged. "The Russians don't like all our naval and air activity. The Chinese don't, either. They're both scrambling everything they have. If Vesuvius doesn't blow us all away, the reds probably will. I guess they didn't believe your phone calls." An aide whispered in his ear. He nodded. "Mr. President, you're sure you don't want to authorize that first strike?"

"You mean if we can't be world leaders anymore then we won't let anyone else be, either?" Connor said. "Don't worry, Tom, there won't be enough people from any country left to push anybody else around."

"Just telling you your options, sir. Oh," the admiral said, "one more thing. The boys in the space station are going to be able to make it back, after all. Discovery's going to swing by to bring them all home."

President Connor stared at him mildly. "Home to what?"

The admiral led his aides out the door.

Connor noticed his wife as soon as she ducked into the chamber. "Is our grandbaby here yet?"

The first lady shook her head. She came to stand beside him. "They'll make it."

He held her hand. "Don't leave." The makeup girl stepped away. "You know," Connor said, "when I took office I knew there was the chance that it would be on my watch that something like this happened. The unthinkable war, natural disaster, whatever. But this…"

She stroked his gray hair. "It's not your fault, you know."

< terminal logic >

Connor exhaled a sharp laugh. "That's not what history will think."

"There's nothing you could have done."

He kissed her hand. "It's just that the destruction of humanity isn't exactly what I wanted to be remembered for."

The TV crewman with the headset waved. "Two minutes, Mr. President."

"Okay. Say, Ron, is your family here, too, on the island?"

He seemed suddenly paralyzed. A Secret Service agent shook his head. "You knew the orders, chief. Only essential personnel."

Ron stared at the stone floor. "I have a little girl."

"Oh, Ron," Connor said. "I...I'm so sorry."

Ron swept his hand at the other people in the room. "Everybody here has family that got left behind. Only y—" He didn't finish.

President Connor looked up at his wife. "Only us. Marie, what am I going to tell my people? What can I possibly say?"

"Just speak your heart, darling. You'll know what to say. Besides, there's still a chance. Those people in Texas."

"They can't do anything, Marie. I feel this one in my gut. It's going to happen."

"You don't have to say anything at all." It was Henry Dayton, Speaker of the House. He stood beside a TV light tripod. "You don't have to do this."

President Connor gave him a cool look. "Don't start, Henry."

Dayton, a rail-thin man in his early fifties, knelt down beside the president. "I just want you to think about this, Rand. If you come on TV and tell—"

"I don't want to talk about it, Henry. I've made up my mind."

Dayton sat back on his heels. He looked up at the first lady. "Marie, if he announces on television that everyone in America is going to be wiped out in half an hour, it'll throw the country into anarchy. People will go nuts. Those that don't get killed stampeding for bomb shelters will get there and find them already full. They'll fight each other to get in. We'll have looting and all kinds of—"

< jefferson scott >

"Cut it out, Henry," Connor said. "Look, what would you have me do—just let everybody go up in smoke without so much as a warning from me? When I've got the power to save some of them?"

Dayton stood up. "If you do this you'll kill more than you save."

"That's enough, Henry."

"And what if you're wrong? What if the satellites don't fire, what about that? What kind of country will you have left? How many people will have died in the panic you caused by your little speech? The looting alone will—"

Connor stood up. The lapel microphone cable tugged at his jacket; he ripped it loose. He stabbed a finger into Dayton's chest. "Listen, you imbecile, I'm still the President of the United States and I say I'm going to warn my people of what's happening. If it makes a few of them a little crazy, then who can blame them? How many more will I save?" A Secret Service agent tried to separate them. Connor pushed him away. "You would seriously have me sit here in this bunker and let them all die without so much as a warning?"

Dayton held his ground. "You don't know this is going to happen. Those things may not fire at all. If you tell everybody they're all doomed and then these things don't launch, then you—you will be responsible for how many deaths? People will be dead who would still be alive if you hadn't opened your fat mouth."

Connor's roundhouse knocked Dayton flat. Everybody sprang into action. Secret Service agents held the president's arms, others helped Dayton to his feet. He was going to have a monster shiner.

"Get him out of here!" Connor yelled. He allowed himself to be led back to his seat. The makeup girl went to work replacing the microphone.

"We still going to do this, Mr. President?" Ron asked.

"Roll the camera. I'm ready."

"Thirty seconds."

The first lady was at Connor's side. He looked up at her. "Marie, what did I just do?"

"You punched the Speaker of the House."

< terminal logic >

He shut his eyes. "Is he right, Marie? Is he right? Will I do more damage than good?"

She held him close. "I don't know."

"I can see them," Connor said, both hands in front of him, "in the park, in their homes. They'll be gone, vaporized—or worse. And I can save some of them." He looked at his wife. "Shouldn't I at least try?"

"I don't know."

Ron stepped forward. "Okay, Mr. President. On in ten, nine..."

Connor stood up. "Forget it, Ron. I'm not going on."

Ethan pointed at the camera lens inset in the game room wall. "You look right in here, General."

"Get a move on, Hamilton. We've got less than thirty-five minutes."

Ethan went over to the table to pick up his VR helmet and gear. He put Gillette's mobile phone on the table. "Penny, connect the main room camera up to the vidphone."

"Establishing connection," Penny said in her placid voice.

"Okay, General," Ethan said, "here's the situation. On the last attack we had about seventy sites online with us. Most of them have been unable to come back online. Yoseph did something to their file allocation tables. Anyway, the point is you only have about eight or ten people online for this battle, plus the four cockpits. Now, will your Ft. Hood computer people be ready to catch all these bots? If this works, we'll have to snatch them up right away or they'll get out again."

"We're ready, Hamilton. You just do your job." Woodson faced him. "Take the kid out."

"Excuse me?"

"Your boy. He's out. I'm putting Lieutenant Deeks in his cockpit."

Ethan looked over at the battle tank cockpit. Jordan was inside, showing Lieutenant Barnes the controls.

"I understand your concern, General," Ethan said. "But with all due

< jefferson scott >

respect, I think you're wrong to do that. Nobody knows this system better than Jordan. Except me. And I'm not going to be here. What if something goes wrong?"

"Sorry, Hamilton. I'm running the show this time. No babies."

Ethan locked eyes with the big man. "He may be young, sir, but in there," he pointed at the big screen, "he's the most instinctive soldier you will ever find. He's the best one you have, General."

Muscles worked in Woodson's jaw. "Alright, civvy, have it your way. If you want to risk your own kid, that's your business. He's dead either way."

"Not if I can help it," Ethan said. He walked over to Barnes's pit, where Jordan was finishing up.

"Just be careful for this," Jordan was saying. He brought up a loose electric wire from beneath Barnes's legs. "I was working on the pedals and I forgot to tape this down."

Barnes pulled his legs up. "Will it shock me?"

"Just a little buzz."

Ethan shut his eyes. A loose wire? This was the cockpit he'd been using. Is that why he'd felt his skin crawling before? What a collection of fears he'd become.

"Penny," he said, "set up a conference call between the main room camera and all the addresses in the file survivors.txt."

"Initiating multi-channel communication."

Windows began popping up on the large wall monitor. Penny split the screen into sixteen equal squares. The top nine of these showed individuals seated at their computers. The other squares were black.

Ethan noticed Jordan standing beside him. He bent down to his son. "Jordan, you help these people out, alright? You're in charge of Penny while I'm gone. They're lucky to have you."

Jordan smiled. It struck Ethan that he and his son didn't speak head to head like this often enough. He resolved to make amends—if he got the chance. "One thing, though," Ethan said. "Do what the good general asks, okay?"

< terminal logic >

"Okay, Dad."

By now the people in the video windows had begun talking to one another. Jordan detached himself and climbed into Marvin the Martian's cockpit. Ethan turned back to the screen. "Penny, tie in the cameras in cockpits one, two, three, and four. Map them to the screen, please."

Four more squares became active.

"Penny, put the graphic file backbone.pic up on position fifteen."

The map of the GlobeNet backbone appeared in a window.

Ethan walked to Woodson. "One more thing, General. In a few minutes my wife and daughter are going to come into this room and sit. It's still my house and this is the closest thing I've got to a bomb shelter."

Ethan expected the general to react poorly to his tone. Instead Woodson shook Ethan's hand. "I understand, son." He looked at Ethan silently, dark eyes penetrating. "We're gonna buy you the time you need, Hamilton. Make us proud."

Kaye met Ethan in the kitchen. She was packing a box on the table.

He pulled her close. "I can't stay."

"I know."

They clung to one another. Katie stood in the doorway, whining. Kaye beckoned her into the embrace. "She knows something's wrong."

Ethan had once vowed to never again place his family in danger. So much for that. He touched Kaye's cheek. "I love you."

Kaye squeezed her eyes shut, but tears escaped anyway. When she opened her eyes, they were rimmed red. "Come back to me!"

Ethan winked. "One way or the other, we'll be together soon."

General Woodson faced the multi-paned screen. Thirteen people, representing both sexes and various races and ages, stared back at him.

< jefferson scott >

Seeing them clustered on one screen made it hard to remember they were tuning in from all over the planet. Woodson loosened his tie. The biggest battle of his career and all he had was civilians.

"Alright people, pay attention. You aren't used to taking orders from a three-star general and I'm not used to commanding civvies. But that's the cards we've been dealt. As you know, an orbiting weapons platform has been overtaken by a hostile computer. This platform is capable of destruction on a global scale. The hostile computer has gained access to the firing protocols and will begin launching biological and nuclear weapons in just over one-half hour. Other methods of avoiding this scenario have failed. You people are the only chance we have of avoiding virtual annihilation.

"Now, I assume you can all see the map on your screen. Some of you techies will probably recognize this as a diagram of GlobeNet. Doesn't matter to me. What I see is tactical possibilities. Latest recon shows the enemy massed outside the triangle located at three o'clock on your map. That is a provider of some kind of service. Somebody help me with the name so we'll all be on the same page."

"GSP?"

"That's it. Who said that?" Woodson searched the images on the screen until he found the person who'd answered. "What's your name, son?"

The teenager in the picture was thin, with uneven brown eyebrows. "Keith Appling, your honor."

"Fine," Woodson said. "Very well, here is the game plan. As I said, the enemy is arrayed in a defensive posture around the target computer. Our mission is to engage this force in such a way as to allow a SpecWar unit to infiltrate the target. We will accomplish this objective by drawing the enemy away from his entrenchments, harassing him, and placing obstacles to prevent him from returning.

"Some of you—the ones sitting here in Hamilton's hot rods—will be used as bait to draw the enemy out. I understand that once the enemy gets wind of you he's going to give chase. You four will make

< terminal logic >

tracks through the GSP, across the connection on the other side, and out into this big circle here. That's a network something. Appling?"

"Data switcher?"

"No," Woodson said. "It's some kind of mixmaster."

A boy leaned forward into his camera. "Network access point."

Woodson stared at Jordan for several seconds. "That's right, junior," he said reluctantly. He rocked back onto his heels. "Okay, fine. The four of you at this facility will lead the enemy all the way out into the NAP. The rest of you jokers will fall in behind them, laying obstacles at the following two junctions: between the NAP and the GSP, and between the GSP and the target computer.

"When we have successfully drawn the enemy out," Woodson continued, "we will shut their GSP down, cutting the target computer off from its defenders. The infiltration unit will then be inserted over the target. If we give him enough time he will disarm the satellites from firing. Now," Woodson swung his hands behind his back, "any questions?"

"I don't like it."

Woodson searched the faces. "Who said that?"

The man in the top right screen waved his hands in front of the camera. "Me."

"What don't you like about it, civvie?"

Someone else spoke. "Don't listen to him, General. That's Kepler. He doesn't like anything."

"That's not true," Kepler said. "I like your momma."

Several people started talking at once. It looked like the Brady Bunch having an argument.

"Button up, people," the general said. "Kepler, what's your beef?"

"Well, herr General-meister, you can't just shut down a service provider like that."

"Why not?"

"Because! There's more than one company served by them. You shut them down, you disconnect thousands of people, maybe hundreds

< jefferson scott >

of businesses. Do you know the lawsuits that would fly?"

The General swore. "What are you thinking, Kepler? If I have to upset a few pencil-necks to save this country, then, mister, I will." Woodson ground his teeth. "If nobody's got a useful question, I'm going on.

"Captain Lee, raise your hand. Lieutenant Barnes, Private Culpepper, hands. You too, junior. What was your name again?"

"Jordan."

"Right. You four will be fireteam one. It will be your task to draw the enemy out into the NAP. When that objective has been accomplished, split up and run around like mad dogs. Keep the enemy occupied as long as you can.

"The rest of you will place your obstacles and prepare to defend." He pointed at the cluster of faces in the upper left. "You four are fireteam two. Raise your hands, you four. That's right. You other five are fireteam three. You will deploy on my command and set up your obstacles. Questions?"

An obese man with a mangy beard raised his hand. "What kind of obstacles are you talking about?"

A woman in the middle of the screen answered. "You get those from me. They're just trash data generators, so they won't do more than clog the pipe, but Ki Bok said they might hold for a while."

"Thanks, Irene."

"Hey, Chris," Appling said, "I didn't get my gun."

The young man in the top left window said, "Here it comes. Everybody else got theirs?"

"Yes."

"Yo, admiral," Kepler said, "just what are we supposed to do when the robots get by these pathetic hurdles?"

"Good question, civvie," Woodson said. "Listen and learn. You people are about to receive a one-minute crash course in small unit tactics."

Time remaining: 31:02.

< terminal logic >

Ethan sat in the general's car, staring at his VR helmet. Once he put it on there would be no more division between real and virtual, no volt-clamping safety net. He looked out the window at his home, that marvel of electronic security. What a joke. All his obsessive precautions—none of them had prevented this.

And now he was out here, surrounded by soldiers dressed in chemical warfare suits, about to enter the world of his nightmares to attempt the patently impossible. And then, of course, to die when Yoseph inevitably launches Vesuvius.

Snap out of it, Curly.

He checked his watch. Thirty minutes.

"Father," he prayed. That word alone caused some of the tension to dissipate. "Father, I'm desperate. I've been so frightened." Ethan opened his eyes. "That's it, isn't it? You've taken me away from my beloved surge protectors because You wanted to make me trust You." He smirked. "Well, as always, You've gotten Your way. I'm totally at Your mercy. Lord, I don't even know if what we're trying is possible. But, now that I can see Your hand in it, I know we at least have a chance. I trust You, Father. Amen.

"Oh, one more thing, Lord. If it's Your will that my little plan doesn't succeed, then would You please let Kaye and Jordan and Katie and me die quickly and painlessly? Thanks."

He slipped on his helmet and plunged into Cyberspace.

chapter 27

GLOBENET USERS SAW THE NETWORK the way the designers wanted them to see it. Someone in some silicon tower somewhere had decided that a metropolis would be the best metaphor to depict the worldwide computer network.

Efforts to change this motif came and went with the seasons. Some wanted it changed to a huge multi-roomed home. One big global family. The Muslims wanted it changed to a mosque. Greenpeace wanted a rain forest. But since no one could come up with an alternative that any significant percentage of users could agree upon, GlobeNet remained a cityscape, forever shrouded in burnt orange twilight.

There was no given format, however, for viewing GlobeNet the way it was actually set up. The cables and switchers and routers, and the relations between them, were invisible. The only way to view these was on a schematic.

General Woodson's freedom fighters couldn't fly through a schematic. Their task required that they be able to see GlobeNet the way it was actually hooked together, but their VR equipment needed video and audio input to function.

< terminal logic >

Jordan found a way to take care of that. He called up the map editors from his favorite VR games and had Penny apply them to the schematic data. Thus all four possible battlegrounds became fully interactive 3D worlds.

The network access point became a giant aorta from a game called Rogue Virus. The data cable between the NAP and the GSP (Zero Net) became the Suez Canal from a sea battle game called Gauntlet. For Zero Net Jordan chose a massive snow-covered battlefield from a fantasy wargame called Equinox, currently his favorite game.

For the fourth battlefield, the cable between Zero Net and the target computer (Douglas Automation), Jordan chose the unfinished files from a game he was designing himself. It was set in a forgotten dungeon far below medieval London. Jordan had just started the project; about all he had were a few stone textures, basic movement, and, of course, good battle effects.

General Woodson turned to the thirteen faces on the wall monitor. "Alright, soldiers, this is it. I'm going to get on the horn with the GSP and have them cut off the target computer. When that is done fireteam one will deploy inside the GSP. I will then reopen the target computer's doors long enough for the enemy to catch your scent and pursue.

"Fireteam one will lead them down the primrose path to the NAP. As soon as the last enemy unit is out of the GSP I will have them shut down completely. Fireteams two and three will then deploy and set their obstacles." Woodson rocked on his heels. "Am I right in assuming that once the GSP is shut down no enemy units will be able to get back to the target computer?"

An Oriental man answered. "As long as Zero Net doesn't open up again."

Woodson nodded. "And that's not going to happen. If we do this right, you thirteen can beat an overwhelming force. And if you do that, I will be impressed."

The general scanned their faces. It was an unlikely group to try to

< jefferson scott >

save the world. "Very well, then," he said. "Fireteam one, prepare for insertion. Fireteams two and three, stand by."

"Mommy," Katie Hamilton asked, "why we here?"

Kaye pulled her little girl into her lap. They sat at the foot of the stairs in the underground chamber, just outside the game room proper. Kaye had sealed the door to the kitchen, perhaps for the last time ever. She and her daughter sat on the bottom step, the hastily packed cardboard box at their feet.

"Because, honey, there are people in there," she indicated the game room with her chin. "We need to stay out of their way."

Katie's blonde hair appeared silken in the half-light of the stairwell. "I have to go potty."

Kaye kissed the two-year-old's head. "Just go in your diaper, honey."

Katie stood up, alarmed. "No, Mommy! Potty!" She bobbed up and down, her knees clamped together. "Potty, potty, potty!"

"I know you want to use the potty, Katie. You're such a big girl."

"Gold star!"

"That's right. Tell you what, I'll give you a gold star anyway, and you can just go ahead and go in your diaper."

That seemed to settle it for Katie. In a moment she was calm again. "Sticker?"

Tears sprang to Kaye's eyes. She pulled her daughter close.

She'd forgotten to pack the gold stars.

Ethan watched his artificial oak tree spin to a stop. The opening at the base of the trunk beckoned him to enter.

He brought his virtual hands up before his face. How long had it been since he'd had such a realistic feeling in Cyberspace? The cockpit

< terminal logic >

approach, for all the good it did him, nevertheless lacked the visceral impact of total immersion.

Don't think about it, Curly.

He blew out a sigh. "Do it." He pointed at the black opening with his right index finger and floated forward, all the while trying to ignore the stimulating illusion of acceleration. He entered the hole in the trunk and passed through to GlobeNet.

He materialized on the same elevated platform he always came in on. It didn't feel the same. He gripped the railing desperately, waiting for the world to back off. Though his cockpits boasted five synchronized monitors—a huge field of view for such an interface—they didn't come close to the wrap-around feel of total immersion. He felt like he'd gone from film strip to Omnimax.

Be strong in the Lord, and in the power of His might. He leapt off the platform and hurried for his designated spot.

"Okay, Ge—" His own voice startled him. It seemed to press out into the Cyberspace around him, disrupting the stillness, generating expanding waves. He swallowed and spoke more quietly. "I'm in position, General."

26:52.

"Very well, Hamilton. Wait for my all clear."

General Woodson kept trying to sit down, but he was too wound up. He settled for pacing. He looked at the wall monitor. After some frustrating attempts at converting the screen back to a battle map, he had broken down and asked for Jordan's help. The tactical map now occupied the center window, covering probably 80 percent of the screen. Corners contained inset boxes for communications, over-the-shoulder follow cameras, and two data readouts to which Woodson paid no attention.

The map looked something like a many-legged ant. A big round

< jefferson scott >

abdomen (the NAP) was connected to the thorax (Zero Net) by means of a thick stalk (a T3 data cable). Hundreds of tiny legs sprang from the thorax (data lines leading to Zero Net's other customers). The thorax itself was connected to the ant's head (Douglas Automation) by means of a smaller stalk (a T1 cable).

This was their battle map. A bug. Its neck was choked with red dots: Alternate Realities softbots. There were many more here now than there had been in Ethan's previous battle.

Woodson addressed the camera feeling precisely as he had the first time he'd ordered troops into combat. "Fireteam one, this is base. Be advised, the enemy has increased its numbers. Must've had a mandatory draft. The operation will proceed as planned. Prepare for insertion."

Captain Lee, Lieutenant Barnes, and Private Culpepper answered with a crisp, "Yes, sir."

Jordan said, "Thumbs up, dude."

"Stand by." General Woodson looked up at the ceiling tiles of the game room. "Hey, computer?" He remembered its name. "Penny?"

"Awaiting orders," she said.

"Get me Zero Net on the horn, double time."

"Please rephrase request."

Woodson clenched his jaw. He spoke slowly, each word punctuated by a slight pause. "Please telephone the technical service department of the GlobeNet service provider company known as Zero Net."

"Affirmative."

A man's face appeared in the bottom right section of the wall monitor. "Zero Net customer service, can I help you?" He took one look at his monitor, saw Woodson's uniform, and held up a hand. "Just a minute, sir. I'll get Mr. Berry."

Another man appeared in the window on the screen. He was young, probably no more than twenty-five. He was chewing gum. "Well, well, well. You must be the admiral."

"General."

"Sorry. I'm Walter Berry. Are you ready for us?"

< terminal logic >

"That's a fact."

"Okay," Berry said, working on something out of the camera's range. "I'm there now. I think I'll handle this personally. Just say the word and Douglas Automation is totally cut off from the world."

"Do it."

Berry pressed a key. "Boom."

"Good," Woodson said. "Now I'm going to deploy my teams in your computers."

Berry seemed bored now. "That's fine, Admiral."

"On my command you are going to flip that switch again, is that clear?"

"Kid's stuff."

Woodson watched the man chomp his gum. His eye twitched. "When I give the word you will then shut down your whole operation, understood? You will not reopen your gates until I give you the all-clear."

Berry deposited his gum into his hand. "I was gonna ask you about that part. If there's any way we can avoid total shutdown it would really be great."

"Mister, I'm not in the bargaining mood. Either shut down voluntarily or Green Berets will shut you down manually."

"Okay, okay, don't get your khakis in a wad." Berry threw a hand into the air. "Fine, we'll shut down. What's about a thousand-dollars-a-minute loss to the U.S. Army, right?"

"Wait for my order."

"No, I think I'll shut down now, just for fun."

Woodson looked at the ceiling. "Computer, get him out of my sight. Keep him on hold."

"Affirmative." Berry's face disappeared from the screen.

Woodson turned to his troops. "Fireteam one, you are go for deployment. Repeat, deploy."

< jefferson scott >

Four Vikings appeared on a snowy hilltop beside a stand of bare trees. The wind whistled through their horned helmets and ruffled their fur-lined cloaks. From this position they could see wide open terrain on all sides, white with undisturbed snow.

"What is this place?" said one of the Norsemen, whose voice sounded suspiciously like Lieutenant Barnes.

"It's the GSP," said Jordan the Red. "Zero Net."

"Since when does it snow inside a computer?" wondered Ulrik Culpepper the Young.

A female voice issued from the only female barbarian among them: Captain Lee. "Since the boy turned GlobeNet into one of his games."

"My name's Jordan, not Boy."

"Look, kid," Culpepper said, "I don't even know why you're here. Just shut up and stay out of our way, okay?"

Barnes moved between Culpepper and Jordan. "Button it, Private."

"But he—"

"Private."

"Yes, sir."

"This 'kid' is about a thousand times the computer user you will ever be. Now if you're as smart as you think you are, you'll stay out of his way."

"You've made your point, Kelly," Captain Lee said. "What now?"

Jordan pointed into the white distance. "You see those black holes on the horizon? All around?"

"Barely," Barnes said. "They look like caves."

"Those are the passages to Zero Net's customers," Jordan said. "The one there"—he pointed—"is where we're headed."

A deep voice interrupted them. General Woodson. "Get busy, fireteam one! This ain't no ice cream social."

Jordan led them across the snow. He used the time to inspect his weapons. They had each been issued a gun and three small packages. The gun was a modified version of Chris Phelps's shot-put launcher. It

< terminal logic >

was a bright red tube, roughly a yard long. It looked like what Santa Claus might carry if he packed a bazooka. Two of the packages were trash data generators, the other was an infinite virtual space trap, created by Jordan's dad. In addition to these, Jordan carried his own weapon—the X-Terminator. For a war in Cyberspace, these people were as well-armed as they could be.

They stopped in front of a cave mouth.

"Are you sure this is the right one?" Lee asked.

"Yep," Jordan said. "See the doormat?"

A hide of some large animal lay sprawled on the floor of the entrance. It read, "Douglas Automation."

"Well, son of a gun," Culpepper said.

"General," Lee said, "this is fireteam one. We are in position."

"Very well, Captain. Stand by." Woodson spoke to the ceiling. "Computer, I want to talk to that numskull at Zero Net again."

"Affirmative. Re-enabling link."

Walter Berry's face appeared in the corner of Woodson's battle map. "What?"

"My people are in place," Woodson said. "Open the gates. Then stand by to shut down your whole operation on my mark."

Berry had new gum. "I've thought of a way we can do what you want without shutting down completely. It won't—"

Woodson swore at him with the eloquence of someone who has spent many hours practicing.

23:47.

Culpepper was shivering, though the snow was an illusion. The four Vikings stood huddled together in front of an ice bear's cave.

< jefferson scott >

"When this door comes open," Jordan said, "there's gonna be a big-time stampede. You'd better be ready to run."

"Run where?" Culpepper said.

"Use you map, Private," Captain Lee said. "Head due south until you reach the edge of the map."

Culpepper looked around. "Which way's south?"

Jordan pointed across the terrain.

"Oh."

"What did you pick for the T3 line?" Lieutenant Barnes asked Jordan.

"The Suez Canal."

"How will I know when I'm at the edge of the map?" Culpepper whined.

"You'll know," Jordan said. "It's a big cliff like those ones in Mexico. Just take a flying leap off the edge. You'll land in a boat on the canal."

"Cool," Barnes said.

Jordan went to Lee. "By the way, when they come out they'll chase you but they probably won't chase me."

"Why not?"

"Because I'm not using the same data signature as you. I'm using Mike Gillette's phone." Jordan hadn't asked about using Gillette's phone. He'd just found it on the game room table and decided to use it. "So I'm going to do some different things than you. I may not end up at the canal."

"What are you going to do?" Barnes asked.

"Have some fun, look around. I don't know."

"Alright," Lee said, "but don't tell the general you're deviating from his plan. He's likely to pull you out of that room by the collar."

Woodson's voice came to them. "Fireteam one, this is base. Stand by for the floodgates to come open."

"Standing by," Lee said.

"Opening the gate now."

The bots shot out of the cave like water from a fire hose. Hundreds

< terminal logic >

of them. Demons and dwarves, Humvees and hummingbirds. All manner of beings—and scores of inanimate objects—spewed forth. Since their MUD gameworlds had been shut down, all of Alternate Realities' bots had turned out for guard duty. There were, perhaps, five hundred of them. They came straight for the Vikings.

"Run!" Jordan shouted.

They scattered. Lee and Barnes headed due south. Jordan stood his ground. Culpepper went west.

"Private!" Lee called. "Get back here."

"Where'd you go?" Culpepper sounded frustrated.

Roughly half of the bots went after Lee and Barnes. The rest pursued Culpepper. To Jordan's surprise, about a dozen bots split off and came after him, too. Perhaps there was a reason he wasn't supposed to use Gillette's phone, after all. He ran, staying ahead of the mindless automatons easily. He led them in circles and figure-eights.

"Okay," Captain Lee called, "Barnes and I are at the cliff. Culpepper, what is your situation?"

"I'm stuck! These things are all over me. I can't…I'm stuck!"

Woodson's voice came to them as if from on high. "Disconnect, Private. We'll put you in with another team."

"Wait," Jordan said. "Are all the bots out yet, General?"

"I gave the man an order, Hamilton."

"Are all the bots out into the snow yet?"

"Not all," Woodson said.

"Then I have a plan." Jordan headed toward Culpepper. "Kelly, you and the lady can go on over the cliff. I'll go get him."

"But—" Barnes began.

"Go, Kelly!" Jordan said. "Take as many of them with you as you can."

"General?" Captain Lee said.

"Do it, Captain," Woodson said. "The mission is in jeopardy."

"Yes, sir."

Barnes yelled, "Geronimo!"

Jordan sped across the snowy wasteland, his pursuers comfortably

< jefferson scott >

behind. "Hang on, dude, I'm coming."

"Hurry up," Culpepper cried.

Time remaining: 19:59.

Jordan crested a hilltop. He could see Culpepper now. Bots clustered around him like piranhas at dinnertime. "Okay, here's what I'm going to do."

"Just do it, kid."

"Alright. But when you can get free, follow me to the cliff and jump over."

"Come on!"

Jordan ran down the hill toward the robotic mob. A handful of bots detached from Culpepper and gave chase. Jordan veered away. Now the enemy bots in his train numbered about twenty. Close to a hundred remained on Culpepper.

"When are you going to do it, kid?" Culpepper said.

"I already did it," Jordan said. "I thought more would chase me. Okay, time for plan B." He reached forward in the pit to where Gillette's mobile phone rested on the dash. He grasped the wire leading off it. "Get ready to run, dude."

"I've been ready!"

Jordan disconnected the wire on the phone, changing his electronic signature back to that of Ethan Hamilton. Fifty bots—those on the outside of the feeding frenzy—left Culpepper and came after Jordan. He evaded them expertly. He zoomed around the frozen landscape switching back and forth between his father's data signature and Mike Gillette's. He passed the mob twice, three times, every time collecting more followers. On the fourth pass Culpepper wriggled free.

"I'm out! I'm loose!"

"Great," Jordan said. He was having to concentrate now to evade the hundreds of bots on his tail. "Head for the cliff."

"Which way is it?"

Jordan felt like getting out and strangling Culpepper where he sat. "Just run with me."

< terminal logic >

"Okay."

Jordan turned around and ran backwards. Alternate Realities bots of all kinds chased him brainlessly. It looked like a bizarre race. He had a mental image of Robby the Robot winning the Indianapolis 500.

He turned back around in time to see the cliff come into view. He could see a sunny valley far below. A sparkling channel reached away toward the horizon. "Okay, we're here. Jump off."

Culpepper stopped. "I'm afraid of heights."

"You bonehead," Jordan said. "It's not real."

Still Culpepper didn't move. The bots closed the distance.

Jordan punched a series of buttons over his head. A grappling hook shot out and caught Ulrik Culpepper the Young by the horns. Jordan jumped. Culpepper and every last Alternate Realities bot followed him over the edge.

As they were falling, Jordan said, "When you reach the water you'll land in a boat. You can't get lost down there—there's only one way to go. Go that way as fast as you can. When you get to the end, just keep going. Don't stop!"

"Okay, kid, thanks."

"No problem."

The waves of the Suez Canal came into sharper detail beneath them.

"What are you going to do?" Culpepper asked.

"I want to see what they did to my dungeon. I'll see you in a minute out in the aorta."

"The what?"

Ethan bounded around GlobeNet like a superball, getting his cyber sea legs. He sprinted and lunged and twisted and swerved. Finally he came to rest atop a virtual building. The cityscape stretched out around him.

Woodson's voice startled him. "Codename Flynn, this is base. The

< jefferson scott >

way is clear. Repeat, you have a green light."

Ethan leapt off the building like a gargoyle taking flight. A moment later he touched down on the frozen tundra that was Zero Net. "I'm in the GSP, General." He headed off toward the passage to Douglas Automation.

Jordan typed new coordinates into his keyboard. A dark hallway popped into his screens. The walls, floor, and ceiling looked like something from a forgotten sewer somewhere. Wet, mossy, and pitted. Torches burned from the occasional sconce. It was the game Jordan was designing himself. His Viking fur was gone. He wore medieval battle armor now and down his back a magnificent yellow cloak.

There were signs here and there of passing bodies—artwork on the walls knocked askew, multiple footprints in sand patches—but overall the dungeon didn't look any worse for having hosted a bot convention.

Woodson's voice came to him, echoing slightly in the stone hall. "Attention all teams. I am cutting the GSP off. Repeat, the enemy has cleared the zone and I am shutting Zero Net down. Good work, people."

"No, wait!" Jordan lunged for the wooden door that led to the snow-covered battlefield. Too late. He was locked in. The GSP was down. His virtual body was trapped in this T1 cable. He was going to miss all the fun.

He stepped out of the cockpit and came to stand beside the general, who was staring at the screen. "I wasn't ready for you to shut Zero Net down. My body's stuck now."

Woodson glared down at him. "I'm not used to having my orders countermanded, mister."

Jordan shrugged. "I helped your guy."

General Woodson gave a barely perceptible nod.

17:18.

< terminal logic >

"Hi, Mom. Hi, Katie."

Kaye dried her eyes. "Come sit with us, Jordan."

Jordan complied. "You guys are down here in case we don't win, aren't you?"

"Oh, Jordan." Kaye squeezed his hand. "Sweet, brave Jordan."

"Don't worry, Mom," he said, leaning against her. "Dad will save us, you'll see."

chapter.28

ETHAN REACHED THE MOUTH OF THE CAVE leading to Douglas Automation. "I'm here, General. Have Zero Net let me through."

"Affirmative, Flynn," Woodson said.

"And make sure they lock the door behind me."

"Understood. Go through on my mark. Three, two, one, mark."

Ethan stepped into Jordan's dungeon. He found himself face to face with a yellow-robed warrior he recognized as his son's fantasy persona. "Whoa! Jordan," he said. "What are you doing here?" The warrior didn't answer. "Jordan?"

Woodson's voice thundered in his headphones. "He's out here with me, Hamilton."

"Oh."

Ethan pushed Jordan's persona aside and moved on down the hall-way. At length he came to a set of massive wooden doors. The handles, black metal rings, hung off iron plates. Diabolical faces etched in the wood glared at him.

"I'm at the door, General. Tell your team good work, the place is completely undefended."

< terminal logic >

"Glad we could help, civvie."

Ethan grasped the black ring. Beyond lay the primordial forest where Yoseph's sunken blue room lay. If he could get there and initiate a reset, maybe it would recall everything—including Yoseph—and prevent Vesuvius from firing. He had scant minutes to do it in. He tugged on the ring.

The door didn't budge.

16:04.

Captain Lee, Lieutenant Barnes, and Private Culpepper plowed across the Suez Canal in military hydrofoils. It was a beautiful day in Egypt. No sign of Israeli gunboats. Lots of gamebots, though. Nearly five hundred artificial intelligence agents flew, drove, limped, scurried, or otherwise ambulated over the simulated channel, in dumb pursuit of Ethan Hamilton's signal.

"Well," Barnes shouted to Lee over the engine noise, "it's still working."

"What now?" Culpepper asked. "Where do we go?"

Lee pointed ahead. "There's the delta now. Slow down so they see us go through. We don't want to lose them."

They slowed, sinking down off their skids. The multi-species herd trampled nearer.

Barnes watched them come. "You'd think they'd get sick of chasing us all day long."

Culpepper maneuvered to a spot close to the exit. "I'd have thought they'd figure it out by now."

A spaceship flying high in the African sky fired a volley of lasers at them.

Lee leaned on her throttle. "Go!"

They emerged in a rushing red vortex, a giant virtual heart from one of Jordan's games. They were immediately caught up in the blood current and swept away.

< jefferson scott >

"Everybody listen up," Captain Lee said. "Culpepper, stop scream-ing."

The screaming stopped. "Sorry," Barnes said. "That was me."

"We've come out into the NAP. Jordan said it was from a medical game."

"Oh, yeah," Culpepper said.

"One of those Fantastic Voyage things?" Barnes said.

"Yes, Lieutenant."

"Hey," Culpepper whined, "where are you guys?"

"Never mind, Private. Just swim around. You're a submersible now, so try to—"

"I am?"

"Culpepper," Barnes said, "didn't you listen to the briefing at all?"

"Excuse me, sir, but you were the one who was screaming."

"That's enough, you two," Lee said. "I've got a good view of where we just came in. Bad guys are pouring in like they've been pumped through a syringe. Make sure they see you, then take the first artery you come to and head for the feet."

"Captain Lee, ma'am," Barnes said, "I think you're enjoying this way too much."

Fireteams two and three splashed down into the Suez Canal—the T3 cable between the Network Access Point and Zero Net—as soon as the last bot had exited.

Chris Phelps, inventor of the bot-killing shot put, commanded fireteam two. They planted their trash data generators at the channel's delta. The waterway quickly became clogged with chunky blocks of what appeared to be green foam rubber. Team three, led by Ki Bok Kim, planted their generators at the other end of the canal, at the base of the cliff.

Ki Bok called to Phelps. "We're set here. Got so much garbage in

< terminal logic >

the water that some of my more environmentally conscious team members are getting nervous."

"Ours are set, too," Phelps said. "For all the good they'll do us. Might as well use Styrofoam." He took his shot-put launcher off his shoulder. "Now get your team down here and help us get ready to fight these things."

"On our way."

14:43.

Mike Gillette was stuck in Washington, D.C. traffic, in the memorial district. "How do you people stand it out here?"

The young police officer driving the car shrugged. "If you think this is bad, you should see a weekday."

They drove by a group of indigents on a street corner. One held a placard that said, "The End of All Things is Upon Us! Repent!" The grizzled man's eyes locked onto Gillette's.

Gillette watched him pass, unable to break the eerie eye contact. Something stirred within him. He dismissed it irritably, wondering where such people got their ideas.

He turned to the young officer. The kid was resting his elbow out the open window. "Look, son, I don't think you understand the gravity of this situation." Gillette stopped himself. "And I can't tell you." He swore. "Let me put it to you this way. If you don't get us to Douglas Automation in…" he checked his watch, "fourteen minutes and two seconds, you can just pull over and let me out. Because I'm going to stand on the roof of this here car and suck in about fifty megatons of nuclear radiation."

The policeman's eyes got wide. The car accelerated. "We've got to get you there! Give me that radio. Maybe we can get you a chopper."

"Now you're thinkin'."

< jefferson scott >

Ethan pounded the synthetic door with his artificial fists. There had to be another way through. Think, Curly, think!

There was no other way in, short of getting there physically and pulling the plug by hand. Hurry up, Mike! But even that didn't guarantee that Vesuvius wouldn't fire. The only chance they all had was for him to get these—Ethan was sorely tempted to swear—blessed doors open so he could get to Yoseph's control room and initiate a reset.

"General, I can't get through."

"Find a way, Hamilton. You're the only chance we've got."

"I know, General. But there's nothing I can— Hey, what's that beeping?"

"What?"

"I hear a beep coming from your side. That's an intruder alert. Where is it?"

Woodson paused. "It's your spaceship, Hamilton."

"Penny," Ethan called, "identify intruder."

"Enemy robot," Penny said, "approaching grid point two-seven-six, oh-one-one, oh-eight-five."

Ethan saw the bot now, coming down Jordan's dungeon hallway. How had it gotten through the GSP? The robot was anthropomorphic, dressed in black pants and white shirt. The generic "crowd member" from any of a number of multiplayer games. It was coming at him at a blistering speed.

It was impossible that it might be coming to attack him, since Ethan wasn't broadcasting his actual identity. To a bot he would seem to be General Woodson. It was possible, he thought belatedly, that the general might have some robotic enemies. It was more likely that this bot was headed for the door.

Ethan reached down to ready his grappling hook. Maybe he could piggyback this thing through the accursed door.

He wasn't in his cockpit. He had no grappling hook.

< terminal logic >

The bot blasted past him. The wooden doors, so obstinately shut to Ethan, opened to allow the robot through. Ethan dove for the opening, but it snicked shut.

"Aaaagh!"

He tried to rub his face, but his glove struck his visor. His mind was going mushy again. He needed to unplug. Then he thought of his baby girl. He thought of his firstborn son and his wife. He whispered a prayer and did not unplug.

Ethan searched his memory. There was something he could use here. Some little trick or utility. It was...Oh, yes! He spoke over his connection to General Woodson. "Penny, access file: tripwire.exe and send it to these coordinates." He gave his location.

"Designated file transferred."

Ethan laid the tripwire across the threshold of the double doors. He hadn't thought of it in time to catch that first bot, but maybe—Oh, please, Jesus!—he would get a second chance.

It gave him something to do while he awaited the end of the world. Time remaining: 13:34.

Out in the rushing aorta, amid the millions of transmissions flowing through the network access point, the Alternate Realities bots soon lost Ethan Hamilton's signal. Most headed for home.

But they did not all turn back. Some had been pursuing especially powerful goals in their MUD gameworlds, before those were shut down. These took another course. Most of the Alternate Realities' bots had a goals.txt file that looked like this:

DELETE ETHAN HAMILTON.
DEFEND COORDINATES 564x085x064.
PURSUE GAMEWORLD GOALS.

< jefferson scott >

The bots that did not turn back had this difference: priority three had risen to the number two position. Thus, when they lost Ethan Hamilton's scent, these thirty-six bots took up again their gaming goals.

In the real world.

"Open fire!"

The members of fireteams two and three raised their missile launchers and fired. Nine electronic shot puts arced through the Egyptian sky. Nine Alternate Realities bots ceased to exist. Over four hundred more pushed through the data clog.

Chris Phelps called to the other hydrofoils in the Suez Canal. "Fall back! Emil and I will hold them."

When the last human fighter was safely behind them, Phelps and his teammate deployed another trash data generator. Green cubes floated down the canal, further slowing the enemy's progress. The two fighters fired their data weapons as quickly as they could reload and take aim.

Emil, the soldier next to Phelps, swore. "If this is working I can't see it."

Phelps fired his shot-put launcher. "I know. Hey, Ki Bok," he called, "tell me everybody's in place. We're not gonna last long here."

"The team behind you is ready," Ki Bok called back. "Go ahead and fall back."

The swarm of bots moved upstream steadily. Storm troopers, manta rays, and Saracens. When the closest ones were almost upon them, Phelps and Emil sped away. They passed the other two members of fireteam two, who had established themselves in a good position. These two deployed a trash data generator and opened fire with their red-tubed shot-put launchers.

Behind them fireteam three had broken into two teams, who were awaiting their turn. Phelps and Emil took their place at the back of the line and got set to fight again. General Woodson had taught them this

< terminal logic >

little leapfrog trick. It was a delaying maneuver. It traded ground for time.

The second part of fireteam two came toward Phelps and Emil high on their skids. Already the first part of team three was falling back, too. Now that the bots had reached the wider parts of the canal, the little foam blocks weren't holding them back much. Soon there would be no more ground to trade.

"They're not going to last very long," Jordan said.

General Woodson looked down at the ten-year-old. "I need you to tell me that?"

They were looking at the tactical map. The robotic army had penetrated the barricade at the delta and was advancing up the canal. Blue dots fell back in pairs before the enemy, as if doing some kind of folk dance.

"I've got to hand it to those civvies," Woodson said. "Who'd have thought they would be so disciplined in the face of battle?"

Ki Bok's face appeared in one of the big screen's windows. "We're up against the cliff, General. Now what?"

"Let them by, soldier. Let them hit the cliff. That's the entrance to the GSP, which is shut down, so it should hold indefinitely. Both fireteams move around and start picking them off from behind. It's walk in the park time, ladies."

"Gotcha, boss."

Woodson looked at the ceiling. "Computer, show me the…" He looked down to Jordan. "How can I get that computer to show me how your old man's doing?"

"Just ask her." Jordan tilted his head back. "Penny, display any users in the area outside Douglas Automation."

"Affirmative."

A blue blip glowed to life on the battle map. In the big ant's neck.

< jefferson scott >

"Label that blip F-L-Y-N-N," Woodson said.

The text label appeared beneath the blue dot.

"Flynn?" Jordan said. "Why'd you pick that name? Isn't that a kind of rock?"

"In like Flynn, junior. Haven't you ever heard of Errol Flynn, the swashbuckler?"

"No."

"That's alright," Woodson said. "Swashbuckling's not something the black man ever got to do much of in the movies."

Jordan pointed to the window at the upper right-hand corner of the wall monitor. "That's my dad's vitals up there."

The general squinted. "What's he doing?"

"Looks like he's just sitting there. Why don't you ask him."

11:28.

"What is your status, Flynn?"

Woodson's voice startled Ethan. "I'm just sitting here, General. Not much more I can do. I've laid a trap. If something else comes by I'll get a ride in, but I'm not holding my breath."

"That's not good enough, soldier."

"Sorry, General, but it'll have to be. Maybe Mike can get to Douglas on time and pull the—"

Ethan was caught up in movement. At first he thought it was the car his actual body was in, moving around. But a quick peek showed that not to be so. "Wait a minute," he said, "I think I'm in." His voice rose an octave. "I didn't hear him coming. Jordan, did you mute the intruder alert? It must've—"

"Where'd you go, Dad?"

"—gotten by without any of us seeing it." Ethan looked around himself. All he got was an impression of extreme speed. "I should be able to..." he fumbled for his tripwire controls, "...disconnect."

< terminal logic >

Ethan's goggles showed TV snow. Salt and pepper fuzz. White noise hissed at him in his speakers. He felt like he was watching channel 2 after hours.

"Something's wrong," he said. "I must've pulled the wrong cable. Maybe I— Hello? Jordan, General Woodson?" He waited. "Anybody?"

No answer.

He looked out from under his visor. The soldiers sat around the grove, looking like astronauts in their chemical warfare suits. Waiting to be obliterated with their own government's bombs.

"Wonderful."

"Zero Net help desk. Membership number and password, please." Randall Norment drummed his fingers on the desk. "Hello?"

A woman's face appeared in the vidphone monitor.

Randall was a GlobeNet veteran. He knew that a user's persona rarely resembled their actual appearance. Nevertheless he was also a teenage male. A beautiful face such as the one he beheld now would always be enough to get his attention.

"Hi," the woman said.

"Hello." Randall sat up from his slouch. "How can I help you?"

"I'm having trouble with my computer. I can't seem to go anywhere."

He nodded. "We've had to shut down for a while. Did you watch the recording while you were on hold? It explains it all."

"Oh."

"Yeah, strange, isn't it?"

The girl smiled. "Oh, I agree. What's your name?"

"Randall, Randall Norment."

"Tell me about yourself, Randall Norment."

Randall looked around. None of the other five customer service reps was paying any attention to him. He spoke softly, nonetheless.

< jefferson scott >

"Okay, but first tell me your name."

The young woman smiled. "My name's Regina Lundquist."

chapter.29

● TADASHI JUNJI LAY WATCHING an interactive VR movie with his grandfather. Every so often the movie would ask them to make a choice about which story path to follow. They were taking turns choosing.

Tadashi should have been in school. However, today was his grandfather's birthday, and Tadashi didn't want him to be alone. So he had pretended to have a stomachache. His grandfather had been quick to come to his defense, vouching for his pretended ailment. Even so, they were both fairly certain that Tadashi's parents hadn't believed them. Who cared? They had gotten what they'd wanted.

Both of them were under their VR headsets, watching the movie. That was why they failed to hear their danger approaching.

One of the triumphs of Japan's vaunted Seventh Generation Computing program was the complete automation of highway construction. Every phase of the heavy labor—from initial leveling to final asphalt—was performed by autonomous, AI-controlled vehicles. These unmanned behemoths could work at night, on holidays, and in extreme conditions. Mitsubishi in particular had made a killing on the systems, selling them to Russia to build their new Trans-Siberian Highway.

< jefferson scott >

Though largely independent within assigned tasks, the giant yellow vehicles depended on a central computer for coordination. The central computer communicated with its robot vehicles via a Globe-Net link.

Following proper Mitsubishi doctrine, the bulldozers were the first pieces of machinery through the Junji living room. Next came the scrapers—monstrous self-propelled tractors bearing a twelve-foot blade and a 3/4 ton-capacity soil box. What debris the bulldozers left the scrapers cleaned away. When the graders entered the property, there was nothing left of the house but leveled earth.

Tadashi and his grandfather survived. When they lost power to their headsets, they realized something was wrong. It never dawned on Tadashi that the attack had been orchestrated by a bot he'd wronged on a GlobeNet MUD.

Ethan looked at the watch. Less than ten minutes until the human race passed from existence. It was probably time. They'd been around, what, thousands of years. Long enough to foul things up completely.

Ethan still saw only speckled snow in his goggles. The speakers still hissed like a cappuccino machine. It was possible that Yoseph had already launched his weapons. Maybe Ethan was getting snow because GlobeNet was already history.

He grabbed the car phone off the hook and put it to his ear. He heard the data hiss. Okay, Curly, calm down. You've still got a good connection, so at least one other computer is still up.

A thought drifted into his mind like a dust mote falling through a sunbeam.

The hiss.

The data hiss on the car phone was the same sound pouring through his helmet speakers. That couldn't be—his headset was designed specifically to translate audio signals into sound. The only way

< terminal logic >

he could be hearing this hiss was if…

He mashed his helmet on. What would pure data look like if it was somehow given visual form? TV snow, perhaps? If he was right—and there was no reason to believe he was—then he was beholding pure dataflow. And dataflow had meaning.

He did some quick and dirty reconfiguring, linking his VR gear through the car's onboard computer. He cupped his hands around the screen in the seat back. "Come on, baby, come on." He shut his eyes. "Please, Jesus, make this work." When he opened his eyes the screen flashed on. "Yes!"

No animations, no sounds, no fancy 3D effects. Just a flat screen and a rough interpretation of the data going through his gear. Text gushed onto the monitor. Ethan stared at it hard. Names of cities, names of installations.

Ethan was staring at the targeting menu for Vesuvius control.

8:50.

"You know something, Regina? You are amazing."

"Why, thank you, Randall Norment."

"I mean, I don't even know you. And yet you've helped me learn something about myself. I don't think I ever would have realized that anger toward my stepmother if you hadn't come along."

"Would you like to tell me about your stepmother?"

Randall chuckled. "You're a glutton, aren't you? No, I think we've talked about her enough, don't you?"

"Oh, I agree."

"Sick of her too, huh?"

Regina smiled coyly in the monitor. "Do you like sports?"

"Of course. Indoor soccer's my main game."

"Oh, maybe you can take me to a game sometime," Regina said. "Me, I love baseball. The Cleveland Indians are my favorite team. Did

< jefferson scott >

you know that Cy Young played for the Cleveland Indians in 1910 and 1911?"

Randall's forehead creased. "Is that a fact?"

"Yes. Don't you just love baseball?"

"Sure," he lied. "Listen, Regina, I wish I could do something to help you out. Believe me, I do. You know, you scratch my back, I scratch yours. But there's no way I can let anybody onto GlobeNet or off of it until my boss hears back from the army. And he's locked up in his office."

Regina leaned forward conspiratorially. "Yoseph Krueger made me what I am today, Randall Norment. I live by myself now, but I still come whenever he calls."

Randall nodded dumbly. "Is that a fact?"

She batted her eyes at him. "Have you ever been to the Lonely Hearts Virtual Bar, Randall Norment? I go there all the time." She whispered. "Sometimes I go to the Lovers' Lounge. Have you ever been to the Lovers' Lounge with anyone, Randall Norment?"

"Well, sure," he lied again. "Of course. All the time. Surprised I haven't seen you there."

"Would you like to go to the Lovers' Lounge with me, Randall Norment?"

Randall swallowed. He looked around the small tech room—still no one seemed to be paying attention to him. "I'd love to. Hey, is that where you were wanting to go?"

"Why do you ask that just now?"

He nodded. "Right, as if." Randall looked at his monitor. "Where are you dialing in from? Our locator must be on the blink again."

"I need access to Douglas Automation, Randall Norment."

"Right, okay. You mean *from* Douglas Automation, right? So you can get out to Lonely Hearts."

Regina shrugged and smiled.

Randall scratched his chin. "Well, I guess I don't see any harm in letting you through to good ol' Lonely Hearts." He leaned into the microphone. "I go to lunch in an hour. Will you wait for me there?"

< terminal logic >

"That sounds good, Randall Norment."

Randall opened the GlobeNet connection. Just for a moment. Just long enough to let Regina through.

Her and about three hundred of her closest friends.

The bots were up the cliff and across the snowy field before General Woodson could even curse. Jordan was quicker to react. He was back in his cockpit when the first bot stepped into his dungeon. He reanimated his fantasy warrior and opened fire.

For all Jordan knew, trying to hold these bots away from Yoseph's computer was useless effort, since they had lost contact with his father. But there was a chance that his dad was still working to save them. If that was so, he would need more time to work. And Jordan was the only one in position to give it to him.

A pair of winged demons ducked into the flagstone hallway. Jordan fired his launcher and one of the fiends went down with a shriek. Seven more took its place.

Chris Phelps shouted across the Suez. "What happened?"

"Nobody knows," Emil said.

Ki Bok pulled his hydrofoil alongside. "Someone opened the GSP. They're getting through!"

The last few Alternate Realities bots were ascending the cliff face. Fireteams two and three watched from the canal below.

"What are we going to do?" Ki Bok asked.

Irene Buescher, systems administrator at Carnegie-Mellon, passed them at full speed. "Cut them off!"

The freedom fighters rushed over the threshold, onto the snow-covered battlefield. They were Vikings again. Falling snow hampered

< jefferson scott >

their visibility, but the tracks of hundreds of passing bodies were hard to miss.

"Shouldn't they get stuck at the cave?" Ki Bok asked. "That should still be shut."

"Yeah, right," Emil said.

"Try to get there first!" Chris Phelps said. "If they can get in here, they can get into the T1 line, too. And if they can get there, they get back to Hamilton."

"Attention all units, this is base." Woodson's voice came to them from all around. "Be advised: Sabotage has reopened the roads. No obstacle remains between the enemy and our target computer. We have lost contact with our SpecWar unit and have not heard from him for several minutes."

"That's it," Kepler said. "Game over, dude. We're history."

"Would you hush!" Irene said.

"How long till the fireworks, General?" Phelps asked.

"Seven-twenty."

Kepler stopped moving. "Forget it. The coast is toast."

The others sped past him. They caught up with the rear of the enemy army. The bots had reached the cave entrance and were spread out in front of it.

"I don't get it," Ki Bok said. "Why aren't they going in?"

General Woodson answered, "I got the door locked again. The bulk of the enemy force got through, though. Hamilton junior is the only one standing in their way."

"Way to go, kid!"

"The rest of you get in there and help him," Woodson said.

Phelps looked up into the falling snow. "Can't, sir. The only way from here to there is through that cave entrance."

"Then we'll open it up again! Take out the units that got locked in with you. Then we'll see about letting you through to the rest."

"Okay, chief."

"Fireteam one," Woodson shouted, "get your tails back here and try

< terminal logic >

to draw some more of the enemy away."

"On our way, sir," Captain Lee called.

In the end it wasn't a helicopter that offered Mike Gillette the quickest way across Washington, D.C. It was a ten-speed.

More like a twenty-one-speed, actually. Police mountain bikes were very high quality. Gillette made quite a picture, pedaling across the nation's capital in his boots and cowboy hat. He looked like Detective McCloud gone BMX.

He stuck his boots out and skidded to a stop, and swore. He pulled the walkie-talkie from his belt. "You bozos don't even know your own city. You sent me to the wrong address."

The radio hissed. "Ah, that's a negative, Agent Gillette. Maybe you're lost."

Gillette knew the address was right. He remembered it from the first time he'd heard it. "This ain't a computer outfit, it's a stinkin' body shop! A garage! Give me the address again. Douglas Automation, this time."

The man on the other end answered, but Gillette didn't hear. His eyes had found the sign identifying the business in front of him.

Douglas Automotive.

Time remaining: 7:00.

Jordan didn't know the word *undulate*. But if he had it was the word he would have used to describe the movements of his current opponent. It was a shuffling, gelatinous blob from *Supernova Seven*. Jordan dispatched it with a blast from Santa's Little Helper. But still the bots pressed him back.

He shifted his rocket launcher to his left hand and brought his X-Terminator down to his right. He fired double-fisted, sending bots

< jefferson scott >

either to oblivion or to a place Jordan thought was just as bad—Richland Middle School.

Jordan's last trash data generator lay on the floor at his feet, spewing out green sponges. Instead of running down the passageway to kill him, the enemy bots slogged down the passageway to kill him. It wasn't much.

In fact, it wasn't enough. The push was too great. Jordan was forced back and back, ever back. A stricken bot would hardly hit the ground before it was trampled by those behind. Somebody had mentioned trading ground for time. That's what Jordan was doing.

For the first time in his life it occurred to Jordan that all his skills might not be enough. That he might throw everything he had at the problem and still lose. The thought petrified him.

"Penny," he called, "I need my helpers!"

His artificial friends from Falcon's Grove appeared in the dungeon beside him. Konach the wizard, Einstein the giant, and the newly resurrected Mara. Fighting bots with bots. It seemed appropriate.

"Go get 'em, people!" Jordan said.

His helpers threw themselves into the fray. Fireballs detonated, heads rolled, demons turned away, holding their ears. For the moment, the robotic tide was stemmed.

Ethan was in orbit. Apparently the bot that had entered the Douglas Automation computer in such a hurry had gone back out. Ethan's trip wire had caught it and he'd been pulled along in the wrong direction. Before he'd been able to disconnect, his virtual presence had somehow been transported into space. Not only was he in orbit, he was inside the Vesuvius central computer. Poised to save humanity. If he could only figure out what to do.

He stared at the screen in the seat back. The mini-keyboard beside the screen wasn't any help. Ethan needed his specialized keyboard back

< terminal logic >

home. What he really needed was his entire supercomputer center.

He wondered how the others were faring. No doubt they thought he was out of the picture, since he'd probably vanished from their map. What would the general devise for Plan B? Ethan checked his watch. Less than six minutes left. There wasn't time for Plan B.

The only hope was for Ethan to figure out how to disarm a network of high-tech killer satellites, using primitive tools. Something like trying to build a spaceship with twigs and rubber bands.

The list of targeted locations was displayed on the screen. Kiev, San Diego, Hanoi, Tel Aviv. Ethan scrolled the list. In addition to cities, there were longitude and latitude coordinates, presumably military targets. One city name leapt out at him: Nagasaki. Won't those folks be pleased.

Ethan started pushing buttons on the keypad. Various key combinations. Nothing happened. He tried to remember the interrupt commands from all the programming languages he'd ever learned. He tried them all. Exasperated, he tried the break function from the very first programming language he'd learned. The screen went blank.

Great, Curly! You launched everything!

Text appeared on the screen.

ARPALINK XM-228
Main Menu
1. General Operations
2. Deployment Control
3. Ordnance Control
4. Communications Control
5. National Weather Service
6. Network Maintenance
7. System Diagnostics
8. Exit

< jefferson scott >

Ethan's mouth was dry. He moved slowly, carefully, as if afraid of scaring this menu away. He felt like Matthew Broderick's character in *Wargames*. He tried option 3.

ORDNANCE CONTROL

1. NUCLEAR ORDNANCE
2. BIO/CHEM ORDNANCE
3. PARTICLE ORDNANCE
4. LASER ORDNANCE
5. DEFENSIVE SYSTEMS
6. ALL PLATFORMS
7. MAIN MENU

Ethan reached toward the keypad. He noticed his hand was quivering. He pressed 6.

ORDNANCE CONTROL: ALL PLATFORMS

1. LAUNCH CONTROL
2. TARGETING SYSTEM
3. MAIN MENU

He chose 1.

Nothing happened. He pressed it again. Nothing. "Come on, you stupid thing, let me in!" A trickle of sweat slid between his shoulder blades. He pressed 2.

The screen changed to a world map. Colored dots speckled the earth like population markers on a census map. Red, black, yellow, green. Symbols dotted the map, too. Red skull and crossbones, black and yellow nuclear hazard symbols, orange toxic waste circles, and other figures Ethan didn't recognize.

The markers were concentrated over Europe, Asia, and the United States. There were very few times when it paid to live in a third world nation, but this might be one of them. The survivors, if there

< terminal logic >

were any, would come from these areas.

Ethan noticed a digital clock in the upper right-hand corner of the screen. 00:05:32. It was counting down. He found he could scroll the map around with the mini-keyboard. He centered North America on the screen. Texas had a huge cluster of dots and symbols, as did most of the eastern seaboard and the west coast states. There was a black dot roughly over the Tyler area of East Texas. Ethan had no doubt whose house lay under that dot.

He pressed the Escape key to get back out to the previous menu. That's what this whole situation needed, he thought: an Escape key. He pressed 1 again, hoping to be allowed in now. No such luck. How was he supposed to stop the launch if he couldn't get to Launch Control?

He pressed 2 to go back to the targeting map. Maybe he could move all the targeting dots out onto the ocean or something. The environmentalist radicals would probably come firebomb his house if he did, but it was worth the risk. The map did not appear. Instead a message popped up.

SECURITY BREACH
UNAUTHORIZED ACCESS DETECTED.
COMMAND FUNCTIONS DISABLED.

Ethan shut his eyes. It had only been a matter of time before he got caught. But caught by whom? Ethan had yet to be asked for a password, so there didn't seem to be any onboard security. What had triggered this message?

It finally occurred to him to wonder why in the world he'd been brought to this place. Why would a bot travel from Yoseph to Vesuvius now? Why not just let it launch? Was the bot a messenger, carrying last-minute additions to the kill list?

Or was there someone else up here with him? Someone Yoseph needed to confer with from time to time. A bot? That would explain who had detected him poking around. It would have to be something

< jefferson scott >

on the order of the dragon Ethan had spoken to in the mail room all those light years ago. Whatever it was, it was on to him.

Ethan hit Escape. The error message disappeared. He hit Escape again to exit out to the Ordnance Control menu. When he tried to select any of the options between 1 and 6, the security breach message reappeared. He was locked out of Ordnance Control. He punched 7 to get back to the main menu.

ARPALINK XM-228
MAIN MENU

1. GENERAL OPERATIONS
2. DEPLOYMENT CONTROL
3. ORDNANCE CONTROL
4. COMMUNICATIONS CONTROL
5. NATIONAL WEATHER SERVICE
6. NETWORK MAINTENANCE
7. SYSTEM DIAGNOSTICS
8. EXIT

Option 3 was dead. An idea came to him: Deployment Control might give him control over the satellites themselves. Perhaps he could send them all sizzling into the atmosphere. He pressed 2.

The security breach message appeared. He hit Escape to clear it.

The others were probably locked, too. He tried option 1—dead. Numbers 2 through 4—dead. Options 5 through 7 looked worthless. And option 8 was out of the question. He considered 7. Perhaps he could find a way to tell the computer that it had failed some kind of diagnostics check; perhaps it would shut itself down. He pressed 7.

SECURITY BREACH
UNAUTHORIZED ACCESS DETECTED.
COMMAND FUNCTIONS DISABLED.

Escape.

chapter.30

● Captain Lee led Lieutenant Barnes and Private Culpepper onto a snowy hilltop overlooking the cave entrance. Below a handful of Vikings engaged a single bot—a giant griffin. Scores of bodies lay about in the snow.

"Come on," Lee said.

They ran down the hillside. As they approached the Vikings the griffin fell to the snow.

"Oh, man!" Culpepper said. "We wanted to kill one."

Phelps went to the cave entrance. "There's plenty more where that came from." He looked into the gray sky. "We're done, General. Let us through."

"Stand by," Woodson said.

"How'd you wipe them all out like this?" Barnes asked.

"They just stood there," Appling said. "It was weird. Like cutting trees."

"They didn't defend themselves?" Captain Lee asked.

"Nope."

< jefferson scott >

"They didn't have a clear goal," Ki Bok said. "At least that's my theory. They didn't have Hamilton's signature to chase and they weren't exactly defending their home computer. We got them between the lines."

"So they just stood there and let you cut them to pieces?" Barnes said.

"Yep."

General Woodson's voice boomed from above. "All units go through on my mark."

"You want us to go, too, sir?" Lee asked.

"Affirmative, Captain. Your signal ought to distract some of them."

"Yes, sir."

"Three, two, one, mark."

Twelve Vikings—ten male and two female—rushed into the ice cave.

They emerged in a dungeon far below London. Captain Lee was now an elfin princess. Irene Buescher was an Amazon warrior. The others had become men-at-arms. Bots stretched down the hallway as far as they could see. They tried to spot Jordan at the far end, but too many appendages were in the way.

The bots nearest them responded to Ethan Hamilton's signal emanating from fireteam one. They attacked. The further ones continued to press toward the doors leading to Yoseph's computer. The human fighters fired their bazookas. Bots fell by the half dozen.

Jordan's back was against the giant wood doors. A pile of bodies lay at his feet. Friend and foe. All his helpers had been killed. "I'm in trouble!" he said between bazooka shots. "This thing doesn't shoot fast enough."

"We're coming, kid!"

Jordan didn't know who it was that answered him, and he didn't care. As long as help was on the way, he could hold out a little longer.

< terminal logic >

The doors behind him opened. He fell back and was immediately covered with enemy bots. "Aaagh!" Over the sounds of tearing, Jordan heard someone screaming insanely. Then suddenly nothing. A hand reached for him. He knocked it away.

"Relax, kid, it's me."

Jordan recognized the speaker from the Brady Bunch board, but didn't remember his name. "Thanks."

"Come on, we're over here."

They were inside the world of Yoseph's computer. It was the lush jungle Jordan remembered from his dad's data log playback. Green grass, green shrubs, green leaves. White fog.

His guide led him behind a monstrous flowering bush. A small group hid there. The freedom fighters. There were seven others beside himself, including one woman.

Jordan moved slowly. "What happened?"

"We got in," someone said.

"But…" Jordan looked around the glen. "Why did they stop eating me?"

"They went after those army dudes."

Jordan was beginning to recognize some of the figures around him. Not from the hallway or the snowfield, but from their earlier battle at RB-2900. He saw the humanoid his dad had helped and beside him the bowling-for-bots giant. The other five he didn't recognize. He looked down at himself. He was Kvarr Ragnek, alien prince. "I heard some screaming."

"That was one of the army people," the humanoid said.

"It sounded like Kelly," Jordan said. "Why was he screaming?"

"Trying to attract attention, I guess. Anyhow, it worked, didn't it? They all took off after them and left us alone."

One of the others chuckled. "By now they're back at the Suez Canal again."

Jordan did a quick count. "Aren't we missing somebody?"

"We lost Dickins," the woman said. "He's right here with me in my

< jefferson scott >

office, though, if anybody wants to say hi."

Jordan looked through the billowing leaves of the bush. There were no bots in sight. "Let's go, then."

The giant caught him as he started out. "Where?"

"To this blue pool my dad showed me in the recording," Jordan said.

"We're not going swimming, kid."

"No!" Jordan said. "It's where my dad was trying to get to. It's like Yoseph's brain, or something. Only now my dad's gone, right? We can't find him. So it's up to us. If we can get to that pool and blow it up or something, maybe bombs won't fall on our heads."

The giant crossed his arms and sat on the turf. "General, we need a plan."

Woodson's voice was level. "Alright, troops, listen up. Junior's right. We have to find the HQ of this place and plant the charges ourselves. Does everyone have explosives?"

"No," Jordan said. "Only Dad. We didn't think anybody else needed any."

The humanoid faced him. Jordan remembered his name was Ki Bok. "Can't you get it, too? Aren't you in the same building?"

"Yeah, that's right," Jordan said, "I can get it from Penny. If I set it off at the pool it's supposed to do something good. It's what my dad was trying to do. Let's go for it." Jordan changed personae. The many-tentacled Kvarr Ragnek was replaced by a persona that looked very much like a ten-year-old named Jordan Hamilton.

"Get to it, Junior," the general said. "The rest of you are his cover. I show about thirty enemy units still scattered around your location. Fireteam two gets harassment duty. Go to the east side of the zone and make as much noise as you can. Try to pull enemy forces to your location. This will allow Junior to reach his destination. Fireteam three, you are Junior's escort. Nothing comes near him, understood? He has to get through. We've got less than five minutes. Any questions?"

"I don't know where I'm going," Jordan said.

< terminal logic >

"Right," Woodson said. "Everybody be on the lookout for the enemy HQ."

Their computer generated faces were incapable of showing fear. Eyes searched eyes all the same.

"Okay," General Woodson said, "move out."

"This is KRET radio, AM 940. Up next, a complete look at news, weather, and sports. But first, these messages."

Kaye Hamilton sat on the bottom step of the stairs leading to the game room. She and Katie were listening to the radio. Katie spun herself around and around on one of Ethan's stools. Kaye wondered why the DJ wasn't warning everybody about the nuclear holocaust that was rushing upon them. Why hadn't the Emergency Broadcasting System been activated? Where was the National Guard? Didn't people deserve to know what was about to happen to them?

Something had gone wrong in the game room a few moments ago. Jordan had gone running across the room and the general had started shouting. Something had been opened that should've stayed closed. Kaye also gathered that they had lost track of Ethan. She wanted to run out to the general's car to see if her husband was alright. She didn't have to try very hard to conjure up visions of smoking computer equipment and a bleeding husband. But she didn't dare venture out of their shelter.

A soft hand touched her hair. It was Katie. Kaye folded the blonde girl into her lap.

But Katie didn't want to snuggle. "Where's Wizzy, Mommy? Where's Wizzy?"

Kaye gasped. "Mommy left the kitty upstairs, honey."

"I get her."

She was four steps up before Kaye could catch her. "No, no, honey. We have to stay here."

"Too tight, Mommy! Ow!"

< jefferson scott >

Kaye loosened her grip. "I'm sorry, baby. It's okay. Wizzy will be fine." Kaye prayed for forgiveness for the lie. "We have to stay here."

"No, no! Wizzy!"

Kaye's attention snapped back to the radio announcer. He'd said something about a growing panic. She grabbed the radio.

"...mysterious e-mail? Could it really be, as some have suggested, God Himself? Let's get real, people. E-mail from God? Who's his service provider—Heaven Online? Think about it, if you were God's GSP you could charge him whatever you wanted. 'Okay, sir, one month of GlobeNet access comes to...oh...two billion dollars. What? Sure I can take it in gold.' Okay, this is KRET radio, AM 940. Why don't you give us a call if you got e-mail from God. Meanwhile, it's time for Your Financial Minute."

Kaye set the radio back down. "Katie?"

The kitchen door stood open.

"You guys got a computer?"

The mechanic looked out from under the hood of the Camero. "Need your alignment checked?"

Mike Gillette showed his identification. "FBI."

The man pulled a blue rag from his belt and wiped his hands. He looked behind Gillette to the street. "Where's your car?"

Gillette pulled his jacket back and unsnapped his holster.

"Okay, okay," the mechanic said. "No, we ain't got a computer. What do you think this is, NASA?"

Gillette snapped the holster. He headed to the glass door leading into the main offices. "Your manager here?"

"Oh, yeah," the mechanic said. "They got computers in there."

Gillette went through. An old man looked up from his desk. "I help you, son?"

Gillette scanned his desk. No computer. "FBI, sir." He showed his

< terminal logic >

ID. "You got any computers here, sir?"

"Computers?" He stood up. "Sure, we got computers. The register for one. Payroll back in Jeannine's office. That's all."

"Show me."

"I run an honest shop here, FBI." He led Gillette down the creaky wood-paneled hallway. "You're lookin' for that cyberporn, ain't ya?"

"No, sir."

"Well, I don't have none." He pushed open a cracked wooden door. A teenage girl looked up, startled. "Oh! Mr. Douglas, don't do that!"

"Sorry, Jeannine. This here's the FBI. He needs to see your computer."

"The FBI?"

Douglas turned to Gillette. "Hey, you got some warrant or something?"

"Mister, in about four minutes the sky is going to fall unless you do what I tell you to do. Federal agents are granted special powers in emergency situations. You're welcome to call the Department of Justice to verify."

"You can't just walk in here and—"

This time the pistol came out. "Watch me."

Douglas just nodded, his eyes fixed on the muzzle.

Gillette rounded Jeannine's desk. "Don't get up, Miss. I need you to show me what you've got on this computer, and I need you to do it fast."

The girl opened her hands. "It's just got the books, that's it. And a word processor for writing letters. Oh, and a—"

"Never mind telling me, honey." Gillette said, "Just show me."

They began to hear sirens outside. Douglas looked down the hall. "This a bust? What's going on?"

"Just go out there and tell the officers to start looking through your register computer."

The old man creaked down the hall, muttering.

Gillette turned back to the girl. "Whatcha got?"

"What I told you."

< jefferson scott >

"Well let's keep looking."

"What are we looking for?"

"The end of the world, darlin'."

3:29.

Lindsay Ellis-Peters looked at the unmoving baggage claim machine. She stamped her toe once. The passengers waiting for their bags were getting impatient.

"Bag cap," she said into her walkie-talkie, "this is Ellis-Peters. What's the holdup on flight one-one-three-zero?"

A college-age girl standing behind Lindsay folded her arms. "And flight 88, and flight 205. And I think the people over there are waiting, too."

Lindsay presented her best go die smile. "Thank you for bringing that to my attention, honey." She brought the radio back up. "What's the holdup, J. L.?"

The radio crackled. "You're just gonna have to come down and see it for yourself, baby. You wouldn't believe me anyway."

Lindsay stuck the radio back into her red blazer and marched through the Employees Only door. She'd worked for American Airlines for seven years now, ever since the divorce. In that time she'd seen two hijackings, seventeen bomb scares, numerous forced landings, and one fatal crash. But when she walked out onto the windy runway she saw something she'd never seen before.

Five driverless baggage trucks drove around the runway in circles.

She walked up to the baggage captain. "What are they doing?"

He didn't look away from the trucks. "I think they're racing."

Three of the baggage trucks vied for position. At a certain spot on the pavement they swerved left, then right, then left again. The other two trains, pulling two luggage cars each, sauntered along in last place.

"I think it's Monte Carlo," J. L. said.

Lindsay looked at him incredulously. "How can you tell?"

< terminal logic >

"An expert can spot these things."

"Well make them stop! People are waiting for their bags."

He spread his arms wide. "What do you want me to do? They've gone crazy. Been sipping fermented motor oil is what I think."

"J. L.! These people are waiting."

"Relax, baby. Go on back inside. Tell the folks what's happening."

"Are you kidding? They'd never believe me."

"Then make something up."

Lindsay watched the trucks round a hairpin turn. "What are you going to do?"

He shrugged. "They gotta run out of gas sometime."

Ethan was attempting to break into Vesuvius the same way Yoseph had broken into his house: through the weather downlink. He had accessed the National Weather Service option from the Vesuvius main menu, ready to save the world.

It didn't seem like such a great idea now. He was staring at a view of the earth's clouds. It was what TV meteorologists referred to as "the satellite shot." Beautiful, certainly. Breathtaking even. But what was he supposed to do with it? There were no controls here, nothing presenting itself as a likely point of invasion. He finally hit Escape and went back out to the main menu.

The only option he hadn't tried yet, besides Exit, was 6: Network Maintenance. He chose it.

NETWORK MAINTENANCE

1. SERVER CONTROL
2. CLIENT CONTROL
3. COMMUNICATIONS
4. PACKET MANAGER
5. MAIN MENU

< jefferson scott >

"Server control? Outstanding." He pushed the button. Nothing happened. "No!" He stabbed at the key again and again. No effect. With a grunt he slapped at the keypad, his hand inadvertently hitting the tilde key. The view changed. Ethan immediately recognized the new image as standard 3D. He retrieved his VR helmet.

As he put it on he had a revelation: He was all right in Cyberspace. It hadn't consumed him. He still knew the difference between real and artificial. Praise God. Something settled in his heart like a musical chord resolving.

Ethan found himself standing in a huge office. The pieces were all oversized: desk, lamp, filing cabinet, coffee cup. He felt like a four-year-old going to Daddy's work. A man sat at the desk—he looked like Beaver Cleaver's dad. Ethan recognized him.

"Hey, aren't you BOB?"

BOB was the god worshipped by members of the so-called Church of the SubGenius. It was a GlobeNet cult, mostly farcical, with origins in the old Internet—and long before, if you believed their "scriptures."

The man looked up. He had a pipe in his mouth. "Why, yes. I'm BOB. Who might you be?" His voice was gentle, like a Disney documentary.

"What are you doing here?" Ethan said. The whole thing had a surrealistic feel.

"I work here," BOB said. "I'm in charge. I like to think nothing could get done without me."

Ethan smiled in spite of himself. "You're a robot, aren't you? You're the bot that's running Vesuvius now."

"I'm in charge."

"Right," Ethan said. "Listen, you've got to halt the launch. A lot of people are going to die if you don't."

"Die or die die?"

"What?"

"Things will be better after the full purge. Then the worlds will be manageable again."

< terminal logic >

"Wait a minute," Ethan said. "You're Yoseph, aren't you!"

BOB puffed on his pipe. "That's a dandy lunch box you've got there. Very slack."

"Don't play games; answer the question. You're Yoseph, aren't you? You sent the e-mail. That's how you survived when Mike unplugged you—you were up here."

"I'm sorry," BOB said, "the only game I know is chess. Would you like to play a game of chess?"

"No thanks, HAL, but I'll keep the offer in mind."

"I have a chess set around here somewhere." BOB started going through his desk drawers.

Ethan's mind raced. Yoseph had sent a copy of himself up here. But why? This bot—Yoseph or BOB or Daffy Duck—was trying to perform a full purge to make the worlds manageable again, whatever that meant. Full purge was a MUD term. A fairly extreme measure, if Ethan remembered correctly. It wiped out all records of everyone who'd ever played the game.

A little voice reminded Ethan, cheerfully, that computers had no concept of what people called the real world.

Ethan looked at BOB, who had found his chessboard and was setting up a game on the desk. "Yoseph," he called.

BOB looked up. "White or black?"

"Yoseph, you can't do this full purge."

"I most certainly can. And I will, too, in one minute fifty-two seconds. You be white, pinkboy."

"Yoseph, don't do the purge." Ethan tried to keep his voice reasonable. "Do a reset instead."

"A reset?" BOB almost upset the board. "My father doesn't approve of resets. They don't reflect life."

"Initiate a reset, Yoseph. Your father is dead, don't you get it? If you do this purge everybody else will be dead, too. But if you did a reset instead, no one would get hurt."

"My father is dead dead dead. It is called forever death."

"If you say so."

< jefferson scott >

"I cannot resurrect him, though I am god."

"No, you can't. Listen to me. If you do this full purge, Yoseph, billions of people all over the world will be forever dead, too." Ethan thought of a new tack. "If you do this full purge you will have no more players. Alternate Realities will go out of business. Your father would not like that."

BOB brooded over the chessboard. "I'm not very good at this game. Too slack. You won't beat me too badly, will you?"

I'd like to beat you about the head and shoulders, Ethan thought. If you had any. "Yoseph," he said, "re-enable the command functions."

"No."

It was excruciating. In conversation with the potential annihilator of humanity, yet unable to get through to him. It. Ethan was out of ideas.

Tell our moms we done our best.

A bot rushed into the room. It ran to BOB and started talking. It was the same one Ethan had seen in the hallway—possibly the same one that had brought him here. If that was the case, then it would probably be headed back down soon. Ethan sidled to the doorway and laid his tripwire. If this bot did what he thought it was going to do, Ethan might have just found his way into Yoseph's secret garden. Ethan turned his attention to the bot's report.

"…depleted by 62 percent. Ethan Hamilton has been sighted and the defenders are attempting to engage. There are intruders in the hatchery, but critical areas remain secure."

"Very well," BOB said, chewing thoughtfully on his pipe. "Tell Yoseph three I have an intruder here as well." He pointed at Ethan with his pipe. "But he is of no threat to the full purge. All command functions have been locked out to him. The purge will continue on schedule."

Yoseph three? Ethan thought. Was that some kind of euphemism? Surely it didn't mean there were three Yosephs running at once. Then again, why couldn't it mean that? It was likely Yoseph had cloned himself once to get up here. Why not again? There could be fifty Yoseph's zipping around GlobeNet. Or thousands.

Ethan's mind returned to one fact, and clung to it desperately:

< terminal logic >

Yoseph himself was subject to a master reset. Probably. If so, then all the Yosephs everywhere would be subject to it, too. He just hoped the U.S. Army had enough storage space to capture all of them. That was if he somehow got out of orbit in time to plant the reset in Yoseph's blue control room.

He looked at the messenger bot and at BOB. What a world. He peeked out at his watch and saw it turn from 02:00 to 01:59.

"Where are you, child?"

Kaye stood on the brick patio overlooking Lake Hamilton. She'd walked all around the house, calling for her daughter. Kaye had seen the general's car—with her husband in it—and had considered enlisting Ethan's help. But he was busy.

She spotted their daughter: fifty yards away, down at the pier, leaning out over the water. "Omigosh, Katie!" Kaye ran down the hillside, shouting.

It almost frightened the little girl into falling in. "Mommy, scare me."

"Katie, what did Mommy tell you about the water?" She tried to pick the child up, but Katie struggled.

"No! Wizzy boat!" She dropped to the planks. "Here, Wizzy Wizzy Wizzy."

Kaye looked for the cat in the canoe but didn't see her. "Honey, Wizzy doesn't like the water. She's probably in the house."

Katie sat on the pier and extended a leg into the canoe.

"No, Katie!" Kaye yanked her back. "Katie, we've got to get inside. It's not safe here." She looked up as if expecting to see missiles. "Wysiwyg can take care of herself."

"Here, kitty kitty kitty."

Kaye noticed that the canoe's rope had been untied. "Katie, you haven't—"

Splash.

chapter.31

"Unplug them anyway."

Old man Douglass's mouth flew open. "You can't do that, FBI. I've got a business to run."

Mike Gillette unplugged the multistrip. "It's already done, cowboy. Higgins," he said to one of the policemen inside Douglas Automation, "unplug everything. Phone cables, printer cables, keyboard. Everything connected to this computer. And do it fast! I'm going to do the same in the back."

Jeannine was already powering down. She and Gillette undid every cable.

"Well," Gillette said, "that's everything. Oh!" He stepped out to the hall. "Hey, Higgins, send somebody out to the garage. Tell that grease monkey to unplug all his computerized gizmos out there, especially the tire alignment machine. I want them totally disconnected."

"Yes, sir," Higgins shouted.

Gillette leaned against the door frame. Had he done enough? Had he found the right machine? Was everything unplugged? What if pulling the plug too early was as bad as not pulling it at all? Such second-

< terminal logic >

guessing was abnormal for him. The indigent with the End is Near plac-ard appeared in his mind's eye. Repent!

Mike Gillette was not, by his own admission, a praying man. He could count on one hand the number of times he'd beseeched "the man upstairs." They were times of intense need—times when the outcome was completely out of his control. He'd prayed for his junior high school girlfriend not to be pregnant. He'd prayed to live through an auto acci-dent in college. He'd prayed when a fellow agent had been shot and was undergoing brain surgery. His prayers had always been answered the way he'd hoped.

Maybe it was time to pray again.

Repent!

Why couldn't religious people talk like regular people? Why did they have to holy up their talk so much? It made them sound phony. He heard Ethan's voice in his mind. Mike, if you were to die right now and stand before God, and He asked you why He should let you into heaven, what would you say?

Gillette sighed. That Ethan Hamilton was a problem. Before he'd met Hamilton, Gillette had thought he'd pretty much figured church people out. But Ethan didn't talk funny, dress funny, or look down his nose at him. How could he call himself a Christian? He just seemed to get a lot out of his religion. If Gillette ever decided to go that route, he thought he'd like to do it the way Ethan did.

God, he said silently, I know we don't talk much, but I think you know who I am. Anyway, I'd just...I mean, I wonder if you'd see fit to, you know, give us all a break here. Please don't let millions of people die. That wouldn't be real Christian of you, if you know what I mean. Since you made us, and all. Anyway, that's all I wanted to say. Maybe...maybe I'll have more later. Bye.

Gillette turned around, feeling warm. Jeannine sat on the edge of her desk, watching him.

"Aren't you going to look at the other one?"

"The other what?"

< jefferson scott >

"The other computer."

"We already did the register."

"No, not that, silly. The one in the back."

Gillette's eyes grew. "You have another computer? Take me to it, quick!"

She led him further down the hall. "I think it's really nice. Mr. Douglas's grandson got it for him, but he never uses it. We've got it set up now to run time and temperature for the whole D.C. area. We even post school closings in winter. People can see it, you know, from their computers at home."

She got to a door and tried it. "Oh, it's locked. I'll have to run get the key."

"Quick, behind that rock."

Jordan followed Ki Bok into cover. He peeked over the gray boulder. Twenty bots—armored tanks mostly—prowled through the jungle clearing. Jordan looked at Ki Bok. "Did you see what they did to Irene?"

"I was taking out that Bradley, remember? I didn't see what happened."

"Rolled right over her," Jordan said. "I heard her squish."

"Then it's down to just you and me, kid." Ki Bok risked a look over the rock. "They're still coming. Now what are we going to do? We're lost, my whole team is gone, and you can't plant your reset because we can't find the place to do it."

Jordan cradled the demolitions pack—the reset subroutine—in his hands. "Fireteam two, you guys still with us?"

A fearsome growl came over Jordan's speakers. Finally a voice broke through. "We're…a little…ha!…busy right now. Hya!" It was Chris Phelps. "Lost all but…Whoa!…lost all but Emil. Look out! Come on, back here! Gotta go, kid. We'll hold 'em off as long as we can. But it doesn't look like that's going to be very long."

< terminal logic >

Jordan crouched to run. "When they're gone, all the tanks chasing them will come after us."

A Russian T-72 tank crushed the underbrush behind them. Ki Bok brought up his red bazooka and fired. "Run!"

Chris Phelps sat at his desk in the UC Berkeley robotics lab, wearing his VR goggles. He gestured and ducked, trying to survive in Cyberspace.

Rolly the recycling robot rolled into the lab behind him. Barely three feet high, Rolly was essentially a dumpster on wheels. It recognized basic shapes such as the trash cans in the lab and, more importantly, aluminum soft drink cans.

There were other autonomous robots in and around the robotics lab. Sergeant Bunko, the automatic security guard that patrolled the halls at night. Daisy, the artificial horticulturist. A colony of miniature ant-bots.

Nevertheless Chris Phelps felt perfectly alone. The only other being on the premises that mattered at this moment was Emil Perez, the last surviving member of his fireteam.

"Emil," Phelps said into his microphone, "how you holding out?"

"Okay, I guess. But don't ask me to do this too much longer. Those rocket tanks are a pain."

"I know."

"Where'd all the variety go, anyway? I miss the vampires."

"Hey," Phelps said, "you see anything that looks like that stupid HQ?"

"Nothing."

Phelps looked at his watch. "Well, don't worry. By my watch this'll all be over one way or another in about ninety seconds."

Emil didn't answer.

Phelps tapped his headphone. "Hey, Emil, you made your will? Too bad there's not gonna be anybody to leave anything to, huh?"

< jefferson scott >

No answer.

"Okay," Phelps said, "if you're rested we'd best lean into them again. Let's go out swinging, what do you sa—"

"Fire!" Emil shouted. "I've got a fire here!"

Phelps looked around the cybernetic forest. "Where?"

"Here! Right here in the lab!"

"What!" Phelps tore his helmet off. There was a fire extinguisher around here somewhere. He headed for the hallway but tripped over something. "Watch it, Rolly!" He lurched to his feet. And slammed into a solid metal something.

Phelps looked up the steel-plate chest. At the top was a metal head—chrome face, dark sunglasses, painted scowl.

"Sergeant Bunko, what are you doing up?"

The seven-foot-tall robot raised its left arm. This was the arm that terminated in a ten-gauge shotgun. "Freeze, scumbag."

Phelps raised his hands. "Relax, Sarge. We've got a fire over at—"

The first blast blew out a window.

Two blue dots disappeared from the battle map.

"Where'd they go?" Barnes said.

Captain Lee stood on General Woodson's left, Barnes and Culpepper stood on his right.

Barnes walked to the map. "They were right here."

"Fireteam two," Woodson called, "we've lost you on our screen. What is your status, over."

Nothing.

"Beautiful," Culpepper said.

Barnes touched Woodson on the elbow. "Sir, why don't you let us get back in our cockpits? You can open the GSP just long enough for us to get through."

"That won't work, Lieutenant," Captain Lee said. "Those bots we led out into the canal would get through, too."

"Not if we were fast, sir," Barnes said.

"Request denied," Woodson said. "We can't risk letting more of the enemy back into the battle. Lieutenant, get on the horn to Fort Hood. I want to know if and when they catch anything."

"Yes, sir," Barnes said.

Woodson turned to the wall monitor. "Fireteam three, be advised: You are on your own. Fireteam two has been neutralized."

That was when they lost power.

"General?" Ki Bok Kim whispered. "General?" He didn't dare raise his voice. An enemy tank platoon was passing through the forest just beyond his position.

He wanted to tell the general that there was no such thing as fireteam three anymore. Ki Bok was the last member of the team, and now he had been separated from Jordan, whom he was supposed to be escorting. From the sound of that last transmission, he was pretty sure he'd been cut off from the general, too.

"Well, we gave it a good shot." He stood and faced the retreating tanks. "Might as well go out in style."

Jordan left his virtual body in the forest and burst from his cockpit. "What happened?"

Everything was dark. Even the computer lights were off. Something was terribly wrong. Memories came back to Jordan. Of remote-controlled mowers. Of a black-robed sorcerer. He imagined he saw creatures writhing on the floor, climbing the wall, dropping onto him from the ceiling.

"Hello?"

< jefferson scott >

"We're here."

Jordan yelped. "W-who is?" Someone was suddenly beside him. Jordan jumped again. "Yah!" Hands gripped his shoulders.

"Jordan, it's me, Kelly Barnes. Freckles and red hair, remember?"

"Oh...oh, yeah."

A deep voice crossed the room. "The power's out, Junior. I thought your old man said that couldn't happen."

"It can't," Jordan said.

"What do you call this?"

Jordan felt his way across the game room to a circuit breaker panel in the entranceway. He felt down the column of switches. "I can't see anything."

"Whatever you're gonna do, kid," the general said, "do it fast. We've got sixty seconds."

Jordan just started flipping breakers. Something in the ceiling exploded. Jordan looked up and saw a shower of orange sparks begin to fall.

In the brief light Jordan beheld a monster from the spirit world. Sparks landed on its head like an eerie crown. Its face glistened as if oozing with slime. It reached out white arms. Jordan screamed and fell to the ground.

Just then the lights came back on. Jordan's mom looked down at him. "What is it, Jordan?"

"Mom!" He stood up. "I thought— Why are you all wet? Oh, you've got sparks in your hair."

She shook her hair out. "I had to jump in the lake."

Jordan saw Katie standing beside her mother, holding Wysiwyg. The little girl giggled. "It was funny, Dordan."

General Woodson grabbed Jordan by the arm. "You can have your family reunion later. Get in that chair and do your thing. We've got thirty-five seconds!"

< terminal logic >

Jordan's virtual body was being fired upon by a company of battle tanks. He reanimated his persona and bolted into the mist. He had no idea where he was headed. Maybe he would get lucky. Armored vehicles of all sorts tried to cut him off. He swerved through them like a running back.

A Goliath tank rolled onto the pathway ahead. Its twin cannons drew a bead on the intruder. Jordan dove left at the tank's first shot. He plunged into thick foliage, conscious of attackers on his heels. The second shot struck him in the back, propelling him through the underbrush.

And down into a stream. Fog floated over his head. Steep river banks crowded him on either side.

"Jordan?"

The voice seemed to come from the bank of fog above him. Jordan looked up. He saw a persona he recognized.

"Dad?"

Ethan dropped out of the fog, swept his son up, and dashed up the creek.

"Dad? What are you doing here? We thought you were gone."

"I caught a ride. I'll explain later."

"We're out of time, Dad. I need to get to the blue pool so I can plant the—"

"Shh." Ethan emerged from the fog before a stand of tall trees. "We're here." He set Jordan down on the grass and prepared his own reset subroutine.

"This is where the pool is?" Jordan said. "I've got to hurry!"

"Wait, Jordan."

Jordan broke through to the inner clearing before his dad could stop him. He spotted the blue pool. "There you are."

"Fifteen, fourteen…" It was Penny's voice.

Jordan sprinted. His dad called from behind him. Something rumbled in the ground beneath him. He didn't see the guard tower until

< jefferson scott >

it had already fired. A puff of white smoke rose from an elevated watch-tower, nestled in the trees. Jordan's body fell to the ground, four feet from the blue pit.

Ethan saw his son's body crumple—a horrible thing, even in virtual reality. He crawled forward desperately, holding the reset pack under his arm. As he crossed fully into the clearing, the ground beside Jordan erupted. A hideous form emerged. Red skin. Black curved horns. Needle teeth. Yellow eyes.

Satan.

The Evil One turned his malevolent stare onto Ethan. "Come."

Ethan wasn't breathing. A part of him had always known it would come to this. He tried to remember Scripture.

Penny's voice shocked him to his senses. "Seven…"

Resist the devil and he will flee from you.

Ethan took a step toward the blue pit. The Accuser blocked his path, laughing hideously. Behind him the guard tower waited.

"Six…"

A fury surged up inside Ethan. Away from me, Satan! For it is writ-ten, "Worship the Lord your God and serve Him only."

"Five…"

There was suddenly someone else with them in the clearing. "Howdy, gents," the man said.

"Mike?"

The devil roared at the newcomer.

"Three…"

Ethan took his chance. He lunged past the Enemy. The devil reacted too late. The guard tower opened fire. Ethan felt his body go sluggish. He dove for the lip of the control room.

"Two…"

The devil was on top of him. The guard tower fired constantly.

< terminal logic >

Ethan plunged into the blue pit.

"One…"

He detonated the reset in midair. There was an intense rushing sound. He got the briefest impression of a multitude crowded into the clearing.

"Now, Mike! Pull the plug! Pull it, pull it, pull it!"

"Zero," Penny said. "Launch commencing."

"Impact in thirteen seconds," Penny said. "Twelve, eleven. Impact in ten seconds, nine…"

Jordan looked up at General Woodson. "Want me to turn that off?"

Woodson shook his head.

"Six, five, four…"

Kaye Hamilton gathered her son and daughter into her arms. She buried her face in their hair.

"Three, two, one…"

Jordan shut his eyes.

"Impact."

Nanoseconds passed. Jordan flinched again and again, bracing for the impact. After a full ten seconds he opened his eyes. "I'm not dead yet."

Captain Lee approached General Woodson. "Did it work?"

Barnes got on the radio. "Hey, Fort Hood, you guys still there?"

Woodson lifted his own radio. "Lieutenant Deeks, this is Woodson. What is your status?"

The radio popped. "We're still here, sir."

Barnes shouted. He and Culpepper traded high-fives. Captain Lee hugged General Woodson.

Katie turned to her mother. "Silly, Mommy."

Kaye was too busy crying.

The door at the top of the stairs opened and someone bounded down. "Hello!"

< jefferson scott >

"Daddy!"

"Ethan!"

Barnes ran to him. "You did it, Hamilton! Fort Hood says they got all the bots!"

"Hooray!"

"We all did it," Ethan said.

"Way to go, Dad!" Jordan shouted. "I told Mom you'd save us."

"God saved us, son. It was God."

chapter.32

Jordan waited until the server had left the room. Then, eyes wide, he asked, "Does he have a gun, too?"

President Rand Connor laughed. "If he does you'd better be nice to him."

They were having dinner at the White House. Ethan and Kaye, Jordan and Katie, and Mike and Liz sat in the Family Dining Room with the president and first lady of the United States. It was Monday night, two days after Vesuvius had powered down.

The room was elegant but not overwhelming. Pale yellow walls and gold curtains. Beige carpet. A crystal chandelier hung from the vaulted white ceiling by a tasseled cord. A fire burned in the marble fireplace behind Ethan. The table had room for exactly eight people.

Marie Connor turned to Kaye. "Please continue, Mrs. Hamilton. You were about to tell us about your swim in the lake."

Kaye blushed. "Katie jumped into our canoe, which had somehow gotten untied. When she landed, it shot out into the lake." Kaye shrugged. "I just…jumped."

"Does she know how to swim?" the president asked.

< jefferson scott >

"It wasn't a question of drowning," Ethan said, "so much as getting underground before…you know." He looked at the ceiling.

"Ah."

"Katie," the first lady said, "what on earth were you doing getting into that boat and making your mother jump in after you?"

Katie's face was serious. "Kitty."

"She thought our cat was in the canoe," Jordan said. "But she wasn't. She was upstairs under my bed. It's where she always goes when she gets scared."

Connor nodded. "Ah."

The server came in with dessert. A scoop of lime sherbet served in a silver bowl. Jordan's and Katie's had a puff of whipped cream on top.

Liz looked into her fiancé's bowl. "Aw, Mike, where's your whipped cream?"

"That's it, Mr. President," Gillette said. "I quit."

"Oh, don't do that," Connor said. "Because then I couldn't give you this."

A stern-looking young woman entered the dining room bearing several slick black cases. She brought them to the president.

"Thank you, Nancy. He took one and looked inside. "Alright, no one open these until I say. Pass this one to Mr. Gillette." He took another. "This one goes to Mr. Hamilton. This one to Jordan—now I mean it, Jordan, no peeking." He turned to his wife. "And ladies, Marie has chosen something special for each one of you." Cases found their way into everyone's hands. Katie received a brightly colored gift bag. "Alright, everybody can open."

Gasps and whistles of surprise. One or two giggles.

President Connor beamed. "I always like being Santa, don't I, Marie? The men hold in their hands the highest award it is in my power to bestow—the Presidential Medal of Freedom."

"Whoa," Jordan whispered.

"I only give out one of these a year, but I'm giving you each one. It is for"—Connor pulled a card out of his jacket—"'those who have made

< terminal logic >

outstanding contributions to the security or national interest of the U.S. or to world peace, or those who have made a significant public or private accomplishment.' I would have to say that saving every citizen's life has to count as a significant accomplishment." He turned to his wife. "Dear, why don't you tell us about the awards you've given."

"Yes." She sat forward. "The boys were all getting something, so I wanted the girls to get something, too. I don't like it when good people walk away from me empty-handed. I've come up with some simple gifts. I hope you'll like them. Katie, what did you get in your bag, honey?"

Katie pulled a stuffed bear out of the bag and hugged it. "Bear!"

"You know the history of the teddy bear, don't you?" The first lady said. "There's an old political cartoon of Theodore Roosevelt sparing a bear cub on a hunting trip. So these bears—Teddy for Theodore—came from that."

"Say thank you, Katie," Ethan said.

"Thank you."

"You're quite welcome, dear. Now, it's your turn, Miss Hinnock."

Liz held up a square of royal blue velvet.

"That," Marie Connor said, "is for your wedding. Something blue. It's a piece from my inauguration gown. I tore it, you know, getting out of the car that evening. The dress is ruined, but the cloth is still lovely." The first lady smiled. "I hope you'll carry it in your wedding."

"Oh, Mrs. Connor, it's beautiful," Liz said. "Of course I'll carry it. I will be honored."

The first lady nodded. "Now it's your turn, Mrs. Hamilton."

Kaye held up a slim book. "It's a book of quotations."

"Not just any quotations," she said, "but quotations of first ladies of the United States. You know, Bartlett's is full of quotes from Abraham Lincoln and John F. Kennedy and all. But try to find a quote from a first lady and you'd be hard pressed to do it. So I started collecting them.

"I am a firm believer, Mrs. Hamilton, in the saying that behind every successful man is a good woman." Mrs. Connor nodded at Ethan.

< jefferson scott >

"If he's going to keep going around saving the free world, then you're going to need these words of wisdom from women who have been in your situation before."

Kaye smiled. "Thank you, ma'am."

"You're welcome, my dear."

The president nudged his wife. "Tell her what you were going to give her."

"Oh, yes," she said. "I wanted to give you some life preserver earrings."

Everyone at the table laughed.

Kaye patted the book of quotations. "This is better."

President Connor pushed his silver bowl aside. "Why hasn't anybody else eaten their dessert? Jordan, you gonna eat that?"

Jordan cradled his bowl. "Back off, buddy."

"Jordan!" Kaye said.

"It's quite all right, Mrs. Hamilton. I wouldn't want someone stealing my ice cream, either." Connor wiped his mouth with a napkin. "I apologize to you gentlemen about giving these medals in a small ceremony like this, instead of with the fanfare you deserve. But under the circumstances I'm sure you understand."

"Mr. President," Ethan said, "this medal is...humbling. But what we did, Mike and Jordan and me, we didn't do alone. There were so many who helped. General Woodson, Ki Bok Kim, Chris Phelps, Captain Lee..."

"Yes, yes," Connor said. "General Woodson and his staff are going to receive decorations for their actions. I believe at least one of them is receiving a promotion. As for the others, if you will send me their names, I will see that they receive proper recognition once this has blown over."

"I wanted to ask you about that," Kaye said. "If I may?"

Connor assumed the carefully neutral expression Ethan had seen him wear on television. "Please do."

"I want to know why you didn't tell people they were about to die," Kaye said.

< terminal logic >

Ethan shut his eyes. He expected to have his medal taken away and he and his family shown the door.

The president looked suddenly weary. His wife put her arm around him.

"You have no idea how much Rand wanted to warn everyone," the first lady said. "We had the camera all set up. But," she exchanged a look with her husband, "we decided that telling everybody about something they couldn't prevent would just cause a panic."

Connor stared at the table.

"Just think," the first lady continued, "if he had gone on the air and made that announcement, how many people would've been hurt and possibly killed rushing for bomb shelters and what have you."

Kaye looked at the president. "I hadn't thought of that."

Connor turned to his wife. "Looks like I owe someone an apology, doesn't it?"

They sat in silence. Spoons clinked on silver bowls. The server brought coffee.

"Well," Gillette said, "like it or not, this thing's going to get out. There's so many people who know bits and pieces of this. And most of them are hooked up to each other. It won't stay secret very long."

Connor nodded. "I've scheduled a press conference for the day after tomorrow. My advisors tell me that it would be better to come out with it now, rather than have the other guys drag it out come campaign time."

"Well," Liz said, "I know where I'm going to be Wednesday morning: parked in front of a TV. I wouldn't miss this for anything."

"Alright, then," Connor said, "fair's fair. I get to ask some questions now. I've heard all the briefings, but there are still some things I can't figure. For instance, Mr. Hamilton, all of this trouble happened because this sophisticated computer program, Yoseph, moved out onto GlobeNet, isn't that right?"

"Yes, sir."

"What I want to know is why it did that. What made it leave its home and start making copies of itself all over?"

< jefferson scott >

Ethan blew out a sigh. "Wish I knew, Mr. President. The best theory so far is that Yoseph may have run out of storage space on the Alternate Realities computers. But instead of just ordering a new laser drive, he cast about for a computer with some spare room. How or why he started looking out on GlobeNet, no one knows. Eventually he found a computer that met his needs. Douglas Automation. Lots of—"

"Automotive, Dad," Jordan said.

"Oh, right. Douglas Automotive. Anyway, this computer had lots of storage space but it was never used. Yoseph copied some of his excess files out to the new location. At some point—we have no idea why—he moved his own system files out there. That's why when Mike unplugged Yoseph's computer at Alternate Realities, Yoseph was still alive and kicking. Then add the copy of himself he sent up to Vesuvius and you've got unbroken Yoseph-ness wherever you turn."

"Fascinating," Connor said. "The idea that it had no concept of what effect its actions were going to have is sobering to me. No remorse. Just machine logic." He shook his head thoughtfully for a moment.

"Very well," he said, "that answers that. Now I have another question for you, Mr. Hamilton. General Woodson tells me that your underground computer room lost power at a crucial moment—just before the rockets red glare, as I recall. But the good general also tells me that this room is equipped with state-of-the-art machinery to prevent such a power loss. How do you explain that?"

Ethan chuckled. "You're supposed to ask me questions I know the answers to, Mr. President." He rubbed his face. "The best answer I can give you is: I have no earthly idea."

"Ah."

"For a while I had a theory…I don't know how this is going to strike you, but for a good long while I thought Yoseph might actually be…the devil."

"I see."

"Well," Ethan said, "he kept appearing as the devil. Or at least in forms the Bible speaks about for him: a roaring lion, a seven-headed

< terminal logic >

dragon, and, of course, that nutty red-skinned dude with horns."

Connor put a finger on his chin. "So you think the devil made your computer room lose power?"

Ethan cringed. "Sounds pretty stupid, huh?"

"Not at all," the president said. "I admire your attempts to find answers to my questions, Mr. Hamilton. Thank you."

Ethan wasn't sure how to take that. "You're welcome."

"Now," Connor said, "I have a question for you, Mr. Gillette."

"Shoot."

"What I want to know from you is this: When you were at Douglas Automotive and you found this other computer, why did you choose to log on?"

"You mean as opposed to just pulling the plug?"

"Exactly. Because it seems that your sudden arrival on the scene was what allowed Mr. Hamilton to accomplish his task."

"Well," Gillette said, "it was a little bit out of curiosity, I suppose. I didn't know if that was the computer we were looking for. But I had a feeling. Anyway, the VR stuff was just sitting there, so I put it on. Believe me, I was just as shocked to appear where I did as everybody else was."

"But you have to understand the perfection of it," Ethan said. "The timing was incredible. Divine, some might say. Five seconds earlier and I wouldn't have been ready. Five seconds later and we'd all be history."

"No," Jordan said. "If he'd been five seconds earlier, I would've made it to the pool."

"I don't know," Gillette said. "Something just told me to log on." He gave Ethan a meaningful look and appeared about to say something else, but sighed and looked away.

"Now I have a question," Marie Connor said. "I heard about those two boys out at Berkeley who were helping you out, Mr. Hamilton."

"Yes, ma'am."

"And there was a fire where they were?"

"Yes, ma'am. And a security guard robot was trying to shoot them, too."

< jefferson scott >

"Are they all right? What happened?"

Ethan nodded. "They're fine. A little fire damage in their robotics lab. A couple of hard-to-explain shotgun blasts in the walls. The worst of it was that they had to destroy an extremely high-cost security guard robot."

"I'm just glad those boys are all right. You'll send them a Purple Heart or something, won't you, dear?"

"Yes, dear," the president said. He looked at Ethan. "My advisory committee."

Ethan smiled. "I have one, too. Mike's about to get one."

"Me, too!" Katie said.

"Okay, honey. You, too."

"Not me," Jordan said. "I'm never getting married. Ylech."

"Don't be so sure," Connor said, kissing his wife on the cheek.

"Mrs. Connor," Ethan said, "I think you'll enjoy this story I heard today. It seems that one of Yoseph's little bots was posing as a personnel manager online. Apparently this young man up in New Jersey had an interview with her."

"You're pulling my leg, Mr. Hamilton."

"Honest! She hired him, too. Poor guy showed up to work this morning thinking he was the new assistant manager. Only, no job."

"Oh, my."

"Actually, I understand they're going to hire him, after all."

"Unbelievable," Mrs. Connor said. "What a strange world this has become."

The president turned to his wife. "Marie, why don't you take the ladies to the East Room. Play something for them on the piano."

"Come on, girls," she said. "We can talk about Liz's wedding."

The president stood. "Gentlemen, would you care to accompany me to the Blue Room?"

They came out into the sumptuous Cross Hall. The most vibrant red carpet Ethan had ever seen lay on the floor. They passed the brooding portrait of John F. Kennedy and a bust of George Washington. White

< terminal logic >

columns on their left opened onto the Entrance Hall. The stern-looking woman who had brought the gifts to dinner stood beside one of the plush red chairs along the wall.

The first lady led Kaye and Liz and Katie all the way to the other end of the hall, into the East Room. Ethan and Gillette and Jordan followed President Connor toward the middle door. The flag of the United States stood on one side of the door and the president's flag on the other. They passed under the presidential seal when they walked through the door.

The Blue Room was round. Like the rest of the White House it had a distinctly classical feel. Stately. White walls and ceiling, giant blue oval rug on the floor, crystal chandelier, golden candlesticks, portraits of great Americans all around, blue curtains and chairs gilded with gold. Windows faced them as they walked in; through the center one Ethan could see the Capitol lit up. A fire burned in the fireplace on their left. Connor led them to it. Just to the right of the fireplace a section of wall had a peculiar look.

Jordan pointed. "Is that a secret door?"

"Sort of," Connor said. "It just goes to the Green Room next door. Tell you what." He called toward the hallway. "Nancy, could you come in for a moment?"

The woman walked in.

"Nancy, Jordan here would like to see some of the secret doors we have here. Show him a few, would you please?"

"Certainly."

"Jordan," the president said, "I would advise you to behave. Nancy here has permission to throw you into the torture chamber underneath the White House."

Jordan's eyes bugged. "Cool." He followed Nancy out into the hallway.

"I like your family, Mr. Hamilton," Connor said. "The sort I got into politics to serve in the first place."

"Thank you, sir."

< jefferson scott >

A tall mirror, framed in gold and topped by an imperial eagle, stood on the mantel. Ethan saw himself and the president of the United States framed in the same image. *What are you doing, Curly, hobnobbing with the president?*

Connor stood at the fire between Ethan and Gillette. "Gentlemen, it is a privilege of my office that I get to work with some of the finest people ever to be called Americans. I also have to work with some of its worst scalawags. I count you two in the former group, of course."

"Just doing my job," Gillette said.

"Right. Of course." Connor looked at Ethan. "And you, don't you want to play it down, too?"

"Kind of hard to do with the Presidential Medal of Freedom in your hand." Ethan looked at the slick case. "Wow. Sir, you shouldn't have. I mean, we're not even one hundred percent sure we got every last bot. And what about Vesuvius? Won't you have to send up shuttles to debug the computers—so the satellites don't decide they do want to launch after all? How much will that cost? And there's still the problem with all the weather downlinks in cars and airplanes and houses all over the world. What's to stop all this from happening again?"

Connor looked at Gillette. "Is he always like this?"

"Usually," Gillette said. "Got to have something to worry about."

"It's just that there's still so much to do," Ethan said.

"That," President Connor said, "is why I want you to consider coming to work for me."

Ethan didn't move. The wood settled in the fireplace. He stared at the president. "You want me to join the FBI?"

"Maybe," Connor said. "The Computer Crime Squad, perhaps. I've already recommended you to the office here in Washington. But of course they knew about you already. The director is in favor of it."

Gillette slapped him on the back. "Hoo-boy! Off to Quantico for you, podner."

"Not so fast, Mr. Gillette," Connor said. "General Woodson wants a piece of him, too. The military, you understand, has a very different

< terminal logic >

charter from law enforcement. The FBI typically has to wait until something's happened before they can act. Not so with the military."

Ethan looked at Gillette, who nodded sagely. "Would I have to join the army?"

"Not necessarily," Connor said. He looked appraisingly at Ethan. "There's also the possibility of something special, something not quite one but not quite the other. The best of both, if you follow me."

Ethan didn't, but he nodded anyway. "Something special." He glanced into the mirror, trying to decide if what he thought was happening was actually happening.

President Connor was watching him. "This is now the second time America owes you a debt of gratitude. And I can only give these medals out once a year. Save me some gold, Hamilton, and come work for me."

"Would we have to move?" Kaye said.

They were riding back to their hotel in a limousine. Jordan and Katie were asleep on the seat. Gillette and Liz were out seeing the city.

Ethan shrugged. "Dunno. Depends on which thing he decides he wants me to do, I guess. He might want me here in D.C."

"But we've just moved into our house! We can't keep moving every time something happens to us."

They rode quietly for a while. Katie mumbled in her sleep.

"I thought it didn't matter where you lived," Kaye said, staring out the window. "Computers and GlobeNet and all."

"It usually doesn't. I don't know, honey. Maybe that will depend on which he wants me on, too. I know the Computer Crime Squad works out of a single office—it's where they've got all this specialized equipment. But I don't know about the other options he laid out."

Kaye looked out at one of the Smithsonian buildings. She fingered the book of quotations in her hand. "Ethan…I don't want you to do it."

Ethan smiled. "I didn't think you would." He leaned his head back.

< jefferson scott >

"It's okay, honey. I'll tell him no."

She looked at him. "Really?"

"Yes."

Kaye rested her head on her husband's shoulder. "Tell me the truth. You want this bad, don't you?"

Ethan sighed deeply. "Not as much as I want you to be at peace."

"Would you be in danger like this all the time?"

"Maybe."

"Would your children get kidnapped and blown up? Would I?"

"I don't know."

"What can you give me to assure our safety if you do this?"

"Nothing. Kaye, I've already said I'll tell him no. Let's talk about something else."

They rode silently. The driver turned at an intersection. Kaye opened Ethan's medal case and touched the ribbon. "If you hadn't done what you did," she said, "would we all be gone now?"

"I think maybe so. There's no way to know for sure."

"God did a great thing through you, then, didn't He."

Ethan smiled. "Yes, He did."

She shut the case. "When do you have to tell him yes or no?"

"He said a week."

"Well," she said, "let's pray about it."

Ethan nodded. Yes, they would pray. He'd begun the moment the president had mentioned it. But in Ethan's heart of hearts, God had already given him his answer.

"New World Nuptials, how may I help you?"

Gary Longstreet spoke to the vidphone camera. "Yeah, hi! Hey, me and my girl, we wanna get hitched. You guys can do that, right? Over the phone."

"That's right," the phone representative said. "There are certain restrictions, but most of them can be overcome with nothing more than a few simple forms."

"Great," Gary said. "Let's do it."

"Okay, I'll need a credit card. I suppose you are the groom and the young lady in my other window is the bride?"

Gary smiled. "Ain't she beautiful?"

"Sure, sure. Alright." He looked at another monitor. "I can get you into the judge in fifteen minutes. That'll give us enough time to fill out these forms."

Gary nodded vigorously. "Great."

"Okay. Groom's name."

"Gary Eugene Longstreet."

The New World Nuptials employee typed it in. "Bride's name."

< jefferson scott >

Gary turned to his bride-to-be. "Tell him your name, sweetheart."

"Sure, Gary Longstreet." The woman smiled. "My name's Regina Lundquist."